VANESSA NELSON

THE HUNDRED - BOOK 2

THE SUNDERING

The Hundred - Book 2

Vanessa Nelson

Copyright © 2019 Vanessa Nelson

All rights reserved. This is a work of fiction.

All characters and events in this publication are fictitious and any resemblance to any real person, living or dead, is purely coincidental.

Reproduction in whole or in part of this publication without express written consent is strictly prohibited.

To find out more about Vanessa Nelson and her books please visit: www.taellaneth.com.

For my brother, G, and my sister-in-law, C. A little bit of armchair travelling for you.

With love.

Contents

1. CHAPTER ONE — 1
2. CHAPTER TWO — 13
3. CHAPTER THREE — 19
4. CHAPTER FOUR — 31
5. CHAPTER FIVE — 39
6. CHAPTER SIX — 47
7. CHAPTER SEVEN — 52
8. CHAPTER EIGHT — 59
9. CHAPTER NINE — 66
10. CHAPTER TEN — 73
11. CHAPTER ELEVEN — 84
12. CHAPTER TWELVE — 99
13. CHAPTER THIRTEEN — 108
14. CHAPTER FOURTEEN — 115
15. CHAPTER FIFTEEN — 122
16. CHAPTER SIXTEEN — 129
17. CHAPTER SEVENTEEN — 141
18. CHAPTER EIGHTEEN — 149
19. CHAPTER NINETEEN — 160

20.	CHAPTER TWENTY	169
21.	CHAPTER TWENTY-ONE	178
22.	CHAPTER TWENTY-TWO	186
23.	CHAPTER TWENTY-THREE	191
24.	CHAPTER TWENTY-FOUR	205
25.	CHAPTER TWENTY-FIVE	214
26.	CHAPTER TWENTY-SIX	229
27.	CHAPTER TWENTY-SEVEN	244
28.	CHAPTER TWENTY-EIGHT	250
29.	CHAPTER TWENTY-NINE	256
30.	CHAPTER THIRTY	263
	THANK YOU	268
	CHARACTER LIST	269
	PLACES	271
	ALSO BY THE AUTHOR	272
	ABOUT THE AUTHOR	274

Chapter One

Yvonne stood on the front step of her house, feeling the remnants of the cleansing spell working their way over her. At least she no longer had purple beetroot juice on her hands and the flour was out of her clothing, even if the kitchen was still cluttered with the partly assembled ingredients for the cake she had been trying to make. She did not think she was going to get to finish her baking. It had been an eventful afternoon so far, and it seemed that was going to continue.

She watched three of her oldest friends ride towards the house and walked forward to meet them. After the revelations of the afternoon, it was soothing to see familiar faces and feel the world settle around her again.

Sillman, the unofficial leader of the Hundred, was slightly in front, as he usually was, white hair a sharp contrast to his dark, beautifully made clothing. He was followed by Suanna, tall and stately in her usual dark clothing, and Mica, his head barely reaching Suanna's shoulder even on horseback, clothing a colourful collection that did not quite match. As they drew closer, she could see that they were all wearing unusually serious expressions. The Hundred only met on solemn and awful occasions, and she braced herself for whatever it was they needed her help with. It must be something terrible to require at least four Hunar.

She braced herself, as well, against dealing with more unsettling information after an afternoon of shocks. First, Guise's unexpected arrival, the goblin lord unwontedly sheepish, swiftly followed by his mother's arrival. The actual star of the Karoan'shae, ruler of goblin kind, had been in her house. That in itself was extraordinary, and yet it paled against the news, delivered by Guise, that, somehow, less than a dozen days ago in a space of time that she still could not remember, she and Guise had formed a bond that was a lifetime commitment amongst goblins.

The closest equivalent in human terms to this bond was marriage. She had told Guise, just before he left, that she did not want to be married. Not to him, not to anyone.

There had been no time to think. First Guise, then his mother, and then her children. Her ears were still ringing with Joel and Mariah's laughter. Apparently, they found the idea of her and Guise being married highly amusing. It was perhaps a better reaction than most, but it was still unsettling.

She tried to push all of that to one side and focus on the people in front of her as her three fellow Hunar drew their horses to a halt. Sillman dismounted with slow, careful movements. He was getting old, but usually had more grace and it caught her attention, and concern.

She moved forward to meet them, smiling. Amongst all the other madness, and everything else that was going on, she was Hunar, and so were they. Oath-sworn to help those in need. However different they were as individuals, they had a common goal.

"Sillman, Suanna, Mica, it's good to see you again so soon. Will you come inside? I've been baking this afternoon."

Sillman turned from his horse, and whatever else she might have said died on her lips. She had rarely seen him look so grave.

"This is not a social call," Sillman told her. "We are here on a matter of great importance."

"I did not imagine otherwise," she said, a trickle of unease growing. The last time she had seen Sillman look so serious, they had been at an open mine, made by slaves who were mostly children, the mine being dug down to the burial site of the first Hunar's ancient enemy. That had been not that many days before. She could not imagine what had happened since to bring that expression back to his face. "What is it? Please tell me."

"Word has reached us of a serious matter," Sillman began. "I can hardly believe it. I can hardly believe that you would do such a stupid thing."

"Sillman," Suanna scolded, "you're making a mess of this."

"I am," Sillman acknowledged. He straightened and drew in a breath, blowing it out while keeping his rigid posture, the lines of age around his eyes and mouth deeper than she remembered. "We have been led to believe that you have formed a bond with the goblin, Guidrishinnal de'laj Krejefell."

For a moment, Yvonne could not say anything. She had only found out about the bond herself that afternoon. Not long enough to understand what it meant. She could not understand how the Hundred could have heard about it so soon.

"Is this true?" Suanna asked.

"I am told it is," Yvonne answered, her face stiff.

"How could you?" Sillman asked, the words pulled from him, rigid posture flowing into anger. "Hunar and goblins should not mix."

For a moment, Yvonne forgot about her own issues and remembered the expression their fellow Hunar, Pieris, had when he was talking about the winter he had spent in the northlands, with a goblin lord who had taught him a lot about their magic. Judging by Pieris' face as he remembered, she did not think he would agree that goblins and Hunar should stay apart.

She had no time to protest, or gather her thoughts. Sillman was not finished.

"It is not possible to be a Hunar and to be bonded in that way. A Hunar must be able to act where there is need, with no thought of the consequence. Family ties are an inconvenience."

A small spark of anger lit inside her. She was the only one of them, as far as she knew, with any sorts of family ties, with the children who were even now somewhere inside the house, keeping out of the way, which was unusual enough that she should have noticed it before now.

"I do not recall this being part of our oaths," Yvonne said. The oaths were simple, and focused on providing service to those in need.

None of the rest of the Hundred might have children, or husbands, or wives, but they had entanglements nonetheless. Elinor, her mentor, had enjoyed her lovers, and had been one of the most warm and generous people that Yvonne had ever met.

"You cannot be a Hunar with this bond," Sillman told her, straightening a little more.

"What?" Yvonne heard her voice, thin and breathless. She felt as if she had been punched in the stomach. "That is not in our oaths," she protested. "I can recite them for you, if you have forgotten."

"We are bound to service. And only that."

"That's ridiculous," Yvonne protested, anger in her tone. "You are telling me that no Hunar has ever been married? Or had children? Or been in love?" Elinor's face rose in her mind, the heat in her gaze when she looked at Adira or Renard. No one had ever questioned Elinor's life, or the love that she had.

"It does not matter," Sillman said, dismissing her words and her inarticulate protest with a wave of his hand.

That hand wave made her more furious. He was treating her as the lowliest apprentice, not fit to hold an opinion.

"I have sworn my oaths. I have upheld them. I have been one of the Hundred for nearly a decade. The highest calling of a Hunar is service. It's in the name," she told him, hearing the flat tone of her voice and unable to do anything about it. Hunar meant servant, in the ancient language that they used for spell casting. A dead language no one apart from the Hundred knew. She felt her jaw tight, forcing words out through stiff lips. "There has been no complaint about my service. Not one. I have put the service of the Hunar above my family and above myself. I have fulfilled my oaths."

"That is not how the Hundred see it," Sillman said, voice as hard as hers. His face could have been etched in stone apart from the blaze of his eyes. He was furious.

A bond with a goblin that she did not remember making. That she had only just found out about.

And it seemed enough to cancel out her years of service. Not just as Hunar, but the apprenticeship she had served before that. Nearly two decades in total. The greater part of her life.

She opened her mouth. Nothing came out. Dozens of words choked each other. She shook her head, unable to believe what he was saying.

"Yvonne of Fir Tree Crossing. By order of the Hundred, you are sundered from our ranks. Your name will be struck from our records. You are no longer Hunar," Sillman pronounced. "Hunar Suanna. Hunar Mica. Will you bear witness to this sundering?"

"We will." Suanna and Mica spoke with one voice. Yvonne realised that they were just as stony-faced as Sillman. Just as determined.

The anger disappeared, crushed by ice that formed through her. It did not feel real. She could not feel the ground under her feet, the air against her face. Nothing was real. No longer a member of the Hundred. No longer a Hunar.

"You have brought this on yourself," Suanna told her, face tight. "We cannot have goblins being part of our secrets."

Yvonne wanted to scream. She was being punished for something she could not remember, and did not understand. And she wanted to shout at Suanna. Guise had more secrets than the entire Hundred put together.

Sillman drew a small piece of parchment from the pouch at his waist. Yvonne recognised the sort. The Hundred used them almost daily. It was a prepared spell of some kind. Her whole body tensed. Sillman had planned this. Brought a spell with him, ready to use. He murmured a word, the activation word for the spell, too low for her to catch, and the parchment dissolved into a cloud of green magic that he blew in her direction.

The green cascaded over her, blasting across her exposed skin, burrowing its way underneath clothes, wriggling across her body to the place on her shoulder where the symbol of the Hunar glimmered faintly in the light. The symbol that sat in the same place on her shirt, no matter what she was wearing. The little spark of magic that identified her to the world as Hunar.

Sillman's magic caught hold of the symbol, the green flaring and clashing, and she bit off a cry, falling to her knees, as the magic cut not into the cloth of her shirt, but into her skin, boring into her flesh, and carving out the symbol that she had carried for so long, that she had earned through the training she had endured, and the final test, and the years since when she had fulfilled her oaths. To help those in need. To act where it was needed. To not demand payment for the service that she offered, as a Hunar.

She wanted to scream. Partly in agony, partly in frustration, partly in grief. She held the cry back between her teeth. The three Hunar in front of her were standing motionless, with stern expressions, watching as the magic Sillman had released bit into her. She had begged once in her life before, faced with feral wulfkin in the filth of a quarrel. It had not done any good. She would not beg again. Not ever.

At length, it was done and the agony faded. Her shoulder felt raw. She glanced down to see blood blooming on her shirt and knew that, if she looked underneath, she would find a wound on her skin in the shape of the Firebird, the Hunar's symbol. Just one more set of scars to add to those she already carried.

"You have made your choice. We wish you joy of it." Sillman said, voice bleak. He turned with the others and got back on their horses, riding away without a backward glance, leaving Yvonne still kneeling on the ground outside her house.

She was hot and cold and shaking and frozen and hurt and bleeding and numb all at the same time. Her mind spun around and around and around as she tried to comprehend what had happened, wondering if it had actually happened. Had three of her oldest friends, three of the people she trusted most in the whole world, really just ridden up to her house and torn the symbol of the Hunar from her?

Light footsteps sounded behind her. She could not move. She was locked in her kneeling position, staring blindly ahead. Her shoulder was sore. She recognised that, distantly, but could not think what she might do about that. Or even if it was worth doing anything about that.

She was no longer Hunar. Sundered, Sillman had said. Dismissed.

The words did not make any sense. Nothing made any sense.

The sounds echoed inside her, into the great void that had opened up, black and endless. That place where the spark of magic had sat, had always been there. That place where there had been a core of certainty. Where she had known herself, who and what she was. There was nothing there. A gaping hole.

"Kalla?"

For a moment she did not recognise the voice, or the word, or understand that she was being spoken to.

Then a shape appeared in front of her, blurred at first. She was crying. She didn't know when she had started crying.

"Kalla?"

She recognised the word now. Kinswoman. In a language almost no one spoke.

A bit of her brain was working, then, even if the rest of her was not.

She blinked, and her vision cleared slightly. A slender young woman with abundant dark hair and bright blue eyes. She knew her. She could not place the name for a moment, too busy trying to stay upright.

"Something bad," another voice said. Deeper. A young man came and stood beside the young woman. Taller, broader, with paler blue eyes and blond hair that needed combing. Brother and sister. They did not look anything alike, but she knew that was what they were. And they were not human, either. She should be frightened of that, she knew. Wulfkin had damaged her, badly, in the past. Right now, she could not think about that. Something terrible had happened.

"We should try and get her inside," the young woman said.

"We can't touch her," the man said. "She's hurt. They did something to her."

"Look at her shoulder," the woman said, voice catching. "The symbol has gone."

The pair of them looked at her for long moments during which she simply tried to breathe.

Mariah. Joel.

Her children.

Family ties.

A great, wrenching sob came out of her throat. She did not know she was capable of making such a sound, but it was out there, harsh and raw to her ears.

"Kalla, would you come inside, at least? It will be night soon, and is likely to get cold." Mariah. That was Mariah. Fierce, opinionated, loyal.

"I'll make some tea," Joel said. Quieter than his sister, thoughtful, and just as loyal as she was.

Tea.

Her mind blanked for a moment and then she remembered the feel of pottery between her hands, the heat from a drink, the taste of tea in her mouth. It was something real. A memory she could hold on to when nothing else made sense.

"Tea," she said, her voice hoarse, sounding nothing like her.

She managed to get herself to her feet, wobbling a bit. Everything was difficult to see, and she realised that it was growing dark. She did not know how long she had been kneeling on the gravel, how long it had been since the three Hunar had been here.

With some gentle persuasion from Mariah and Joel, she turned away from her last sight of the Hunar and towards the house, moving with stiff, uncooperative limbs around the side of the house and into the kitchen, which was still warm from the afternoon's baking. It was a mess. The table held ingredients that she did not remember selecting.

She got inside the back door and her feet refused to move her any further forward. She leant back against the wall next to the door. Her knees gave out, and she slid down to the ground.

She was no longer Hunar.

The words were still not making much sense, but she repeated them. She was no longer Hunar.

There was an odd, clacking sound and she realised that she was shivering, her teeth rattling together. She was cold, freezing despite the heat in the kitchen. The bleeding wound at her shoulder was the coldest part of her.

Movement in the kitchen drew her attention. Mariah and Joel. She would know them anywhere. Or so she had thought. She remembered the blankness earlier, when she had not really known who they were.

But now, they were in their wulfkin form. Great, four-legged beasts with thick fur. They came and lay beside her on the stone floor, one on either side, and she slid the rest of the way down the wall to lie in between them, their warmth chasing away some of the ice that was in her body.

She was no longer Hunar.

―⁂―

There was a woman screaming.

She sounded like she was being torn apart from the inside, by something so awful that she could not speak the words, only utter those piercing shrieks, visceral and unfettered.

"Kalla."

The word shocked her.

Close to her ear. Too close. How had anyone got that close to her?

She snapped awake, coated in sweat, breathing too hard and too fast, and the screams died.

She realised that she had been the one screaming.

And with that realisation, the memories flooded in. The ones she could turn away from when she was awake. The quarrel. The prickle across her scalp, the sharp lines of pain where the razor had cut her skin as they crudely shaved off her hair. The filth all around her. The stench of feral wulfkin. The eerie light in their eyes. The utter helplessness of not being able to fight back. Of not being able to move. Of not having any choice. Of wanting it all to end. Just end. So that she didn't have to live in her torn and broken body, or hear the pain of the others. Other girls like her, taken to satisfy the whim of feral wulfkin.

Her lungs were full of the stench, ears hearing again the helpless cries.

Memories from when she was nothing. A wounded and terrified girl.

The damage had not ended with the quarrel. She had escaped the quarrel only to be turned away by her family. They did not want her. Damaged goods, her father had said. And they certainly had not wanted the two wulfkin children clinging to her.

And she had known then that, even if her family would have taken her, she could not leave the children. They were helpless, too young to fend for themselves. Keeping them alive had been her sole purpose.

She had not cared about herself. She had been broken. Nothing.

Before she had found the Sisters in the Stone Walls. Before she had met Elinor. Before she had trained. Before she had been a Hunar.

Hunar no longer.

A great wrenching sob rose up out of her stomach and worked its way out as a wordless cry that had her doubled over on the hard floor.

Shapes moved in the gloom. One in human form, the other in wulf shape. Her breath caught again, the old terror rising. But there was no malice in either of these shapes. They were twined through her very being and she knew them. Now that the shock of waking, the shock of memory, was gone, she knew them. Joel, keeping himself still and low to the ground in his wulf form. Mariah, in human form, crouching next to her brother, tears on her face caught by the faint moonlight from the kitchen window.

They were in the kitchen. And she was on the kitchen floor.

She could not remember how that had happened.

Her mind turned on those puzzles, trying to remember how she had got here.

Sillman. Suanna. Mica. The hard faces. The words spoken by Sillman. Suanna's condemnation. The will of the Hundred. The tearing out of the Hunar's symbol from her shoulder. Sundered.

"I'm awake," she told her children, voice rasping. She scrubbed her face with her hands. It must be past middle night. "Did someone mention tea?"

Joel made a low sound in his throat, rose slowly, and padded away to the pantry, emerging a moment later in his human form, fully clothed. He did not like to shift form in front of anyone else. It was too personal, he had said once.

Mariah rose to her feet. Apart from tangled hair, there were no signs she had spent the night on a floor, in her wulf form.

Yvonne looked up at them both and wondered how they had grown to be such remarkable people, when she was sitting on the floor of her kitchen, tears a breath away, unable to move.

"You made cake as well, Kalla," Mariah said, and held out a hand. Joel held out a hand, too.

Yvonne put her hands into her children's and let them pull her to her feet, her weight almost nothing to their superior strength. They were warm and real. She gave their hands a squeeze before she released them.

"A nightmare," she told them. "Sorry."

"Sillman hurt you," Mariah said, her voice low and intense.

Yvonne's hand strayed to her shoulder, which still stung. She glanced down and saw the large stain on her shirt. It covered most of her front. Blood. Starting where the symbol of the Hunar would normally sit.

"Yes," she answered Mariah, not sure what else to say for a moment.

"Why can't you be Hunar anymore?" Joel asked. He had set the kettle to boil, and was keeping himself very still and quiet near the stove. Too still and too quiet. He was just as angry as his sister.

"I don't …" her voice trailed off as her throat closed. She shook her head and moved across the room to one of the chairs, landing in it with a thump and resting her elbows on the table surface, head in her hands.

"We couldn't hear everything," Mariah told her.

Yvonne didn't look up, didn't want to see what was on their faces, just kept her head down as they bustled around.

It made no sense in her head. And she still could not remember forming the bond with Guise. In a castle dungeon, where they had been put so that Guise could kill her, drugged by the castle's lord.

"They know about the bond," she said, sitting back at last and blinking. The table, which had been a mess, was clear, everything put away and the surface cleaned, lit by a pair of candles at one end. There was a tea pot, mugs, a jug of milk and plates piled high with baking in front of her. "Did I fall asleep?" she wondered.

"We cleared up a bit while you were sleeping," Mariah told her.

"How did they know about the bond?" Joel asked, sitting opposite, brows drawn together. "They must have known before you did." He handed her a mug of tea, made the way she liked.

"I don't know." Yvonne held the mug between her hands, letting the warmth creep through her. It was too hot to hold for long, but she needed the heat of it to remind her she was alive.

"Guise wouldn't tell them," Mariah said definitely. She tossed her hair back as Yvonne raised an eyebrow. "I don't like him. But he wouldn't do that."

"No, he would not." Yvonne added that to her list of certainties about Guise. He would not hurt her. He would not lie to her. And he would not have told near-strangers about something as important to goblins as this bond.

But, before the afternoon, she would have said she trusted the Hundred with her life, and that there was nothing that would come between them. They were all Hunar. Bound together by training, by oaths, by knowledge. All with a common purpose. Help those in need. A purpose that had been a bright spark inside her, reflected in the symbol she had been proud to wear, reflecting the oaths she had taken.

The oaths were gone. Ripped from her.

Her list of truths had been shortened. Yet, somehow, she was still confident about Guise. More confident, she realised, than her faith had been in the Hundred. Apart from Elinor. And her children. And a few others. Perhaps. She mentally reviewed the names and faces that came to mind and shook her head.

The list was shorter. Elinor was gone, and the rest of the Hundred did not want her anymore.

She wasn't part of the Hundred anymore. The spark inside was gone. Sundered.

Chapter Two

At some point during the course of the night, she must have made it up to her own bedroom because she woke up late in the morning to sunlight on her face and the sense that something was fundamentally wrong with the world.

For a few breaths, she could not remember. There was no reason that she could think of why her whole body felt so heavy, and she wanted to turn back into the pillows, pull the cover over her head, and sleep away the rest of the day.

She moved slightly, gathering the pillows to her, and the pain at her shoulder woke her up more fully. She peeled back the neck of her nightgown and peered at the bandage there. Shoulders were awkward to deal with, and the bandage was lumpy and poorly formed, but at least it covered the injury that she now, vividly, remembered dealing with in the small hours. The dried blood crusted around the wound. The jagged edges of a Firebird, carved out of her flesh by magic, the symbol of the Hunar taken from her.

She was no longer Hunar.

That meant, as far as she could tell, that there was no reason she should get up. There was no reason why she could not stay here, in this comfortable bed, warm and safe for the moment, and just let the rest of the world pass by. The Hundred had decided that they could do without her. Perhaps they were right. Perhaps she was unfit to be Hunar.

The pain of that made her gasp, curling tight around the nearest pillow, face damp. Unfit. Dismissed.

Before she could think of any other reasons to stay in bed, light steps sounded outside her door. There was a knock, followed by Mariah's voice.

"Kalla, Joel is making eggs for breakfast. How many do you want?"

There. That was a reason to get up. Joel was an enthusiastic but amateur cook, and had set fire to a kitchen in the past.

She did not really want any eggs. She did not really want to eat anything, or to get out of bed, but the memories of the kitchen fire prompted her to sit up.

"Two, please," she answered Mariah. Wulf hearing was far superior to a human's, and she did not need to raise her voice to answer.

"I'll tell him. It's all right, nothing is burning yet."

Mariah's footsteps left, fading down the corridor, and Yvonne sat for another moment. She wondered how long it would be before one of them was back, wanting to know why she wasn't out of bed. For most of their lives with her, she had been up long before them, even after a disturbed night.

She found clean clothes, dressed and went downstairs to find that, far from burning the kitchen, Joel had done an excellent job. Poached eggs, her favourite. As well as the eggs there was fresh bread that one of them must have got from town that morning, and tea made already.

"I'm due at the docks later," Joel told her. "Four barges, maybe more, are coming in. But I don't need to go just yet. Do you want to do drills after breakfast?"

It was another familiar thing in their lives. Unless there was a good reason otherwise, like a disturbed night, every morning there would be drills. Her children were proficient in weapons, though they probably would never need to use them, with their wulf strength.

She thought about the question as she sat down and could not think why drills would be important. She was no longer Hunar.

"Not today. I need a bath," she added, almost on reflex. She caught the two of them exchanging glances, but neither said anything.

"I was supposed to be working on a wedding dress today," Mariah said, "but I can stay here with you."

Yvonne shook her head, mouth full of food.

"No," she said when she was able to. "Do what you have agreed to do. Some quiet would be nice, actually."

They were not convinced, their doubt evident, but they did not press her. Years of habit, perhaps, when she was the one making the decisions.

"These are excellent eggs." She smiled at Joel, or attempted to at least. "Did you get the bread?" she asked Mariah.

"I did. First batch of the day," Mariah added, proud of herself. For someone who hated early mornings, it was quite an achievement.

The children left not long after, more slowly than normal and turning back now and then as they rode their horses away from the house and across the bridge. She returned their waves, and then turned back into the house as they crossed the bridge. Quiet. She had wanted quiet. And now she had it, the house seemed enormous, full of shadows and unseen threats.

But it also had the extraordinary luxury of a bathhouse, and nearly unlimited hot water.

She stayed in the bath until her skin was wrinkled and the water, once piping hot, had cooled to the point it was becoming uncomfortable. She was warmed through, finally. She had not known how cold she had been until she slid into the bath, the heat a shock.

The remaining horses, Lothar and the spare horse who no one had given a name to, at least not one they could agree on, were surprised and pleased to see her. She spent some time grooming them, picking out tangles in their manes and tails, making sure there were no stones in their hooves, and generally making a fuss of them. Then she looked at the saddles and bridles and felt heavy again, at the thought of more chores and more tasks undone.

It did not all need to get done today, though. Her throat tightened as she realised that. She was no longer Hunar. No longer at the call of anyone in need. She no longer had to be ready to move at a moment's notice. No one would be requesting her aid.

Someone had put a bench out by the stables, near the fields, where the sun would catch it in the afternoon. She settled there, watching the horses graze, letting the sun keep her warm after the bath and trying not to think of anything. In particular, she was trying not to think about the afternoon before and all its extraordinary events, or the nightmare that had pulled her screaming from her sleep or the dull ache at her shoulder as her flesh healed.

She tried not to think about what would happen now, about how she might fill her days, about what job might be appropriate for a former Hunar. There was no precedent. No Hunar had ever been dismissed before, as far as she knew. They had all died in service. Elinor had said once that even if the older Hunar weren't able to help much in their later years, they could still do something.

She shifted slightly on the bench, and her sword hilt poked her in the ribs. She couldn't think why she had put her weapons on, apart from the fact it was habit. Years of going nowhere without a weapon to hand.

Ordinary people did not carry weapons, though.

Ordinary people had full and busy lives that did not involve magic or sword fights.

She could not imagine what such a life might be like. But she supposed she would need to find something to do with her time.

Just as she was wondering how to fill the rest of her day, Lothar raised his head and made a low sound. A warning. Someone was approaching the house.

She turned and saw a rider coming along the road at a headlong pace, his horse almost leaping the small stone bridge rather than crossing it. It looked like one of the law keepers or, rather, the Antonine Rangers that were masquerading as law keepers in the town.

She watched as the rider drew his horse, its sides heaving with exertion, to a halt at the bench near the bridge. The Hunar's bench, set up to provide a place for her to meet supplicants. When she had been a Hunar.

Before he could ring the bell that had been placed there, she rose to her feet and waved, drawing his attention. He turned his horse towards her and rode on at a sharp trot, sliding off as he came nearer.

"Grayling's compliments, Hunar. There's sign that the kidnappers are back and he could use your help tracking them."

The sharp pain of hearing the title she no longer held almost drowned out the rest of his message.

Kidnappers.

For a moment her mind was blank. She could not remember. And then she did. The young girl, the ladder marks outside her window. The stories of other young girls being taken in similar fashion all across the lands. And the herbalist, who had seen men with horses trying to take the girl and had, instead, taken the girl away from them.

Grayling, the head of the town's law keepers, wanted a Hunar's aid.

She opened her mouth to refuse, to tell the deputy that she was no longer Hunar, and no longer of use to anyone, when the memory of the girl's hand in hers rose up. The cold, wet hand that she had thought was long dead when she pulled her from the water. The girl was not dead. Indeed she was now back with her family. Other families were not so lucky.

Grayling might have asked for the Hunar, but he really wanted a tracker.

Still, she had her mouth open to say no, that she could not help. That the magic of the Hundred was denied her. The bright spark she had carried for so long was gone. Grayling would need to solve this mystery on his own.

She did not want to speak. Did not want to say the words aloud. Even thinking about her dismissal made her flinch inside and want to creep away, back into the house, where no one could see her.

The deputy was waiting, frowning, clearly wondering why she was standing with her mouth open, not answering.

She closed her mouth, swallowed, and opened it again to tell him she could not help.

Before the words could leave her, a trickle of warmth crept through her. Familiar and reassuring. The little bit of magic that she used to track people. A birthright, Elinor had called it. It had always worked differently to the Hundred's magic, relying on instinct more than formal spell working. It had not left her when the Hunar's symbol had been ripped out. Instead, it was there, waiting to be used.

Perhaps she wasn't quite so useless after all.

"Your horse is done," she told the deputy, "rest for a bit while I get ready, and then you can follow on. There's water," she added, pointing to the trough and the well that would provide clean water for him, too.

Lothar was happy to come to her call and to stand to have his saddle put on, ears forward. He knew there was work to be done.

She should have cleaned the saddle after all, she realised, as she gathered a waterskin and tied it on.

Chapter Three

THE DEPUTY WAS FOLLOWING at a steadier pace, his horse still blown, but had told her Grayling was at The Tavern. Yvonne had flinched when he had said that. It was a public space. Always busy. There would be witnesses to the blank space at her shoulder.

She drew her cloak around her as she rode through the town, trying not to meet anyone's eyes. The people of Fir Tree Crossing knew her as the Hunar, and she was met mostly with wary respect. She wondered what would happen when they learned she didn't have that title anymore.

One of Sephenamin's people was outside The Tavern, waiting for her, and waved for her to stay on Lothar when she would have dismounted. The wulfkin cerro was on the other side of the river, along with some of his range, the messenger said, and the ferry was being held to her convenience.

Torn between relief that she wouldn't have to walk through The Tavern and curiosity about what had been found, Yvonne rode down to the riverside to where the ferry was waiting for her. Little more than a large, flat assembly of logs, it was a quick way across the river, rather than riding for half a day along the nearest road to reach the closest bridge. It was usually manned by a human ferryman, who would steer fearlessly between the river barges.

Today there was a quartet of wulfkin to steer them across the river, the human oarsman sitting on the riverside, smoking something noxious in a long-stemmed black pipe. He seemed content, so Yvonne assumed that he had been well compensated by either Grayling or Sephenamin. Or possibly both.

The journey across the river was the smoothest and quickest she had ever made, with the wulfkin moving in harmony as though they had done this many times before. Perhaps they had. Perhaps Sephenamin often commandeered the ferryman's raft for business of his own. Unlike humans, wulfkin had the strength to swim across the river. However, they were competent rather than enthusiastic swimmers, and doubtless preferred crossing the river dry and warm.

She had only been across this particular river once before, in an early exploration. The other side was ancient and extensive woodland that stretched for what seemed an endless distance. There was a King's Highway, of course, that served the bridge, and cut through part of the forest. Trying to get from the bridge to here, through the forest, would likely take more than a day.

The townsfolk kept the riverbank at the other side clear of shrubs and trees to a distance quite far back from the river. Yvonne had never quite understood why, as it was unlikely that any army approaching from outside would be able to get across the river. Habit, perhaps.

The cleared riverbank was helpful now, though, as Lothar stepped off the ferry and onto grass, shaking himself from head to tail and giving a low, disgusted snort as he walked up the riverbank to where a group of horses, riders and wulfkin were waiting. Yvonne followed him, feeling her body heavy and slow, part of her still thinking about the comfortable bed she had left. She was here now, though, and with the possibility that she might be able to do something.

Grayling and Sephenamin were standing a little apart, waiting for her, the tall law keeper's plain, dark clothing and serviceable weapons mirrored among his people. No longer young, he carried an unmistakable air of command, something he shared with Sephenamin. The cerro was a full head shorter than the human, pale eyes gleaming faintly with wulfkin power as she made her way over to them.

"Thank you for coming," Grayling said. He was tense with a mix of what looked like excitement and anticipation. "Did my deputy give you the details?"

"No. Just that you needed someone to track for you," Yvonne answered, realising that she should have asked the deputy for more information. She was not normally so lax. But nothing about today was normal. "Something about the men with horses?"

"The descriptions Viola gave us," Grayling began. Yvonne remembered the grieving woman, a herbalist, who had intervened to save a young girl from kidnapping. "We've been keeping an eye out for them. One of my deputies saw a pair of riders who fit the description. I asked Sephenamin if he could help."

Yvonne nodded. It was sensible. The wulfkin were master trackers, and capable of keeping up with horses for a whole day if they needed to.

"They are from the Ashnassan tribe," Sephenamin added, nose wrinkling in distaste. "We know their scent. Found it in the town."

Yvonne could not help a shiver at the name. The men of the Ashnassan were fierce warriors, trained from birth, fanatically loyal to their tribe, and protective of their territory. They generally stayed near their home territory, not far from the border with the Forbidden Lands. No one outside the tribe saw the women, who were kept within their territories along with their children.

If it was the Ashnassan, they were quite a distance from home. Unusual, but not unheard of. They would take paying jobs, from whoever paid best.

Yvonne had managed to avoid them until now, and could happily have continued to do so. The Ashnassan had a general disdain for anyone outside their tribe, and no use for the Hundred.

"We lost the scent over the river, but there's a camp set up not far from here. Well, there was," Sephenamin finished.

"We went to visit them earlier today. All gone." Grayling was as frustrated as Sephenamin, it seemed.

"We could track them so far," another wulf said. Ella. One of the most powerful wulfkin in Sephenamin's range, and their most gifted tracker. Mariah liked to tease Joel about his fascination with Ella. She was lean and graceful in the way of many wulfkin, and also striking to look at with bright blond hair and the slightly heavier bone structure all wulfkin had. Ella had always seemed, to Yvonne, to be a strong and competent individual, usually calm. Today, she was frowning, as frustrated as her cerro.

"Did they use scent to disguise their trail?" Yvonne asked. Or, rather, she heard her voice asking the sensible question. Her conscious mind didn't seem to have fully woken up yet, but she had been involved in tracking fugitives before and knew the questions to ask.

"Possibly them," Sephenamin said, lip curling fractionally, "possibly those damn goblins."

"The Karoan'shae palace nearby," Grayling said, in response to Yvonne's confused expression. "It's been shut, closed, for years, according to the townsfolk. But it started getting deliveries a few days ago."

"Goblins often disguise their scent trails," Sephenamin added, his lip still curled, "although it seems ridiculous. We know where they're going."

Yvonne's heart skipped. She had forgotten. In her long-ago research on Fir Tree Crossing as a suitable home for her family, she had come across reference to one of the Karoan'shae palaces nearby. The Karoan'shae maintained several such buildings across the human lands. Places for the Karoan'shae to stay while they were out of their own lands, where they could guarantee the sorts of comforts and luxuries that they were used to. Very few goblins were like Guise, prepared to stay at King's taverns or hotels, no matter how well-equipped they were.

This particular palace had been shut up for years, as Grayling commented. She had dismissed it from her concerns when considering the town. It was on the other side of the river, and far enough away from the town itself that there should be no issue. Besides which, goblins and Hunar rarely mixed and, therefore, it was unlikely there would be any need to be concerned about the existence of the Karoan'shae palace so close. Now, she wondered. Guise's mother might be there. Guise himself might be there.

She did not want to face either of them.

She did not want to think about any of it. She did not want to think about anything apart from the task at hand.

"Can we go to their camp? I might be able to pick up something from there," she suggested, calling Lothar across to her. As she took hold of his bridle, pain ran through her shoulder, and she hissed in a breath. She had been injured before. Anyone who led the life of the Hunar was familiar with being injured. But this injury, the tearing out of the symbol on her shoulder, still stung and seemed worse as she moved to get on her horse again. Her cloak slipped as she got on Lothar's back, revealing her shoulder for a moment before she was able to gather it back around her. A quick glance around showed everyone else busy with their own preparations. No one was paying attention to her. She was not ready for her change in status to be revealed. Far from ready. She wasn't sure she would ever be ready for people to see the truth of it. Dismissed.

But she might still be useful.

Around her, Grayling and his men were getting on their horses. Only a couple of the wulfkin were on horseback. Even in human form, they could move as quickly as any horse and rider. And they loved a good hunt.

The camp that the wulfkin had found was tucked away in the deep forest, by the side of one of the streams that ran into the larger river. There was not much to see anymore. Trampled grass. Broken branches where more space had been cleared, perhaps to tether horses. Hoof prints in the ground.

Whoever the men with horses were, whether they belonged to the Ashnassan or not, they were long gone and had done an excellent job of hiding their presence.

Not quite good enough, though.

The others hung back among the trees, letting Yvonne walk around the campsite, Lothar happy to chew the grass by the stream's edge.

As she walked, she began to gather impressions, with that extra sense she had, the magic that was nothing to do with the Hundred. A few men. A handful at most. Perhaps three. Perhaps four. Well-trained. Disciplined in a way she associated with soldiers. Not mercenaries. The kind of discipline that came with dedication to a single cause, a single King, rather than hiring out to whoever paid the most.

An odd thing for a group of kidnappers.

"Why would the Ashnassan be involved in kidnapping?" she asked aloud, not really aware she had spoken until Grayling answered from his position under the trees.

"They've kidnapped before. Young women. When they wanted brides."

"Nine-year-old girls?" Yvonne's stomach churned at the thought.

"Never so young," Grayling said, his voice tight.

"But they have kidnapped before," Sephenamin confirmed, his own voice dark.

"They are the most disciplined group of criminals I've ever tracked," Ella commented, reflecting Yvonne's thoughts. The wulf was crouching in the shadows near Sephenamin, her eyes glowing faintly, reflecting her unease. Close to the change.

The reflection of power in a wulf's eyes always sent a shiver across Yvonne's skin, an instinctive reaction. But this was Ella, not a feral wulfkin, and she was perfectly in control. So, Yvonne took a breath, keeping herself still and calm.

"Yes," Yvonne agreed. "Three, possibly four men. There's very little left of them here."

"Can you track them?" Sephenamin asked directly.

"Yes. There's just enough here. If they've stayed together, it will be easier. They're very closely connected."

"We don't think they know they're being hunted," Grayling added. "We didn't see them in the town."

Yvonne wondered how they had found the camp then, with nothing to alert them to the tribe's presence.

"I was out running," Ella explained. "I scented them. They don't belong," she said, quite definite in her opinion. "They didn't see me," she added, perfectly confident in her abilities.

"It might have been time to move on, then," Yvonne speculated, taking another slow walk around the campsite. If it was the Ashnassan tribe, they rarely stayed in the same place for long outside their own territory.

She heard a sharp breath from Grayling as she drew nearer to him and glanced across to see his gaze fixed on her. Her cloak had slipped again, showing her shoulder. And the plain fabric of her shirt, no symbol in sight.

She drew the cloak back across her shoulder and felt the muscles of her face freeze.

"I don't want to talk about it," she told him baldly, conscious of the audience around them.

He looked at her for a moment more before inclining his head. Antonine Rangers. Far from home. They would understand loss, she thought, and changes in status, even if she didn't. Not yet.

The great hollow inside her welled up, threatening to overwhelm her. She shoved it back. There was work to do. Now was not the time to fall apart.

"You can track the group, so let's do that," he said.

"Yes. They went that way." She tilted her chin in the right direction and went to fetch Lothar, spending a moment scratching behind his ears, settling herself, before she got back in the saddle.

No one was in the mood for idle conversation as they rode away, and Yvonne pressed Lothar to as quick a pace as was safe among the trees. It helped that the warriors they were hunting had gone before them, making a narrow, nearly invisible path through the forest.

She could hear the other horses behind her, stretched out in a line through the trees. There were wulfkin running to either side, managing to keep pace with the horses, running with loose, easy strides that looked like they were no effort at all.

Still, everyone was behind her, so that when Lothar cantered out of the forest into clear ground, and into the ambush, they were the first ones under attack.

The first she knew was the shape of a man rising out of the grass in front of her, sword in hand.

Lothar turned, without her prompting, and met the man side-on, so that he took the sword slice across his shoulder rather than through his neck. He let out a squeal of pain, then another of fury and Yvonne felt him gather himself, powerful hindquarters lowering before he lashed out with his front legs, catching the attacker by surprise.

When Lothar came back to earth, he was standing on three legs, quivering under her. The attacker was on the ground, head twisted at an angle no human could survive.

She slid off his back, gave him a pat to send him away, trying not to think how badly hurt he must be to be walking on three legs, then drew her sword and turned in time to meet the next attack.

The quiet of the forest was broken by the sound of steel on steel and the soft, deadly snarls of the wulfkin.

The four men she had been tracking had multiplied. Several times over. She counted a dozen, in between fending off attacks.

And they were skilled. Definitely soldiers. Trained, disciplined, holding their forms even as they faced furious wulfkin and the might of the law keepers.

Ashnassan.

Bronzed skin marked with tattoos to celebrate the points of their life. Their first kill. The children they had fathered. The battles they had won. The more tattoos, the more dangerous the tribesman.

And every one that Yvonne could see had tattoos covering one complete side of their faces.

No novices here. All experienced warriors.

Formidable opponents. Her pulse sped up, mouth dry. The weight of her sword was familiar in her hand. Years and years of drills kept the point up. Not the first time she had faced trained warriors. She was trained, too.

Between sword strikes, Yvonne caught glimpses of the Antonine Rangers in action. Unlike the tribe, men and women fought side by side among the Rangers. They were all skilled and disciplined, holding their own, moving with a smooth and deadly grace that rivalled the wulfkin.

The wulfkin were partially shifted, using their enlarged hands with their dagger-like claws to strike their enemy, ducking under the sword strikes as though this were a mid-summer dance, snarling their fury at the tribesmen daring to attack them.

The grass churned underfoot, sprayed with blood. Bodies fell. Another pair of tribesmen, eyes staring blindly at the sky. A low sound of fury and pain from one of the wulfkin, dancing back out of the fight, one arm limp by his side, a pair of Rangers closing in on the space where he had been, a wall against the charging tribesmen.

Yvonne ducked under another sword strike, not as fast or as graceful as either the Rangers or the wulfkin, and brought her own sword up to catch the strike meant to take her head.

Her mind refused to focus. Thoughts scattering, despite the danger. She was remembering moments in her training, Elinor a stern instructor, the feel of the wooden practice sword thudding against her flesh for the third time, the numb sensation all down her arm. The first time Lothar had been injured when they were trying to complete a task, a crossbow bolt lodged in his hindquarter. He had killed that attacker, too, she remembered. The feel of moving her bruised body off the ground, clothes covered with bits of grass and dirt, Elinor's voice coolly telling her where she had gone wrong in her fall, before her mentor had swiped forward with the long staff in her hands, taking Yvonne's feet out from under her again. She had fallen better that time.

The sharp cut of air in front of her nose brought her back to the here and now long enough to see Grayling catch the sword that had been aimed for her, the Ranger putting himself between her and the oncoming tribesman.

She stumbled back to give him room, feet catching on the churned-up ground, staggering a few more steps until she was steady on her feet.

The fight was nowhere near done. There were still too many tribesmen standing. Too many injured wulfkin, and one Ranger propped up by a tree near Lothar, a hand pressed to her side.

Yvonne looked at her sword. Clean. None of her strikes had landed. And Grayling had needed to rescue her. She was not helping anyone.

The void inside swelled again, skin itching, heart still racing too fast. It had been years since she had felt so useless, so helpless, unable to defend herself. Vulnerable.

She backed away, slowly, heading for the Ranger. There were bandages in Lothar's saddlebags. Perhaps she could tend the wound, even if she could not help with the fighting.

Lothar snorted a warning, starting forward on three legs, the other still held up, and Yvonne turned, sword raised in automatic reflex in time to meet another tribesman who had somehow managed to get behind all the rest of them.

He stayed a few paces away and grinned at her, sword held loosely in his hand. His arms were bare to the elbows, skin spattered with blood, forearms twisted with tattoos, one side of his face covered with markings. One of the more senior warriors in this group. Perhaps even in the tribe. And shockingly young. Younger than her, no lines on his face, but with hard, assessing, dark eyes.

"And why are you here, little girl? Not a fighter, are you?"

The tip of her sword dipped. His words rang through her. Why was she there? Why was she in the middle of this fight, when she could barely keep herself alive, when her distraction had already got her horse injured?

Lothar made another sound, this one of pain, as he tried to put weight on his other leg, the wound at his shoulder bleeding freely.

He was not giving up, though. Her old warhorse, long past his prime, was hobbling forward to meet his enemy, ears flat against his head. If he had fangs, they would be bared.

His determination brought the tip of her sword back up. If he was not giving up, nor would she.

The tribesman chuckled.

"I do like a woman with spirit."

"Do you like children, too?" she asked. Her voice sounded too cool to be hers. Icy. Focused. Not at all like the twisting mess of emotion inside.

"I like the ones who can fight back," he told her, grinning again. The Ashnassan were known to kidnap women to be their brides. She wanted to be sick.

"Nine-year-old girls," she snapped back at him, some of the ice melting into anger. "Taken from their homes."

"Nasty work. But it pays well."

"Pays," she repeated. "You're still being paid."

"We don't work for free."

"And who wants nine-year-old girls so badly they pay you for them?" she asked.

There was something important about the number nine. Something critical that her mind was trying to scream at her, but most of her attention was now on the tribesman advancing towards her. His good humour was fading into focused, lethal intent. The eyes that she had thought were hard when she had first seen him were now as cold as winter's night.

And just as she thought she was going to have to fight him, to defend herself and her injured horse, a sharp whistle sounded out of the trees around them, and his expression changed to shock.

"Until next time," he told her, before turning and running back into the trees.

She moved to follow him, but he was out of sight already, moving faster than she would have thought possible.

Turning, she found that the rest of the tribesmen were vanishing, too, melting away as though they had not been engaged in vicious fighting moments before, leaving their dead behind.

"What was that?" Ella asked. She was still partially shifted, her hands and claws mired with blood, breathing hard after the fight.

"Retreat," Grayling answered. He was breathing hard, too. Oldest of them, Yvonne thought, as the light caught the grey in his hair. "Wounded?"

He was more focused than she was, still, Yvonne thought, remembering the Ranger propped up against the tree. She went to Lothar, only thinking to sheathe her sword when she was at her horse's side, and took down the saddlebags. She put a gentle hand on Lothar's neck, taking a quick look at the wound. A long, deep slice, it had gone through skin and into muscle. It wasn't life-threatening, though, however guilty the sight of her horse's blood made her feel, and he would wait a little longer.

"Bandages. Some salve," she said, to no one in particular, heading for the wounded Ranger.

The woman was pale, face beaded with sweat, grimacing as she kept pressure on the wound in her side.

"Stabbed," she said, breath short and choppy, as Yvonne knelt beside her.

"All the way through?" Yvonne asked, opening the saddlebag and fetching a pair of scissors.

"No. Deep, though."

"We've a field kit, too," Grayling said behind Yvonne's shoulder.

"Will you lie down?" Yvonne asked. "It will be easier to treat you."

The woman glanced across at Grayling before she complied, stretching out on the ground beside the tree, staring fixedly up to the sky while Yvonne cut her clothes open a little further to see the wound. Deep, bleeding freely. Not life-threatening, just painful.

By the time she had spread salve around the wound to try and prevent infection, packed it with clean cloths to soak up the blood, and tied a bandage around the Ranger's waist, the Ranger propped up against the tree again for that last part, the others had made their own assessment of the rest of the injuries and were thoroughly inspecting the dead.

"They were waiting for us," Sephenamin observed. He was standing a few paces away from Grayling, neither of them looking at each other, both focused on the pair of Rangers going over the nearest corpse.

"Someone told them we were coming?" Grayling speculated.

"Unlikely. There was no one in the forest apart from them and us," Sephenamin answered.

Yvonne poured a cleansing potion over her hands before packing the salve and unused cloths away in her saddlebags. The Ranger was looking marginally better, a little less white around her mouth, and let two of her fellow Rangers help her up and across to one of their horses. It was going to be a long journey home for her. She would heal, though.

It was going to be an even longer journey home for Lothar, Yvonne realised, chest constricting. She could only hope that no one attacked them on the way home, as she was not sure she could defend herself just now.

Chapter Four

Not sure she had much to contribute to the discussion Grayling and Sephenamin were having, she took her saddlebags with the medical supplies across to Lothar. He was still standing on three legs, quivering slightly, trying to put weight onto his front leg from time to time and quickly lifting it again.

"I'm sorry, old friend," she told him, sliding a hand down his neck. She didn't want to look at the wound properly, but knew she had to. A deep, clean slice through skin and muscle, it looked like it might have hit bone.

She poured a bit of water onto one of the cloths and wiped, gently and carefully, around the edges of the wound, trying to see the extent of it. Lothar made a soft sound of protest, the water stinging, and she put her hand back on his neck again, making a soothing noise.

The feeling of helplessness returned. No good in a fight. Too distracted, and too slow. Her tracking magic had worked. Yet she felt hollow inside. She had a pouch full of prepared spells, including healing spells. Spells written in quiet moments as a Hunar, preparations which had saved her life, and others, more than once. A written spell required only one word to activate it, rather than the delay and focus of speaking the spell at the time it was needed.

There were at least a dozen strips of paper in her pouch. And she was frightened to try them, to take one out, to speak the word, to find that the parchment remained intact. She didn't want to find that, apart from her tracking magic, everything else had been taken from her with the Hunar's symbol.

The fear gripped her. Helpless. Vulnerable. She wanted to hide. To find a place she could not be seen, to huddle into the ground and cry again.

She could not. This was Lothar, her old and loyal companion, and he needed her help. He did not need a coward who wanted to run away. He needed her to try one of the healing spells, to see if they worked.

She could do that. She could try, at least.

Before she could pull one of the healing spells from her pouch, Lothar's head lifted. There was someone behind her.

Turning, she was not surprised to find Grayling and Sephenamin a few paces away. They were trying to look as non-threatening as possible, deliberately out of easy reach, standing a little apart and slightly turned away from her.

She had an unexpected impulse to laugh, or bury her head in Lothar's mane and let the tears out. She must be in a bad way if an Antonine Ranger and a cerro were trying not to frighten her.

"We are taking the bodies back to town," Grayling said.

"There is no sign of how they knew we were here," Sephenamin added.

"It could have been magic," she told them, although she was fairly sure they knew that already. The Ashnassan were known for having access to crude magic. "Or it could just be bad luck, that they were meeting here anyway."

It was a reasonable suspicion, now that she thought of it. This was an anonymous bit of forest, away from civilisation and any casual passer-by. And, until recently, there would have been no one passing through this bit of forest, or even close to it, as the Karoan'shae palace had been shut and boarded for several years.

"I suppose we'll never know," Grayling said, sounding frustrated, his jaw tight. There was a deep crease between his brows as he looked around, silver in his dark hair catching the light. "At least we didn't lose anyone. Although I am sorry about your horse. That's a nasty wound."

Yvonne glanced back at Lothar, and her heart twisted. He was too old for this. And he deserved better than a rider who had been so distracted.

"We can help you home," Sephenamin said. The offer was unexpected enough for her to turn and meet his eyes. They were shimmering with a trace of power, the predator quite close to the surface. Her pulse skipped and her breath caught, old fear rising, before she realised that the predator was not directed at her. "The least we can do."

"I'm not sure I deserve it," she said, something in their manners making her more unguarded than normal.

"The woman who single-handedly destroyed a quarrel?" Sephenamin said, smile pulling his mouth, predator fading once more. "A remarkable and worthwhile achievement."

"It needed doing," she answered, uncomfortable with the praise. She had managed to destroy the quarrel in large part because of the power of the Hundred. Power which she did not have anymore. There was no trace of it left inside her, just that void.

"That it did," Grayling agreed. "It should never have been allowed to go on for so long."

"Getting your horse home is the least we can do," Sephenamin said. His eyes strayed to the bare patch on her shoulder, where the symbol of the Hunar had been. She had forgotten to pull her cloak back again.

She could not help the small flinch she made, heat rising in her face. The shame of it burned almost as much as her shoulder had, when the symbol had been torn out of it. She did not want to be here. She did not want to look at them, and see the pity on their faces. Or the questions. She did not want to explain anything.

"It doesn't matter to us," Grayling said. The frown had faded, and he met her eyes with a direct look, serious and honest. "It wasn't a Hunar's magic that found the girl in the marsh."

"And it wasn't a Hunar's magic that made you go into the quarrel," Sephenamin said, equally sincere. She opened her mouth to argue with him. She wouldn't have been anywhere near the quarrel if she had not been a Hunar.

"You think you're the first Hunar to find a quarrel?" Grayling asked, voice slightly bitter. "It's happened before. And the Hunar summoned the local law keepers, keeping out of the way while the law keepers did the work."

Yvonne stared at him for a moment, her attention caught, brought out of her own embarrassment. That did not sound like a story he had heard. It sounded like something he had lived through. And she could not imagine any of the Hundred simply standing by while law keepers went into a quarrel.

But then, she had not been able to imagine a situation where three of her oldest friends in the world would look at her with hard and unyielding faces, where

Sillman would, without flinching, send a piece of magic towards her that scored her shoulder and tore out the symbol that she had worn for so long, and worked so hard to achieve. So, perhaps, it was her imagination that was lacking. She believed Grayling. There was no hint of a lie or hint of deception about him.

"I am sorry," she said, not entirely sure what she was apologising for. The weak Hunar who had stood by and let law keepers go into the quarrel. Or that he, and the other law keepers, had had to see the inside of a quarrel, and what wulfkin were capable of when they gave in to their wild nature.

"It's not your fault," Grayling said, voice gentle.

"No. It's the fault of stupid, hot-headed idiots who think we should go back to nature. Nature. As if our ancestors behaved that way," Sephenamin said, lip curling up to show bright teeth, voice shaded with fury and bitterness. "And the fault of cowards who do not stand up to them."

Yvonne thought about the town where the quarrel had been. Full of artists and craftspeople. Full of beauty. Not a place which should have held the ugliness and violence of a quarrel.

"You did the world a service by destroying it," Sephenamin told her, voice calmer. "Do not ever forget that."

Her skin itched with fresh embarrassment. Not used to praise. The warmth of it soothed some of the raw hurt and she ducked her head, stroking Lothar's neck, her horse solid and real under her fingers.

Not Hunar. Perhaps not useless, though.

Lothar had been surprisingly cooperative when the wulfkin gathered around him and simply picked him up, carrying him back through the forest. In fact, Yvonne was sure she had seen him licking one of the wulfkin's ears on the way.

She had ridden back to the ferry crossing on one of the wulfkin's horses, her cloak gathered around her. Grayling and Sephenamin might be accepting of her change in status, but she was not willing to broadcast it to the world. Not just yet.

Back across the river, Lothar objected to being picked up and carried again. Perhaps unwilling to show weakness in front of so many witnesses. So, Yvonne got off the borrowed horse and walked him through the town and then on towards the house. She waved off the offers of company. Walking on, she suspected that Grayling or Sephenamin, or possibly both, would have someone keeping an eye on her until she made it to the house's boundary.

The house wasn't really that far from town. Long enough that it was far easier on horseback. And far enough that the slow, painful pace that Lothar could manage, using three legs, made the journey stretch.

Long enough for her to think about what had happened, to remember, again, how useless she had been in the fight with the tribesmen. To feel guilty, with every awkward pace that Lothar took, about the injury to her horse. She had not had time, not yet, to make a proper assessment of the wound and clean it properly. He was walking, on three legs, with his head low and every now and then made a soft, low sound of pain as he tried to put weight on the other leg.

And in between the guilt, and the helplessness, was the blank space ahead of what she should do tomorrow, and the next day, and the day after that. When she had been a Hunar, she might not have known what would happen, but she was confident that something would. Someone would need her help. There was always someone in need. And, despite the worries about money over the years, it had always worked out, one way or another.

In the waiting, there had rarely been quiet moments. There were always things to do. She had never known when she might be needed, and so all the tasks around the house needed doing, all the mundane matters like laundry and mending and restocking the pantry and tending to the horses' welfare.

She was not Hunar anymore. There would be no more supplicants. She didn't need to keep the house ready, her saddlebags prepared, or go through the long list of things that needed doing around the house and garden. Not yet. And not all at once. There was time. She had time. And no idea what to do with it.

There had never been a time in her life when there was nothing to do. When she did not have some purpose. It was unsettling.

And then there was Guise. She had all but forgotten him, in the aftermath of the Hundred's visit. But he had said they had created lifelong bond. Her memory was still blank. She still had that space, between waking up in the filthy dungeon at Coll Castle, and finding the Hundred in the castle's great hall, surrounding the body of the castle's lord. There were fragments of memory, fleeting impressions that suggested she had been terrified. She could remember Guise's red eyes. The grating sound of iron on stone, as the manacles that had held him to the wall loosened. And the core deep certainty that he would not hurt her.

She stopped for a moment, standing still in the road. That was more than she had remembered before. Although, she still could not remember why and how he had come to be in manacles.

The gap in her memory resonated with the void inside. No more magic of the Hundred. No clear memory of the event that had brought her here. The loss of her magic stung. The gap in her memory was frustrating. And she could do nothing about either of them.

Lothar snorted, tugging the rein, wanting to keep moving. She gave him a gentle pat on his neck, careful to avoid the wound, and kept walking.

Somewhere along the way, she had walked through water without knowing it, and her feet were wet. She had performed a service for a family of tanners in Silverton, before her lost memory and the mine, and had found time to send them a request for new boots, which she was now able to pay for. Until then, she was left with the worn out and leaking boots that she had on now, and the damp seeping between her toes, the misery of cold, wet feet.

The sky was dark overhead, with the peculiar almost black colour that promised heavy rain, and no breeze to move the clouds along. It perfectly suited her mood, brooding and grim. She envied the clouds. At least they had a purpose.

Even as her throat closed, and her eyes stung, she could feel the phantom beat of wings inside, and caught the sound, faintly, at the furthest edges of her hearing, of the shriek of a mythical bird. She looked up and around, almost losing her footing as she tried to see where that cry had come from. The Firebird, the first Hunar's legendary companion. She had thought the Firebird was a myth, even though most of the legend of the Hunar had some basis in truth. Until the Hundred had formed a circle at the mine and the Firebird had risen in all her extraordinary colours and, with the beat of her wings, had destroyed the mine that had cost the lives of so many youngsters, burying the Hunar's ancient enemy again, safely sealed in soil.

Before she could think about that too much more, she realised that they were, at last, back at the house. They crossed through the boundary, the ward stones shivering in reaction to her presence, and made their way, slowly and painfully, to the stables.

To her surprise, both Mariah and Joel were there. She had not been paying attention to her surroundings at all. It was dangerous to do that, but she did not really care. Not now.

"We were following the tribesmen," she told her children, hand on Lothar's neck. "We ran into an ambush." It sounded so simple, and so logical, when she said it aloud. The bare facts of the matter. And yet, the guilt still twisted inside her. She had ridden her horse into a trap, and he was injured.

"Sit down for a moment, Kalla," Joel said. "We'll look after him."

Mariah led her to the bench near the stables, the one that she had been sitting on when Grayling's deputy had arrived. It felt like half a lifetime ago. She turned slightly and watched as her children unsaddled Lothar, brushing him down with exquisite care, tending to his wound with the same care. She had done something right with them. Their movements around the warhorse were steady, calm and assured. In short order, his wound was cleaned, dressed with salve, and he was back in his stable with fresh water and feed.

"You're back early," she commented, when Lothar had his nose in his feed bucket.

"Only a little. There was the delivery for you at the Tavern," Mariah said. "We've left it in the kitchen."

"And we went to the bakery again," Joel added, "so we don't need to cook tonight."

"You don't cook anyway," Mariah told him.

It was all wonderfully familiar, and the thought of not cooking, and finding out what the delivery had been, brought Yvonne to her feet and following her children into the kitchen.

The parcel on the table was large and bulky. She could not think who would send her such a thing until she unwrapped the plain cloth to reveal three sets of leather boots, beautifully made, and a short note from the Cressins, the tanners from Silverton. Boots, for her and her children, made by all three family members.

Mariah and Joel lost no time in sitting down to take off their own boots, trying the new ones on. They fitted perfectly. Of course they did. She would expect nothing less from so skilled a family.

She sat down with her own new boots in front of her, not wanting to try them on with wet socks, feeling her eyes burning again. The boots were payment for a Hunar's service, and she was not a Hunar anymore. She was not sure what she was.

Chapter Five

She woke with the echo of a scream running through her head and sat up, heart skipping as she tried to identify the threat. It was the middle of the night, the faintest sliver of moonlight outlining the objects in the room. There was nothing moving apart from her. And there were no outside sounds, either.

It had been in her head. For a moment she wondered if she had been back in a nightmare, in the quarrel, with the steel bars against her skin. But her throat was not raw, and she was not shaking, as she usually was in the aftermath of one of those nightmares.

She tried to remember what the scream had been and realised it had been the echo of the Firebird, ringing through her head even in her sleep.

Unexpected anger rose up. She was no longer Hunar. She should not be troubled by the things that only Hunar should know and should deal with. She had been dismissed.

But the echo of the Firebird's scream was still ringing in her head. And she knew, somehow, that if she went back to sleep now she would be waking again soon with the same cry in her head.

The rest of the house was quiet. The scream had only disturbed her.

Although her body felt heavy with fatigue, she did not want to lie down again, so she got up and dressed in the dark. She added her weapons as an afterthought before making her way, as quietly she could, out of the house. Mariah and Joel might have heard her, but they were leaving her alone, keeping to their own rooms.

Outside, the night was cool with the final lingering traces of winter in the air. Summer had not quite established itself. The world was shown in black and white and grey, with deep pools of shadows. Her human eyes were not well adapted for darkness.

She found herself making her way along the path that led to the gate to the road, letting herself through, the latch and hinges making no sound thanks to Joel's work. She kept walking until she reached the benches that had been set up, what felt like a lifetime ago, for the Hunar to receive supplicants. They would need to remove those benches, she thought. Now that she was no longer Hunar. There would be no more supplicants. There might be visitors, though, and it would be rude to make them wait at these benches for her attention.

She had not lived here long enough to have had much use for the benches. Just the Cressins, searching for their missing son. She looked down at her feet. She had, without thinking, put on her old boots that were still damp from the day. She wondered what the family was like now. Now that their son was back. The parents she had met had been aged with grief. She wondered if that extra age would have faded, and whether they were able to let him out of their sight yet.

The benches had been set up next to the small bridge that led across the river. It was only just wide enough to need a bridge across it, the water running deep and fast, flowing into the Great River that ran past Fir Tree Crossing.

On the other side of the river, fields stretched towards the town. There were a few copses of trees, providing firewood for the house.

She drew her legs up, so she was cross-legged on the bench, and sat for a while, trying not to think. She did not want to consider what she might do with her day, or the next day. And she didn't want to think about her injured horse, and how long it might take him to heal.

Before she could replay the ambush, and Lothar's scream of pain, in her head too often, movement in the fields caught her eye. Not the livestock, which were scattered about, dark shadows in the grass, sleeping comfortably. This was a person, moving rapidly and with purpose through the sleeping animals.

Part of her supposed that she should be concerned. Normal visitors did not cross fields to get here, but took the road. Normal people did not walk through fields of livestock if they could help it.

She stayed still, watching, as the figure climbed over the nearest fence, onto the road, and then across the bridge. A slender figure, draped in black cloth, with their features hidden by another swathe of black cloth so that they were simply a dark blot in the uncertain light.

Yvonne straightened slightly, interested. She thought she knew this person, despite their only meeting being a fleeting one, in a warehouse in Three Falls, where this person had shot a poisoned arrow at Guise.

"A lovely night," the other said, by way of opening to the conversation. She had an accent-less voice. Impossible to place her country of origin. Impossible to tell, in fact, if she was human or goblin. The school at Abar al Endell had accepted non-human students from time to time. And this particular assassin was known not only to Guise, but to friends of his.

"At least it's dry," Yvonne answered.

"Yes. Travelling on wet nights is not pleasant. May I sit?"

It was a very civilised question for a mid-of-night visitor. Yvonne inclined her head, watching as the assassin copied her pose, sitting cross-legged on the other bench, finding that she was curious as to what the assassin could want.

"Guise isn't here," Yvonne said.

"I know. He's at the Karoan'shae palace on the other side of the river."

"You are better informed than I am," Yvonne commented, hearing some bitterness in her tone. It was difficult not to blame Guise, at least in part, for the situation she was in just now, her shoulder aching as she thought, again, of the moments when Sillman had pulled the Hunar's symbol from her.

"He would tell you if you asked," the assassin said, apparently quite relaxed. "He's quite smitten with you."

"What do you want?" Yvonne asked, not wanting to discuss that. There had been no time, not really, to think about what had happened when Guise had come to visit, closely followed by his mother. No time to really think about the fact that she was, apparently, bonded to a goblin in a way that humans would not understand. She had never wanted to be married, despite Elinor's wish for her to live a fuller life. Even all these years after the quarrel, the memories were still vivid.

"You're causing quite a stir among the Karoan'shae," the assassin said. "No one has tried bonding with a human for quite some time. At least, not that they will admit to. And some of the purists think it should be stopped now, before it has time to continue."

Yvonne bit back several hasty replies, staying silent while she thought through some of the permutations of that. She was aware, as all humans were, that there were goblins who believed they were superior to humans, that they were the older race, and entitled to go where they wanted and do as they pleased. Goblins who believed that any human in their way was simply an obstacle to be removed. She could well imagine that those goblins would react badly to the news that one of their own, and not just one of their own but a high-ranking member of the Karoan'shae, had apparently bonded with a human. And not just any human, but, so far as they knew, a Hunar. Goblins and Hunar did not mix well.

"Is Guise in danger?" she asked, her voice calm. Guise could more than take care of himself. And, unlike her, he had a lifetime of experience with the Karoan'shae.

"I believe so. You may be, too. They will most likely go after him first, but he is careful, and you're an easier target."

"Why are you telling me this? Last time you saw Guise, you shot him with poison." Yvonne was more curious than angry. Goblins were very difficult to kill. The poison had made Guise ill, and vulnerable, but she did not think, looking back, that he would have died from the poison alone.

The assassin shifted her position slightly. A tiny movement, but she had been still and controlled throughout the conversation until then, and the movement caught Yvonne's attention. Something she had said had hit home.

"It's complicated," the assassin answered at length.

Yvonne resisted the urge to roll her eyes. The assassin could kill her quite easily. "If you want me to take a message to Guise, you're going to have to do better than that."

The assassin shifted her position again.

Yvonne let the silence continue, somehow sensing that would be more effective than pressing for answers. Assassins from Abar al Endell would be used to people being nervous, and over-talking, around them. She supposed she should be nervous, but was confident that if the assassin had wanted her dead, they would not be speaking.

"We did not part on the best of terms," the assassin said. She sounded reluctant, her body stiff. "A youthful and foolish episode, on both our parts. It nearly cost me my blades, and caused Guise a lot of trouble with his family."

Yvonne absorbed that in silence. She had suspected a past relationship between Guise and the assassin. It fit perfectly with what she knew of him, although it was highly unusual for one of the dedicated assassins to enter into such entanglements.

"He never cared for me the same way as he does you," the assassin said, abruptly and unexpectedly. "Even being young and stupid, there was no possibility of any bond being formed. We both knew, really, that it was in fun."

Yvonne's face was burning, her skin itching with discomfort. She was not sure how to respond, and what to respond to. Unexpected laughter bubbled up. She was sitting next to one of the world's deadliest assassins, and the assassin was trying to reassure her. It was one of the strangest conversations she had ever had.

"So, you want me to warn Guise that someone in the Karoan'shae wants him dead?" It would hardly be surprising for him. Far from following the normal path of high-ranking members of the Karoan'shae, Guise spent the majority of his time outside goblin lands, travelling across human lands and generally, it seemed, pleasing himself. He had an appetite for gathering information and secrets, and a careless attitude to human laws.

"Yes." There was a lot more behind that one word than Yvonne could guess at.

"And by telling him that I got this message from you, you are pointing out to him that you can get to me at any time," Yvonne added. The words simply spilled from her without much thought. It was one of her more serious flaws, talking without thinking.

"Something like that. I can see why he likes you." The assassin rose to her feet in one smooth movement, made a slight bow that reminded Yvonne strongly of a high-ranking goblin, and then moved away, disappearing into the shadows under the trees.

Yvonne tipped her head back, looking up at the sky. There were scattered clouds hiding most of the stars, the patches of sky between them inky dark, the sliver of the moon casting just enough light to see by. It was still the middle of the night, with dawn a few hours away.

And she was suddenly exhausted. The restless beat of phantom wings inside her had gone. The assassin was gone. There was nothing keeping her here. And there was a comfortable bed inside, and the prospect of as long of a lie-in as she wanted.

At some point during the day, she would need to renew the spells on the ward stones. Just in case. And consider what, if anything, she might do about the assassin's message.

The next morning, the children let her lie in, and she woke when the day was half done from a deep and dreamless sleep. Her body was still heavy, and she did not really feel like doing anything in particular. Not drills, not chores, not any of the dozen or so tasks that still needed doing around the house and its grounds.

She went down to the stables and checked on Lothar, pleased to see that her old companion was out in the field, and able to put a little bit more weight onto his leg as he came towards her. Stable rest would have been far better for him, but she could only imagine the fuss he had made seeing the other horses let out that morning.

The wound was healing well, even though it was early in the process. One of the children had cleaned it again, and dressed it with more salve. Yvonne felt oddly numb. It should have been her tending to her horse, and she should have felt guilty about sleeping in while his injury needed dealing with. But she did not feel guilty. Despite the long sleep, she still felt tired, tempted to go back to bed and ignore the list of chores and the daylight.

Instead, she took a bath, washing her hair and then, when she was clean and dressed with her hair left loose to dry, going to her room to find the set of hairpins that had been a Mid Winter Feast gift from Mariah and Joel several years before.

The bedroom she was using had a dressing table and stool which she had never used, the ancient mirror covered with a cloth as she did not want to see her reflection every day. She pulled the cloth aside, the mirror browned and spotty with age, and stared at her reflection for a while. Pale skin, shadows under her eyes despite the extra sleep. Black hair, normally pulled back from her face. She had been wearing her hair in a single plait down her back since it had started growing long enough after the quarrel. It was an easy, practical style that she could manage half asleep and in the dark. Mariah had often lamented that she did not experiment more and try different things.

Yvonne looked at the hairpins she had set out on the dressing table, and thought about the various styles worn by women around the town, and by Mariah. They seemed to manage to put their hair up, however long, using only a few pins, and have it stay there for the whole day. Her only previous experiment with hairpins had been comical. But she could do a single plait.

She pulled the heavy length of her hair over one shoulder and braided it loosely. It was strange having the weight of her hair at the front rather than the back, but it also partly hid the blank space on her shoulder where the symbol of the Hunar had been.

She tied off the end with a piece of ribbon, and then thought about the chores that needed doing and how having her hair in front was going to be a nuisance.

Before she could pull off the ribbon and redo her hair in the normal style, light footsteps sounded at the stairs.

"Kalla, are you awake?" Mariah asked, coming to a halt at the open doorway of Yvonne's room. "Frida wanted me to remind you that she hasn't told you about the potters, if that makes any sense? She said you should visit any time."

Yvonne looked back at the reflection in the mirror and thought again about the chores that needed doing. Sitting with the dressmaker and hearing the tale about how the two potters in Fir Tree Crossing had come to be such enemies seemed a far better way of spending the rest of the day than mending fences, cutting back weeds, or any of the other dozen things that needed doing. And she would not need to redo her hair.

"Thank you. I think I will go now."

"You look nice," Mariah commented, following her down the stairs.

"I can't work out what to do with hairpins," Yvonne admitted. It was such a silly thing, such a frivolous thing, and yet she felt quite ashamed in her admission.

"I would love to show you," Mariah told her. "Although I don't think they are very practical for sword fighting."

"That is true. And thank you for looking after Lothar."

"Joel did that this morning," Mariah said. "He's back at the docks. Apparently, Sephenamin challenged Grayling to a competition between the range and the law keepers."

Yvonne paused a moment in her walk through the kitchen on her way to the stables, and had an impulse to go to the docks. She could not imagine that ending particularly well. And then she remembered. She was no longer Hunar. Other peoples' welfare was not her concern. Joel's was, of course, but she could not interfere where the cerro had led. She had many years' practice of standing aside, unable to help her children, and it did not get easier, no matter how necessary it was. She might be their guardian, but she was human, and humans were not welcome in wulfkin business.

"There was a lot of laughter," Mariah added, perhaps sensing her worry. "The law keepers are doing very well."

"Are you home for the rest of the day?" Yvonne asked.

"No. I just came back to get some ribbons. We are doing another wedding dress," Mariah said, as though that explained everything. She held up a cloth packet that must have come from her room. A collection of the ribbons that had been used to wrap gifts, that Mariah had carefully preserved and hoarded for use.

It made sense. It was perfectly logical. And yet Yvonne had a strong suspicion that Mariah had come back to check on her.

"I'll be fine," she told Mariah. She took the spare horse's saddle and bridle, and made her way to the field. Joel's horse was still there, slightly to her surprise.

"He's been running to and from town most days," Mariah told her. "While you were away, there was a competition in the range. A silly thing."

"Yes. I remember you saying. Is Joel trying to get faster?" Yvonne asked.

"I think so. I don't see the point, really." Mariah put her bag of ribbons into her saddlebag and waited while Yvonne saddled the spare horse.

Yvonne was smiling, welcome and unexpected, as she got on the horse. Mariah was not a fighter, but Joel was a powerful wulf, which meant he was also competitive. She could easily imagine his frustration at having been beaten by others of the range and the previous competition, and determination to do better in the next one. He was just as stubborn in his own, quiet way as Mariah was, and she loved them both. The hollowness inside shrank as her heart swelled.

Chapter Six

Having left her horse at the Tavern, Yvonne made her way through the town to the dressmaker's shop. She recognised a few faces as she passed and exchanged polite nods and brief greetings as she went, careful to keep her cloak gathered around her. Word would spread eventually, it always did, but she did not want to face questions just now.

The street to the dressmaker's shop looked the same. She was careful to walk in the middle as she went past the potters' shops, her feet staying on the thick white line that looked like it had been freshly painted.

Before she arrived at Frida's shop, she came to a halt in the shadows of one of the nearby buildings, apprehension crawling over her skin. She was not ready. Not nearly ready. Frida was sharp-eyed and quick-minded, and would notice the lack of the Hunar's symbol at once. And Yvonne did not want to answer any questions.

"Mistress Yvonne." The voice snapped her out of her momentary panic and she blinked, finding Frida at the door of her shop, a hand lifted in greeting. "Do come in. I promised you a tale. There's fresh scones. And the kettle's ready."

Yvonne could not remember if she had eaten anything that day. Fresh scones sounded lovely. And non-threatening.

She went up the pair of steps into the shop and stopped as soon as she was past the threshold, feeling out of place again. It was a working space, that much was clear, with racks of fabrics and several chairs and stools of different heights, a large table at the back set near a window at the rear of the building that must overlook the river, letting in more daylight for the dressmaker and her staff to work.

And although it was a working space, it was full of things that she found utterly mysterious. She recognised the ribbons, threads and pincushions, but there were other objects. What looked like large, wooden mushrooms. Other wooden shapes collected together in a wicker basket. A set of shelves with rows of boxes and bottles with names that made no sense to her eyes.

"Why don't you sit at the table, and I'll get the tea," Frida said, stepping past Yvonne. "The girls are at our client's house today, so it's nice to have company." Yvonne turned her head and measured the truth of that in Frida's face. There was no hint of dishonesty. They were nearly of even height, Yvonne noted, both tall for women, the dressmaker slender and upright despite the grey in her chestnut hair. Frida kept going, through a door that Yvonne hadn't seen until now but which must be a small kitchen, as Yvonne could hear the dressmaker moving about and the clink of china.

She moved to the table, as instructed, and found a chair that let her have her back to the wall, and a view of both the river outside and the front door of the shop. Unsettled by her unfamiliar surroundings, she relaxed fractionally with the solid stone at her back.

Frida appeared moments later with a tea tray that held the promised scones, finely crafted mugs, and a large teapot.

"Those aren't from Handerson or Keffle," Yvonne said. It was probably rude, but it was the first thing that came to mind.

"No, indeed," Frida answered, smile pulling her mouth. "These were made by their master, before they were even apprentices."

Yvonne's brows lifted. The pair of potters along the street, with shops either side of the thick white line, each had children old enough to marry and start families of their own. Which meant that Frida's pottery was perhaps twenty years old. Perhaps older.

She lifted the mug that Frida had poured for her, and turned it in her hands. It was some of the finest work she had ever seen, and that included the work produced by Handerson and Keffle.

"This is beautifully made," Yvonne said.

"Yes. Seward was his name," Frida said, with a fond, remembering smile. "He was too old for me," she continued, with a gleam in her eye and a smile dancing across her face that suggested age might not have mattered. At all. "He was a good man. Kind. And blind."

"He had Handerson and Keffle for his apprentices?"

"Both at the same time," Frida nodded, the smile and gleam fading. "Old fool. It never seemed to occur to him that there was only space in his shop for one senior potter. And still, he trained them both."

Yvonne took a sip of her tea, cradling the mug between her hands, craving the warmth, listening to all that Frida was saying, and not saying.

"There's a master's fair every year. At the harvest festival. You won't want to miss it," Frida added. "So many beautiful things. The guild masters from Hogsmarthen come to judge the apprentices' work and award their guild status."

"And Keffle and Handerson were in the same year?" Yvonne asked, although she was sure she knew the answer.

"Of course. Old Seward, he wouldn't choose between them both. Even though there was only one place. The guilds don't put two apprentices into the guild at once. Not in a town this size." Frida shook her head, staring out the window to the river.

Frida was a master storyteller. She kept her pacing even, with little bits of information thrown in here and there, as she told the tale of the young apprentice potters, each desperate for the single prize, and not only that, but each having their eye on a girl they wanted to marry. Not the same girl, Frida added, with a roll of her eyes. There was that.

And then, the day of the fair. The day to present their wares before the guild. And someone had smashed their master pieces. Both of them. Into little shards.

Each blamed the other.

They had, separately, gone back to the workshop and the kilns, hoping to make something of the day. Tempers were high. Beer may have been involved. The apprentices had fought.

Seward had tried to break up the fight, calm them down, and put himself between the pair.

There was no one else there at the time. So, no one apart from the pair of them now knew what had happened, but it had ended with Seward dead on the floor of the workshop and the two apprentices bloodied and bruised.

They hadn't spoken directly to each other since then. The law keepers of the time, who Frida noted were not nearly as fair-minded as Grayling, had decided that someone had to be to blame. Handerson had been sent to prison, for a handful of years, because no one could prove anything other than it was a stupid accident. Keffle, with a wealthy merchant in his family, had been spared.

And when Handerson had returned to Fir Tree Crossing, he found that Keffle had passed into the guild and set up shop. So, Handerson took the shop opposite. Apparently, he had been a model prisoner and completed his master piece in prison. Prison had left its mark, though. Even to this day, he didn't sleep well, or eat well.

When Frida finished her tale, she was staring out the window again.

Yvonne found that she had eaten the scones Frida had put in front of her, and drunk the tea.

"I'm sorry for your loss," she said, voice soft. Twenty years ago. And Frida still used Seward's pottery every day.

"Thank you." Frida shook her head, brushing a tear away. "I need to talk about it every now and then. And then I want to march down the street and shout at them both for being so stupid. But, what's to be done. It was so long ago."

"And did they ever learn who destroyed their apprentice pieces?" Yvonne asked.

"Ah. That, mistress, that is the real issue. Right there. No. No one ever found out. They both deny attacking the other's work. And it makes sense. Because the pieces were in the same place. And they are both too full of pride to destroy their own work."

"And not quite as good as their master," Yvonne commented, lifting the mug to inspect it again.

"Well, there are some tricks only known to masters," Frida said, wry twist to her words, "and they killed theirs before he could finish teaching them. And no one else wanted an apprentice with that history. Not even with all of Keffle's money."

"So, they have had to settle for being excellent potters, rather than exceptional ones," Yvonne concluded. "That must rankle."

"Every day," Frida answered, with a dark satisfaction in her tone. "I take my tea out on the step quite a lot," she added. With mugs made by her lover, and the potters' former master. An unsubtle reminder of what they had lost. What their hot heads had cost them.

Yvonne's mouth curved in an answering smile. It was a sort of justice.

Then her shoulder twinged. The potters might have brought about their own downfall. At least in part. The fight that had led to Seward's death. She could not remember what she had done to deserve her own dismissal.

"And Keffle's son is courting Handerson's daughter. That must rankle, too."

"If the idiots aren't careful, they're going to lose their children over it," Frida commented. "But they'll still blame each other."

Yvonne shivered lightly. "I could not imagine losing my children," she said.

"I doubt you ever will," Frida answered, voice warming. "That Mariah is a fiery one, but she's got as good a heart as you could wish for. I don't know Joel as well."

"He's wonderful," Yvonne said, throat closing for a moment. She wanted to cry again. "They both are."

And in the dark of her mind a familiar thread of doubt surfaced again. She had done her best, and still wondered if they would have been better with a wulfkin range as their family. There was so much she had not been able to teach them, and she could not follow them into the ranges. They might have found a possible home now, but it had taken years.

Chapter Seven

All the trades were closed for the day as Yvonne made her way back to the Tavern, pleasantly full of tea, scones and conversation, her mind busy with the story Frida had laid out for her. The short-sighted generosity of the master potter, taking in two apprentices. The bitterness evident today, with the white line between the shops and one of the town's law keepers watching the potters. The prospect of more trouble ahead if their children did decide to marry. The rivals risked losing their only children if they could not put aside their differences, and the bitterness.

And she could not help wondering what had actually happened all those years before. Who had destroyed the apprentices' pieces for the guild fair? She could not help thinking that someone else had been involved. What had actually happened when Seward had died? That one of the pair had escaped prison was clearly unfair, but what would a fair outcome have been? It was a mystery two decades old, though, and one unlikely to be solved.

She hadn't been paying much attention to the path she had taken, or her surroundings, and found herself in the main square. It was deserted at this hour, in the quiet hour or two when most businesses had closed for the day and most people were home for their evening meal. Too early for the taverns to be throwing out drunks.

Almost deserted, she corrected, seeing a familiar figure striding across the square from the law keepers' offices. Grayling was heading straight for her.

Curiosity kept her still, waiting for him, and she found that she had forgotten to gather her cloak around her, the bare place on her shoulder visible next to the thick plait of hair. She had an impulse to draw her cloak around her again and checked it. Grayling had seen the blank space already.

"Mistress Yvonne, I'm glad to have caught you. I could use your help, if you have time?"

She had another impulse. This time to tell him that she was no use to anyone. The words stuck behind her teeth. She could not quite bring herself to say them. Instead, she found herself nodding, and then walking with the law keeper across the square to his offices.

He showed her into his office, and she took the same chair as she had on her first visit here, when she had been surprised to see that the town's law keepers were Antonine Rangers.

"Tea?" he offered. "Or, no, I have something more appropriate." He reached into the bottom drawer of his desk and produced a large, square glass bottle half full of amber liquid, two glasses and, more surprisingly, a metal flask beaded with condensation and carrying a preservation spell that made her eyebrows lift. "It's a liqueur from the desert people. Made with almonds, apparently. Here." He poured her a measure, and opened the metal flask to remove a piece of ice as long as Yvonne's little finger, then passed the drink across to her, making one for himself.

She swirled the liquid in her glass. The ice was clear, the sort of purity normally found high in the mountains. "Where did you get the ice?"

"The flask. Water goes in. Any water. And clear ice comes out."

"Remarkable. I've heard of such things. Never expected to see one." An extraordinary thing for a humble law keeper to have. And expensive. The sort of fine magic that went into creating such things was only performed by the more accomplished mages. The ones who usually worked for kings. And who occasionally worked with Antonine Rangers.

"A gift. A long time ago." There were echoes in his voice of a past he did not want to talk about any more than she wanted to discuss the bare patch on her shoulder.

The liquid, when she took an experimental sip, was sweet and smooth, a complex mix of flavours cooled by the ice.

"This is delicious. Like drinking a dessert."

"Far better than the spirits most taverns serve," Grayling agreed, leaning forward to top up her glass.

"You wanted my help?" Yvonne prompted. Not for one minute did she believe that the town's law keeper had invited her into his office to drink excellent liqueur.

"We didn't manage to get any information from the tribesmen," he told her. That was hardly a surprise, as they had not been able to question any. The few that had remained were dead, and unable to talk. "But I had sent out some scouts to the nearest towns and other law keepers. They've come back with reports. Another pair of nine-year-old girls gone missing. Separate towns. And several days apart, distance-wise."

"Ladder under the window?" Yvonne asked, chill creeping across her skin. Nine-year-old girls. There was something important about that age, if only her sluggish mind could remember it. The Ashnassan had almost succeeded in taking a nine-year-old girl from the town not that long ago, stopped only by the efforts of Viola, the herbalist, still grieving the loss of her daughter. A daughter now returned, although damaged.

"Yes. And no one saw them taken." Grayling took a sip from his own glass, staring into the middle distance for a moment, expression bleak. "I cannot think of a good reason for anyone to be wanting nine-year-old girls."

"Nine," Yvonne echoed, sitting up in her chair, realisation spreading across her skin in prickles.

"That means something?"

"Nine. It's the age when any witches, or those with power, usually come into it. Girls anyway. Boys are usually later, perhaps eleven." Yvonne set the glass on the table with a thump, tangling her fingers together. She remembered the parents of the girl from the town. The mother with a touch of sight.

"So, someone is gathering up nine-year-old girls with potential for power?"

"It makes sense," she said, her face numb. It did make sense, at least as to why those girls had been targeted. "I'd bet that if we could check with all the parents, we'd find that there is a witch or two in their family, or someone with the sight."

"And then we just have to work out why someone needs girls with potential for power."

Yvonne lifted her glass and drowned the rest of the contents in one swallow, coughing as the alcohol burned down her throat.

"You know the reason." Grayling's eyes narrowed.

"I may not be Hunar anymore, but there are some secrets we are sworn to protect. You need to tell the Hundred," she told him.

"I can try and get a message to them," Grayling said slowly, "but wouldn't it be better from you?"

"No. They don't want to see me. They've made that clear." Her hand strayed to her shoulder as a twinge of pain reminded her of the lost symbol.

"Alright. I'll send a message. And to the other law keepers."

"They won't help," Yvonne said, hearing the bitterness in her voice. "Most law keepers are like most kings. They only really care about what happens in their borders."

Grayling made a face. He agreed with her. He did not like it, but he agreed with her. He finished the rest of his drink and set his own glass on the table, eyeing the bottle. Yvonne knew that look. She had worn it more than once herself.

"It doesn't help," she told him. "Well, it helps a little bit," she corrected herself. "But the nightmares still come back, and the next day is awful."

"I know," he said. He put the bottle, and the metal flask, back in his drawer.

Yvonne sat back in her chair for a moment, thinking about what he had said, and not said. The Ashnassan, paid by someone else, were targeting nine-year-old girls. The lord of Coll Castle was dead. But the tribesmen were still being paid, were still being sent after girls. Someone else was involved.

Trying to think of potential allies, she wondered about writing to the Sisters in the Stone Walls. Only for a moment. The Sisters would take in any refugees that she found, no matter how badly damaged, but the Sisters would not get involved in affairs outside their own territory. It was the main reason why the various kings and rulers around them had left them alone. The Sisters were as neutral as they possibly could be.

No one would be properly looking for the girls, crossing borders, and following the trails where they actually led.

Yvonne rode back to the house barely paying attention to her surroundings, her mind turning over what she and Grayling had discussed. And what she had not, and could not, tell him.

Nine-year-old girls. Children coming into their powers for the first time. A lot of the Hundred had been approached over the years by near-hysterical parents, terrified of what was happening to their children. Those parents who had lost touch with their ancestors, and had forgotten the long history of witches or mages or sorcerers or those cursed with the sight in their family line.

And then there were the families where the power seemed to run strong, where they had not forgotten their ancestry, and, more than that, also remembered the dangers that faced young children. A lifetime of potential in a small, and vulnerable, body.

A very long time ago, before many of the current lands had been formed, around the time of the first Hunar, there had been a warlord in the desert who had kept a dozen wives, all of them taken as nine-year-old girls. The ones who showed power, and promise, he kept. The ones who did not show any power, or promise, were never seen again. He had ruled, it was said, for over a hundred years until one of his wives had slit his throat in the night, and had then been executed for her trouble, despite the relief the population had felt, freed from his tyranny.

Very few people were as well informed, and well educated, as the Hundred. But those families with strong lines of power, the very few of them that were left, knew enough to keep their children safe the moment they started showing promise.

And now someone was collecting nine-year-old girls again. Taking them away from their families. She agreed with Grayling. There were no good reasons for that.

The Hundred might act. But she could not go to the Hundred.

The Sisters would not help. The Sisters kept a carefully neutral stance, confining themselves to the Stone Walls. A difficult path, Yvonne had always thought, even as she understood that it was necessary. The Sisters had resources, in land and knowledge and magical power, that many kingdoms would envy. Keeping out of politics kept the Sisters and those within the Stone Walls safe from interference or challenge.

But it left Yvonne without allies. Isolated.

There might be a few law keepers like Grayling, prepared to look beyond their own territories. They would not get far, though. Most law keepers were proud of their position and jealous of their borders.

She knew what it was like to be taken. To be helpless. She had been a few years older than nine, and the nightmares still woke her from time to time. She could not leave these girls to whatever fate their captors had planned.

There was the empty space inside where her magic had been, ripped out with the Hunar's symbol, the lack of it a gnawing ache along with the healing wound on her shoulder. The magic, and the symbol, had been part of her. She did not know what she might be, how she might live, without them.

She shook her head, turning her mind away from the future, back to the more immediate issue. The missing girls, and how she might find them.

She had her tracking magic, and a pouch full of prepared spells that might work. Perhaps.

It was little enough, along with the weapons she carried.

She was not Hunar anymore. People tended to help someone carrying a Hunar's symbol. They were less likely to help an anonymous woman.

It did not matter. She could not stand aside while the girls were in danger. She needed to act.

Her feet twitched, wanting to move, reminding her of the new boots she was wearing. Perfectly fitting. Beautifully made. By parents who had asked for a Hunar's help, and a youngster who had been taken by the slavers, all the way to Three Falls.

She had never spoken to Alexander, beyond sending him back to his parents. Never had a chance to ask him who had taken him. And now, with the tribesmen collecting girls, it might be a critical question.

Silverton was not that far away. And from there, she might have a trail to follow. Information to uncover.

She wanted to leave now. And could not. Lothar was injured. It would be weeks before he could travel.

Without the symbol of the Hunar to protect her and her warhorse, she would be vulnerable in ways she had not considered for years. Nor did she have unlimited resources of wealth to buy guards for her back, or use as bribes for information.

For a moment she considered asking Mariah and Joel for help. They would both be willing, she was quite sure. And yet. They were building lives here. Far away from slavers, and whatever fate might be in store for the girls. She did not want to put them in danger, or, at least, no more danger than already existed for wulfkin.

There was one person who might help. With seemingly unlimited resources. Well-connected, with a network of friends who were just as adept at collecting information as he was.

And who also, apparently, was now her husband.

She might not want to see him, not yet, not before she had found time to research what a goblin bond was and what it meant, but she knew that he would help. Knew it with the same certainty as she knew he would never hurt her.

She needed to find Guise. Most of the time, she would have had no idea where he might be or how to find him. He had always found her before. But, thanks to a night visit, she had a place to look. The Karoan'shae palace not far away.

She needed to speak to Alexander. She needed to find Guise.

Her spine straightened, shoulders lifting slightly. There. She had a plan.

Tomorrow. She would go tomorrow.

Chapter Eight

She wasn't sure if Mariah and Joel were more relieved or worried when they got back to the house to find her cleaning the horses' harnesses. She had her travel saddlebags packed, tucked away in the kitchen out of sight from Lothar. Her warhorse was no fool, though, and knew something was up. Rather than grazing peacefully in the field, he was at the edge of the field closest to the stables, ears forward, keeping a close eye on her.

"Are we going on a journey, Kalla?" Mariah asked. It sounded like a perfectly innocent question, but she knew her daughter.

"More girls have gone missing," she told them, without warning. "Grayling is going to get a message to the Hundred."

"But you can't stay home, and just let them deal with it," Joel said. There was no criticism in his voice. "Where will you go?"

"I never got a chance to speak to Alexander," Yvonne told him, feeling shaky with relief. She had been worried that her children might try and talk her out of her journey. She felt vulnerable without the symbol of the Hunar at her shoulder.

"And you can thank him for the boots as well." Mariah shrugged slightly when Yvonne looked at her. "I don't want you to go," Mariah said, with all of her usual conviction, "but we know you can't stay here while there are children in danger."

"Yes." That one word was all she could manage for a few moments as she finished cleaning the last bridle. Then she turned to her children. "Family hug," she suggested, and was immediately surrounded by her children and the clean scent of wulf.

They held on to her for the usual five heartbeats, then let her go. For the first time, there was no panic at the end. No unwanted memories trying to shove themselves back into her mind. Just the lingering warmth of the hug.

"I've made stew," she told them. "It should last a couple of days." Then she laughed. "Or perhaps just one meal, depending on how hungry you are."

"But you're not just going to see Alexander, are you?" Mariah asked as Yvonne left the stables and went to make a fuss of her horse.

"It's not really our business," Joel said.

"Well, it's probably a good idea that you know where I'm going to go, at least to start with," Yvonne said, scratching Lothar behind his ears. He shoved his nose into her chest in a familiar gesture that made her step back a pace against the force of it. "Silverton first. Then, there is a Karoan'shae palace not far from here. I'm going to try and find Guise." She had not told them about the assassin's visit, and did not do so now. She was certain that the assassin was not interested in her children, or her in particular. "If I'm going to find out what happened to the girls, I'm going to need resources."

"Resources," Joel repeated slowly, unexpected mischief in his eyes. Yvonne felt heat in her face and ducked her head, giving Lothar an extra scratch.

Joel was the quietest of them. It was easy to forget, sometimes, just how much he did see. He would be out of her legal guardianship soon, although she hoped he would stay with her, and Mariah, for a good while longer. Despite his young age, he was already powerful and showed all the signs of potential for being a very powerful cerro. Perhaps powerful enough to rival Sephenamin, although Yvonne did not think that the local cerro would be concerned about that. Sephenamin was unusual in many ways. And Joel had no interest whatsoever, at least for the moment, in having his own range, with all the problems that went with that.

Lothar had been unsettled when she had put saddlebags on the spare horse and ridden away that morning, both Joel and Mariah promising to remain with her warhorse until he settled.

The business of navigating through the town, on a horse not used to being ridden, had kept her mind occupied, but once out of Fir Tree Crossing and riding the narrow path across the marsh towards the King's Highway that would take her to Silverton, the pain that had been building up in her chest burst out into tears.

It was the first time, in all their years together, that she had ridden out on a task without Lothar. And it was just as awful as she had expected. He had been hobbling, distressed and determined, along the fence after her, calling out, knowing, as he always did, that something was wrong and realising, as she kept riding away, that he was not going with her.

Her heart cracked with the pain of it, and then she had to grab hold of the spare horse's reins as he took fright at something in the undergrowth. He was not used to being ridden, or being out on his own, being mostly used for luggage and companionship for the other horses. A perfectly acceptable and adequate animal for those purposes. A poor and chancy substitute for Lothar.

She wiped her face, brushing away tears, and focused instead on the horse and her surroundings. Without Lothar's keen senses, and the Hunar's symbol, she felt exposed, the nape of her neck prickling under the normal, single braid, and the scarf that covered her scars. Not for the first time, she wondered if this was the right decision. And told herself, again, that it was the most logical choice.

At the pace the horse could manage it would take most of the rest of the day to get to Silverton, and she could only hope the horse could hold his pace for the journey after that to the palace.

―――*ℓℓ*―――

On his own, without his normal companions, the horse was reluctant to move fast, or far, and Yvonne ended up camping overnight in an abandoned barn, riding on into Silverton in the morning. As she passed by the last few fields before reaching the town, she was conscious of the curious stares from the farmhands out and about. A woman riding alone, with a sword, was an unusual sight. In the past, she would have let her cloak slide back from her shoulder to show the

Hunar's symbol. Now, she drew the cloak around her a little more tightly and nudged the horse to a slightly faster pace.

The main tavern, the one that doubled as a marketplace, was more than happy to serve her what turned out to be a very good breakfast, accompanied by tea rather than small beer. She left the horse to a temporary rest outside the tavern and went in search of the Cressins. She did not have far to go, hearing laughter as she made her way along the village's single, main street.

The family were engaged in what looked like a cleaning of the workshop, most of their equipment outside the building, the three of them busy going back and forth, with a lot of teasing among them.

For a moment, Yvonne wanted to walk away. The laughter was easy and care-free, and nothing she had to ask of them was easy. Alexander was completely relaxed, moving with his parents, working with them. The worn-out, terrified youngster she remembered was gone, replaced with a confident young man with an open smile, surrounded by people who loved him, curling brown hair probably too long for his mother's liking.

Even so, it was Alexander who spotted her first, and raised a hand in greeting.

"Hunar. It is good to see you."

She closed the distance between them until she was only a few paces away.

"It's just Yvonne," she said, her throat tightening for a moment. They would spot the bare patch on her shoulder soon enough, even partly covered with her cloak.

"Are you here on business?" the wife asked.

"Of a sort, yes. I am sorry, but I wonder if I might speak with Alexander for a few moments?"

"You want to know what happened," Alexander guessed. He shrugged slightly at her expression of surprise. "It's all right. I don't mind talking about it."

"Why don't you sit for a bit, and I'll make some tea," his mother said. She and her husband were still lean, dressed in plain, serviceable clothing suitable for their craft, but the exhaustion and fear they had carried, that had brought them to a Hunar's gate, were gone. The couple seemed to have lost ten years at least since she had first met them.

So, Yvonne sat in the morning sunshine with Alexander, and his parents, and asked him to tell her how he had been kidnapped, who by and what had happened.

As it turned out, he did not have a huge amount of information for her. He had been taken at night, and the kidnappers had bundled a cloth over his head, so he didn't have much of a good look at them. He had been carried over the shoulders of a horse, like a sack of grain, for a while, and then thrown into the back of a wagon with other youngsters who were just as bewildered as he was. They had then been taken, in that same wagon, with infrequent stops, and only ever at night, to the warehouse in Three Falls where she had found him.

Yvonne swallowed the rest of her tea, now cold, and thought that over. There had been no deviation on the way. He was quite clear about that. There had been a half dozen of them in the wagon. He was the last one. And the wagon had just kept going, with those infrequent stops, all the way to the city. The kidnappers had not really spoken to them, apart from ordering them in and out of the wagon. They hadn't been fed much, either, something which made his mother shake her head in disapproval.

Just as she thought she had got all the information he could provide, he frowned slightly.

"I think the men who grabbed me were different from the ones who were watching the wagon," he said, slowly, as though only just realising it. "I haven't thought about it until now, but they smelled different, and I'm sure they spoke a different language amongst themselves."

"Was the language something like this?" Yvonne asked, then said the few words that she knew in the Ashnassan tongue.

"Yes. That's what it sounded like. And they had a sort of musty smell. A bit like horses, only sweeter."

"You know who they are," his father said, face grim. "And I'm guessing you're here because someone else's child has been taken."

"I don't want you to worry," Yvonne said, although she knew it was almost certainly futile. They had lost their son once. No matter how unlikely it was that the kidnappers would come back for him, she could only imagine the fear of that. "But, if you want to feel safer, I am sure Grayling will find a place for you. No one has been taken from Fir Tree Crossing. The one time they tried, they did not succeed."

"We might just do that," he answered, exchanging a brief glance with his wife. "It would be good to have a break from here anyway."

"Superstitious idiots," his wife muttered, not quite under her breath.

"You've had trouble?" Yvonne asked.

"They've decided we are bad luck, for some reason." The husband was just as disgusted as his wife. "I think they'd be singing a different tune if it was their child taken."

"Has something else happened?" she asked.

"No. The wise woman died, as we told you. And then Alexander came back," the wife said, unable to help the smile on her face as she looked at her son.

"Nothing has happened," her husband confirmed. "But it's always been a peaceful place. And we're not welcome anymore."

"My grandmother and my mother helped birth half the elders in the place," the wife said, voice shading to bitterness, "and now no one wants to talk to us."

"I'm sorry," Yvonne said. It was not her fault, she knew, but this family had lived their lives here, and probably expected to see out their days here as well, all of them. "Fir Tree Crossing seems a good and honest place. And I am sure there is room for more excellent craftsmen. My children and I are very grateful for our new boots. I particularly like having dry feet," she added, drawing smiles from the family.

"Fir Tree Crossing," the husband said slowly, speculatively, and looked around the tools and equipment that they had removed from their workspace for cleaning.

"We don't have all that much. The wagon would take it. And we don't need to rush the journey," his wife said.

"It's just as well. The oxen don't go fast," Alexander said, nose wrinkling.

"I can see you as far as the King's Highway," Yvonne said. The offer of assistance was as natural as breathing. She could provide some aid, and she sensed that the decision had been made, and they were going to act on it quickly.

"Well, now you've given us the idea, we best get on with it," the wife said.

And so, Yvonne's horse had a longer rest than planned while she helped the family bundle up their possessions into the large wagon they had, fetching him while they hitched up a pair of placid looking oxen, and spending the rest of the day journeying with them to the King's Highway, which was the easiest overland route back to Fir Tree Crossing.

They stayed overnight at the King's Tavern, the family making their way on in the morning at a steady walking pace, the oxen completely untroubled by the odd journey. Yvonne pressed her horse a little faster. The King's Highway led, a little further along, to a bridge across the river that she needed to cross to get to the Karoan'shae palace, to try to find Guise.

Chapter Nine

At length, there was a fork in the path. The trail that she had been following, a reasonably well-maintained wagon road, kept going, but there was a wide, smooth road that turned away from it and led into the forest, passing between giant, ancient trees. The horse did not want to go that way, perhaps more sensible than she was, snorting and dancing sideways as they moved onto the new road. A shiver of foreign magic crossed her skin, the slightly static sensation she associated with goblin magic.

They were in goblin territory now, and her stomach tightened with nerves. It was one thing to plan this, in the safety of her own house. It was another thing to find herself here, in the late afternoon, miles from any human habitation and riding in the shadows of trees that soared above her head, trunks patterned with bark that carried a scent which teased her senses. It was a common ingredient in perfumes and soaps. This entire forest would be worth a fortune in human terms, and yet every tree she could see was untouched, none of the bark stripped or sap drawn out.

It was a potent symbol of wealth, this forest, the trees slightly too uniformly planted to be natural. It reminded her of the enormous fountains in the southern city of Abar al Endell. A deliberate display of wealth. All that water going to waste, near the desert. And here, a fortune left untouched in the trees.

The horse danced sideways again, calling her attention back. Bad enough she was in goblin territory. Worse still if she was thrown off her horse and had to walk the rest of the way to the palace. And, from the way the road stretched ahead of her, with no end in sight, she suspected it would be a long walk.

After some time, when she estimated it was near evening, the trees ahead thinned a little and she caught her first glimpse of the palace in the wider gaps between the trees.

Her first thought was that it was huge. Bigger than any single building she had seen in her life before.

It stretched out ahead of her, a giant construction several storeys high, made of what looked like ordinary grey stone, but which glimmered slightly in the daylight. As she rode closer, she could make out more details. There were windows in the upper storeys which sat out from the building at a seemingly impossible distance. There were towers here and there, some rising an immense height into the sky, others on the ground, offset from the main building, squat and round, windows gleaming in the late afternoon sunlight. Some of the windows were massive, single spans of glass that must have preservation spells to maintain them. Others were small, diamond-shaped panes. Still others were stained glass, images that she could not make sense of.

It made no sense to her eyes. It looked like there had been a half dozen, or more, architects involved in its construction, and they had each thrown their ideas into the building.

The trees fell away around her, giving way to an expanse of cropped grass that must require either an army of gardeners or a hefty dose of magic to maintain, the road she was on following a slight curve up to an enormous pair of doors, standing ajar in the fading afternoon sun.

Her stomach tightened again, and her horse danced sideways again, throwing up his head and snorting in protest as she pushed him forward. She missed Lothar. He would have protested, too, she was sure, but he would have gone where she asked, ready to act if he spied any enemies.

The horse gave another snort as they drew to a halt in the shadow of the doors. At least three storeys high, the doors were made of dark wood bounded with iron, as beautifully crafted as she would expect from a goblin building.

They were also deserted. Despite being slightly open, there was no sign of anyone. No servants, not even a grounds-keeper.

She left the horse with its reins on the ground, hoping that its training would hold and it would not bolt and leave her behind, and went towards the half dozen shallow stone steps that led up to the doors, looking for a bell, or something to summon the housekeeper. There must be one, for a building this size.

As soon as she set foot on the first step, a shadow moved behind the door and a goblin stepped out into the light. He had the pale grey skin and clean bone structure of the Karoan'shae, and was dressed in the same navy blue livery as the coachman who had driven Guise's mother. Yvonne froze for a moment, wondering if the assassin's information had been wrong and that, far from finding Guise, she had instead found where his mother was staying.

He looked her up and down, hands tucked behind his back, expression tight. Displeasure or disgust, she wasn't sure.

"Good day to you. I am looking –"

He interrupted, saying something in the goblin tongue too quickly for her to catch. She knew a few words, nothing more. Every goblin she had met had been fluent in several languages, including the one most humans used. In all the scenarios she had imagined on the journey here, finding a servant who did not understand her had not even crossed her mind.

"I don't understand," she said, keeping her voice calm and steady. "I am looking –"

She did not get a chance to finish, again, as he moved, lifting an arm and pointing behind her. She turned, hand going to her sword hilt in reflex, wondering if someone had crept up behind her. There was nothing there. Just her horse, looking less than impressed, and the long path back through the giant trees.

When she turned back to the goblin, he was already moving away, back towards the doors.

"Wait," she called, taking a step forward.

He whirled back towards her, red flickering in his eyes, and she froze. He had one hand under his coat, doubtless on a weapon of his own. He might be a servant, but goblins considered fighting a form of art.

Many also considered humans to be far beneath them, too. And she no longer had the symbol at her shoulder. So there was no need, none at all, for this goblin to be polite to her.

Facing formidable opponents was something she had done too many times before. She squared her shoulders, refusing to let her unease show, and stared back at him.

"Guidrishinnal de'laj Krejefell," she said, speaking the words as clearly as she could, and hoping she was not mangling the pronunciation too badly.

His lip curled up, showing a long, gleaming incisor, the red still in his eyes, and he said something else, in a sharp tone. Doubtless declaring that a prince of his people would have nothing to do with a shabbily-dressed human woman.

Yvonne sighed. She agreed with him. It was ridiculous.

He waved his hand again, indicating the path.

"Fine. You want me to leave. I understand. But I need to speak to Guise."

More words, in a sharper, more menacing tone.

"I really don't want a fight," she told him, and some flicker across his face made her pause. "Oh, so you can understand me. You just don't want to speak to me. Fine," she said again, nervousness and tension melting into anger. "But at least tell me where I can find Guise. Guidrishinnal de'laj Krejefell, I mean. I need to speak with him."

Another torrent of words, and another gesture behind her.

The hilt of her sword dug into her palm. She would not draw it unless she had to. It would not be wise. But she was tempted.

"If you will not speak with me, then find me someone who will. I need to know where to find him," she told the servant, anger riding her.

He stepped forward, drawing a sword from underneath his coat in one smooth move, and flicked the end of the sword back towards the road.

"No." She drew her own sword, ready to defend herself. "Tell me where to find Guise."

He bared his teeth in a silent snarl a wulf would have been proud of, and flicked his sword towards her. Doubtless thinking that she would move back.

Instead, she met his blade with her own, the hiss of clashing steel breaking the peace of the afternoon.

He said something else, still speaking goblin, in a low, furious tone.

"No. I'm not leaving," she said.

He moved again, with that flowing grace goblins could manage, sword slicing forward, trying to make her retreat. She ducked around the sword. He was not trying to kill her. Not yet.

His eyes widened in surprise as she did not immediately retreat, and she felt a grim satisfaction. She might be a shabbily-dressed human woman, but she had been trained well, and met his next attack with the flat of her sword, slapping his weapon to one side, taking a step back to draw the long knife that sat at her other hip. He was taller, more powerful, than she was.

But not as skilled. And fast losing his temper, the red flaring in his eyes.

He attacked again, and she used the wild movement to catch his blade between hers, twisting the weapon out of his hand, and then resting her sword point just under his chin.

He froze, breathing hard, eyes full of bright sparks of red, fangs descended, and snarled something in his own language.

"Oh. I know some of that. Filthy human, yes?" she asked. She was slightly out of breath from the exercise. A few days' absence from drill practice and she was losing condition. Hopefully, there would be no more fighting.

"Mristrian. I am delighted to see you."

That voice. She would know it anywhere. Her memory never quite captured it perfectly, and every time she heard it again after an absence, like now, it curled through her, an invisible draw towards the speaker.

Guise.

She did not move her sword, turning her head to see him standing several paces away, a trio of other goblins behind him, all of them tall and lithe, with the pale grey skin and refined cheekbones of high-ranking members of the Karoan'shae. She blinked. Not just other goblins, but ones she had met before, when Guise had been injured. Friends of Guise, people he respected and liked. Brea, her husband Thort, and their daughter Jesset. And all of them, even Guise, were dressed in work clothes, not their usual outfits at all. Linen shirts, worn loose over heavy cloth trousers tucked into calf-length boots. Each of them was liberally splashed with mud.

She blinked again, wondering if she had imagined the scene, but they were still there.

"I see Prestin has been making you welcome," Guise added, voice dry. He took a pace forward, bent, and picked up Prestin's discarded sword. Despite his work clothes and the dirt on them, he moved with his usual smooth grace.

"Very welcome," she answered, matching his dry tone. She turned back to see the red still in the servant's eyes. "Careful. I'm still holding a sword at your throat. More insults would be unwise."

"You will have an apology, mristrian," Guise assured her, voice cooling as he turned his attention to the servant. "Prestin, this is the lady Yvonne. Mristrian, Prestin is the steward here."

Not just an ordinary servant, then, but one in a senior position of some responsibility.

"I am pleased to make your acquaintance, Lady Yvonne," Prestin said, demonstrating a perfect command of the humans' language, remaining quite still under the point of her sword.

"I knew you could understand me," Yvonne told him, resisting a momentary impulse to stab him.

"I apologise for any misunderstanding," Prestin added. Typical goblin. It could be an apology for the insult, for his pretending not to understand her, or for some other transgression of goblin manners she could not guess at. It was also the most lukewarm apology she had heard for some time.

Yvonne lifted a brow, and clamped her jaw shut against any more hasty words. As tempting as it was to say more, she was in unfamiliar territory and he was a high-ranking servant. There might be repercussions. She drew back her sword and sheathed her weapons.

"Lady Yvonne, it is good to see you again," Brea said, cutting across whatever Prestin, or Guise, might say next. She stepped forward, just as graceful in her work clothes as she had been in the flowing desert robes Yvonne had seen her in before, with her right hand up, palm outward, and Yvonne remembered just in time that was a friendly greeting among goblins, stepping away from Prestin, putting her own palm out to touch Brea's, then repeating the process with Thort and Jesset.

Exchanging the greetings, Yvonne realised that all of the goblins had their long, black hair tied back, out of the way of the mud that covered their clothes. For once, her serviceable hairstyle and her own, plain clothing were not out of place.

"Have you come to help with the negotiations?" Jesset asked, eyes bright with curiosity. "You would be a great help."

"Ah. No. I ... I am here to see Guise," Yvonne answered, heat rising in her face.

"Oh –"

"Jesset," Brea interrupted her daughter smoothly, and put a hand through her daughter's elbow, tugging gently. "Enough for now. Lady Yvonne has had a long ride to get here and would doubtless like some refreshment. Prestin, see to it."

"My lady," Prestin answered, bowing fractionally. He eyed the sword that Guise was still holding, clearly decided against asking for it back, and disappeared back into the palace.

"If you will come this way, mristrian," Guise said. He stabbed Prestin's sword into the ground, and Yvonne winced as the steel twisted. There were probably rocks or stones under the surface. It would take a smith some time to fix the sword. Perhaps Guise had not believed Prestin's apology, either.

Chapter Ten

Guise was silent as Yvonne fetched her horse, then walked with him around the side of the palace, back in the direction that Guise and his friends had come from.

Despite his greater height, they fell into step easily. She was grateful for a few moments' quiet. As well as the voice, Guise also had a presence in the world that drew her, and she needed to find her balance again.

The gravel path they were walking on continued around the side of the palace, and Yvonne could see two other paths cutting across the perfectly maintained grass lawn. The furthest one dipped out of sight as the land sloped away. Guise turned down the nearest path, which led away from the palace towards a copse of trees that had been deliberately planted. Yvonne had never seen that particular combination of trees in nature. A large, mature tree with broad, deep red leaves was surrounded by fractionally smaller trees with leaf colours ranging from pale yellow to vibrant green.

As they crossed under the first tree's canopy, another fizz of magic crossed her skin. Another boundary.

A moment later and she saw what this boundary had contained. It was a modest-sized dwelling, compared to the palace, barely larger than the house she was currently renting, set amid beautifully maintained gardens that were a riot of colour and scent. Her horse lifted his head and blew out a breath, some of the tension leaving him.

"This is the annex," Guise explained, leading them through the garden, around the house, to an area of grass that also held a large wrought iron table and a half dozen chairs. "Please, sit. I'll get some water for the horse."

It was only then she realised that they were alone. Brea, Thort and Jesset had disappeared somewhere along the way, or possibly stayed at the palace.

Rather than sitting down, she took the horse's saddle and bridle off, putting on a rope halter with a long tether rope, and gave him a quick brush before Guise was back with a large wooden bucket of water and another, smaller bucket of plain feed.

As Guise set the buckets down, Prestin arrived, carrying a tray which held a large tea pot and, Yvonne's nose told her, a variety of food.

"That will be all," Guise told him. Prestin made a tiny, calculated bow and left, shoulders square, walking with an unhurried pace.

"He's charming," Yvonne said, unable to help herself, just before Prestin was out of earshot. He checked slightly in his stride, back stiff, but kept going.

Guise laughed, shaking his head slightly.

"He is not part of my household," he told her, as though that should explain everything. It probably would have done, for a goblin. Yvonne was more interested in the food than in understanding that, and followed his gesture as he waved her to a chair, busying himself with unloading the tray, setting a laden plate in front of Yvonne moments later. A spread of cured meats, cheese, bread and fruits that she knew were tart and sweet at the same time.

"Please, eat," Guise prompted. With his hair pulled back from his face, the clean lines of his jaw and forehead were in stark relief, making him look more like a warrior than the finely dressed gentleman he usually portrayed to the world. No one would mistake him for anything other than a member of the Karoan'shae, though. It was in the clean lines of his face, the pale grey skin and the way he carried himself. The unconscious air of someone used to privilege. She had thought him arrogant at their first meeting. She still thought so, but now knew that the arrogance was tempered with many other things, like a keen mind that revelled in secrets and knowledge.

While she had been considering his changed appearance, he had made up a plate of his own, and there was no talking for a while.

Yvonne discovered that she was truly hungry for what felt like the first time in days, finishing everything on her plate. The food was almost as good as the offerings at Modig's hotel in Three Falls, and she told Guise so.

"True. But Modig's kitchens are superb."

Yvonne agreed, sitting back in her chair with the large mug of tea Guise had poured for her, turning the mug around in her hands. It was made of fine, almost translucent china, the sort normally used for dainty teacups and tea services. She could barely imagine the skill of the craftsman who had created this, or how much it was worth.

"You've come from Fir Tree Crossing today?" Guise asked. He was holding his own mug of tea.

She blinked as she looked at him. Not only was he more casually dressed than she was used to, he also seemed more relaxed than she had ever seen him, more expression on his face than he usually showed to the world. Perhaps it was the effect of being in his own territory.

"No. The King's tavern near Silverton. I went to see Alexander."

"The tanners' son, yes. How is he faring?"

"Better than I had hoped," she answered. "Although, the townsfolk in Silverton have been less than friendly. The family are on their way to Fir Tree Crossing now."

"I am glad the boy is well. So, from Silverton to here?" Guise prompted.

She set the mug down on the table top with care, not wanting to damage the china. "I know why the tribesmen are kidnapping nine-year-old girls," she said without any preamble.

He did not move much, but in the space of a single breath his posture changed from relaxed to focused.

"Tribesmen?"

"I assumed you knew," she said, shaking her head. "Men with horses were seen in Fir Tree Crossing. The wulfkin found traces of people camping in the forest near the town. On this side of the river. We followed. Ashnassan." She saw his lip curl at the name. "They attacked. We defended. They retreated. Lothar was injured." She looked away, eyes burning, remembering again the squeal of pain, not wanting to show weakness or be thought foolish for her upset over her horse. "They were being paid for the girls. They didn't get anyone in the town, but Grayling has two more reports of girls being taken."

Guise was quite still when she looked back at him, eyes brilliant green.

"How can I help?"

Not the question she had been expecting. She had been expecting him to ask what the Hundred were doing. Or about the blank space on her shoulder. Not that simple, direct offer of help.

She had an impulse to get up and leave. She did not belong here, in this beautiful garden, in goblin territory. Without the badge of Hunar at her shoulder, she felt utterly out of place.

She did not know what he saw in her face, but his serious, intent expression lifted into a slight smile.

"I, and my resources, are at your disposal, mristrian."

"Nine years old is when girls come into their powers. Usually."

Guise's expression darkened again.

"We need the others," he said abruptly. "No, sit there just now. I'll summon them."

"Wait." The word was out before her mind had time to catch up. And, of course, he waited, settled back in his chair, and became still.

And now she had his full attention again, she had no idea what she really wanted to say. Something about the Hundred. Something about how she shouldn't be here. Something about how she didn't know what to think about this bond they had apparently created, and she still could not remember, and did not understand.

Her mouth opened. No words came out. Instead, her hand lifted to touch the blank space at her shoulder, a twinge of the still-healing wound under her shirt reminding her of Sillman's implacable face.

"I was dismissed. Sundered," she said, face and voice tight. She could not look at him. To her horror, her eyes were hot again, her throat constricted.

"Sillman?" he asked. His voice seemed calm, unsurprised, and she glanced across to see sparks of red in his eyes. Not calm, then. But not surprised, either.

"How did you know?"

"Call it an educated guess," he answered, sitting forward in his chair and extending his hand, palm up, on the table between them. Inviting her to put her hand in his.

Not quite sure why she did so, she leant forward as well. The sensation of another's skin under hers was odd. Not unpleasant. Just different, requiring her attention. The strength and faintly rough texture of hands used to hard work, despite the gentleman's clothes he usually wore. Warmth under her fingers, when she had not realised she was cold.

"I didn't even realise it was possible," she said, words pouring out of her, voice rising in pitch. "But they had already decided and there was nothing I could do and I can't go to them for help. I can't. But..." She bit off whatever else she might say and ducked her head, ashamed of her outburst.

"Whatever you need, mristrian," he told her, as serious as she had ever seen him.

"I don't understand you," she told him plainly, her hand still resting on his. She had said the same words to him only a few days ago. Before Sillman had arrived and torn the Hunar's symbol out of her.

His fingers curled up, slowly, giving her time to pull away, and he clasped her hand for a moment before straightening his fingers again. And gave her the same answer he had before.

"I know. But I would very much like it if you did." It might be the same words, but the tone was different. Deeper, richer, that incredible voice pulling her forward.

Her breath caught, seeing the faint shimmer of gold in his eyes, and her pulse skipped, the old, old fear rising. She knew he would not hurt her. This was Guise. And yet, she could not hold his eyes. Or keep contact with his hand.

Heat rose in her face. She was frightened of a simple hand clasp. Still gripped by her past. And not able to do anything about it.

She pulled her hand away, fingers cooling as she sat back in her chair, picking up the priceless, delicate mug as though that could be a shield between her and the many things she did not understand or want to think about.

"Brea and Thort would be delighted to help, too. Let me fetch them," he said, all business as he rose from the table and strode away across the garden.

She finished her cooling tea in a too-large mouthful, almost choking as she tried to swallow it all. Guise, Brea and Thort were formidable. Between them, she was sure they would find answers to where the girls were being taken. And yet, she wanted to saddle her horse and ride back to Fir Tree Crossing as fast as possible.

Away from golden eyes, the rough texture of skin against hers and a bond she did not understand.

Before she had time to do anything, Guise was back with, of all things, another tea pot, this one larger and plainer than the first. He was still in the work clothes, although she noted he had managed a cleansing spell and unbound his hair, so that it fell in a gleaming black wave across his shoulders.

"More tea, mristrian?"

She heard herself agree, and watched as he poured her a fresh mug. Leaving enough room for milk without being asked.

By the time he had poured himself more tea and taken his seat again, across the table from her, Brea and Thort were striding into the garden, dressed as they had been when Yvonne had first met them, in flowing garments more usually found in the desert.

"You were working," Yvonne said, cheeks heating up. She had interrupted something. Doubtless something important, if all of them were involved, along with Brea and Thort's daughter.

"Digging ditches," Brea said, settling in a chair, Thort sitting beside her. "Your arrival was a very welcome interruption, Lady Yvonne."

"Call me Yvonne, please," she answered by reflex, then tilted her head. "Digging ditches?"

"Seems unlikely, I know," Thort agreed, with an easy smile, handing two fresh mugs to Guise, who filled them for the couple. "But the lower field is prone to flooding."

"And the entire damned circus is arriving soon, so the field is needed," Brea added, as though that explained everything.

"There's only so much we can do with magic. There's just too much soil."

"So, we had to actually dig," Brea finished, with a delicate shudder. "I swear I still have dirt under my fingernails." She held out one hand to inspect her nails which were, of course, clean.

"The circus?" Yvonne asked. The one part of that exchange she had not fully understood.

Brea and Thort exchanged glances, then looked at Guise.

"You didn't tell her," Thort said.

"We were discussing other matters," Guise answered, apparently calm. Yvonne was not fooled. She had seen that posture before, many times. It was a mask. An excellent mask, used to disguise whatever it was he truly felt.

"The Karoan'shae are coming here in about two weeks," Brea told Yvonne, shaking her head slightly. "Why they had to pick here is beyond me. There's at least a half dozen places closer to the borders."

"My mother's choice," Guise said, voice light, and still wearing that mask.

Yvonne's attention caught on that. Helgiarast se'laj Krejefell was the current star of the Karoan'shae. In human terms, the goblin queen. And she had determined that the Karoan'shae would meet here. At an inconvenient distance from the goblin lands. At the closest goblin palace to Fir Tree Crossing.

It was very possible that Helgiarast had other reasons for choosing this place, reasons that Yvonne could not possibly guess at. And yet, some instinct told Yvonne that was not the case. The current star of the Karoan'shae had, Yvonne thought, been annoyed by her son's bonding with a human. Doubtless others would be, too.

"I nearly forgot," she said, putting her tea down again. "I had a visit from your assassin friend. She didn't leave a name."

"What did she want?" Guise had gone perfectly still. A predator. And yet she was not frightened of him.

"To let me know that you're in danger."

"No news there," Brea commented, taking a sip of tea. "May I guess that she came to visit you at night, and wasn't particularly straightforward?"

Yvonne found an unexpected laugh in her chest, and let it loose.

"Still wearing black," she confirmed to Brea. "She's visited you, too?"

"Some years ago." Brea shook her head slightly. "I told her to use the gate next time, like any civilised person."

Yvonne laughed again. She could easily imagine Brea facing down the black-clad assassin.

"She came to your house?" Guise asked, voice silky soft.

"To the meeting place outside," Yvonne answered, stumbling a little over the words. She had been about to say the Hunar's meeting point, correcting herself in time. "We had a very interesting conversation."

Whatever Guise might have said was interrupted as Brea threw back her head and laughed, whole body shaking with mirth, not stopping as Guise lifted a brow at her. Some kind of cousins, Yvonne remembered.

"You have quite excellent taste," Brea commented to Guise, wiping her eyes. "Interesting conversation indeed."

"She did not threaten you?" Guise asked, still in that silky soft voice.

"Of course not." Yvonne shook her head, picking up her mug. "If she had wanted me dead, I would be dead."

"You seem quite calm about that," Thort commented.

"There was no real threat," Yvonne answered, looking down at her tea as she shrugged her shoulders. "And plenty of people have tried to kill me, one way or another."

"Guise said you had news?" Brea said in the awkward silence that followed.

Yvonne summarised the discovery of the Ashnassan, giving more detail than she had to Guise. She told them about her conversation with the tribesman, but missed out Lothar's injury on this telling.

"You're sure that the tribesmen aren't keeping the girls?" Brea asked.

"No. I can't be sure. But it doesn't fit. They aren't interested in girls that young," Yvonne answered, the excellent food she had eaten curdling in her stomach. "And they are being paid. Enough to risk collecting girls from the middle of towns."

"Shame that they retreated," Thort said, eyes narrowed. "More information would be useful."

Yvonne remembered the tribesman's expression when the whistle had sounded, calling them away. He had not expected the order to retreat.

"There were reports of a scout party near here," Guise said slowly, eyes narrowed in concentration.

"On goblin lands?" Brea asked, eyebrows lifting.

"Near the borders," Guise said, a line between his brows. "They have been careful to stay outside."

"Will they still be there?" Yvonne asked slowly. "It's not that far from here to where they were attacked," she added. She had gone the long way around, with her visit to Silverton, but if she had taken a direct route through the trees, she estimated that the ambush site was less than a day's ride away.

"Latest reports suggest so," Guise told her. "We've left them alone so far as they have been keeping to themselves. Perhaps it's time to visit," he speculated, teeth bared for a moment, then tipped his head up, assessing the sky. The light of day was fast fading. "Perhaps tonight."

Even as the knot of tension inside loosened, Yvonne glanced across at her horse, dozing in the fading sunlight, and shook her head slightly. Lothar would have been able to make a mid-of-night raid. The spare horse was done for the day.

"We'll find you a horse," Guise promised, following her line of sight.

"I'm not sure how much help I will be," Yvonne said, voice and throat tight, remembering. Her distraction. Lothar's injury. Grayling intervening, blocking the strike that could have killed her.

"Do you still have some fireball spells?" Guise asked, a familiar gleam in his eyes.

She lifted a brow. Throwing fire in a forest was not usually a good idea. And, apart from tracking the Ashnassan, she had not tried to use magic for the past few days. Since she had been dismissed from the Hundred. For a moment she considered telling Guise that she might not be able to work magic now. The words stuck in her throat. The great hollow inside her, left by the tearing out of the symbol, did not ache as much. She had been able to use her tracking magic. And the spells she had in her pouch were already primed. They just needed the word to activate them.

"Yes," she answered, trying to put as much confidence as she could into that word. Part of magic was believing that you could do it, Elinor had said more than once. She drew in a slow breath. She just needed to activate the spells. She could do that. All she had to do was say the command word, and it was right there, behind her teeth.

"Excellent."

"We'll need all of our weapons," Thort commented.

"And to let Jesset know," Brea added.

The pair of them rose and were about to move away when Brea turned back briefly. "And there are matters which you should discuss, Guise."

Yvonne watched the pair as they left the garden side by side, a matched pair nearly equal in height.

"I would like to know more about the assassin's visit," Guise said, voice quiet, before she could speak.

"That is not what Brea thought you should discuss," Yvonne answered, casting her mind back over the conversation. "Something about the Karoan'shae coming here?" It was a guess. Guise tilted his head slightly, acknowledging the point.

"A trade of information, then," he suggested.

She shook her head, reluctant to tell him more about the strange conversation with the assassin. "I'm not going to bargain with you," she told him plainly.

To her surprise, he accepted her answer with good grace, dipping his chin in recognition, before his expression turned more serious. He turned to look across the garden.

"There is to be a confirmation. A new Head of House," he began abruptly. "They are usually carried out in the territory of the current star. But my mother has decided the confirmation should happen here."

"Jesset said something about negotiations?" Yvonne prompted, frowning, wondering why the confirmation of the head of a house would require bartering, even among the Karoan'shae.

"A renewing of alliances. Agreements which were made with the old lord need to be confirmed."

Yvonne's brows lifted. So. The old lord had made agreements with others in the Karoan'shae, and they had all known him. And the new Head of House, whoever they were, now had to renegotiate the old agreements. No wonder goblin politics were so complicated.

"If the new head cannot make the same agreements, what happens?"

Guise's eyes gleamed, fangs bared for a moment. "Then the circus becomes very bloody." He shook his head, looking across the garden again, serious once more. "The old lord had nominated an heir. But there are a half dozen other candidates."

It sounded like the prelude to civil war. The houses that made up the Karoan'shae all circling each other, wary of the other families. And a struggle for power inside the house as well.

"Does this happen often? The confirmation, I mean," Yvonne added.

"Not that often. The heads of houses are either killed quickly, through their own foolishness, or live long enough to secure the place for their heir. The old lord's death was unexpected. A riding accident. He had done nothing more than nominate an heir."

"You liked him," Yvonne realised. Something in the way Guise had spoken. "I'm sorry for your loss."

"It's common for children of the Karoan'shae to be passed around the houses for a few years. It lets us make our own connections," he told her, voice shading to bitterness. "I spent a few years in his house."

There was something he was not telling her, she knew. Something important. Probably more than one thing, knowing Guise. She opened her mouth to ask, then closed it again. There was more than enough information to keep her occupied for a while.

Thinking over what he had said, and what Brea had said, and not said, a chill ran through her.

"The whole Karoan'shae is coming here?"

"Not all of them. Someone has to keep house," he said, his attempt at humour falling flat. He was not looking at her again.

"Your mother chose this place," Yvonne said, voice flat. "Near to human lands. Does she expect me to be there, too?"

"What my mother expects, and what she shall get, are quite different things," he answered. "I must change." He rose to his feet abruptly and stalked away through the garden. It was almost rude of him, leaving Yvonne with an uneasy knot in her stomach and a head full of questions. She was also quite sure that, whatever her son might believe, the current star of the Karoan'shae was not used to being denied.

Chapter Eleven

RIDING INTO THE GATHERING night with a group of near-strangers was something she had done before. Trouble seemed to sleep during the daylight hours. But she had always had Lothar before, her dependable warhorse giving her at least one ally in any group she was in. She missed his solid presence.

Now she was surrounded by a trio perhaps just as lethal as the Hundred. Perhaps even more so. Guise was restored to his usual impeccable attire and, as usual, she felt shabby beside him with her threadbare clothes and well-worn weapons.

Brea and Thort had changed again, not into the loose, desert clothing they had worn when she first met them, but into outfits more like a warrior's uniform, each of them bristling with weapons. From the way they carried themselves, Yvonne was quite confident that they were just as competent, if not more so, than Guise in the goblin art of war.

The horse they had found for her, of goblin breeding, naturally, had been less than impressed at a human rider and a great deal of her concentration in the early part of the journey was taken up with trying to stay on her horse, and come to some kind of an understanding with it. She could only hope that it would not simply throw her aside and run into the forest at the first sign of trouble. Even if she did manage to stay on the horse, she did not think she would be much use if there was any fighting, apart from the few fireball spells in the pouch at her belt.

Realising that they were going to be travelling at night, she had taken a few moments, while Guise was changing, to dredge her memory for a spell that would enhance her sight. She did not think it was close to goblin's night sight, but it was a lot better than her normal, human eyes could manage. And working that small piece of magic had settled some of her nerves. There was still some power at her command.

There was very little discussion of what they would do when they found the Ashnassan. Yvonne was too preoccupied with her horse to contribute much, in any event, but she also suspected that the others had worked together often enough that they didn't need much conferring.

They had ridden for long enough that it was truly dark before Brea spotted a campfire ahead of them. A small clearing in the forest. The tribesmen were not making any effort to disguise their presence. But then, they were very close to goblin territory, and in a deserted part of the forest. Perhaps they did not think they would get visitors.

Even so, the tribesmen were ready for them when they rode into the small clearing.

There was a cooking pot suspended over the fire, the clearing full of the rich scent of a meal almost ready. They had been settled here a while, then, as Yvonne knew from experience just how long it took to cook decent meals over a campfire.

At the edge of the clearing, just within the firelight, three riding horses were tethered. They had the lean, angular look that Yvonne associated with desert horses.

In front of the fire, a pair of tribesmen were waiting. Armed and wary, they were standing together, just far enough apart to use their weapons. They were dressed for the cooler night, with long-sleeved tunics hiding whatever markings they might have on their arms. Their faces bore a few marks, though, telling Yvonne that they were relatively junior warriors. Not the obvious choice for a scouting party near goblin territory.

Three horses meant three warriors, though. The Ashnassan did not travel with spare horses. If these two were junior, she wondered how senior the missing warrior was.

"I'll find the other one," Thort said, and slid off his horse, looping its reins loosely around the saddle horn before disappearing into the night, blending into the dark so well that even Yvonne's enhanced sight could not follow him.

"You're far from home," one of the tribesmen said. He had his hands on his hips, close to weapons hilts. "What's your business here?"

"I could ask you the same thing," Guise said. He dismounted and sent his horse away with a pat, taking a few steps closer to the tribesmen who were still standing close together, watching his approach. "Your people have been engaging in unsavoury activity," he commented. And that was the Guise she knew, Yvonne thought. Full of the arrogance that came with being a high-ranking member of the Karoan'shae, with a lifetime of unlimited resources behind him.

"You're going to need to be more specific," Yvonne commented. "They've done a lot of unsavoury things."

She hadn't quite meant to say that, but saw, by the reactions of the tribesmen, that she had struck home. Outside their own territories, the Ashnassan were renowned not only for their fighting prowess but also for a variety of crimes. Petty theft of small items such as jewellery and, on occasion, food. Kidnapping. And horse stealing which, in many lands, was considered far more serious than mere kidnapping. Good horses were invaluable.

"You're quite right, mristrian," Guise said, inclining his head in her direction. He turned back to the tribesmen. "A number of young girls have gone missing. You will tell us what you know."

The men laughed, shaking their heads, as though he had told them an excellent joke.

They were a pair of humans, facing an armed goblin, with two other armed goblins to support him. The tribesmen might ignore a human woman, not considering her as any kind of threat. No one ignored the threat of a single armed goblin, let alone three.

The tribesmen were too confident.

Yvonne got off her horse as well. She did not know it well enough, and it could be dangerous to stay mounted rather than on the ground.

Glancing at Brea, who was alert, her eyes constantly moving around the clearing, Yvonne judged that the lady was more than capable of watching their backs. As she had expected. So, Yvonne moved forward to stand near Guise. Far enough apart that they could both draw their weapons.

"Where are your friends?" she asked, and sensed a slight shift as Guise tensed, picking up her cue.

"We've got trouble," Thort told them, coming back into the firelight and dragging an unconscious man with him. "This one was keeping watch, but I'm sure I heard horses coming towards us."

"Expecting company?" Guise asked the two tribesmen, who were still standing, at their ease, next to the fire.

From the smirk on their faces, Yvonne guessed that, yes, they were expecting company, and in numbers great enough to tackle three fully armed goblins.

"Do you know what the girls are taken for? What purpose they will serve?" she asked them. "Did you ever think about that? You have mothers, and sisters, and wives, and perhaps children of your own. These girls are only nine."

The smirk faded slightly on the one on the left, but the other seemed completely untroubled.

"It pays well," the untroubled tribesman told them.

"Not anymore," Yvonne told them.

"And who are you to say that? Don't think you'd be quite as brave without your goblin friends," he said.

"I would not be so sure," Guise said. "The lady is both brave, and powerful. She is also right. Kidnapping children will not pay well anymore."

"And who are you to make that promise? You just keep to your own kind, and leave us to our affairs."

"I am Guise," he said, and drew his sword. "And you have just reached the end of my patience. Thort, we need this one alive." He pointed to the one on the left, the one that looked like he might have a conscience. "Mristrian, I think we are about to have company."

Her stomach knotted. All the doubts surfaced again. Her ability to use magic without the symbol of the Hunar. Her ability to even hold her sword, after the last fight. She shoved them aside. Now was not the time. And the spells just required an activation word. One word. She could manage that.

And if she could not manage to at least hold her sword after the hours and hours of training that she had endured with Elinor, and the hours and hours of practice since then, then Elinor and Renard would have wasted the time they had spent on her training. And she could not bear to let Elinor down.

So, she swallowed down the doubt, drew a breath. "Ready," she confirmed, voice steady, drawing a pair of spells from her pouch and stepping back to give him room.

Two tribesmen against two goblins was nowhere near a fair fight. Guise disarmed, and killed, the bolder of the two in a few controlled moves, while Thort simply clubbed the other one on the head and then bound him, and the one he had dragged from the forest, with rope that Brea handed to him from her horse.

The goblins were efficient. When they had finished tying up the unconscious men, Yvonne could hear hoof beats approaching, but whoever the tribesmen had expected was not there yet.

Following Guise's lead, three goblins and a human retreated back into the forest, out of the firelight, and away from the direction that the hoof beats were coming from, taking their horses with them, so that when a large group – perhaps two dozen, maybe more – of Ashnassan warriors rode into the clearing, they were met with the sight of one dead and two unconscious members of their tribe, the horses grazing peacefully at the end of their tethers.

Yvonne was struck, once again, by the discipline of the group. They were all holding ranks, keeping to their assigned tasks, despite the scene in front of them. And all surrounding their commander. A leader travelling with at least two deputies. Yvonne recognised one of the deputies as the tribesman she had spoken to in the forest outside Fir Tree Crossing.

And she knew the leader of the group, by description and reputation. A tall, wiry man who claimed to have both goblin and witch blood in his heritage, although no one had ever proved it. He had dull blond hair pulled back in an untidy knot, and a stare that made her shiver slightly even from this distance. Another predator. The warrior known to his men as Slayer. The leader of the Ashnassan. A fearsome warrior, and fanatically devoted to the Ashnassan's gods. Far outside his own territory, and perilously close to goblin borders.

The Slayer assessed the clearing with a keen, sweeping glance and barked a few orders to his men. Yvonne had never learned their dialect completely, but could pick out a few words. He was not pleased that the men were bound, rather than dead.

All at once, the night felt a lot colder. As well as his skill as a warrior, the Slayer also had a reputation for enforcing discipline in his ranks by killing those of his men who had offended him. She had always assumed it was an exaggeration, struggling to believe that any leader would be so cruel. Or that a warrior people like the Ashnassan would willingly follow him.

Even as she watched, one of the deputies, the one she had met before, slid off his horse and approached the bound men, drawing a long knife from his boot. His expression, partly lit by the fire, looked grim, but determined.

Before she knew what she was doing, she was stepping forward, out of the trees and into the light.

Guise, Brea and Thort stayed where they were. A tactical advantage.

"You again," the deputy said, lip curling. He seemed less than pleased to see her.

"What have we here?" the leader asked. His command of the common tongue was flawless, though heavily accented. He moved his horse a few paces forward and eyed her up and down. "Are you supposed to be a woman?"

"Are you supposed to be frightening?" she asked, lifting her chin. He was human, and wouldn't be able to hear the heart thudding in her chest. Or the thoughts circling in her head. Why had she stepped into the clearing to save the bound tribesmen? She was no longer Hunar, and they had not asked for her help anyway. And yet, she could not simply stand by and watch cold murder.

The Slayer bared his teeth in what might have been a smile.

"You've got some fight in you. I like a woman with spirit."

Yvonne's stomach curdled. The Ashnassan had not kidnapped any women for brides for quite some time. No one quite knew what happened to the women they did take, as none had ever escaped. Yvonne's own memories supplied some idea of what might happen to a woman who fought back against a predator like the Slayer, or his deputy. She could see the glint of anticipation in his eyes.

"Easy to say when you're up there, sitting on your horse." She heard the words out of her mouth, tone hard and challenging, and could not regret them.

"I'll say it standing on the ground, too," he told her, teeth bared again. He was less amused now. "Perhaps demonstrate."

"Try it, and you'll feel the edge of my blade," she told him.

The amusement had gone from his eyes. Another bully and coward, furious when he didn't get his own way. Or perhaps he wasn't used to a female talking to him at all, let alone answering back.

There was a warm curl of anger sliding through her, warming her fingers and nose which had become chilled in the night air.

"Perhaps little girls are more to your taste?" she asked, voice hard. "Nine years old. They probably don't fight much," she added, the warmth spreading through her. Still a pure, unfiltered rage. She could hear Elinor's voice in her mind, memories from long ago, teaching her how to focus through her emotion. It had almost always been fear at the beginning. The anger had come later.

"You do not know what you are talking about. Or who you are talking to."

"You're the one they call Slayer," she said, voice still hard. She wished she could match Guise's bored tone, but she was too angry for that. "And you and your men have been taking nine-year-old girls. I'm told it pays well."

His eyes slid over to the bound men on the ground, and his expression shifted.

Yvonne's breath caught, a cool wash of fear chasing away some of the warmth of the anger. If she had thought that the deputy was dangerous, with his dead eyes, then this man was lethal. The entire side of his face was covered with markings, and she would bet that his markings extended down both arms and across his chest.

When he looked back at her, there was nothing human left in his face. He was stripped back to the predator under his skin.

The fear had faded, though, and she was burning through with fury again. She met and held his stare, unflinching.

The predator bared its teeth, and the Slayer moved, sliding off his horse with the coiled, lethal grace of a wildcat.

She stayed where she was, hand resting near her sword hilt, spells tucked out of sight in her other palm. Her spine was straight, breathing even, pulse loud and steady.

He had not drawn his sword yet. Perhaps he didn't think he needed it to defeat her. Foolish man.

He jerked his head, and his deputies melted back, along with the rest of his men.

"You're an insulting little thing," he told her, words sharp and cut off. He made to circle around her. She took a step back, catching his intent at once. If he circled her, and she followed his movement, keeping him in front of her, she would be caught between him and his men. And, while the anger held her tall and straight, she was not stupid enough to believe she could take them all on.

"It's impossible to insult someone who trades in children," she answered back, voice as sharp as his. He was avoiding her goading, demonstrating a level of self-control she would not have believed possible from the stories about him. Perhaps more encouragement was needed. "Tell me, what do you get for each child?"

"More than you'll ever see in your life."

"Times must be hard in your homeland if you're out here doing someone else's filthy work," she said. There. She had managed something like Guise's bored, arrogant tone. He didn't expect that, and even in the poor light she could see the flush of colour run up his neck and across his face.

"We serve a higher purpose," he growled at her, menace in his voice sending a chill up her spine. "For the glory of Nassash."

"For the glory of Nassash," the rest of the tribesmen repeated. A fine tremor ran through her, apprehension crawling over her skin. The Ashnassan tribe were a religious people, with faith in a number of gods, as fanatical about their religion as they were about their war skills. And the Slayer was more devoted than most. Or so his reputation said.

"Nassash wants you to play with girls?" she asked, lifting a brow. She had managed to hold on to Guise's bored tone despite the threat in front of her. Judging by the pulse she could see in the Slayer's neck, the tone was quite effective. She could understand why Guise was so fond of it.

The Ashnassan held faith in several gods, not all of them mighty warriors. Nassash was the one they set above the rest, though. A formidable warrior. A conqueror. Unflinching and undefeated in battle. The Ashnassan made offerings to Nassash to help them in battle. And made offerings to the other gods to appease them, to stop them inflicting their weaknesses on the warrior, and the tribe. Weakness was not tolerated among the tribe.

Her mind snagged on that. Weakness. "Playing with girls hardly seems worthy of warriors. Now, remind me, is Nassash the impotent god, or the one with the bad leg?"

His sword was in his hand almost before she realised it, and he was stalking forward, eyes flat and deadly, white teeth bared, one side of his face shadowed with all the tattoos he bore.

She took another step back, throwing one of the spell parchments in front of her and saying the activation word, putting her will behind it. A circle of fire ran around his feet, trapping him for the moment, the flames too high to step over, and not enough room in the circle for him to leap out.

"Magic bitch," he snarled, then jerked his head to his men. "Kill her."

The rest of the tribe slid off their horses and advanced, weapons ready.

They were ten paces away from her, close enough for her to see that they were all senior warriors, displaying a remarkable range of tattoos, when there was movement behind her.

"Mristrian." Guise's voice. Of course he would choose that moment to make an entrance. She didn't dare turn to look, yet she could picture his pose. Tall and straight, hands tucked behind his back, not a weapon in sight.

"My lord," she answered, feeling formality was called for.

"You have the matter well in hand, I see. And yet, my companions and I would welcome some exercise. May we join you?"

Yvonne almost turned to glare at him over her shoulder. May they join her? She was tempted to throw a fire spell in his direction. Except he would probably step around it with the same grace as he did everything else.

"Your participation would be welcome," she said instead, voice smooth.

"Oh, excellent. I haven't had a really good fight for a while," Brea said, coming to stand to one side of Yvonne. The lady was already baring her weapons, a pair of wickedly sharp, curved swords, her fangs glinting in the night air.

"This should be interesting," Thort added, stepping up to his wife's side. He had a great sword in one hand and a long dagger in the other.

"Are we too much for you?" the Slayer asked, still in his circle of flames.

"I'd hate to disappoint my companions," Yvonne answered, ducking the implied insult. "You know how much goblins adore fighting."

"You are too kind," Guise said, as though she had just paid him a great compliment. He stepped up to her other side, weapons ready.

Three armed goblins, ready and waiting. It should have been enough to make any sane human pause, no matter how many numbers he had around him. Goblins trained in the art of war from their cradle. Trained warriors like the Ashnassan should only have to glance at the three goblins to know they were facing masters.

The tribesmen did not hesitate. They surged forward, weapons raised.

Yvonne threw a spell into the midst of them, the concussive force knocking several off their feet. The rest closed the gap and kept coming, met by Brea and Thort, the pair as elegant as she had imagined they would be.

"Do you have any more of those fire spells?" Guise asked. He wasn't even breathing hard, fending off a pair of tribesmen with ease.

"Yes," Yvonne answered, and threw the necessary spell, catching a quartet of tribesmen in the circle, the fire catching hold of another's trouser leg, the man screaming in pain and rolling onto the ground to put the flames out.

"For Nassash!" the Slayer yelled. He sprang into the air, higher than should have been possible, and escaped his fire circle, landing lightly on the ground and advancing to Yvonne.

There was no time for more spells, or for retreat.

Her sword was a familiar weight in her hand, long dagger in the other, and she shifted her weight, ready for his attack, heart racing, mouth dry.

He came at her with no finesse, just brute strength.

She danced back, away from the onslaught, and ducked around his next wild swing. He was furious, not thinking straight, demonstrating none of the skill his warriors were known for. If she could keep him angry, there was a chance he would make one mistake too many.

"So, Nassash likes little girls?" she taunted, voice light. "You really should pick your gods more carefully."

He let out a yell of fury and frustration and swung his sword at her like a club, seeming to forget it had a sharp edge.

She moved away from the blow, feet following familiar patterns learned over hours of training. They were almost around the other side of the fire now, and she was aware of Guise nearby, fending off two tribesmen at once, but keeping pace with her. He was there to assist. If she needed it.

The anger faded, a different warmth taking its place. It was a rare day that there was someone guarding her back.

She turned her shoulder so that she was nearly back to back with him. Nothing would get to her from that side, she knew. Guise would see to it. She could focus on the Slayer.

"I will take your head to Nassash's great temple and place it on a stake there," the Slayer told her, teeth bared, words barely comprehensible through his anger. "And you will know the penalty for mocking his name."

"I'll be dead, though," Yvonne pointed out, voice cool. "But perhaps Nassash would like your head instead? It's quite ugly. But he is a strange god. Likes little girls and ugly warriors."

"He does not need the girls for his own glory." Rage made his voice shake.

"Really? So he's just acting as a lackey for someone else?" Yvonne asked, keeping her voice calm even as her heart skipped. The tribe were gathering the girls to what they believed was their god's will. And yet, their god did not want the girls. "A more powerful god, perhaps?"

"There is no god more powerful than Nassash."

Yvonne wanted to growl in frustration. That was the problem with religious fanatics. One track mind. It was almost impossible to get decent information out of them.

"But he's taking orders from someone else," she pointed out, struggling to keep her voice calm.

"We are gathering wealth that reflects his glory," the Slayer corrected her. "Golden crowns that we shall use to celebrate him."

Golden crowns. Finally, some useful information. The currency of the kings of Valland. And rare enough that a large quantity of them might be traceable. If they were genuine.

"Golden crowns?" She made her voice sceptical. "You are being fooled. They are rare as your manners."

"The authenticator did not think so," he answered, voice a low growl.

An authenticator. Someone who could be traced. And questioned. She did not need to look at Guise to know he would be taking in the information, too.

The Slayer was calming down again, she noticed, almost too late.

The next sword swing was smooth and controlled, and if she hadn't been on her toes already, could have sliced her in two.

As it was, she slapped the sword aside with her own blade, and thrust forward with her dagger, the point of it running down the Slayer's arm. He had not expected her to know how to use either weapon, she saw.

He let out a bellow of fury, grabbed something from his pouch and threw it at her.

The small bladder of liquid burst on her shoulder and all at once she could not breathe, her eyes streaming, nose burning, lungs seizing up. The stench was extraordinary.

Even so, she had her sword up, and met his next attack, coughing helplessly as the oil soaked into her clothing. It was touching her skin. Her entire body seized in reaction, skin crawling. If she had been able to, she would have leapt out of her own skin.

Skunk oil.

Distilled from the fierce creatures found in the Ashnassan homeland, it was favoured by some mercenary bands. It was the most awful thing to ever cross her nose. She had dealt with decomposing bodies that smelled better.

Her lungs were seizing again. She did not want to breathe anymore. Did not want any more of this awful stench inside her as well as out.

But she had to keep her sword up.

"Allow me, mristrian," Guise said, voice edged.

She managed to nod and cough, choking on the smell. It must be many times worse for him. Goblin senses were sharper than human.

She stumbled back, letting him take her place facing the Slayer.

There were a pair of tribesmen behind him, circling her, looking for an opening, even though their noses were wrinkling in distaste at the smell.

She glanced down and found that her whole arm was soaked with the oil.

She looked back up to find that the tribesmen were trying to keep their distance from her.

Without more thought, she charged towards them, oil-coated shoulder in the lead, waving her stinking arm like a weapon.

The tribesmen let out squeals more normally heard from teenage girls, and backed away from her. She followed them.

They backed all the way towards their fellow tribesmen, who were still trying to hold off Brea and Thort. The other tribesmen looked in horror at her charging towards them, arm outstretched, the dark oil clearly visible.

It was not the worst idea she had ever had.

The tribesmen retreated away from her, those closest to her with streaming eyes as they caught a stronger dose of the stench of the oil.

They retreated so far around the fire that they came across Guise and the Slayer. The Slayer was attacking Guise with the same single-minded focus that he had used with Yvonne earlier. Guise looked utterly at ease, moving with his usual grace. His breathing was still even, despite the approaching stench from Yvonne's shirt.

The Slayer was distracted by the approach of all of his men, and the growing smell.

He looked around the clearing, at the one dead tribesman, the two bound men, the three goblins, with red eyes and fangs, and gave a sharp whistle to his men, a sound Yvonne recognised from her first encounter with the Ashnassan, when Lothar had been injured. The Slayer must have been there. Close enough to call off his men, away from Antonine Rangers and wulfkin. Now, he sounded a retreat from three goblins.

His warriors were surprised, but, as with the first time, the whistle had them retreating, back towards their horses.

They melted away into the forest in moments, leaving Yvonne gasping for breath and fumbling in her belt pouch for a cleansing spell. Or six.

It took three full doses of cleansing spells before she could breathe normally, and another two before the stench had faded to a level that was almost acceptable to her dull, human nose. It was only when she had released the fifth spell that she realised she had been using magic without thinking about it, the power there, ready to be used, as it had been when she was Hunar. Her breath caught. The great void inside her was gone, as if it never had been, and she had not noticed. She did not feel quite the same, the bright spark of Hunar power not there. But, she had used magic. Her hand strayed to the bare patch on her shoulder and she felt her spine straighten. Not useless.

By the time she was able to breathe, Guise, Brea and Thort were gathered around the original three tribesmen they had found, expressions grim.

Yvonne checked which way the air was moving, and moved downwind from them, careful to keep a short distance away.

As she came closer to the bound men, she saw why the goblins were looking so grim.

The pair of captives had their throats cut, blood pooling into the ground beneath them. Somewhere in the fight, the tribesmen had carried out their leaders' orders and made sure that the captured men could not talk.

"Does anyone have a better scent or perfume?" Yvonne asked, after staring at the corpses for a while. "I don't have a change of clothes."

Brea's nose wrinkled and she shook her head slightly.

"It's almost bearable just now. From a distance," the lady said. "I have a mint scent that might work." She strode away to her horse, coming back with a vial, holding it out to Yvonne at arm's length. The vial was made of glass embedded with silver flecks, small enough that it fit into the palm of Yvonne's hand. Yvonne's eyes widened as she took it.

"This is too much," she protested. It was one of the most expensive perfumes that the artisans in Kelton made. A single ounce cost at least one golden crown.

"It should improve your, ah, aroma," Brea told her, waving her hand in Yvonne's direction. "Please. Use as much as you need. It will make the journey back more bearable for all of us."

Yvonne ducked her head, colour surging into her face, and opened the vial. The fresh, green scent of mint cut through the lingering trace of skunk oil.

All the goblins breathed a sigh of relief, shoulders relaxing.

"I'll ride downwind," Yvonne offered, wrinkling her nose. She tried to hand Brea the perfume back, but the lady waved it away.

"Keep it until we get back. You will probably need at least one other application."

Yvonne nodded, and tucked the vial into her spell pouch which had, mercifully, escaped the skunk oil. Her skin was still crawling underneath her clothes, despite the many doses of cleansing spells. She wanted a bath, a vast quantity of soap and a scrubbing brush. And even then, she was not sure she would feel clean.

Chapter Twelve

In the end, she had needed to use the entire bottle of Brea's perfume on the journey back, the goblins' eyes streaming as they reached the annex. Guise had provided her with a rough sack, soaked in lavender oil, to dispose of her clothes, and brought her saddlebags, which she had not unpacked, to the bathing room.

After a long bath with as much soap as she could wish for and a change of clothes, she had felt marginally cleaner, skin smarting from the scrubbing brush, still convinced that traces of the stench lingered in her hair even though she had washed it four times.

She had simply burned the clothes she had been wearing, the lavender from the sack partially masking the stench. No amount of cleansing spells would get rid of the skunk oil. It left her with no spare clothes, which could not be helped.

Guise had shown her to a comfortable room on the upper floor of the annex and left her there for the rest of the night. When the door had closed behind him she had not thought she would be able to sleep, mind too full of the events of the night.

To her surprise, she had slept soundly, waking when the sun was already high outside.

In her threadbare shirt and worn trousers, trying to calculate if she had money enough for a new set of clothes, she came out of her room and almost tripped over the parcel on the floor outside her door. Wrapped in plain cloth, it was soft to the touch when she picked it up, and heavier than she had expected. There was a folded piece of parchment on top, which she opened to reveal a few words in handwriting that she knew. Guise.

I hope these will be suitable replacements.

Frowning slightly, she took the parcel back into her room, closing the door behind her, and opened the cloth to reveal a new shirt and trousers, in heavier and finer fabric than anything she had owned before now. The shirt was made of a pale blue, the sky on a summer's morning, the trousers of densely woven black cloth. And they smelled, faintly, of lavender, and not of the lingering stench of the oil.

She had changed into the new clothes before she quite knew what she was doing and, once she had tried them on, knew that she was keeping them. The fit was excellent and they felt familiar as soon as she put them on, as though she had owned them for years and not minutes. There was even a scarf, of the same colour and fabric as the shirt.

She came downstairs to find the house deserted. It was possible that the others were out digging ditches again, or on some other errand. It was possible that there were still lingering traces of skunk oil in the air, clear to their sensitive noses but not to hers. In any event, it seemed that she had the place to herself.

Just as she was thinking that she should go and see to her horse, there was a knock at the house's front door. In the absence of anyone else, she went to answer it, freezing for a moment in astonishment when she saw who was on the other side.

"Good day to you, Yvonne," the wulf said.

"Renard. It is so good to see you," she said, and stepped forward to give him a brief hug, breathing in his scent, clean and familiar. The undertone of wulf, of course, but also saddle soap and weapons oil. One of Elinor's lovers, Renard was the only wulf, besides her children, who did not belong to any range.

"I wish it were under better circumstances," he said. "Is there somewhere we can talk?"

She blinked. Renard was not normally abrupt. And he would usually have returned her hug instead of standing stiff and unyielding. Concerned, Yvonne stepped back to let him into the house, and led him through to the front sitting room, which looked out onto the garden.

"Would you like some tea? I think I can find the kitchen."

"No." The single word was as clipped as his previous tone.

She closed the door behind them and turned to find that he was standing quite straight, which put him at even height with her, with his hands behind his back, his normally expressive face still, lines of age pronounced around his eyes and mouth. He had lost weight since she had last seen him, his clothes slightly loose, and there was more grey in his hair now than blond, reflecting his pale grey eyes. If Elinor's house had been full of laughter when Adira was in it, Renard brought a deep intensity with him. He was usually full of warmth, though, and his cool manner worried Yvonne.

"How did you find me?" she asked, curious.

"The law keeper. Grayling. He told me where to find you." Renard looked around him, doubtless noticing the same things that Yvonne had. The flawless craftsmanship. The priceless artwork. "I can see why you did not want to stay in Fir Tree Crossing." Before Yvonne could react, he turned his attention to her, and lifted his brow. "And new clothes, as well."

"Replacements," she said, her face and mouth stiff, hiding the hurt. It seemed that Sillman, Suanna and Mica were not the only ones of her old friends behaving strangely. "The tribesmen used skunk oil."

His nose wrinkled in remembrance. A wulf's sense of smell was far sharper than her own. Sharper even than a goblin's.

"But you did not come all this way simply to insult me," she said, back straight. She had thought that losing the symbol of the Hunar was painful. It had been. It seemed it was not the worst pain she had to bear, though. Renard had never been so cool with her. Not once. Not even when she had flinched from him, newly arrived at Elinor's house, the memories of the quarrel still fresh and raw in her mind.

"I do not insult. I merely observe."

"Your observation is flawed," she told him. She remembered her first riding lessons, Renard a patient and forgiving teacher, very far removed from the stiff and angry wulf in front of her. "What do you need?"

"An explanation. Elinor is dead. And you have made no attempt to discover who is responsible."

Yvonne felt as if she had been hit in the stomach, her whole body flinching at the accusation. She had to lock her knees to remain upright, feeling the colour drain from her face as she stared across the room at Renard.

"It was an illness," she said, hearing her voice tremble. "It affected her neighbourhood, and she died of it. A Hunar is not immortal." She clamped her jaw shut against any more words, not trusting what she might or might not say.

"And you think a simple illness could kill Elinor? Did you never think to question it?"

"Honestly, no," Yvonne said, and moved to the nearest chair, her knees giving out as she reached it, and she sat down with a thump that jarred her back all the way up to her teeth. "The Hundred are human. They get ill. They can die."

"You keep saying *they*," Renard said, teeth bared in a silent snarl. "Do you not accept even this responsibility?"

"I was sundered," she told him, and it was not just her voice shaking now. Her whole body was trembling, fine tremors that she thought might break her. It was too much. The patch on her shoulder ached as fiercely as her heart. Elinor was dead. The loss and grief of it still rang through her, every single day. And she had never questioned, not once, that Elinor's death had been anything other than stupid circumstances. It would be so typical of Elinor to go out and about amongst the sick and the needy, and to get ill herself.

"What happened?"

The difference in tone drew Yvonne's attention out of her own misery, and across the room to Renard. He had settled on a chair opposite her, and was leaning forward, eyes intent. That awful coldness had gone. Instead, there was the quiet intensity that was so familiar, and which Elinor had loved.

For a moment, Yvonne could not answer, choked with grief and anger and humiliation. She shook her head, swallowed and knotted her fingers together.

"I don't remember all of it. Not yet. But it seems that I am part of a goblin bond. And that, it seems, is not permitted for one of the Hundred."

"Did Sillman say so?" Renard asked.

"How did you know it was him?" Yvonne asked.

Renard did not answer at once, staring at the elaborate design on the floor covering for long enough that Yvonne thought he had forgotten the question. At length, he sat back, and looked up at her, his eyes bright with power. "There is nothing in the oath of the Hundred that stops any type of bond being formed," he told her. "It was an argument that Elinor had with him often. Sillman seemed to think that all members of the Hundred should live without any kind of family or personal connection. Elinor would tell him that a lot of the past members of the Hundred had been wives, and husbands, and mothers, and fathers, and it had not impaired their ability to do the work."

"I did not realise you disliked him so much," Yvonne said, slowly, turning that new information over in her mind. She had always known that Elinor and Sillman did not see eye to eye. It had always seemed to her, at least, that it was healthy that they did not always agree with each other, and that different opinions were voiced. It was one of the main reasons why she missed Elinor, in any discussion with the Hundred. Whatever anyone else might think, Sillman had a habit of overruling them to get his own way. But, even though Elinor and Sillman had not agreed with each other, there had, it seemed to Yvonne, been a mutual respect. It had never occurred to her that Elinor, or her lovers, might dislike Sillman.

Even as she thought that, she realised how naive that was. Adira and Renard were very different from each other, and Elinor had loved them both in different ways, but with every part of her being. Yvonne did not think that Sillman had ever loved anyone like that. He had never been able to understand Elinor's lifestyle choices.

"He is hungry for authority, and manipulative," Renard said, voice calm, words measured. A damning assessment of Sillman. "He would be extremely dangerous if he was not bound by his oath as Hunar."

"I've never thought of it that way," Yvonne said, honestly.

"I know. But you have not lived as long as I have, or known Sillman for as long as I have." Renard rested his head against the back of the chair and, for the first time that Yvonne could remember, he looked every one of his advancing years. Wulfkin could live as long as goblins, and Hunar, and Renard had already had a long life. "I think I owe you an apology."

"It is not necessary. I am glad you came. I have missed you." It was true, even with the unsettling prospect that he had raised. "Do you really think that Elinor was killed?"

"Yes," he answered baldly.

"Why?"

"I wish I had a good answer for you. You're right. The Hundred are human. They get sick. They die. But. There's just something."

Yvonne untangled her fingers and sat back in her own chair. If it had been anyone apart from Renard, she might have dismissed the suspicions. This was Renard, though, and he had not lived as long as he had, without the protection of a range around him, without having exceptionally good instincts for danger, and for when something was not quite right.

And now he had raised the matter with her, she felt a stab of guilt. She had simply accepted the story she had been given. She had never questioned it. None of them had, but of all of the Hundred, she had been closest to Elinor.

Before she could tell Renard any of that, movement outside drew her attention. Guise was walking through the garden, on his way back to the house, moving with his habitual, fluid grace. He was dressed in his usual manner, elegant clothes perfectly moulded to him, hair loose around his shoulders catching the light as he walked.

Yvonne's stomach twisted again. She was in Guise's home. Or, at least, one of them. And he was surrounded by people he considered friends and who also worked with him in gathering information and secrets. She did not feel as though she belonged, no matter how much they had accepted her.

In her mind she made a contrast with Elinor's house, which had always felt like home. Where she had never felt like a stranger. Where she had always been welcome.

And Renard believed that Elinor had been killed.

"I will find out what happened," she told Renard. She felt the promise ring through her as if it were the word of a Hunar, the echo tightening her throat again.

She turned back to Renard and had another shock. She had already noted the grey in his hair, and his loss of weight. Now, he seemed to have aged even more. There were fine lines around his mouth, cheekbones prominent. He was also paler than she remembered.

"Are you quite well?" she asked.

"I am not quite myself just now." He closed his lips together in a thin line, eyes flickering with anger. "I find myself unable to do much without tiring. Age finally catching up to me," he added, voice bitter. "I would investigate if I could," he told her, lip curling up in silent anger, eyes bright with power. "But even riding here today has tired me."

Yvonne swallowed her concern with difficulty. Renard was as stubborn, and proud, as any other wulf she had known. For him to admit weakness meant it was serious. Far more than he was letting her see now, still holding himself upright in the chair.

"You should go and stay with Mariah and Joel," Yvonne said. "They would be delighted to see you." They would also spoil him, she knew. Renard was a firm favourite with them both, and they would see that he was warm and fed, and he would not resist them in the same way he would resist her. They were as close to his kin as any other wulf, and still children in his eyes. He could rest for a little while.

The anger and bitterness faded into a smile. "And I can keep them from destroying the house, yes, while you find a killer?"

Yvonne laughed, warmth in her face. She hadn't actually meant to appoint him as a child-minder, but, now he mentioned it, it was a good idea.

"So that is Guise," Renard commented, before she could say anything. "And you cannot remember creating the bond with him?"

"I had been hit over the head by a vettr," she told him, skin crawling as she remembered the stone creature and its tiny, malicious eyes. "There's a blank space. It's so frustrating. I can remember every other part of my life, including the bits that I don't want to remember, and yet I can't remember this thing that got me dismissed from the Hundred." Yvonne heard the bitterness in her own voice by the time she reached the end, and could do nothing about it. She was bitter. She was trying not to be angry with Guise, because that was not fair.

"It's not the only blank space, though," Renard commented. "Elinor told me that you don't remember everything about your testing."

Yvonne opened her mouth, about to deny that, and then closed it again. She trusted Elinor. She trusted Renard.

"I thought I did remember everything," she said.

"Elinor seemed quite certain that something of significance had happened," he said. "She talked with you about it in the day or two after your testing, and then tried to speak to you again and, she said, you had no memory of it."

Yvonne frowned, trying to remember. She remembered standing in the temple, with sun-warmed stones under her bare feet, looking up at the painting of the Firebird on the temple's wall. She remembered arriving at the temple the day before, and being left overnight for the test.

"You're right," she said, a chill crossing her skin. "I can't immediately remember everything that happened."

Even as she tried to remember, she heard, in her mind, the echo of the Firebird's scream and imagined she could feel the stir of air from the downbeat of those great wings.

"Don't try and force the memory. It will come in its own time," Renard said. "For now, if it is not too much trouble, tea would be most welcome."

He looked tired, and frail, and those were not words that she was used to associating with him. And, being a wulf, he would be hiding the worst of it. Trying not to show her worry, she left him and went through the house, looking for the kitchens.

She found Guise on his own in the house's kitchen, preparing a tray with a teapot, mugs and food.

"Mristrian. I heard you had a visitor. I thought you might want some tea."

"It's Renard," she told him, watching as he moved around the kitchen, as comfortable here as he was everywhere else. "He thinks Elinor was killed."

Guise paused and glanced across at her, expression unreadable. "And you will go, and find out what happened to her," he said. "What do you need?"

She could not speak for a moment, at the unexpected and immediate offer of assistance.

"I'm running low on funds," she said at length. "Thank you for the new clothes. I could not get the smell out of the old ones."

"I am glad you like them. That smell never leaves," he added, nose wrinkling. "Funds are easy to manage. Anything else?"

For a moment she was torn. As well as Elinor's death, there were missing children to find, even if she had no clear idea of where to go to start that work. She thought briefly about asking Guise to come with her to Elinor's town. But, Elinor had been her mentor, and her friend, and Yvonne had the strongest wish to make this journey, and start this investigation, on her own.

"Nothing I can think of just now, thank you."

"Shall I carry this through for you?" he asked, lifting the tea tray.

"You just want to meet Renard," she realised, words out before she had thought. The faint smile told her that the guess was accurate. She shook her head slightly. She found herself curious as to what Guise and Renard might make of each other. "He would be pleased to meet you, I am sure."

Chapter Thirteen

Yvonne was not surprised to see that Renard had composed himself, with no sign of his earlier weakness, when she came back into the room, Guise carrying the tea tray.

Guise set the tray down and made a bow.

"You must be Renard. I have heard a lot about you. It is an honour to meet you."

"And you must be Guise," Renard answered, voice laced with humour. "I have heard a lot about you, too."

They all settled in chairs for one of the strangest rounds of tea that Yvonne had ever had. Renard and Guise were both on what she recognised as their best behaviour, at the same time each trying to get the measure of the other. By the time the tea had been drunk, she could not tell who had the upper hand nor, she suspected, could they. If either of them was frustrated by it, they did not let it show.

"Do you need somewhere to stay? There is plenty of room here," Guise said.

"No. I should go. I have some distance to travel, still. But I do have a gift for Yvonne first," Renard said.

"Nothing is necessary," Yvonne began, cut off by Renard's lifted hand.

"It was Elinor's last wish. A gift from both of us." Renard rose to his feet. "You will need to come outside."

Curiosity roused, Yvonne followed him out of the house, and along the path that led back towards the main palace. There were two horses standing outside the main doors of the palace, each resting a leg. Prestin was nowhere to be seen which, Yvonne thought, was probably just as well. It was unlikely he would have approved of horses making the place look untidy.

"This one is yours," Renard said, taking the rein of the nearest horse.

"I don't understand," Yvonne said, the words sounding stupid even in her own ears. Renard was famous not only for being a wulf without a range, but also for being one of the best horse trainers alive. He had trained Lothar, and taught Yvonne to ride.

"Lothar is due his retirement," Renard said, voice gentle. "Elinor mentioned this was troubling you. And so, she asked me to find you a replacement."

Yvonne had accepted Lothar as a gift, many years before, not really understanding the true value of what she was being given. He had been a faithful and loyal companion, and had saved her life on more than one occasion. She had been dreading the task of finding his replacement, however necessary it was. But now, with many years of being Hunar behind her, and of travelling the world, she had a much better idea of what a horse trained by Renard was worth.

"It's too much," she said, protesting on instinct. "He is worth a fortune."

"Only if I choose to sell him," Renard said, his voice still calm and gentle. "And I never would. He is one of Lothar's relatives. A little bit green, still, but I think he will serve you well. Come and meet him."

Yvonne took a step forward, assessing the horse even as he was assessing her. He was a dull, dapple grey. Almost unremarkable in appearance. But then, Lothar was also unremarkable in appearance. She held out her hand, careful to keep her fingers tucked under, and let the horse blow breath on the back of her hand, taking her scent. He snorted, ears flicking back and then forward, and then lifted his own head, sniffing her hair.

"His name is Baldur," Renard told her. Another word for warrior, she thought. Renard chose his horses' names carefully.

Another warhorse for her. A gift. From Elinor and Renard. She stroked the velvet-soft nose, scratched behind his ears and stroked his neck, feeling the vibrant life under her fingers, eyes prickling again. A last gift. She loved him already.

Renard agreed to take her spare horse back to the house, to Mariah and Joel, and also to carry a letter for them. Yvonne wrote a few lines, as quickly as she could, and hoped that her children would not mind that she did not have time for individual letters. She did not think they would, used to receiving brief, often hastily written notes from her over the years, and made Renard promise to give each of them a hug when he saw them.

Yvonne watched Renard ride away with the usual sense of conflict. She would have liked to spend more time with him. It had been too long. And yet, she knew that Mariah and Joel would love to see him and more than that, Renard had been hiding just how unwell he was. He would be able to rest at the house. And unlike most cerro, Sephenamin would be honoured, rather than threatened, she thought, to have Renard within his range.

And she had the unexpected gift of a new horse.

Baldur watched his master ride away, apparently calm, ears flicking forward and back a few times, before he turned and shoved his head into Yvonne's chest. It was something that Lothar would do and Yvonne laughed, reaching up to scratch the horse behind his ears, laughing again as he tilted his head to give her better access.

"There is a practice arena behind the stables, if you want to get to know him," Guise offered. "He is a fine horse."

"Yes, he is," Yvonne agreed and led him to the practice arena, keeping her movements calm and relaxed, not betraying any of her tension and excitement. A new horse. Renard had not given her much information, but then he had not given her much information about Lothar either, all those years ago. She needed to learn her horse for herself, Renard had said. Getting to know Lothar had involved her ending up on the practice arena floor several times and, looking at the springy stride of the horse walking next to her, she suspected that the same would be true here.

She forgot about the potential audience, and Guise's interested gaze, as she checked over Baldur's harness, making sure everything was in place, before she slowly and carefully got on his back. He did not move, at first, standing stock still as she settled in place.

She asked him to walk forward, using the gentlest and most subtle of commands, as Renard had taught her, and he sprang forward into a headlong gallop.

The fence around the arena flashed by as he raced, seemingly trying to outrun his own skin, and she sat still as she could and let him run.

At length, he was done running and slowed, changing to a lively trot that jarred her teeth. She stayed still and quiet. That pace was likely as uncomfortable for him as it was for her.

When she did not react, he slowed further, to walk and then to stand, and shook himself from his nose to his tail, before turning his head to glance back at her, ear tilted towards her.

"Yes, I am still here," she told him. He snorted. She asked, again, for him to move forward, with the gentlest of pressure, and this time he moved forward into a smooth walk, neck extended and relaxed ahead of her.

It was a while later before she was satisfied that they had the beginnings of an understanding.

She slid off his back and gave him a pat, smiling when he put his head into her chest again, demanding that his ears be scratched. He also liked to be stroked under his chin, she discovered.

She walked with him to the nearest exit from the practice arena, and discovered that she did have an audience. Guise had been joined by Brea and Thort, Jesset sitting on the fence between them.

"I am jealous," Brea said, candidly. "Very few people get a horse that has been trained by Renard. He is very picky about who he lets his horses go to."

"He's an excellent trainer," Yvonne said, giving her new horse another pat.

"And you will be leaving soon," Thort prompted.

"Tomorrow," Yvonne said. Now that she had made up her mind, and had the unexpected but welcome gift of the horse, she did not see any reason to delay. She could do little to help where she was, and there was a killer to be found.

"More travel," Jesset said, nose wrinkling.

Yvonne laughed. "Indeed. I enjoy it." It was true. She liked having a place to come back to, but she did like travelling. The new sights, sounds and faces. She had always considered the ability to travel, and indeed the need to do so, as one of the benefits to being Hunar, and realised that, as well as the pain of the sundering, she had been worried that she would be confined to Fir Tree Crossing. Perhaps that would not be the case.

She took the horse into the stable, the others disappearing about their own business, and spent some time grooming him until he was sleepy and relaxed. The stable hands had been keeping an eye on her from a distance. Out of curiosity, she thought. A warhorse trained by Renard was something worthy of note.

She left Baldur half asleep and perfectly content, and made her way back towards the annex, pausing to douse herself with a cleansing spell on the way. The afternoon had left her covered in horsehair and sand.

Guise was standing in the garden as she approached, his hands tucked behind his back, staring into middle distance. He had been waiting for her. She wasn't quite sure how she knew that. He turned towards her as she approached.

"I have the funds for you, a gift and a request," he told her. He held out a leather pouch that was heavier than she expected and clinked when she accepted it, the sound of coins moving together. She tied it onto her belt for the time being. It would need to go into her saddlebags for the journey. Then he drew something from his pocket. It looked like a disc, about the size of a gold coin, made of gold and silver. "If you need anything, show this to the cloth merchant in the blue house in Willowton, and they will give you all the aid you require."

It was no surprise that Guise had a connection in Elinor's town. Willowton was reasonably large, large enough to host a busy marketplace and to have travellers passing through, with information gained on the road.

Yvonne took the coin from him, thanking him, aware of the familiar push and pull. This must be how members of Guise's network of associates and contacts recognised each other. She had searched the body of one of his former associates, though, and did not remember finding it. However, the merchant, Ubel, had been trading in slaves and out of favour with Guise. Perhaps Guise had already demanded his token back before Ubel's death.

By taking it, she felt oddly complicit in whatever activities he engaged in. It might be nothing more harmful than collecting information. And yet, there was a darker side. The associate whose body they had discovered, Ubel, had been involved in smuggling children. As disgusted as Guise had been about that, Yvonne was quite certain that he would not have objected to other smuggling, and perhaps was involved in it himself. She had never been quite certain what his business was, and remained reluctant to ask.

"A request?" she asked, remembering that there had been a third thing.

"I am needed here for now. I would normally make enquiries myself."

"The authenticator that the Ashnassan were using," she guessed. It was the one, tangible lead from the tribesmen. She had almost forgotten it with Renard's unexpected visit, and his suspicions about Elinor's death. She hesitated a moment, torn again. There were nine-year-old girls somewhere, kidnapped for unknown reasons. And Elinor had been dead for more than a year.

Even though she had made a promise to Renard, she knew what Elinor would have told her to do. And what Renard would tell her, too, if he had known about the girls. Find the children first. Always.

It was the most logical course of action. Yet she hesitated. Every part of her was telling her that Elinor's death needed to be investigated. Soon. It would not wait. Not even for terrified children.

She needed to find a way to do both. Somehow.

"Yes. The cloth merchant I mentioned will be able to make enquiries in Willowton, if asked to do so."

Yvonne tilted her head, considering him. The request was sincere, and well within her capabilities. Talk to a cloth merchant about a coin authenticator. It should not be difficult. And yet, it was a request that drew her further into his world and his network of contacts. A network she had been careful to stay clear of before now.

Willowton was known for its financial and legal offices. If the Ashnassan had not used an authenticator there, then one of the guild might know where to look. And Guise was proposing to use his own network of contacts to get the necessary information.

This network might get her closer to whoever was paying the Ashnassan far faster than she could herself, particularly without the symbol of the Hunar. Closer to the pay master, and closer to finding the girls. There was no question of refusing.

"Do I need to show the merchant this?" she asked, holding up the gold disc.

"At first, yes. If there is any difficulty, you should feel free to use whatever persuasion you require. The merchant is far less skilled than Prestin," Guise told her, baring his teeth in what might have been a smile with no humour in it.

"But should aid you with no difficulty. Or payment," he added, almost as an afterthought. "I will follow when I can. A few days, I hope."

She opened her mouth to tell him that it was not necessary, and then stopped. Trying to control what Guise did was like trying to will the sun not come up in the morning. He would do what he wanted, when he wanted, and at least he was giving her warning of his arrival.

For now, she had funds at her disposal, the unexpected treasure of a new horse and an investigation to start. More than enough to keep her busy.

Chapter Fourteen

Coming back to Elinor's house was just as painful as Yvonne had thought it would be. Everything was different. And everything was the same.

The outside looked different. The windows were shuttered, the front door closed, the wooden gate that led round the side of the house to the small courtyard at the back and Elinor's herb garden, also shut. Elinor's house had never been closed. Not while she lived.

The house sat directly on one of the side streets in Willowton. It was close, but not too close, to its neighbours. Elinor had been as much the heart of her neighbourhood as she had been of the Hundred, and Yvonne saw a few glances cast her way as she got off her horse and made her way to the gate.

If the front of the house had looked strange, the back was, in some ways, worse. There were no other horses in the stables. The herb garden had grown wild in the year since Elinor had died, in a way that Elinor would never have permitted.

Yvonne kept herself busy for a while, making sure the stable was comfortable for Baldur, and that he had enough food and water, before she approached the back door.

The kitchen was deserted. Of course it was. There was no one else here. The heart of the house. Yvonne had only to look around the room to remember. Elinor's voice teaching her a new recipe, standing next to the cook pot. Elinor and Adira, laughing together in the morning sunlight at the kitchen table, Elinor's red hair catching the light, contrasting with Adira's dark hair. Elinor settled opposite Renard on a winter's evening, the room lit by candles, while he repaired a horse's bridle, his movements unhurried, glancing up occasionally to meet Elinor's eyes across the table. Yvonne sitting at the table with Joel and Mariah, teaching them their letters, watching them try and form them with clumsy hands.

Elinor had accepted two wulfkin children into her house with the same warmth as anyone else, even though Willowton did not have a range of its own. The land around the town was mostly flat, open land used for farming crops and livestock. There were no patches of wild land for at least a full day's travel in all directions. And wulfkin needed wild land. Needed to run and hunt now and then. They might visit Willowton, and be welcome by its residents, but no wulfkin wanted to stay for too long.

Elinor had told her once that she had chosen the house, and the town, before she met Renard. And the arrangement suited them both. There was no local cerro to object to Renard's visits.

So, Willowton continued without a range. And, when Mariah and Joel were growing older, Yvonne had taken her children to places with other wulfkin, with ranges that could teach them what they needed to know as wulfkin. Things that she could not teach them.

They had always come back here from time to time. Back to the welcome of Elinor's house.

More than any other place in the world, this was where she had felt safe, and wanted, and loved. No matter the hour, no matter the circumstances, Elinor had never turned her away. And Elinor's help came with no strings attached.

Yvonne was not surprised to find that her face was wet with tears. She set her saddlebags down on the kitchen table and scrubbed her face with her hands. There was a makeshift bed in the alcove by the kitchen fire and she was tempted to use it. She didn't want to go further into the house, to hear the echo of the emptiness, to realise that Elinor would never again run up the stairs to her bedroom, in search of something. Would never again call through the house that the meal was ready. Or turn from the kitchen stove, holding out a spoon for Yvonne to taste whatever she was cooking.

Elinor was not here anymore. If Renard was right, it was because somebody had killed her. And that could not be allowed to stand.

For all her kindness, for all her warmth, Elinor had also been a stern task mistress, requiring commitment and perfection from her student. She had also taught Yvonne early, and valuable, lessons about taking all her mixed-up emotions and channelling them into something useful. Those first lessons had all been about Yvonne's terror. Now, she used those same lessons to channel her grief, and anger, into focus. There was a killer to be caught.

So, she made her way out of the kitchen, going slowly through the house, not going into any of the rooms, simply opening the doors and making an assessment as to whether anything was different, and what that was.

Not much had been disturbed, which was surprising. Elinor had owned this house outright, but this was a busy town and a large property like this was valuable, and in demand. Still, no one had tried to move in. And no one had looted Elinor's possessions. The few things that looked like they had been disturbed were Elinor's wardrobe, which may have been someone looking for an appropriate outfit for her funeral. Yvonne remembered Elinor's body, still and solemn, laid out on the funeral parlour, in a dark-coloured dress that she rarely wore. Whoever had gone through her wardrobe had not known her all that well, or had wanted something that looked formal for the occasion.

The only other piece of furniture that showed any sign of disturbance was a dresser in Elinor's bedroom, where the dust had been disturbed. Yvonne went across the room to check it, not surprised to find the drawers empty. Renard had kept some belongings here and, doubtless, had come back for them at some point.

She left the shutters closed at the front, that looked onto the street, and the front door boarded, and opened a window or two at the back to let some fresh air into the house.

As she made her way back downstairs to the kitchen, she could not see anything that might point to Elinor having been killed. But she trusted Renard.

Back in the kitchen, she put the kettle on to boil and took a mug out of the cupboard. Her hand reached automatically for a second one, and she had to stop, curling her fingers into a fist, and then close the door. She had another moment of grief as she then reached for the sugar bowl, movements familiar from many repetitions. Elinor had possessed a sweet tooth, and refused to drink any tea without sugar. Two rounded teaspoons in each mug. Yvonne's fingers lingered on the sugar bowl for a moment, tempted to add sugar to her own tea in memory of Elinor. She drew her hand back. She hated sweet tea, and it would not be an appropriate tribute to Elinor's memory to do something she disliked.

Settled in her usual chair at the table, she kept expecting to hear Elinor's voice. There was nothing here that she could see which pointed to Elinor's killer, although she was not entirely sure what she was looking for. But, Elinor had apparently died of an illness that had affected the neighbourhood and so the obvious place to start seemed to be to speak to the neighbours.

Making sure that Baldur was comfortable and content in his stable, she sealed the back door of the house and then the gate with a spark of magic, and set off to visit Elinor's neighbours.

They were pleased to see her, their own grief drawing more tears to Yvonne's eyes. Elinor had lived in that house for a long time and had, in fact, helped birth a number of her neighbours, who now had children and, in some cases, grandchildren, of their own. They were bewildered and grieving.

Over the next two days, Yvonne had countless cups of tea with the neighbours, and asked them what had happened. No one found the questions odd, many of them saying that they had talked it over several times themselves, almost unable to believe Elinor was gone.

All the neighbours told the same story. Around the springtime, a fever had taken hold in the neighbourhood which nothing really seemed to help. Elinor had, of course, visited her neighbours, tended to those who were sick and brought them food from her own table. Stews, soups or baking. At some point, she had got sick herself. A few other people had died. A very old, and frail, man. A young baby, too small and weak to stand against the fever. And a young girl, not quite into her teenage years, who had spent time helping Elinor tend to the sick.

And, after a few weeks, Elinor had not appeared one day. Her nearest neighbour had gone into the house the next day, braving a Hunar's wrath. Elinor had been dead, curled on her side in her bed, her skin still hot and feverish.

The neighbours had tried to revive her. They had sent for healers. Nothing had worked. She was gone. And, despite the warmth of her skin, had probably been dead for a half day or more before she was found.

The neighbours were, all of them, honest people. They had done what they could. They had simply accepted Elinor's death as part of the price of the fever.

Shortly after her death, the worst of the fever had passed. No one else had died, although a few people had been weak for a long time after. And no one else had become ill since then.

It all sounded perfectly natural. Perfectly normal. Illnesses did come and go, and did claim victims.

And yet, Renard was convinced there was more to it.

So, as well as the questions about the fever, and the illness, Yvonne asked them about any strangers in the area. Any visitors that Elinor might have had. Anything else unusual that may have happened.

They all told her about Renard visiting. He had come a short time after Elinor's death to collect her horse, but when he had spoken with the neighbours then, he'd said he hadn't gone into the house. He'd come back a couple of months ago to collect his belongings. That matched what Yvonne had seen in the house. And taking the horse as a first priority was very like Renard. He had trained all of Elinor's horses, too, and would not want one of his horses left alone for too long.

There had been no sign of Adira after Elinor's death, which a few of the neighbours found strange. But that, too, sounded very like Adira. As one of the senior Sisters in the Stone Walls, Adira had many demands on her, and would see that her duty was to stay with the living who needed her, not the dead, who were beyond her help. She had been at Elinor's funeral, though, to say her goodbyes, as heart-sore and grieving as everyone else.

And then, on the afternoon of her third day in Willowton, when she was at the point of never wanting another cup of tea again, the couple she was speaking to told her something new.

"One of your lot came to see her a few months before that. Not long after Mid Winter," the husband said. "But, I assume you knew that."

"Oh, that's right," his wife said. "And they had that awful row."

"No, that was the other one. A bit later."

"At Mid Winter?" Yvonne asked, before the two of them could veer off to other subjects, as they had been doing for most of the conversation.

"Oh yes. I remember it. We were just taking the decorations down," the husband said, looking around the kitchen they were sitting in, face reflecting sadness. Everything was plain and functional. No decorations.

"Do you remember who came to see her?" Yvonne prompted.

"Which time? I mean, that handsome young man has been a few times. The older one with the sad eyes. Oh, and that surly faced woman who looks down on everybody. She's been a few times, too," the wife said.

"And the high and mighty one. He's been a few times," the husband added, doubtless thinking he was being helpful in supporting his wife's story.

"So, which one came just after Mid Winter? The first visitor?" Yvonne asked.

"That would be the white-haired one," the wife said. "You know," she said, turning to her husband. "The one who dresses like he's a king."

"Oh, yes. Thinks he's too good for us. Never so much as a hello."

"And did he stay long?" Yvonne asked. It was completely reasonable that Sillman would have visited Elinor, even though Mid Winter was a strange time to be travelling, particularly as Sillman lived a fair distance from Elinor. They would normally communicate by letter over the winter months.

"A few days, I think. Not like the other one."

"Oh, yes," Yvonne said, as though she was just remembering. "You said there was someone else. Another Hunar. Who was that?"

"The sour-faced woman," the wife said, with relish. "They make a right pair, her and the white-haired one. Both look down on us."

Yvonne's breath caught in her throat. Sillman had been here for a few days. And not that long afterward, Suanna had been here.

"I know you don't like to gossip," she started, leaning forward slightly, and lowering her voice, "but, you didn't happen to hear what the argument was about?"

"Not much of it," the wife said, leaning forward in a conspiratorial manner, eyes sharp, "but Elinor said something about betrayal. I'd never heard her so angry before."

Yvonne's heart constricted. It was true. Despite the red hair, which some said went with a fierce temper, Elinor had been kind, stubborn but rarely provoked to temper. Yvonne could not imagine what had happened to make her argue with Suanna so loudly that the neighbours had noticed.

And a betrayal. It could mean nothing. But, still stinging from her last encounter with Sillman, Suanna and Mica, Yvonne did not believe so.

Chapter Fifteen

Yvonne returned to Elinor's house with her mind full of the information she had been given. Elinor had done nothing out of the ordinary. No visitors for a few months before the illness, apart from Sillman and Suanna. An argument with Suanna loud enough that the neighbours had noticed. Mention of betrayal.

Her search of the house the day she had arrived had been nothing more than a simple look around, assessing whether anything looked out of place. Whether there was anything obvious that might have triggered Renard's suspicions. However, Elinor had been a skilled sorceress. And, with the knowledge that two of the Hundred had been here in the months before Elinor's death, Yvonne decided a more thorough search was needed.

Searching using magic was exhausting and time-consuming. She would only be able to manage one room at a time, and would have to rest between times.

She started with the space that she thought she would find most difficult. Elinor's bedroom.

It was just as difficult as she had feared. No one else had used magic in this room since Elinor's death, so Elinor's presence was still vivid and real. With her magically enhanced senses, she could trace Elinor's last moments. The fear. The grief. The anger.

Yvonne found her face wet with tears. Having these last, vivid traces of her mentor in the air felt like losing Elinor all over again. Everything that had been unique about her. All that compassion, all that love, all that stubbornness. Private moments that no one should be privy to, but which Yvonne had to witness, to try and find clues as to what had happened to her.

Yvonne remembered the argument that the neighbours had overheard. Betrayal.

The anger she could sense, one of Elinor's last emotions, carried a sharp edge to it. Elinor had been furious and bitter in her last moments.

She had not deserved that, Yvonne thought. Elinor had been kind, had spent a lifetime helping others. Her last moments should have been many, many years away, and spent in peace, with the knowledge of a life well lived, rather than this mess of fury and grief.

It was hard. One of the hardest things she had done, to set aside Elinor's feelings and to search her most private space. It wasn't long before Yvonne's magic found a hidden compartment in Elinor's nightstand. It opened to Yvonne's touch, keyed to her. Her breath caught. Elinor had expected her to be here. Had expected her former pupil to search her room, and find this compartment.

The space held letters, simple folded over parchments, addressed to Adira, Renard and Yvonne, and a leather-bound notebook.

The names on the parchments were written in Elinor's handwriting, the words misshapen, as though she had been writing with a trembling hand.

Yvonne set aside the letters for Adira and Renard. The letters were not sealed, but they were not her business, and whatever Elinor had wanted to say to them was between them.

She sat at the end of Elinor's bed and opened the letter addressed to her. It had been sealed with a tiny spark of magic bearing Elinor's signature but which, like the handwriting, was slightly misshapen.

I am dying, the letter began, without preamble.

There is nothing I can do about it, and I am furious that I did not see it sooner. Someone has done this to me and, if you're reading this, you need to be careful. There's something rotten in the world. People I trusted behaving strangely. I've left you what I can. It wasn't enough to save me. Be careful. Question everything. Remember your training. And try to remember your final test and everything that happened that night. It could save you. And everyone else.

The letter was signed simply with the scrawling, stylised E that Elinor had always used in place of a signature.

Yvonne read the letter twice more, stomach twisted. Elinor had known she was dying. Renard was right. Elinor's death had not been natural.

"Could you not simply have told me who did this?" Yvonne asked the room. "This is not another lesson. This is your life. If someone did this to you, I want to find them and bring them to justice. A little help would be nice." She clamped her jaw shut. She was talking to the empty air of a dead woman's bedroom. There would be no answers here.

There was the notebook, though. A quick flick through revealed it was full of notes. Scraps of information. It would take her most of a day or night to read through.

She tucked it into a pocket, along with her letter. The spell she had performed would not last forever, and she needed to search the rest of the room.

While the magic was still intact, she made another search of the room and found nothing more. Nothing that would help her, anyway. There were a few letters that had come from Adira and Renard, tucked into a box of correspondence along with other letters from some of Elinor's friends, and a few letters from the Hundred, including a few from Yvonne herself. The box was full, with no room for anything else.

Yvonne did not read the letters from Adira or Renard. What they had said to Elinor was private, and would stay that way. She did take the box of correspondence with her down to the kitchen and set it on a high shelf, sealing it with some magic, the simple spell draining more energy from her. Adira and Renard might want their letters back.

The searching spell wore off, the effort of carrying it for so long leaving her shaky and lightheaded. She needed something to eat, and some rest, before she did anything else.

She made herself tea, remembering the endless cups she had drunk over the past couple of days, and looked at the sugar bowl again. She could use the energy, but she could not stand the taste of sweet tea.

The lingering trace of the spell curled around the sugar bowl, holding her attention for a moment. There should be nothing there for the spell to cling to.

Her energy ran out, and she sat down with the mug of tea, staring at the sugar bowl as though the spell would magically return and answer the many questions she had.

Before she could do more than drink the tea, staring at the innocuous-looking sugar bowl, there was a knock at the front door, that led onto the street.

Immediately on alert as, from the outside, the house looked boarded-up and deserted, Yvonne put a hand on her sword hilt and went through the house, stopping to one side of the front door.

The knock sounded again.

"Hunar, come quickly. There's someone outside who needs to speak to you. They're not quite themselves."

Yvonne recognised the voice as belonging to one of the neighbours, although she could not immediately place which one, and unbolted the door, stepping out into the street to find a few people had gathered around someone lying prone on the road surface. A middle-aged man, who looked ill, and whose harsh breathing Yvonne could hear even from several paces away.

"He was trying to get to Elinor's door," the neighbour who had been knocking said. She and her husband lived a few doors down, Yvonne remembered. They had served her a particularly fine scone along with the tea when she had visited them. "He says he has a message for the Hunar." The neighbour glanced across the street at the man, and then back to Yvonne, lowering her voice. "He doesn't sound right."

"Thank you for letting me know," Yvonne said. She pulled the door shut behind her, and crossed the street to the man, crouching beside him. His eyes were staring at nothing, moving in random patterns, and his mouth was working, although no sound was emerging.

"What's wrong with him?" one of the other neighbours asked. "Is it the fever back again?"

"No," Yvonne said, keeping her voice calm and measured. "It is the sight. If you give him some room, I will talk to him."

The neighbours backed away quickly. The sight was not contagious, but it was unsettling, and Yvonne could understand their impulse to move away, although she noticed that they stayed within range so they could see and hear everything. Wary, but also curious.

The man's head turned towards her as she spoke, even though his eyes were unfocused, not really seeing her.

"Elinor is not here," Yvonne said. "But I will listen to you."

"You," the man said. At least, it was his lips moving, and his throat that the word emerged from. But, like all the other times Yvonne had spoken with someone in the grips of the sight, it was a harsh, deep voice that did not belong to the person speaking. And, as with other times, the voice resonated with something else that made the hairs stand up all over her body. There was power twined with that voice. An ancient power. And it knew her. The sight, whatever it was, had recognised her.

"I am Yvonne," she told him, "and I'm listening."

"You. Must listen. He is risen. Too late. He is risen."

Yvonne's skin crawled at the weight of the words, which landed on her shoulders like the heaviest obligations she had ever undertaken as Hunar.

"No. We buried him," she said, careless of the audience. There was no doubt, in her mind, who they were talking about. The first enemy of the Hundred. The first Hunar's brother, as powerful as he had been. And now buried under half a mountain's worth of soil.

The man's mouth moved again, lips slack for a moment, then forming soundless words before the voice emerged again. "He. Is. Risen."

The man's eyes rolled back in his head, and he slumped to the ground, limp and unconscious. Yvonne, reluctantly, put her fingers on the man's wrists. She did not want to get too close to the sight, even though she knew it was irrational. It was simply a voice. However powerful, it could not actually harm her.

Human skin met her fingers. There was no power there, just a pulse. The man's heart was beating too fast, but he was simply human.

"Is he dead?" one of the neighbours asked.

"No. He's collapsed. Does anybody know where he lives?"

The neighbours edged closer, to get a better look on his face, now that he was unconscious and no longer terrifying. They conferred amongst themselves and then agreed, reluctantly, that they did know him. He had a farm on the edge of town. He also had a wife, and a pair of teenage sons. One of the neighbours sent their children off at a run towards the farm, to let the wife know where her husband was, and that he would need help getting home.

Yvonne looked at the man's clothing, his pale skin and the sweat beading on his forehead, and thought that he probably had not been home for a while. He had not had a bath for some time, his skin sinking across his bones suggesting he had also not eaten for quite some time. She wondered how long it had been since his wife had seen him, and how long he had been wandering, in the grips of the sight. Trying to find a Hunar. Elinor, perhaps. But the sight had recognised her. She could still feel the echo of that first word. You. It rang through her. The sight had wanted to speak with her.

It was not the first time.

It took some time for the wife and sons to arrive, with their pony and cart. One look at the wife's face and Yvonne knew that she had been worrying herself for at least a pair of days, and likely had not slept much.

"Has he done this before?" Yvonne asked.

"Once. Just before the Hunar died. Gave me a right fright. I mean, I know the sight runs in his family, but he'd never shown any signs before."

"Can you remember what he said then?" Yvonne asked, stomach twisting. Around the time Elinor had died, no one else had reported any messages being given to them.

"It was nonsense." The wife shook her head, trying to remember for a moment. "He is coming," she said, at length, speaking slowly as though she was trying to get it right. "Does that make any sense?"

"Messages from the sight rarely make sense at the time." Yvonne looked down at the man and wondered why he had been given that message, for Elinor, such a long time before the messages that Yvonne had received.

She became aware that everyone around her was quiet. Waiting for her lead. She might not have the symbol of the Hunar on her shoulder anymore, but they had all known her as Elinor's apprentice. Mariah and Joel had played with a lot of the children when they were growing up.

"He should be absolutely fine," she told the wife, and saw her shoulders ease, the lines of strain fade from her face. "I've never heard of the sight leaving a lingering effect. The worst of it is not knowing what happened. He looks like he's been walking a while and not eating. You could all use some rest, I think."

"That's the truth," the wife agreed. She beckoned her sons forward and they helped her lift him into the cart, heading away, back to their home, with little fuss.

Yvonne stood and watched them go, her own words echoing oddly in her mind. The worst of it is not knowing what happened.

The first thing that came to mind was her final test. That long-ago night, in the Forbidden Lands. With Renard's prompting, and Elinor's letter, she realised that the only clear memories she had of that night was the first sight of the building, made of pale, sandy stone, rising up from the desert. And then, much later, standing barefoot on the sun-warmed stones, looking up at the great wall and seeing the extraordinary depiction of the Firebird.

Nothing else.

She had hours of time missing from her final test, the most important night of her training, and, until Renard had told her, she had never noticed.

Chapter Sixteen

By the time she got back into the house, the neighbours all settled and returned to their own homes, night was falling. It would be a long time before she got any rest, though.

Her middle was hollow. She needed food. Her hands worked, finding the ingredients for a simple meal. She still had a few hard-boiled eggs from the supplies she had brought with her, and Elinor's preservation spells had kept some vegetables fresh, even a year after Elinor herself was gone.

As she worked preparing her meal, her mind turned on the new message from the sight.

He is risen.

And, before that: he is coming.

She had not known who the message referred to when she first heard it, not really considering that the long dead brother of the first Hunar, and the first enemy of the Hundred, was a real threat.

Hundreds of children and youngsters kidnapped and sold into slavery, many of them dead, worked to death, had proven her wrong. The first enemy of the Hundred might have been buried, at depths that were almost unimaginable, but his influence had somehow crept out. She was still struggling to comprehend the extent of the organisation required to identify, kidnap and transport so many children. And the cunning behind it was chilling. The organisation had taken children from all across the lands, from places that no one had heard of, and had gone unchecked and unrecognised as they crossed borders into different territories. The rulers of lands, and their law keepers, were almost exclusively interested in their own affairs.

And the Ashnassan were involved somewhere. She wondered what progress Guise was making with his enquiries.

And she could avoid it no longer.

He is risen.

The long-buried brother of the first Hunar. Whose greed and ambition, and whose bitter rivalry with his brother, the first Hunar, had almost destroyed the world. For most people, the stories of the first Hunar and his brother were simply that. Stories. The Hundred knew a different truth, taught to them in their final stages of training. The first Hunar and his brother had been quite real. Unimaginably powerful sorcerers, they had fought their entire lives until the final battle, when they fatally wounded each other. There was a reason why the Forbidden Lands were sealed off, and why even desperate outlaws did not take refuge there. The scars left on the land by the battles fought between the brothers were felt even now.

The first Hunar had been buried, with all honour due to him, in the heart of the Forbidden Lands. There was a path to his final resting place that only the Hundred knew.

His brother's body had been taken and, the story said, cast into the deepest pit that could be found, the pit sealed over, never to be found and never to be seen again.

Until now.

Until someone, somehow, had felt the influence of the brother. Had somehow come up with the idea of un-burying him, and bringing him up to the light.

She remembered the grey soil of the mine that the children had been digging. The black tendrils that had snaked out from the deeper pit at the bottom of the mine. The tendrils, soaking up the blood of the fallen, had transformed into creatures capable of killing. And that was with the brother still buried.

He is risen.

Buried no longer.

It did not occur to her to question what the sight had told her. It might be cryptic. It might be frustratingly short on details. But the sight had never been wrong.

It had taken all of the Hundred and all of their strength, and the stunning appearance of the Firebird, to bury the brother again.

And they had failed.

A chill crept over her, the hollow in her stomach spreading, muscles tensing, wanting to run. The first enemy of the Hundred had been formidable enough to reach out from his grave. And he was still not defeated. Even with the might of the Hundred.

Her breathing was too harsh and too fast, fingers twisted together as she struggled for calm. The first enemy was not here. Not in front of her right now.

Her first impulse was to write a letter to the others. To the rest of the Hundred. To let them know.

But she was not Hunar anymore. They had dismissed her.

Even as she thought that, her eyes landed on the sugar bowl. Renard suspected that Elinor had been killed. The letter Elinor had left, perhaps written on her deathbed, confirmed his guess. There was also the notebook, that she had not had time to read properly. And the sugar bowl, which had drawn the attention of her spell, telling her something was out of place.

It was some hours since she had last used magic. With a meal almost ready on the stove, she had enough energy for another spell.

Her body felt weighted to the chair, every part of her reluctant to move. If she confirmed Renard's suspicions, that Elinor had been killed, then she would need to find who had done it. And, with no other strangers visiting Elinor in the months before she had died, that would mean speaking to Suanna and Sillman and finding out what business had brought them here, and what had happened to provoke Elinor's argument with Suanna.

Suanna might be austere, and not the warmest of people, but Elinor had always maintained that she worked hard as Hunar, and had always respected that. Yvonne had always trusted Elinor's judgement.

It was only now, sitting in Elinor's kitchen, facing the truth that she had been killed, that Yvonne wondered, for the first time, if Elinor's own judgement had been flawed.

She did not want to think about that, or open the notebook and read Elinor's words, and so she rose to her feet and went to the sugar bowl, casting the necessary spell to reveal the nature of its contents.

The spell revealed poison. It was not a surprise, and yet her breath still caught in her throat, her heart racing too hard once more. Poison.

Elinor's sweet tooth was famed among those that knew her. It was the one constant. She did not always drink wine. She did not always drink spirits. She always, always had sugar in her tea, and she drank tea every day, a habit that she had passed on to Yvonne.

With the spell still active, Yvonne went through Elinor's kitchen, making sure that the poison had not been left elsewhere, including in the food she was cooking.

There was only one other trace of poison. Elinor had a sack of sugar in the pantry that was laced with poison. It made sense. Someone had poisoned the entire sack of sugar, and Elinor had, unknowingly, tipped it into the sugar bowl, and then into her tea.

The Hundred might be sorcerers, but they did not, as a matter of course, check their food or drink for poison. And certainly not in their own homes, with wards around that would alert them to intruders.

The spell could not tell her what the poison was, of course. And she did not have the skill necessary to work it out. It needed someone with experience in alchemy. Guise might be able to tell, she realised, remembering his interests in the poison that had been used on the slaves. He had seemed to know what he was doing with the various bits of apparatus.

The Hundred all had some basic training in poisons. Mostly to spot the symptoms and how to treat them. There were two or three possible candidates for this particular poison. It could not have had a strong taste, or Elinor would have spotted it. It also needed to be slow-acting, and to mimic a natural illness, otherwise her neighbours would have been suspicious and Elinor herself would have noticed before it was too late.

A slow-acting, tasteless poison added to a foodstuff that Elinor used every day.

Yvonne sat back at the table, with the sugar bowl in front of her, and felt her heart crack again. Her mentor, her place of safety, the person who had seen the potential of a Hunar within a broken and terrified girl. Killed. Poisoned in a cool and calculated way.

Someone who had known Elinor. Someone who had known her habits. That list was, in fact, quite long, as she had been warm and welcoming to everyone around her. All of her neighbours. Everyone who visited the house. Every one of the Hundred. Yvonne's mind flinched away from the idea, but she knew it had to be considered. That one of the Hundred had poisoned one of their own.

She remembered Elinor's letter and her urging to be careful. With the evidence in front of her, that warning took on new meaning. Yvonne could not breathe for a moment, chest constricting with the idea that Elinor had died, furious and alone, knowing who had killed her, and that it was one of her own. Unable to do anything. If there had been anything to be done, Elinor would have done it, Yvonne was quite sure. But, by the time she had realised that she had been poisoned, it was too late. Too late to do anything apart from write those short, cryptic lines and tuck them away along with her notebook.

And Yvonne might still not know, if Renard had not come to visit. Not for the first time, Yvonne wondered what had prompted Renard to visit. She remembered that he had seemed ill, and her chest constricted again, wondering if he had ingested the same poison. He had not shared Elinor's sweet tooth, at least not for sugar in tea, but he would have eaten food that she had prepared. And Elinor had been generous in sharing with her neighbours.

The fever.

Her breath caught again. The fever. The illness that had spread. The one that they had all thought was perfectly natural. The one that had claimed other lives in the neighbourhood. The other lives that had, perhaps by design, disguised Elinor's death as something natural, and not to be concerned about.

Elinor had been strong. Healthy. It would have taken time for the poison to work through her. Not all of her neighbours were strong, though. It was perfectly possible that someone else had shown symptoms long before Elinor, while Elinor continued to take her baking to her neighbours. She would have sat with anyone who wanted her, shared what she had, in an effort to help. And, unknowingly, been responsible for other deaths as well as her own.

In the middle of the grief, Yvonne felt a welcome rush of fury. Bad enough that someone had poisoned Elinor. Worse, still, they had made her complicit in the deaths of others. Yvonne spared a moment to hope, fervently, that Elinor had not been aware that it had been the sugar that had been poisoned or that she had, all unknowing, passed the poison around her neighbours.

Someone needed to pay.

There needed to be justice. For Elinor. For the others who had died because a coward had decided to end Elinor's life in this calculated manner, not really caring who else they might hurt.

She looked at the sugar bowl again. The spell had faded, so that it simply looked like an ordinary bowl of sugar, sitting in front of her on the kitchen table.

She needed somebody with more experience in poisons.

She also needed to know, her chest aching at the thought, whether it had been one of the Hundred who had provided the poison.

And that meant contacting the Hundred. She half rose from her chair to go and get writing materials, not sure what on earth she would write, and then stopped, settling back in the chair. She had a different way. One she had almost forgotten.

She opened her spell pouch and took out the small, beautifully made bird that Pieris had crafted. Goblin magic and Hunar magic combined. As she had been before, she was surprised at the weight of it. The densely made thing cradled in the palm of her hand but weighed as much as a bottle of spirits.

It was keyed to Pieris, and only him. She remembered the neighbour's comments about the Hunar with sad eyes visiting. That could be Pieris. So easily. It could also be Firon. But, she thought, only those two. She had no means of reaching Firon quickly, just Pieris. And she could not believe that Pieris was capable of the cold, calculating decisions that had to have been made to put poison into Elinor's sugar bowl, and then to wait for her to die.

Besides which, Pieris was the one, out of all of the Hundred, that knew most about spells and about poisons. If anyone could work out what this poison was, it would be him. And he should also be able to work out how long Elinor had been poisoned for.

The bird sat on the table in front of her, awaiting her instruction. Her mind went blank for a moment, unable to think of any form of words that would emphasise the urgency of the matter and not alert anyone else to what she had discovered. She spoke the command word before she knew what she was doing. The bird woke up, its beautifully formed, delicate wings fluttering, lifting its beak, ready for her instruction. It was an extraordinary piece of magic and reminded her so much of Pieris, with his attention to detail and his love of learning.

"Take a message to Pieris. I am at Elinor's house and there is something terribly wrong. He needs to come at once."

She gave the bird the command phrase that released it and watched as it spread its little wings, turned once or twice, and then rose up into the air. If she had not seen it come to life from its dormant state, she might have believed it an ordinary bird. She got to her feet, the effort surprising her, went to the door and opened it to let the bird out, watching it fly away into the night sky. It was later than she had realised. She had been sitting at the kitchen table, contemplating darkness, far longer than she had realised.

There was no guarantee that the bird would reach Pieris, or that Pieris would respond. He had not been there when Sillman had pulled the symbol of the Hunar out of her, but Sillman had made it clear the decision was one of all of the Hundred. Her breath caught for a moment and she wondered if she had made a terrible mistake. It was done. She could not call the bird back. And part of her did not want to. Someone had killed Elinor. Justice was needed. Answers were required.

The food she had prepared was over-done. She did not really want to eat, but needed the energy. She settled at the table with a pair of candles lit, Elinor's notebook in front of her, and her writing equipment nearby. She needed to prepare some more spells, and find out what she was dealing with. What Elinor had known.

It was time to begin hunting Elinor's killer.

She was walking along an unfamiliar corridor, warm stone under her bare feet, dressed in an unfamiliar outfit of loose, wide-legged trousers and long-sleeved over tunic that hung down to her knees, split at the sides so that she could walk. An outfit worn by some desert people. Even though she did not recognise them, they felt like her clothes.

Her hair was loose, drifting around her face, hanging down her back, still damp from an earlier bath.

There was a doorway ahead, a stone archway that led to a large courtyard in the centre of which was a fountain. No water flowed through the fountain just now, the basin cracked, damage visible even in the poor light. The whole space looked old, worn and abandoned, plants growing through cracks in the stone.

Looking up, she saw a clear sky with a blanket of stars overhead and a full moon gleaming silver and white.

There was a sound behind her. She should have been alarmed. Alone at night with no weapons. But this felt like a place of safety.

She turned.

There was a shadow in the corridor she had just come from. A darker blot against the wall.

And a voice that seemed familiar, reaching out through the night towards her. "Finally. Daughter. Be welcome."

Yvonne woke with a cry in her throat, her heart racing, body coated in sweat. She stumbled through the words of a light spell, casting the miniature candles around the room. It was somewhere in the middle of the night. There was no one else in the room. No shadows waiting for her.

And she was dressed in her normal nightclothes, the fabric thin and worn from use, her hair in its usual single braid down her back.

She was in her room at Elinor's house. There was the familiar dresser, and the hooks on the back of the door. The rug next to the bed. The nightstand with a glass of water that she had poured in the kitchen downstairs. The floor was wooden, not made of stone.

Something prompted her to get out of bed and go to the chest that sat at the foot of the bed. It had always been in the room, even though she had not used it for many years.

Now, she lifted the lid. Spare bed linen met her eyes. A blanket for colder months. Moving by instinct, she lifted them out and set them at the end of the bed, until she had emptied the chest. And then, she found the notch at the side of the base and lifted the false bottom out.

Underneath the false bottom was a small space that held clothing she recognised immediately. Wide-legged trousers and a long-sleeved, loose tunic of the style worn in the desert. Made of undyed linen, she had no waking memory of wearing them, and yet these were the clothes from her dream. And they were hers.

She lifted them out of the space and checked that there was nothing else there before returning the false bottom, then the spare linens and blanket.

She sat on the side of the bed, the unfamiliar clothes in her hands, and tried to remember. She still had a vivid, waking memory of standing barefoot in front of the wall, looking up at the picture of the Firebird, seeing her gleam as the light picked out the gold flecks that had been used to decorate her.

Sitting in Elinor's house, holding clothes she did not remember, she could feel again the press of air against her face from the downbeat of the Firebird's wings and hear, again, the shriek of rage as the Firebird rose into the air.

She had felt that press of air and heard that shriek at the mine, surrounded by the Hundred and Guise. And yet. She did not think that this memory was from the mine, when the Firebird had buried the first Hunar's brother again. This felt like an older memory, from a time she did not remember.

Elinor's letter. Try to remember. The final test.

The test that all apprentices had to undergo, in order to become Hunar.

Her mind brought up snippets of that day. Elinor's voice, telling her to go into the temple. To stay there until morning. Elinor would not tell her what to expect. Yvonne had gone into the temple with a knot of worry and apprehension in her stomach, moving forward with the certainty that this was something she had to do, pulled forward by the magic that she could sense. The magic of the Hundred.

And the next morning, Elinor hugging her for longer than was comfortable, crying with pride. Yvonne was Hunar.

Hunar. No longer the broken girl who had stumbled into the Stone Walls. No longer the clumsy apprentice, learning how to use the weapons Elinor had supplied her with.

Now she was Hunar, the call and pull of the magic inside her feeling like it had always been there. A Hunar used their power and knowledge to help others, to bring justice where it was needed. It had been the end of a long period of training. And the achievement was hers. Elinor had told her that, more than once. Hunar were chosen. Not all who were tested were accepted.

That morning, Elinor had been full of joy and pride for her former apprentice. She remembered the tears on her mentor's face, the hug, the warmth of the rising sun.

She remembered, too, a change in Elinor's expression. Something about the story that Yvonne had told her, what had happened over the night, had disturbed Elinor. And she had told Yvonne never to tell that story to another living being.

Yvonne shook her head. She could not remember what had happened. Not anymore. But, that morning, she had remembered, had told her mentor, and her mentor had told her not to speak of it again but, instead, to tell everyone another story, if they asked.

In the end, very few people had actually asked. She had not given any explanation to anyone outside the Hundred. When Dundac had asked her, the only one of the Hundred to do so, she had started to tell him Elinor's story but stumbled to a halt, unable to continue the false tale. Dundac had not seemed to notice anything amiss, simply saying that he had been overwhelmed, too, but had, in the end, fallen asleep in the temple.

In the quiet and loneliness of Elinor's house, she was crying again.

Something had happened that she could not remember, but which set her apart from the rest of the Hundred.

Dundac had fallen asleep. He had described having nightmares. Disjointed bits of monsters and the cry of a great bird overhead. From the bits and pieces of information she had picked up over the years, the rest of the Hundred seemed to have had similar experiences. Falling asleep. A restless, disturbed night. Waking the next morning.

Something about spending the night in the first Hunar's temple was enough to determine whether or not they were accepted as Hunar.

As she stared down at the unfamiliar clothing, she remembered another detail. When she had come out of the temple that morning, and seen Elinor, the symbol of the Hunar was on her shoulder. She had been accepted. And that was how Elinor had known.

There had been something about Elinor's reaction, though. Something that was important but which she could not remember just now. A chill worked its way up her spine. There was too much she did not remember. And did not know. Not yet.

As the sun rose outside, she ate leftovers from her meal the night before at the kitchen table, with the sugar bowl and Elinor's notebook in front of her. Two mysteries.

The notebook was some kind of journal, that made no sense to Yvonne's eyes, even knowing Elinor. Random dates, not in sequential order, and notes of things that had happened on those days.

It seemed as if Elinor had been trying to keep track of something, and had written notes rather than relying on her usually excellent memory. But the events she noted seemed to have no connection. A conversation at Mid Winter Feast. A bowl she had bought at a mid-summer fair. Part of a conversation with someone, although Elinor had not noted down who the conversation was with. And threaded through the rest, notes of when and where she had seen some of the Hundred, or where others had reported seeing the Hundred.

Pieris in Abar al Endell.

Suanna in the Royal City. Noteworthy as she hated the place.

Dundac in Hogsmarthen. A long way from the Royal City, where he normally lived. But about the same time as Suanna had visited the Royal City, Yvonne noted.

Sillman in Hogsmarthen.

Sillman in Willowton. Reference to a discussion Elinor had had with him. Related to a supplicant Sillman had been helping.

Yvonne finished her meal no closer to understanding the notebook than she had been the night before. A few hours' disturbed sleep and the strange dream, that might not have been a dream, had left her with an itch between her shoulder blades and a growing conviction that there was something rotten within the Hundred, and a sense that whatever it was needed to be dealt with. Soon.

There were too many mysteries to be solved in one day. Still, she had to start somewhere.

With her questioning of Elinor's neighbours done, her mind spinning with the information they had given her and the fragments of her final testing chasing each other around in her mind, she decided to focus on something that seemed a straightforward matter.

Find the cloth merchant Guise had mentioned. Ask him about authenticators.

She took Baldur for a short, much-needed ride, just enough to stretch his legs and mean that he would not be kicking the stable down until she had a chance to give him a proper run. Then she had a bath. It was one of many things she had always loved about Elinor's house. The luxury of a bathhouse.

Coming out of the bathhouse, clean and surrounded by the familiar scent of Elinor's soap, she looked at the stretch of land behind the house. From the street the house did not look like much. Through the gate at the side, and it was clear that it was the tiniest part of the plot.

Elinor had been a keen gardener, growing most of her own vegetables and fruit.

In her absence, the plot had grown wild. There had been attempts, here and there, to tidy up, and quite a lot of the ripe crops were missing. Yvonne suspected that the neighbours had been behind that. She did not blame them. Elinor would have wanted the produce to be used and not left to rot, and had always shared with her neighbours.

The signs of neglect were as difficult to see as the emptiness of the house was to hear.

So, she left Baldur content and snoozing in his stable and made her way to the trade streets that crossed the middle of the town. She would set Guise's contact on the hunt for the authenticator, and the Ashnassan's mysterious employer, and then she could turn her own attention to finding Elinor's killer and whatever was rotten in the Hundred.

Chapter Seventeen

Guise had simply said that the cloth merchant was at the blue house. It was only as she was walking towards the trade streets that Yvonne wondered if she should have asked for better directions. She could not remember a cloth merchant with a blue house from her time living here.

One look at the street and she realised it was unnecessary. There was only one blue house.

It stood on its own, surrounded by a thick band of green plants, and rose two storeys above the ground. And it was, indeed, blue. The deep, cobalt blue of the most expensive dyes available, a uniform colour around the entire building, which was larger than her house or Guise's annex. The paint alone was worth a fortune.

Both the lower and upper floors had large windows. The upstairs windows were slightly open, and she could hear the clack of wooden looms from the upper level as she drew closer. Her brows lifted. Few merchants had their own cloth woven on site, mostly using weavers who worked at their own, small looms in cottages around the town and in the surrounding villages. To insist on cloth being woven in their own building usually meant that it was high quality, using the most expensive yarn.

Then she shook her head. This was Guise's contact. Of course he would be using expensive yarn. It was probably silk from Abar al Endell. Or the finest wool from the remote villages in the northlands.

The doors to the building were open, the sound of voices drifting out to the street.

She climbed the few steps to the front door, stepped across the threshold and stopped, blinking, as her eyes adjusted to the interior.

The room she had stepped into probably took up about half of the ground floor on its own, and it was a riot of colour. Bolts of cloth as tall as she was were propped against the walls. About a half dozen large, waist-high tables were spread around the space, most of them with one or more bolts of cloth on them, at one of which an assistant was talking with a customer. Then there were racks, too. High wooden shelves stuffed full of more cloth.

Her first thought was that Mariah would absolutely love this place. Her second thought was that if Mariah ever came into this room, her daughter might never want to leave. Before she had time to think further, a slender young man dressed in a beautifully fitting dark suit approached her.

"Good day, mistress. How may we help you?"

"I need to see the merchant, please."

"The owner is not on the floor just now. But I can ask. Who shall I say?"

"We have a mutual friend," she told him. The assistant's eyebrows lifted, but he drifted away to one side of the room where a large wooden door was almost hidden between bolts of cloth in different shades of red, and disappeared.

Not expecting an immediate response, she began a slow circuit of the room, pausing at a bolt of cloth in a tightly-woven black fabric. It would make excellent trousers, she thought, and glanced at the price ticket, then quickly backed away from the fabric. Now she understood how the merchant could afford to paint his entire house in cobalt blue.

Before she had time to look at any other prices, the assistant was back.

"The merchant will see you now," he said, and led her through the room to the discreet doorway.

The door opened onto the building's stairwell, the clack of the looms overhead louder as they passed across the hallway, through an open arch and into a large room at the corner of the building. It was set out as an office, with another of the waist-high tables, a dressmakers' dummy and a large desk that would look perfectly at home in a lawyer or banker's office.

The only other occupant of the room was a curvaceous woman, slightly shorter than Yvonne, wearing an exquisitely-made gown of deep red that showed off her curves as she moved around the desk towards Yvonne.

"Good day to you, mistress. You wished to see me?"

"I did," Yvonne said. How like Guise to not mention that his contact was a woman. Thinking back, she realised that he had, in fact, gone out of his way to hide that fact when he had told Yvonne about the merchant. She wondered how many other women were in his network, and shut down that thought before it could go anywhere.

"A mutual acquaintance?" the merchant prompted.

"Indeed." Yvonne dug in a pocket and produced the disc that Guise had given her. The merchant looked at it, eyes narrowed for a moment.

"The only one of Guise's contacts who even remotely resembles you, mistress, is a Hunar by the name of Yvonne."

Yvonne wondered just how many of Guise's contacts knew who she was, or knew each other. "I am Yvonne."

"But not a Hunar?"

"Not anymore, no," she answered, jaw set.

"I see. Be welcome. I am Lita. Have a seat and tell me what you need."

"You are extremely well informed," Yvonne commented as she took a seat facing the desk.

Lita moved around the desk to an imposing chair that might look like a throne in other circumstances. The placement of the chair and the desk put her between two windows at the corner of the building, casting her face into shadow. No accident, Yvonne was sure. The rulers in Abar al Endell used a similar technique. She wondered how often Lita had travelled there.

"I try to be," the merchant answered, voice light. The sharp glance she sent Yvonne belied her tone, though.

"The Ashnassan tribe have been kidnapping girls. Nine-year-old girls. They are being paid for it. In golden crowns. Apparently, they have been using an authenticator to verify the money they are being paid with."

The merchant barely blinked at Yvonne's words. "And you want me to find the authenticator."

"Technically, Guise wants you to find the authenticator. He has some family business to attend to, or he would be here himself."

"And sends you to do his bidding," the merchant said, mouth lifting in a semblance of a smile. If she had fangs, they would be bared.

"I also want to know the identity of the authenticator."

"I have a reputation to uphold. I cannot simply go about asking questions like this."

"Really?" Yvonne drew out the word, internally smiling. She was, despite herself, beginning to like this sharp-eyed, sharp-minded woman. "I cannot imagine it's the worst task Guise has set for you."

"That is true. He actually sent me to Three Falls once." The woman shivered in convincing horror. "I didn't see a straight seam for days."

"You were looking in the wrong place," Yvonne answered, remembering her visits to Three Falls. It might be a cesspit, but the wealthy were usually very well dressed.

"No. Seriously. Even those fancy robes the priests wear. Crooked hems. Every single one. It was ..." She drew in a slow, deep breath. "Unsettling."

"You don't happen to know Frida, of Fir Tree Crossing, do you?" Yvonne asked. She thought that Frida would find a kindred spirit in this woman, even though they were very different.

"Only by reputation. An excellent reputation. Did she make those clothes for you?" Lita asked, eyes narrowing as she inspected Yvonne. Yvonne was amused, and glad that she had worn her gifted clothes, rather than the threadbare spare set she had. It was a definite advantage to having magic. Cleansing spells would keep the clothes fresh as long as she needed them.

"No. These are from Guise's tailor." At least, Yvonne thought, she assumed so.

"I should have known. No one hand-stitches collars quite as well as he does," Lita said, sighing in apparent envy. "Do you know how many golden crowns the Ashnassan have been getting?"

The abrupt change in subject, and business-like tone, made Yvonne smile again.

"No. The person giving us the information was too busy praising Nassash to give much useful detail."

"Ugh." Lita's nose wrinkled, and she gave an exaggerated shudder. "Do you know, I had some of those barbarians in the other week. Looking for red velvet."

"What in the name of reason could they want with red velvet?" Yvonne asked, brows lifting in unfeigned surprise.

"I did not ask. We simply showed them the door." Lita was looking thoughtful. "But one of them did wave a golden crown at me. As if that would help."

"You don't like paying customers?" Yvonne asked, keeping her tone light.

"I don't like cowards who kidnap women." The merchant glanced to one side, face no longer cast in shadow for a moment and Yvonne saw the tension in her neck and jawline.

"I'm sorry," Yvonne said. That depth of bitterness and pain usually came from personal experience.

"My older sister. We went looking for her. Got as far as the border. They threw her body back across."

"I am sorry for your loss," Yvonne said, bowing her head a moment. She did not ask what state the sister's body had been in. She had too many bad memories to carry already.

"You really mean that," Lita said, voice reflective. "Sincerity is a rare and undervalued grace. If you will give me a few days, I will look into the authenticator for you. I will enjoy disrupting the barbarians' plans." From the light in her eye, Yvonne thought that enjoy was far too mild a word. "Where shall I send the information?"

Yvonne gave Elinor's address, hesitated, then continued. "Please be careful." She held up a hand in a pacifying gesture. "You know your business, yes. But the Ashnassan leader is brutal. He killed his own men to stop them talking."

"You are not at all what I expected, Mistress Yvonne. You must call again," Lita said, rising to her feet and coming around the desk. "We shall have some red wine and discuss Guise's failings."

Yvonne's mouth curved as she rose to her feet. "We may need more than one bottle."

Leaving the quiet of Lita's office, Yvonne headed along the trade streets towards the main market, her mood darkening again as she went. The authenticator would be found. Of that she had no doubt. Which left her free to concentrate on finding Elinor's killer.

She had not decided her next steps yet, but if she was going to stay in the house for a bit longer, she needed food. Even if it was not an official market day, there were still plenty of grocers, butchers and bakers with permanent stalls around the square.

The bustle of the square took her by surprise. She had completely lost track of the days on the way here and arrived on one of the official market days, when farmers and craftsmen could pitch their stalls around the square and sell their goods. The square was packed with traders, townsfolk and visitors. For perhaps the first time, she welcomed the crowds as a distraction from the grim knowledge and unpleasant speculation chasing each other around in her mind.

Completing her errands did not take long. She would usually have made her way home, anxious to be away from the press of people. As Hunar, crowds were often difficult as they were full of potential supplicants. No longer Hunar, she still found the press of people difficult, too many bodies and voices and faces all around her. As well as the discomfort of a crowd, there was always a never-ending list of household tasks waiting for her.

Today, she lingered near the market, not wanting to go back to puzzles she had no answers for, to the empty house and to the silence where there should be the noise of footsteps, laughter or just Elinor's quiet presence.

She settled on the low wall that bordered the market place, separating the stalls from the taverns on this side, cloak tucked around her. Just one more weary-footed shopper among others also taking a moment's ease on the wall. A couple nearby were having a good-natured argument about who had struck the better deal with their purchases. A pair of elderly women were exchanging the latest gossip, shaking their heads in despair at the antics of the young folk. There would be a child along soon, trying to sell her a cup of water even though there was a public water pump not that far away that anyone could use. Ordinary, everyday distractions. It was all wonderfully normal and familiar.

It wasn't enough to keep her mind busy, though, so she looked further, eyes flickering over the crowds, and saw something impossible.

Off to one side of the market square, in an alleyway leading from the main street, standing in the shadows of the buildings on either side, was a man who should not exist.

She recognised the young, striking face and black hair. She had last seen his body on the floor of his castle, surrounded by red robes, blackened blood pooling on the stone floor, the Hundred in a group around him.

The lord of Coll Castle. Who had harboured something that she could not identify. Something that had turned his blood black, had given him claws and blackened teeth, had shaded his eyes.

He was dead. The Hundred had seen to it.

And yet, his very image was standing within bow-shot of her, in Elinor's home town.

She got to her feet, took a step forward and froze, body not willing to move. The world seemed to spin and slow as she stood, stupidly staring, at something impossible. One of the market-goers, laden with goods, bumped into her, trying to get past, and she apologised on reflex, stepping to one side.

By the time she had looked up again, the figure in the alleyway was gone, and she was left wondering at her own sanity.

A dream. A voice in her mind. Clothes that were familiar to touch, yet she could not remember wearing. And now, the face of a dead man. The Coll lord was dead, killed by the Hundred. His blood had soaked into the castle floor. His body had been burned, along with the rest of the dead from the castle. She had seen the scorch marks on the ground.

The scarf around her neck was abruptly too tight, fingers trembling, body tensing.

It was not possible that she had seen him. It simply was not. It must be someone who looked like him. There. That was more possible. She was not going insane. And she would prove it. She would find that young man. She would look into his face and see normal, human eyes looking back instead of black. He would have pale skin without black veins running through it. His hands would be finished by normal fingernails, not claws.

She was walking away, in the direction he had gone, before she realised what she was doing. She did not stop, or hesitate. She was not going insane. The Coll lord was not back from the dead.

Of course, when she reached the alleyway, there was nothing there. She followed it along its entire length, one hand on her sword hilt, looking for trouble in every shadow that she passed so that, by the time she reached the end of the alleyway, she was tense, peering into every shadow. And she found nothing. There was no one else in the alleyway. Not even a stray cat.

She must have imagined the whole thing, even though her mind did not normally play such tricks on her. But then, nothing was normal. She was staying in Elinor's house, every single piece of furniture, every room, every scent, reminding her of Elinor. She had discovered poison in Elinor's sugar bowl, and was seriously considering the possibility that one of the Hundred might have put it there. And she had found strange clothes in the room she had always used, hidden away under a false panel she had not known existed.

Perhaps she was going insane.

She made herself walk away, head back to the house, to walk towards something familiar, even if everything had changed.

Too soon to expect any kind of reply from Pieris, even if he was going to answer.

There were still a lot of things she could do. Elinor's house had been empty for too long. There were chores to do. The housekeeping spells had faded slightly in Elinor's absence. The wards needed checking. She needed to find a way of delivering Elinor's last letters to Adira and Renard. And she had a lively young horse who needed better exercise.

Even so, she kept a close eye on her surroundings as she walked.

Not going insane, she kept telling herself. There had been someone in that alleyway. There was an explanation for everything.

The extra vigilance saved her life.

Chapter Eighteen

She felt the displacement of air and moved, instinct and training kicking in. Dropping her bag of food, she rolled on the ground and came up to a fighting stance, sword ready for the attacker who had been waiting for her in a shadowed doorway.

He grinned, apparently delighted that he had not killed her with his first stroke. The Ashnassan deputy. The one who had faced her while the Rangers and wulfkin fought his fellows. The one who thought she was a bit old for his taste, but that kidnapping young girls paid well, and that was justification enough. The one who Grayling had rescued her from, when she had been paralysed in the aftermath of her sundering. And the one who, she suspected, had slit the throats of his fellow tribesmen because his leader had ordered it.

"Well, aren't you the interesting one?"

"You again," she said, in a disgusted tone. "When are you just going to leave me alone? I want nothing to do with you."

"Well, that's a pity, because I've got orders." The tribesman grinned at her, showing a gap in his teeth. "Seems you've been sticking your nose in where it's not wanted."

"You're going to have to be more specific," she told him. "I ask a lot of questions. Who wants me dead this time? The Slayer?" It was a good guess, given how she had taunted the tribe's leader on their one meeting.

"Don't know. Don't care. The money's good. Which is a pity. I can think of much better uses for you."

Yvonne's stomach knotted. It was far from the first time that anyone had made that threat against her. And the Ashnassan had a grim history with women. She could almost hear Elinor's voice, from her early training, reminding her to use that fear and turn it into focus. Into anger, if that helped.

"Such a limited imagination," she said, keeping her sword ready. He would not be easy to fight. He was trained, and had seen her fight before, so would not make the mistake of thinking she was an easy target.

"But I know what I like," he answered, grinning again. He was confident. He had reason to be. She knew her own skills and strength. He was a stronger and more experienced swordsman.

She had no space for fear. Anger sped up her heart, tightened her grip on the sword, narrowed her focus. This man had participated in the kidnapping of young girls, not caring who wanted them, or for what.

"I will give you one chance to live," she told him. "If you leave now. If you promise to never attack me, or my family, again. You may walk away, and I will not pursue you."

His only response was a disbelieving laugh and the forward thrust of his sword.

"When you go to meet your lame and impotent god, be sure to tell him what an idiot you were," she told him, blocking his attack.

If he had been confident before, he was now both confident and angry.

Not for the first time, she thought she should probably learn how to hold her tongue a bit better. There never seemed to be time to learn, though. The middle of a sword fight was certainly not it.

He believed he was better. He had seen her fight before. But she had not been this angry before. Rather, she had been shaken by her dismissal from the Hundred, and feeling displaced. And then, in the forest clearing with the Slayer, she had been more intent on getting information and staying alive than fighting.

Now she was in Willowton. The closest thing she had to a home town, where she had learned, slowly, to walk down the streets without jumping at shadows. Where she had seen her children grow into confident, curious youngsters, starting to become the remarkable people they were today. And the anger she had, which had almost nothing to do with him, kept her sword point up and her movements fluid and easy.

She felt a grim satisfaction when she disarmed him, his sword flying across the street, too far for him to reach, and saw the shock on his face.

"How did you do that?"

"Practice," she told him. "Lots of practice." She had the point of her sword at his throat. "Who sent you to kill me?" He opened his mouth, but whatever he might have said was lost as an arrow flew past Yvonne's shoulder and embedded itself in his throat, cutting off any words. He was dead before he had time to realise it.

Yvonne turned, pulling a spell from her pouch as she moved, throwing the parchment into the air with its activation word. A rough and ready defence against further arrows. Not a moment too soon. Another arrow flew, and tangled in her web of spells.

"Bloody sorceress. Thought she didn't have her power anymore?" The voice came from an archer, a short distance away, his bow ready with another arrow. She drew another spell out of her pouch. Another counter to arrows.

"Slayer must have been told wrong," another voice said.

"She can still be killed," yet another voice said.

Slayer. The Ashnassan leader. Who had thought she had lost her magic, despite the fire she had used at their one meeting. Her ears caught on the odd phrasing. Someone had told Slayer she had no power.

No time to consider that further just now. Her eyes narrowed. The archer had company. She looked past him to see more of the Ashnassan gathered. A half dozen at least.

"Were all of you sent to kill me?" she asked. "How flattering."

Unlike the deputy, now staring sightlessly at the sky, these attackers were not interested in conversation, and simply came towards her, weapons raised. She bit her lip against further, unwise words, instead pulling a different spell from her pouch.

The concussive spell knocked most of them over, leaving only a few for her to deal with while the others got their feet. It still seemed unfair odds, but she was past caring.

She drew her long knife, felt the balance of her weapons, and lost herself in the fight, in the clash of steel on steel, in the leering faces of the men around her, trying to kill her. There was only the fight. Only the feel of the weapons in her hands. The ground under her feet. Her balance, controlled and easy. The smooth movement of her sword and blade.

They were overconfident, despite having witnessed her earlier fight. They rushed her, again and again, and she beat them back, again and again. She struck out with her sword, defended with the knife, over and over, until the air was thick with blood and they were all wounded to one degree or another. No blows had landed on her. Not yet.

She was tiring, though. All the training in the world did not give unlimited energy. Mouth dry, pulse beating in her throat, emptiness where her stomach should be. She could not give in.

Her vision wavered and she clenched her jaw. Her mind was still sharp, still focused. Her body was tiring. Her arms were heavy, muscles beginning to strain to hold her form, to keep the sword up, to stop these men from killing her. She needed to survive. She needed to find out what had happened to Elinor, and to bring justice to her killers. And she needed to see her children grow. To find their own places in the world.

Defeat was not an option.

Just when she thought she might have to resort to more spells, a shrill whistle sounded. Not the retreat of the tribesmen, but the harsh sound of the law keepers' arrival.

The Ashnassan vanished, melting away as though they had never been there and leaving Yvonne standing, panting for breath, in the middle of the street, a dead body at her feet.

She looked down at the dead man and thought he would probably be pleased at her predicament. Fighting in the streets was frowned upon in Willowton. It was a law-abiding place, most of the time, and she had a feeling that the law keepers would be far less forgiving to an anonymous woman with a sword than they would be to a Hunar.

Her guess proved accurate, the law keepers insisting on questioning her and asking her to repeat her story over and over until her voice was hoarse and the sun was fading.

Trying to explain what had happened without telling them that she had been Hunar was difficult, but claiming to have been Hunar would have its own issues, as she had no way of proving that and, she knew, from long and bitter experience, that some accomplished liars and dishonest people claimed to be Hunar. Some even went so far as to paint a symbol on their shirt. She would not blame the law keepers for disbelieving her.

Eventually, they were satisfied. There were a few witnesses who backed her story. And the law keepers could not find any bow or arrows nearby to explain the man's death. The law keepers let her go, taking her battered food shopping back to Elinor's house.

Her body had seized up with all the standing around and trying to walk evenly was an exercise in torture, her muscles protesting. She needed a hot bath and to stretch and, even then, tomorrow was not going to be a pleasant day.

Despite the aches, she was still paying attention to her surroundings, wondering if the tribesmen would try again, which meant that she saw the shadow outside Elinor's door while she was still some distance away. She transferred her bag of shopping to her shoulder, and put her hand on her sword hilt, walking forward with as easy a stride as she could manage, until she had assessed the possible threat.

When she recognised the man standing outside Elinor's door, she stopped a few feet away, not sure she wanted to continue.

She had not been expecting to see Pieris for a few days, if at all, and yet here he was, standing outside Elinor's door, looking travel-worn and about as heartsick as she felt.

"Yvonne." Despite his grim expression, his voice was bright and his strides, when he came towards her, were loose and light. Before she quite knew what was happening, he had pulled her into a hug.

"It's so good to see you," he said. "But what on earth is going on? Sillman says that you're no longer Hunar. That's ridiculous. Tell me it's not true?"

"Not here," she said, moving towards the gate. "Come in."

He followed her through the gate. As it closed behind them, she saw Baldur's head poking out from the stable, his eyes showing white, nostrils flared.

It was all the warning she had before somebody slammed into her side, propelling her into the side of the house, one arm twisted up behind her back, her face pressed into the stone. Behind her, she could hear a scuffle and Pieris' outraged, inarticulate protest.

Her captor breathed into her ear. An almost sweet smell that she recognised immediately. Ashnassan.

"Haven't you had enough of a beating for today?" she demanded.

"Someone wants you dead. No body, no money," the man said in her ear.

"Not my problem," she told him. Her pulse was racing in her ears, unwanted memories too close to the surface, unable to move. Panic was a breath away.

He leant further forward, perhaps to whisper something else in her ear, and she slammed her head backwards, catching him by surprise. He made a furious sound, his grip on her arm loosening so that she was able to wriggle free. She turned, her back against the wall, and kicked out mostly on instinct, finding his knee, which buckled under her foot, sending him tumbling to the ground, clutching his face. There was blood streaming between his hands. She had probably broken his nose.

She found she did not care. And had no time to care, anyway, as there were more attackers.

Pieris was struggling with a pair of tribesmen, who looked like they were trying to hold him, rather than harm him.

Yvonne had no more time to look at him, as another pair of tribesmen were approaching her, their swords drawn. She met the first attack with the flat of her blade, the impact ringing up her arm, reminding her that her muscles were already tired. Her arm ached as she swept her sword down. One of her attackers had been careless enough to leave his side undefended, and her sword sliced through his clothing, biting into skin. He stumbled back with his own cry of pain.

Yvonne did not care. That was twice the tribesmen had tried to kill her today.

With her free hand she fumbled in her spell pouch, pulling the first one out that she could find and throwing it ahead of her with the activation word.

The concussive force of the spell threw the attackers back and dislodged one of the tribesmen holding Pieris so that he was able to break free. He used the hilt of his sword to knock one unconscious, then crossed the short distance to Yvonne, standing shoulder to shoulder with her, his own sword raised.

"They really want you dead, don't they?"

"They've been kidnapping nine-year-old girls," Yvonne said. "Grayling was going to try and get a message to the Hundred."

"First I've heard of it," Pieris said, his voice grim. "I thought we destroyed the slaving operation."

"No. The mine was only part of it. Can we catch up later? They're still trying to kill me," she pointed out.

Apart from the one Pieris had knocked unconscious, and the one with broken nose and shattered knee, the rest of the Ashnassan were back on their feet, weapons drawn.

"Eight men just to kill you. Seems extreme," Pieris said, voice tense.

"There was another one, too. They killed him."

Before anyone could move, or say anything else, there was a sharp knocking which sounded like it was coming from the door of the house.

"Whoever you are, go away. I'm rather busy just now," Yvonne shouted over her shoulder.

"Are you all right, mristrian?" A voice she would know anywhere. Guise.

"Have you got your sword with you?" she asked.

Pieris took a couple of steps back and opened the gate to let Guise come through.

"Now, these are better odds," Pieris commented, closing the gate behind him.

"You have been much occupied, I see," Guise commented, drawing his own sword.

"I've already fought this lot once today," Yvonne said, sounding grumpy even in her own ears. "Apparently, they want me dead. They won't tell me who is paying them, or why. It's getting annoying."

"Most annoying," Guise agreed, his voice darkening. "If you will permit me, mristrian, it has been a long journey and some exercise would be welcome."

"Go ahead," she told him, and took a few steps sideways, resting her shoulders against the wall of the house and watching as he approached the tribesmen.

"No one said anything about fighting a goblin," one of the tribesmen said.

"We're not getting paid enough," another agreed.

They took a step towards the gate, only to find that Pieris was there, barring their exit.

"I suppose we could turn them over to the law keepers," Pieris said, reluctantly.

"They killed one of their own earlier. The law keepers are looking for them anyway," Yvonne said.

"It would be much better to get some answers from them," Guise commented. He was standing a few paces in front of Yvonne and Pieris, between them and the tribesmen, sword ready. Yvonne could not see his face, but from the wary glances the tribesmen were giving him she suspected there was a hint of red in his eyes and his fangs were out.

"Well, then, if they survive, we can turn them over to the law keepers," Pieris suggested. "Seems fair."

"We don't want any trouble," one of the tribesmen said.

"Cowards and bullies," Yvonne muttered. Faced with an opposition they did not think they could easily defeat, they were showing their true natures. "Happy to kidnap defenceless girls. Not so brave faced with someone who can fight back."

"Agreed," Guise said.

"How about, we tell you what we know, and you let us go?" one of the tribesmen suggested.

"That's not how this works," another tribesman said.

The speaker had been quiet until now, keeping back, almost invisible until he spoke with an unmistakable air of command. Like some of the others, he was wearing an elaborate headdress that hid his features. She did not remember seeing him earlier.

With all attention moving to him, he straightened and tugged off the headdress, revealing the sharp features and dirty blond hair of the Slayer. The Ashnassan's leader.

"You ruined my outfit," Yvonne said. It was the first thing that came to mind, even if it was ridiculous. "Skunk oil. A tactic of cowards and bullies."

"A useful diversion," he contradicted. His men were looking nervous, as well they might. It was one of the core principles of the Ashnassan code that they did not run from a fight unless they were ordered to, and they had been actively considering running away from the angry goblin in front of them.

"This is the leader? The legendary Slayer?" Pieris asked. "Good. We might get answers from him."

"I'll never talk," the leader answered, sneering.

"Everyone talks. In the end." Guise's voice was flat, leaving no room for argument. Yvonne did not think she had ever heard him sound so bleak. Yvonne's mind gave her a picture of Guise's back, crossed with scars, even if she could not remember when she had seen that. She doubted that whatever had left those few, simple scars would have made him talk, but there were plenty of methods of torture that left few visible marks.

"Well, you could at least tell me why you keep trying to kill me," Yvonne said, hearing the irritation in her own voice and not caring. "I haven't done anything to you."

"Someone wants you dead," the leader told her, lip curling, "and they're prepared to pay for it."

"I know that," she told him, irritated. "I'm not completely stupid. Besides, your men have already told me as much. But you must have more information."

"Maybe I do. But I don't have to tell you."

"If you want to have any chance of living, you do," Guise said.

"Well, it seems we are misinformed," the Slayer said, eyes travelling between Guise and Yvonne. "We didn't think he cared enough to protect you. He didn't do much last time."

Pieris laughed. It was not a happy laugh, full of bitterness. "He formed a lifetime bond with a human," Pieris said, voice dripping with acid, "and risked being ostracised from his own people. Of course he's going to protect her."

Yvonne was not sure who was more astonished, the Ashnassan or her.

Pieris' words were a punch to her stomach, forcing into the open things that she had not wanted to consider, and not had time to consider. Guise turned and glared at Pieris. Whether from exposing his own secrets, or the secrets of his people, Yvonne was not sure.

"Well, we were definitely misinformed," the Slayer said. He looked a fraction paler underneath his tattoos and layers of dirt. He smiled in what he probably thought was a charming manner, though the resulting expression made Yvonne's stomach churn. A bully and a coward.

"I would very much like to know who you have been talking to," Guise said, voice silky soft. Yvonne knew that tone. There was usually bloodshed after it.

Proving that although he might be a coward and a bully he was not a complete idiot, the leader paled further and swallowed. "I can't tell you. I gave my word."

"Then you're no good to me, and you will die," Guise said. The Slayer looked at Yvonne, eyes wide.

"Don't look at me," she said. "You have been happily taking money to kidnap young girls for who knows what purpose, and then to try and kill me. I have no mercy to give you."

She was sick to her stomach with it all. All the greed, and the cowardice, and the lies. Her body was heavy with the effort of the day, muscles aching. There was a painful knot in her throat. Young girls, taken from their homes, and she had a horrible feeling that no one, not even the Hundred, was looking for them.

She had no appetite for slaughter, and stayed out of the fight, keeping her back to the wall of the house, watching as the tribesmen, spurred on by their leader, tried to rush Guise and overpower him. If they had paused to think, they would have realised that was pointless.

Even in the midst of a brutal, bloody fight, Guise moved with the grace of his kind and of a trained fighter, seemingly always aware of his surroundings, where his enemies were. And where his allies were. For, to her surprise, Pieris joined the fight rather than staying back with Yvonne. In the fading light, he was pale with determination, eyes dark hollows in his face, mouth bracketed with lines of disgust, and yet he showed as little mercy as Guise in dispatching the Ashnassan.

For their part, the tribesmen kept trying to kill Guise even as he cut through their numbers. Yvonne had to give them credit. None of them tried to run. They kept fighting to their last breath. Their gods liked strong warriors, she remembered, feeling sick again. So, faced with overwhelming odds, they fought until they could fight no more, and hoped for better in their next life.

With a sense of inevitability, as the fight drew to a close, Yvonne heard the shrill sound of the law keepers' whistles and knew that she would have to deal with yet more questions from the law keepers. They would doubtless be even less impressed with her second fight of the day, and the much higher death count.

Not all the tribesmen were dead. The Slayer was holding on to his side where Guise had stabbed him through, staying upright by willpower alone. And there was the unconscious one, and the one with the shattered knee, who had not tried to fight an enraged goblin. The others were dead.

"Was it worth it?" she asked the Slayer, voice hard. There were moments before the law keepers arrived. "You could have run away, like you did before."

He stared back at her with flat, predator's eyes. "We're not being paid to run."

There was no more time to ask the dozen or so questions that sprang to mind. The gate to the street flew open, the law keepers arriving. She slumped back against the wall, tired even before the questions began.

The air in the courtyard was thick with the flat taste of blood, the flagstones washed red with it. Even standing against the wall, she had not escaped. She wanted a bath. And about half a dozen cleansing spells. And something to settle her stomach.

But she could not have any of that. Not yet. There were questions to answer.

It was, though, a quite different experience dealing with the law keepers when she had a fully-fledged Hunar and a goblin lord whose story matched her own. The law keepers might be openly sceptical of the tale that the Ashnassan tribe had attacked her more than once on the same day, but they took the surviving tribesmen into custody, the tribesmen happy to go. One of the law keepers wanted to come in and search the house, stopped by a lifted brow from Guise and Pieris' vehement refusal.

It was dark by then, the end of what had felt like an extraordinarily long day. And it was not over yet. There had been no time for discussion or questions.

She picked up her bag of shopping, wondering if any of it was still usable, and gestured towards the back door. "Why don't you make yourselves comfortable. I need to see to my horse. Oh, and don't have any sugar."

Chapter Nineteen

Somewhat to her surprise, they did as she asked, Pieris taking the bag from her and going into the house with Guise.

It said something for Renard's training that Baldur settled quickly with a bit of fussing and a thorough brush down, so that she was able to leave him, calm and contented and eating his food, far more quickly than she had imagined possible. She promised him a good run the next day, then looked at the bloody mess that was the courtyard. Cleansing spells were needed. Both for the courtyard and for her. She dug a few out of her pouch.

The law keepers had, at least, taken the bodies away, so it was simply blood that she needed to deal with.

The cleansing spells took what felt like the last of her energy, leaving her weak and lightheaded. More was needed, but she had nothing left to give. Not now.

And then she could not put it off any longer. She had to go into the kitchen and face Pieris and Guise, and doubtless a lot of questions and things that she would rather not think about.

Her eyes drifted to the gate. Baldur was eating but, she was sure, would be persuaded to leave. The Ashnassan threat was gone. She could simply get on Baldur's back and ride away. Her feet stayed where they were. She had never run from anything in her life. And Elinor's killer had not yet been caught. There was still work to be done.

So, she made her way into the kitchen and stopped in the doorway, blinking in surprise at the scene she found there. Both Pieris and Guise were in their shirt-sleeves, preparing a meal from the battered contents of her bag and the food that she already had in the kitchen. The sugar bowl was sitting, untouched, on the kitchen table, along with the sack of sugar that had been in the pantry.

She closed the door behind her. Guise looked up from where he was chopping carrots, and nodded to one end of the table.

"I brought some wine."

There was, indeed, an open bottle of wine, and three glasses, sitting at the end of the table, along with a small dish of savoury biscuits that he must have brought along with the wine.

"Where did you hide that?" she asked without thinking. Pieris choked on a laugh, which he turned into an unconvincing cough, and Guise's eyes gleamed.

"I had a bag with me, which I had left at the front door." He tilted his chin, indicating the wall next to the back door, and she saw that there was, indeed, a bag there. More than large enough to hold several bottles of wine.

"Oh." Yvonne could not think of anything else to say. It was a perfectly reasonable and rational explanation.

Instead of thinking anymore, she went to the end of the table and poured three glasses of wine from the bottle. She took a few of the biscuits and her wine glass to her normal chair, settling to the strange sight of a Hunar and a goblin lord preparing a meal in Elinor's kitchen.

Her throat closed up without warning, her eyes prickling and burning. Elinor should be here. She should be here to see the extraordinary sight of Pieris preparing his own meal. She should be here to help make sense of why Yvonne was no longer Hunar. She should be here to try and help Yvonne make sense of this bond that she apparently had with Guise. And, most of all, she should be here because nobody should have killed her. Nobody should have wanted to end her life, in so cruel and so calculating a manner.

A large square of fine cloth appeared in front of her and she blinked, only then realising that she was crying. She took the handkerchief from Guise, unable to form any words, and mopped her face, drying her eyes as best she could. Except that the tears would not stop.

She had not cried this much since Elinor had died, once the shock of the news had worn off and the grief had taken hold and would not let her go.

The handkerchief was soaked through and she was still crying.

She wanted to move, to leave, to go and hide. She was not a person who cried easily, and she hated others seeing her tears.

But the other two did not react, just carried on preparing the meal as though it was perfectly normal for them to be doing so. Their movements were sure and steady, the normality of their tasks settling her.

By the time they were done with preparing the meal, and had tidied everything away again, and the kitchen was full of the scent of cooking, her eyes were dry and she had taken a few sips of the excellent wine that Guise had brought with him. It flowed across her tongue, filling her senses, full of warmth. Another excellent, and extraordinarily expensive, wine.

"Do you always travel with wine?" she asked

"Wherever possible," he told her, surprising her with the easy answer. "I don't like beer very much anyway, and in some places it's truly dreadful."

Yvonne found herself agreeing with him wholeheartedly. She did not like beer either, but she suspected he already knew that, whereas his dislike was new information for her.

"Well I, for one, am glad of your snobbery," Pieris said, raising his glass in a toast to Guise. He took a sip of the wine, raised his eyebrows in appreciation, and then set it on the table, his eyes travelling to the sugar bowl that was sitting, apparently innocuous, at the other end of the table along with the sack it had come in. "I had a quick look at it. Poison. And it's in the sack."

"Yes." Yvonne's throat closed up for a moment and she couldn't say anything more. Guise and Pieris took seats at the table, Pieris gesturing Guise to one of the chairs that visitors used and away from the one that had been Elinor's usual place. In their respective seats, they sipped wine and waited. There was a quality to their waiting that suggested they would sit there all night if they needed to, until she was ready. She took a long, steadying breath. She knew them both. They were not her enemy.

"Renard came to see me," she told Pieris. "He said Elinor had been killed. He wasn't sure how, or why he was so sure, but he was quite sure."

"And so you came here," Pieris said. His face stilled for a moment while he thought, and Yvonne remembered the description from the neighbours. Sad eyes. He had lived far longer than she had, and the years were showing in his face just now, in the lines around his mouth and the touch of grey in his hair. "None of us thought there was anything wrong with her death. We are not immortal."

Yvonne's mouth twisted in what might have been a smile, remembering saying the same thing to Renard.

She told them about the questions she had asked over the past few days, speaking to the neighbours, trying to work out who had been to visit Elinor and what might have happened. She told them about the illness, and the other deaths. She told them the little that she knew of Sillman and Suanna's visits, and heard Pieris' sharp, indrawn breath as he reached the same conclusion that she had. That one of the Hundred was responsible for Elinor's death, however unthinkable that might be.

When she was finished speaking there was a short silence, and then Pieris spoke, voice heavy.

"Sillman decided you could not be Hunar any longer. What reason did he give you?"

Yvonne shifted in her chair, her skin crawling, uncomfortable with the question and the silent, intent scrutiny from Guise, not that far away from her.

"I'm sorry," Pieris said, "I don't mean to be cruel. But I think it's my fault. I told Sillman about the bond." He shook his head at Guise's glare and Yvonne's astonishment. "I could see it. The connection. Goblin magic." Yvonne's breath drew in. Pieris had spent a winter with a goblin lord, studying goblin magic. Among other things. And Pieris loved learning. "I was jealous." His voice was harsh, and he was looking fixedly at the table, rather than meeting their eyes. "I had a winter. Just that. No more, and no less. And you were getting a lifetime's commitment."

Yvonne remembered Pieris' voice as he had spoken to the Ashnassan leader earlier, pointing out that Guise had entered a lifetime's commitment. She remembered, too, Pieris' face as he had told them about his winter in the mountains, about learning goblin magic from a goblin lord. The yearning. The love. He had memories to treasure, yes, but it had been, as Pieris had said, just one winter.

"Elinor always said you had an enormous heart," Yvonne said, voice hoarse. "I still don't remember." She touched her forehead briefly.

"I'm not surprised. It took all of us to put your skull back together again," Pieris said. "I'm not likely to forget that in a hurry."

Yvonne's eyes burned again. The Hundred had worked to save her, when she had nearly died after she and Guise had been caught in the castle. And, despite that, Sillman had still dismissed her from the Hundred. She half-opened her mouth, wanting to ask Pieris why he hadn't spoken to his goblin lord, Jaalam, then closed her mouth again. It was not her business. The Hundred, generally, did not make a habit of prying into each other's business. It was something she had always appreciated, until now. Freedom to live her own life, within the confines of the oaths.

"I did wonder how Sillman had found out," she said. "Particularly as I didn't know myself."

She saw Pieris flinch and a darker expression cross Guise's face, too fast for her to follow. A lifetime's commitment, and one it was not easy to get out of. There had been no time to research what that meant, or to consider what questions she might ask him and whether he would answer. Staring at the surface of her wine, she could not help wondering how long it would be before he regretted making that bond, even if he had been poisoned at the time.

"You sent a message to me," Pieris said slowly. "Did you contact anyone else?"

"No. I don't know who I can trust," she told him bluntly, "and I had an easy way of getting in touch with you. Besides, of all the Hundred, you know most about poison and magic, and this seems like both." And she wanted an ally, she acknowledged, in the quiet of her mind. Wanted to believe that whatever evil had taken Elinor had not spread through the whole of the Hundred.

"A logical choice," he agreed.

"Where are the others?" she asked him, hearing the tension in her voice.

"I don't know. I assume Suanna, Dundac, Mica and Sillman are back at their homes. Annabelle and Idal never seem to stay in the same place for long. And Firon ..." Pieris' voice trailed away. "He's been adrift for a while."

Sad eyes. That was her first thought at Firon's name. She could barely remember his presence at the mine, or afterwards. He had withdrawn into himself further than she had thought it was possible for any creature. All the Hundred had secrets. Most wore them far more lightly than Firon. Or Pieris.

Still, if Pieris was right, none of the rest of the Hundred were anywhere close to Willowton. She could deal with Pieris if he threatened her, she thought. If it was just him.

Her eyes travelled across to Guise and she amended her thought. Between them, she thought that she and Guise could deal with most of the Hundred, if they needed to.

───ele───

It was one of the stranger meals of Yvonne's life. Guise and Pieris had done an excellent job with the ingredients, and the meal itself was delicious. The conversation, though, was difficult. She told them about her enquiries with the neighbours in more detail, about what they had said, what they had seen, relating to the illness, and listened to Guise and Pieris speculate on what the poison could be. They narrowed down the options fairly quickly, as she had. The poison had to be tasteless, slow-acting and hard to detect. As she had speculated, in her own mind, they also speculated that it would have to be one of those poisons that, once you realised you were being poisoned, it was too late to do anything about it.

She considered telling them about Elinor's letter to her, about the fact that Elinor had known she had been poisoned and was dying. In the end, she did not tell them, the conversation continuing without much input from her. She was not sure how much good it would do either of them to know that Elinor had realised she had been killed. Elinor had not left any clue as to who she suspected.

She also found space in all the speculating to let Guise know that Lita was searching for the authenticator.

"I liked her," she told him plainly. His mouth lifted, eyes bright.

"I thought you might. She is exceptionally good at what she does."

"I imagine so."

At some point, late into the night, she left the two of them comparing notes on different poisons, a small sample of sugar in a glass between them, and made up beds in two of the rooms.

She came back into the kitchen to find that Pieris had not really noticed she had gone, though Guise looked up at once. She saw something in his face that made her stop, and want to leave again. He usually wore a mask of sorts. Calm, often expressionless, rarely showing any feeling beyond polite attention or, when the occasion called for it, anger or disdain. In other words, exactly what a human would expect from a high-ranking member of the Karoan'shae. And yet, this high-ranking member of the Karoan'shae had formed a bond with a human. Not just any bond, but a lifetime commitment that, he had said, was the highest honour among his people. A bond which Pieris was deeply jealous of, as he had not been offered anything of the sort from his goblin paramour.

And, stepping into the kitchen, she had seen behind the mask for a moment. She did not want to name what she might have seen, but it had been full of the sort of quiet intensity she had seen in Renard's face from time to time as he looked at Elinor. A warmth that drew her even as she wanted to run away.

As she ducked her head away from what she had seen in Guise's face, she realised that he only showed this side to people he trusted. He seemed perfectly relaxed, sitting in Elinor's kitchen, exchanging ideas with Pieris. But, she could detect a slight wariness in his manner. If she had not known him so well, she would have missed it. He wasn't quite sure about Pieris, someone he barely knew. It made sense. Among the Karoan'shae, trusting the wrong person would get you killed. Few humans bore that risk.

Pieris looked up from his examination of the sugar, unaware of anything apart from the puzzle in front of him. And she knew, then, that he had nothing to do with Elinor's death, and this poison. He would help her find out who had killed her friend, and his.

"I have made up beds for you both," she said, coming into the room. "The rooms at the top of the stairs, to either side. If you want to stay," she added, suddenly wondering if they had other plans.

"That is good of you, mristrian," Guise said. "If there is room enough in the stables, I will bring my horse around as well."

"Plenty of room," she confirmed. "Pieris?"

He had become absorbed in the sugar again and, from the intent expression on his face, and the slight resonance around him, Yvonne knew that he was using magic. She moved across the kitchen to get a glass of water, her body heavy and stiff from the earlier fights. She wanted a bath, but it would have to wait until the next day. She needed sleep more.

"Will you be all right if I go and get my horse?" Guise asked.

Her brows lifted in surprise. She was not used to that level of consideration. But then, of course, nothing was really normal.

"Of course."

His eyes drifted across the room to where Pieris was completely absorbed in his task, examining the spelled sugar. Clearly, Guise did not think Pieris would be much help in his absence. Yvonne bit her lip against an unexpected smile, the flicker of humour welcome and unexpected. "I'll wait for you to get back before I go to sleep," she told him.

Sometime after Guise had left, Pieris lifted his head from the study of the sugar bowl. "I think I know what it is, Guise." He blinked, looking around in surprise. "Where did he go?"

"He went to get his horse. He should be back soon."

Guise returned just as Pieris was clearing away the sugar, putting the contents of the bowl into the sack and sealing it with a spark of magic, returning the bag to the pantry, out of view.

Before Pieris could involve them in another lengthy discussion of the poison, and the implications of it, Yvonne suggested that they reconvene in the morning. It was far into the night, and her eyes were burning from tiredness as well as the aftermath of crying. She thought again about a bath, but an extra cleansing spell would have to do for now.

Pieris accepted the suggestion and went upstairs, an abstracted expression on his face. He would be turning the puzzle over in his mind all night, Yvonne knew, even in his sleep.

Yvonne followed Guise up the stairs, hiding a yawn behind her hand.

Guise hesitated before going into his own room, his expression serious as he turned to her, waiting a moment before he spoke.

"Nothing needs to change, mristrian," he told her, voice low so that it would not carry to Pieris, even if he was listening behind his door. "No matter what others might say. You do not need to be wary of me."

It seemed to come out of nowhere, but she knew he was thinking about her arriving in the kitchen earlier, and turning away from him, not wanting to meet whatever it was in his face.

She looked up now and was caught by his eyes, the green mixed with a gold that she had seen a few times before. There was the warmth she had seen earlier, and once or twice before, the mask removed for a moment. And, despite the warmth in his face and his voice, she knew that he meant every word. He did not lie to her. It was one of the basic truths of her life.

An impulse to reach out, take his hand, surprised her, and the surprise held her still. It must be the gold. And the warmth in his face. And that voice. And the quiet honesty. And the way he spoke to her, as he always did, as if she was his equal.

"I am not frightened of you," she told him baldly. It was the truth. She wasn't sure what she felt, but she knew, had always known, that he would never hurt her. "But, thank you. I can't ..." To her dismay, her throat closed up again.

"We have a killer to find," he finished for her, gold fading to green in his eyes. She missed the gold. "Good night, mristrian."

"Good night, Guise."

Despite the ache in her chest, and her tired eyes, she went to bed with a lighter step, no longer quite alone. A poison to identify. A killer to find. Work to do.

Chapter Twenty

A night's sleep and a long bath had done a lot to restore her calm, although her body was stiff and sore from the fights the day before. She went through a minimal set of drills, slightly less sore by the end. Time, and keeping moving, would be the best thing for the muscle fatigue, she knew.

Pieris and Guise wanted to make enquiries about the poison, both hesitating as they looked at her. She had laughed. They did not want her with them, either of them. Guise, because most of his contacts would shy away from strangers. And Pieris, because the symbol of the Hunar was enough encouragement for most people.

They would meet later. She had a horse to exercise, anyway.

So, they set off about their errands, and she decided she did not want to stay in the house too full of silence and memories. The house had been empty and unoccupied for too long. Renard had not mentioned what should happen to Elinor's house, and none of the neighbours had known, either. There was nothing in the house to indicate Elinor's wishes. The matter could not be left to lie, though, and so, while Pieris and Guise set out to make their enquiries, Yvonne headed to the law offices in town. Elinor had been a meticulous and organised woman, as well as a kind one. It was likely she would have left some kind of instructions with the town's law clerks.

Walking into the building was like stepping into memory. Most of this town held potent memories for her, and this was one of the most profound.

She had only been in this building once before, when she had been partway through her training as Hunar and she was, finally, legally old enough to assume the legal guardianship of Mariah and Joel. A legal arrangement to reflect the reality that they were all living, under Elinor's roof. She remembered the moment she fixed her signature to the document, the red and white ribbons, symbolising justice in this town, fluttering as she handed the parchment to Elinor for her signature as witness. It had been some months in the planning, Elinor dealing with the lawyer, but the moment had finally been there, and she was kin, in the eyes of the law, to Mariah and Joel.

The lawyer had given her copies of the parchment to take with her. One for each of the children, and one for her to keep. Despite their young age, Mariah and Joel had both treated the documents with profound care, keeping them safe. Yvonne's copy was one of the few things she kept with her at all times, rolled into a leather case, tucked into her saddlebags when she was travelling. She had never needed it for anyone else, but in the first years after the guardianship was put into effect, she had put her hand on the case from time to time as though checking it was real. The family she had chosen, the one she made for herself.

Her throat closed up as she looked around her now.

The building had not changed. The great doors, rising at least two stories above her head, made of slender wooden frames and glass panels, stood open. The unsubtle message was that law was available to anyone. Like many things, that did not match the reality.

The doors opened onto the town's Great Hall of Justice, a vast space with wooden floors that echoed with the footsteps and voices of the people in the hall. The ceiling rose high above, wooden beams interspersed with painted scenes from legends, and history, of law keepers delivering justice, and judges delivering their verdicts.

There were low wooden benches set around the walls at various intervals, allowing ordinary folk to wait for consultation, or for justice. The hall also doubled as the town's court on regular occasions, and at the far end from the doorway there was a raised platform with a great wooden desk draped with the red and white cloth that was the symbol of justice most widely recognised across the lands. On the wall behind the desk, which would comfortably seat five, was a vast painting of one of the symbols of justice. A man dressed in floor-length robes with a broken sword in one hand and a pen in the other.

There were doorways set into the walls to either side of the hall, which led to offices through the building. Outside the hall, the building was a bustle of activity, she knew, belying the apparent calm of this space.

A short distance away from the judge's desk was a plain wooden desk with a clerk sitting behind it. She headed towards that desk.

She had another shock of recognition as the clerk looked up. She remembered him from her first visit. She did not think she had ever seen a human so old before, and yet he was still here, his skin paper thin, eyesight requiring the help of a pair of eyeglasses balanced on his nose. He might be dressed in plain, ordinary clothes, but eyeglasses were extremely expensive, usually available only to the very rich. But then, she supposed, if he had been here for as long as she suspected, his knowledge may be of immense value to the town. He may not have had to pay for the glasses himself.

"Good day to you," she began.

"Mistress Yvonne. How nice to see you again. I was so sorry to learn of Hunar Elinor's passing. Such a great loss."

"Thank you. She is greatly missed."

"You'll be wanting to see to her affairs," the clerk said, rising to his feet with surprising grace for one of his age. "She left instructions. If you'll follow me."

As the senior clerk moved away from the desk, one of the juniors who had been hovering around the doorways came forward and took his place at the desk.

Yvonne followed the senior clerk through the nearest doorway and up a flight of stairs she also remembered. Her first visit to this building had been to one of the largest offices available, on the top floor, with bright sunshine pouring in, the air full of the smell of ink and dry with the dust of parchment.

The senior clerk took her to the same room she had visited before, which also looked exactly as she remembered, even including the finely dressed gentleman sitting behind the desk, surrounded by books and parchment. He had some more lines on his face since her first visit, but his eyes were still as sharp as she remembered.

He rose to his feet at once and came around the desk, extending his hand. An old custom still practised here.

She shook his hand and exchanged greetings as the senior clerk made his excuses and went back downstairs.

One of the lawyer's juniors appeared from a side door and held a chair for her to sit in, offering her tea, or something stronger, disappearing again when the lawyer instructed him to bring tea for both of them.

"I was deeply sorry when I heard about Elinor," the lawyer said. "I regret, I was in Hogsmarthen at the time of her funeral."

Yvonne's throat closed up in memory of the funeral. She had not realised it was possible to cry so much, or to carry so much pain inside her chest.

"Thank you. She is greatly missed," she said again. "I wanted to know if she had left any instructions about what to do with her possessions? The house has just been left as it was, but I am sure that is not what she would have wanted."

Not for the house to remain empty and unoccupied. Yvonne could not remember a day, during her time with Elinor, that there had not been one of the neighbours coming in for a chat, or for advice, or overnight visitors. Not just Elinor's very different lovers, but the rest of the Hundred had stopped by from time to time, and Elinor's friends outside the Hundred, people who she had kept in touch with. It was from Elinor that Yvonne had got into the habit of her letter writing, no matter how much her children teased her. A Hunar's life was hard, Elinor had told her often, and it was important to treasure friendships.

"She had indeed left instructions." The lawyer rose to his feet again, and went to one wall of the room, which contained floor-to-ceiling shelves, holding a series of strong boxes that were not only bounded with locks and iron, but also with magic. He brought one back to the table, slightly larger than many of the others, and set it on the side of his desk, opening it. It was full of papers. "You may not realise it, but Elinor was quite a wealthy woman."

He handed her some of the papers in the box, and she looked at them, uncomprehending for a moment. The idea that Elinor, with her simple life, had been wealthy had never crossed her mind. She might have had a house much larger than she needed, with a good bit of ground behind it, but that was the only outward sign that Yvonne could ever remember that Elinor might have had independent wealth.

"She was shrewd as well as kind," the lawyer said. "She made investments."

Yvonne looked at the papers in her hand and tried to read them, her mind tangled almost at once with the formal legal language. There were references to some of the largest merchant companies. The ones who had regular trade routes between the Royal City to the north, and Abar al Endell to the south. The ones whose merchants were always finely dressed, and generally wearing jewellery a single piece of which Yvonne knew would feed her family for a year. Or more.

"I don't understand," she said. She had thought she knew Elinor. Knew all her secrets. Elinor had been the most transparent of all of the Hundred. The idea that she had been secretly wealthy was shaking Yvonne's memories of her, and her certainty.

"Elinor had been a member of the Hundred a very long time," the lawyer said, voice gentle. He broke off as his junior returned with a tea tray, and then dismissed the junior, telling him to shut the door and rising himself to pour the tea. Only when that was done did he continue. "She was one of the most selfless people I knew. But, most people will give some kind of payment for a Hunar's service."

Yvonne nodded, even though he was telling her things she already knew. Then she blinked, realising what he was, in fact, telling her. The long life of the Hunar, combined with consistent service and consistent gifts in return for that service.

"You're saying that she took the gifts she was given, for her service as Hunar, and invested them?" It made sense. It fitted with what she knew of Elinor. Elinor was not interested in fancy clothes, or any of the other trappings of wealth. She liked her life. She liked being part of the community she served. She liked her neighbours, and the fact that they would pop in and see her. And she had loved her service as Hunar. "She did not need the money, so she put it aside," Yvonne finished.

"Indeed," the lawyer said.

"And she said she left instructions? Some indication of what should be done with it all?" Yvonne asked, setting the papers down in front of her.

"Naturally. She has left nearly all of it to you," the lawyer said.

Yvonne grabbed the arms of her chair as the room spun around her. "What?" she heard herself say, her voice faint.

"She considered you almost as a daughter. There are gifts for Adira and Renard, but everything else is yours to do with as you see fit."

Yvonne stared at the papers in front of her, at the names she recognised, and at the sheer quantity of them. Not just one investment, but several. And among the papers the lawyer had not yet shown her, she could see a pair of ledgers that bore the symbol of two of the oldest, most well-known banks that operated across the lands. Countries might go to war with each other, but only a very foolish ruler would threaten the banks.

She touched her forehead, the room around her still spinning slightly, and then took hold of her teacup as if it was an anchor.

"Will you talk me through everything?" she asked.

"That will take a long time. Let me tell you, in general terms, what is involved, and you may come back as many times as you need."

Yvonne tilted her chin, accepting the suggestion, and settled back in her chair to listen as the lawyer started to tell her about Elinor's secret wealth.

She left the law offices sometime later, still feeling lightheaded. Elinor had, indeed, been shrewd. The investments she had made were worth sums of money that some of the smaller kingdoms would envy.

It had still not quite sunk in that it now all belonged to her. That she would never, ever have to worry about money again for as long as she might live, and, indeed, for as long as Mariah and Joel might live, too. There would be no need for renting properties in future. She could buy something outright, and still have more than enough money to live. There would be no need to keep repairing old things, if they did not wish to. There was no need for mismatched furniture. For clothes worn so often that the fabric was tissue-thin.

Her chest hurt again. Elinor had set down the instructions some years before, the lawyer said. She could not have known that Yvonne would be sundered. Elinor could not have foreseen that the status of Hunar would be taken away from her former apprentice, and that Yvonne would be left floundering, wondering what to do with her life.

Elinor would not have cared, Yvonne knew. She would still have opened her house to Yvonne, and to her children, regardless of whether she wore the Hunar's symbol at her shoulder or not.

And she would be delighted now, Yvonne knew. Delighted that the investment she had made, the money she had set aside during her life, that she did not need, would now enable Yvonne to think for herself and for the first time in her life, about what she wanted to do, where she wanted to be. And it would enable independence for her children.

The pain eased, replaced with lightness. Mariah and Joel could decide what they wanted to do. They would not need to be beholden to anyone.

As she descended the shallow steps from the building, movement at the other side of the street caught her eye. Or rather, stillness among the movement. There was someone standing there, apparently watching her. A male figure, dressed from head to toe in dark clothing that reminded her of an assassin's garb, apart from his headgear. His face was shadowed by a wide-brimmed hat so that she could not tell the colour of his skin, or his likely origin.

She paused at the bottom of the steps, staring back at him. She was confident that she had not seen him before, and that he had not been there when she arrived at the law offices earlier. And yet. She felt a resonance in her chest. A sort of recognition. As if she should know him.

A horse and carriage drove past, cutting off her view for a moment, and by the time the carriage had passed, he had disappeared.

She crossed the street, looking both ways, but was unable to see him, or to pick up any trace of him with her other senses.

Her skin prickled, some instinct warning her that this had not been an accident.

She was about to make her way back to Elinor's house, or her house as she supposed she should call it now, even if that did not feel right, when she saw an elderly woman slump against the side of the nearby building, a harsh gasp in her throat, and her eyes rolling up in their sockets.

No one else was paying the woman any attention, walking around her on their business. Yvonne went to her side.

"Mistress," she said, "are you well?"

The woman turned a lined and beautiful face towards her, eyes blank and unseeing, lips moving but nothing emerging for a long moment. Her hand reached out, fingers hooked into claws, and caught Yvonne's forearm.

"Mother." Another woman's voice, worry carrying clearly. "What happened?"

"It's the sight," Yvonne said, keeping her voice low and calm. "Don't worry. Don't try to touch her just now, she won't know it's you."

"I know," the daughter said, bitterness startling Yvonne into looking up. The daughter was staring at her mother with a frown. "She's been getting these turns almost every day now."

"What does she say?"

"Nonsense. Words that make no sense." The daughter's lips closed together, face pinched. "He is coming. He is risen. It makes no sense."

Yvonne ducked her head back to the older woman, wanting to hide her expression from the daughter. The woman was still staring at nothing, mouth still working.

"He is risen," the mother said, voice the same harsh, rasping sound that Yvonne was used to hearing from people in the grip of the sight. "You must remember."

"Remember what?" Yvonne asked. She could not help it. She knew that the sight would not give her an answer, but she still tried, every time, to get more information.

"Remember." The voice rang with the same harshness as everyone in the grip of the sight but it also carried a thread of power that felt familiar, although she could not place it just now.

The older woman collapsed, as if every bone in her body had melted, only Yvonne and her daughter holding her up, preventing a hard fall onto the ground. Between them, they lowered her gently until she was sitting with her back against the building. She was breathing normally, skin pale, but Yvonne judged she had simply fainted and would recover in time.

"Do you live nearby?" Yvonne asked.

"No. My husband will be along in a moment, though. We've got a cart around the corner."

"If you want, I will stay with her while you get your cart."

The daughter sent Yvonne a sharp, hard look before she nodded once and left.

Before the daughter had returned, the older woman stirred, putting a hand to her head and wincing in pain.

She looked around herself in surprise, quickly followed by resignation.

"It happened again, didn't it?" she asked, then looked up at Yvonne, eyes narrowing. "You're Elinor's girl, aren't you? Haven't seen you in town for a while. Sad business."

"Yes, it was."

The daughter returned at that point, with a burly man who seemed to be her husband, and the pair of them managed to get the older woman into the cart, ready to go home.

"Be careful, mistress," the mother said, reaching out to touch Yvonne's cheek, her fingers warm. "You are all light in my eyes, but I see darkness ahead for you."

Before Yvonne had time to ask what she meant, the daughter was driving off. Determined to put as much space between her mother's latest turn and her person as soon as possible, Yvonne judged.

She was frowning as she started walking, one hand on her sword hilt. Remember. She blew out a breath, frustrated. Too many unanswered questions. Too much change, the shock of Elinor's wealth still not quite real.

She needed a bit of time and space to think.

Chapter Twenty-One

Baldur had a fabulous gallop. It was smooth, long-striding, and felt like he could run for hours, if he needed to, and a sharp contrast to the propriety of the law offices. There was no dainty china here. Just a powerful horse willing to move, fearless in his headlong run, his speed measured by the sting of air against her face. The hills outside the town, which had seemed such a vast distance away when they set off, were growing ever closer. Yvonne was breathless, and light with joy, when the ground began to rise towards the hills and she drew him gently back to a walk.

She looked around, discovering that they had, somehow, outpaced Guise and his goblin bred horse. She patted the sweaty neck in front of her, and murmured some words of praise into the black-tipped ears that flicked back in her direction.

Her joy was shadowed, for a moment, as she remembered Lothar, his absence an ache that would take a long time to fade. They had travelled together for years, with little opportunity for fun, the older horse happy to pick up his heels when given a chance. Lothar's gallop was steadier, equally comfortable to ride, and had always given her the same profound sense of freedom she had felt on Baldur's back. As though she were flying across the land.

Baldur snorted as they made their way back towards the town. She and Guise were the only people in sight, the land between them and the edges of town given over to free grazing for herds of cattle. There would be a herdsman or two somewhere around, making sure no predators got close to the livestock, but the humans were tucked away just now.

The cattle had barely flicked an ear as Baldur, followed by Guise's horse, had galloped between them, Yvonne letting Baldur choose his own route. There were no calves about to trip under his feet, and he had made his way through the herd at a speed that whipped the wind across her face.

"He must have some goblin blood in him," Guise commented, turning his own horse to ride back towards the town with her. "That would explain the speed."

Yvonne laughed. It was so in keeping with a goblin's arrogance, that the fastest things, and the most powerful things, could only come from their lands. She suspected he was right, though, and that Renard had mixed some goblin horses with his breeding line. Renard wanted the best horses, and would go to the far corners of all the lands to find them.

The cattle were just as disinterested as they rode back towards town, most of them continuing to graze, or chew, tails flicking now and then.

"I want to visit the law keepers when we return," Guise said. "See what the Ashnassan might say."

Yvonne's good mood faded, brought back to reality. Speaking with the surviving tribesmen was sensible.

"They might be more inclined to speak without their leader," she suggested. Perhaps. The leader's wound had looked serious. He might be in a separate room, out of earshot. Or, he might be dead. Having the Slayer wounded and vulnerable would be a perfect opportunity for an ambitious warrior to take over. "There will be other deputies," she added. The tribe was large, and the warriors they had faced the day before only a handful of their elite. The deputies would also be the most obvious candidates for trying to take over the tribe's leadership.

"We are looking for others around the town," Guise said.

For a moment, Yvonne was tempted to ask him who was doing the looking, and what methods they were using. She had avoided asking in the past, shying away from knowing too much, from having her suspicions confirmed. Meeting Brea, Thort and Modig had made her more curious. Brea and Thort, at least, did not seem like criminals. Modig she was less certain about, as it was almost impossible to live any length of time in Three Falls as an honest person. There were too many criminals there.

She kept her questions to herself again. Not because she thought he would refuse to answer. Rather, she was still afraid of what she might learn if he did answer. It seemed impossible that he should continue to be so well informed without involvement in some criminal dealings.

She was not sure she wanted to get drawn further into his life, or his complex network of connections and relationships. They might be connected by a bond. He had said the night before that nothing needed to change. There was an uneasy feeling in her stomach when she thought about that, almost as though she knew, deep down, that change was needed, even though she could not work out what that change would be like. There had been plenty of change, the absence of the symbol at her shoulder a constant ache, even though the wound had healed.

"I hope that Pieris has some luck tracking down the source of the poison," she said. She was trying to be practical about that. There was nothing she could do, and she did not like feeling helpless. It had definitely been more sensible to leave Pieris to his task of questioning the apothecaries around the town, with the symbol of the Hunar at his shoulder. Questions that she normally would be asking herself, without need for assistance. It rankled that someone else was undertaking her tasks. That it was necessary. Even when the person was Pieris.

"Well, if he does not succeed, then we can go," Guise suggested, an undertone in his voice that suggested he would quite like questioning some people.

Yvonne opened her mouth to reply and stopped, her attention caught by something up ahead.

They had crossed the common grazing and were now on the road that led into the town, the first buildings not that far away.

There was a man standing in the road ahead of them. Of itself, that was not unusual, but she was sure she recognised him.

"Do you see him?" she asked.

"The man ahead of us, who looks remarkably like the Coll lord?" Guise asked, voice grim. "Yes, I see him. Why would you think otherwise?"

"I thought I saw him in the marketplace yesterday, but he disappeared. I thought I was imagining it."

"Not unless we are having the same imagining, which is most unlikely," Guise answered, his voice still grim. Without looking at him, Yvonne knew that he would have one hand on his weapon. Baldur had picked up on her unease, his body tense underneath her. She made a soothing noise and stroked his neck, then rested her own hand near her sword hilt, transferring her reins to her other hand and keeping them loose and relaxed so that Baldur would not react prematurely.

"I wonder if the Hundred have a different definition of dead from the rest of us," Guise said. Yvonne had a strong feeling that, no matter what happened, he would be asking some very pointed questions of the rest of the Hundred, including Pieris, when he saw them next.

They were close enough to the man that they could see that it was, indeed, the Coll lord. Her stomach clenched, remembering their first meeting, the lord's unpredictable temper and the unhealthy power he carried. She drew Baldur to a halt, Guise stopping alongside her.

The Coll lord looked ill, his skin paler than she remembered, the black veins more prominent. For all that, the disdainful sneer was exactly the same.

"You're missing your robes," she said. The splendid red robes, fit for a king, that he had worn in their first meeting.

"Something which I will soon remedy," he said, his voice grating in her ears. It sounded like his throat was constricted.

"Did you not like being dead?" she asked him, and heard Guise's sharp intake of breath, and the ghost of a laugh under his breath. Antagonising the supposedly dead lord was probably not a good idea, but they were not being held by vettr now, and it did not look like there was anyone else around.

"I never was dead," he contradicted her. "Foolish little things made a mistake."

"More likely, your master is not done with you yet," Guise said.

The lord gave a silent snarl, lips peeling back to reveal blackened teeth, and said something too quietly for Yvonne to fully understand, but which sounded familiar. Her pulse skipped. The words spoken were in a dead language that very few living people knew had ever existed, let alone spoke. It was the language of the Hundred. The language that they had adopted from the first Hundred, and the first Hunar, which they used for spellcasting and the oaths that they took. She could not think of a good reason why this lord, with black blood in his veins, should know the language.

She wanted to tell Guise, to warn him, but had no means of doing so without alerting the lord, and she did not want to do that. Guise had questions of his own, though.

"Why are you here?" Guise asked. Yvonne's attention snagged on that excellent question. The lord had, supposedly, been killed and burned some distance from here, and there was nothing particular about this town that should have drawn his attention. It was one of the reasons why Elinor had chosen it when she had first settled here. Willowton was generally peaceful, with law-abiding citizens, and ruled over, from a distance, by one of the more benevolent rulers, who was not in the least interested in expanding his kingdom or starting a war. In fact, the only remarkable thing about this place was that Elinor had lived here.

It had been Elinor's home for a long time, Yvonne thought. Long enough that she had become something of a local legend. And, if someone wanted to be sure of finding one of the Hundred, and knew who to ask, this was the most obvious place to try.

"If it's Elinor you're looking for, you are more than a year too late. She died." Yvonne was proud that her voice did not shake.

The lord's lip curled in another sneer.

"I'm not here for her. We have unfinished business." His black eyes moved past Yvonne to Guise and an odd, hungry expression crossed his face.

A piece of her memory unfurled. She remembered being in the cell with Guise, terrified and hurt, and a vettr telling them that they were looking forward to playing with Guise when she was dead. She had not been the lord's focus. Not then, and not now. He was far more interested in the Karoan'shae lord.

"Well, you're not dead," Yvonne said, calling his attention back, "which I would definitely count as unfinished business. I don't suppose you would stand still and let me stab you?"

"You mock me?" The sneer had vanished, replaced by fury. It was not the reaction she had expected. It was, however, extremely interesting.

"Someone does not have control of his temper," she said to Guise, turning her shoulder on the corrupted lord.

"So it would seem," Guise agreed. "Which makes you wonder, doesn't it, just how desperate his master must have been to use such a flawed vessel?"

Yvonne had no time to reply to Guise, or to ask him why he was so certain that the lord had a master who was directing his actions, as the lord demonstrated his short temper by surging forward, towards them, sword in hand.

He was moving far more quickly than Yvonne would have thought possible. Luckily, Baldur had excellent reflexes and moved sideways, out of reach of the wildly swinging sword, his ears back, expressing his displeasure.

The failure of his first, wild attack provoked a scream of rage from the lord, and he whirled, sword raised again.

Guise put his horse between Yvonne and the oncoming attack and kicked out, finely crafted leather boot catching the lord on his shoulder as Guise's horse danced out of the way, never in any danger from the wild attack.

The lord screamed again, and said another phrase in the language that he should not know. This was more dangerous, though, as it sounded like an attempt to cast a spell.

"Behind me," Yvonne told Guise. She didn't wait to see if he moved, pulling a spell from her pouch and activating it with a word so that when the lord's fire spell was released, it was met with her counter-spell and died in a shower of sparks a safe distance from her.

"He uses magic the way you do," Guise pointed out.

"Yes. And speaks the same language," she answered, pulling another spell from her pouch. She only had one more counter-spell.

"Someone has been giving him lessons," Guise suggested.

"So it would seem," Yvonne agreed. And there was a very small number of people who could have been giving him lessons. "I didn't think that anyone outside the Hundred knew that language," she told him.

They had to break off their conversation as the lord sent another fire spell in their direction, equally furious when Yvonne's counter-spell destroyed it.

Before Yvonne could suggest anything else, or do anything else, Guise had pressed his horse forward and was charging the corrupted lord, sword raised. Yvonne could not see his face, but knew that his fangs would be out and his eyes would be tinged with red. It was a sight that any sane person would run from.

The corrupted lord was not sane. He held his ground, another sneer on his face, as Guise charged towards him, moving out of the way at the last minute, moving with that same speed that Yvonne had noticed earlier. Whatever was running in his veins, blackening them, was making him faster than a normal human. And more powerful in magic, as well. Yvonne's counter-spells had worked, but the fire spells that he had thrown towards them had been among the strongest that she had ever seen.

She pulled another spell from her pouch and rode forwards, following Guise's lead. He was circling behind the lord, who was turning to follow Guise's movements. Definitely more interested in Guise than in her. Yvonne could not really blame him. Guise was, she thought, far more interesting to look at.

She threw the fire spell at the ground in front of the lord, forcing him to step back, showered in dirt. He turned his attention back to her, teeth bared and another, silent, snarl.

"You're not supposed to be able to do that," he told her. "You're supposed to be useless."

"Sorry to disappoint you." Her stomach twisted. Very few people knew about her change in status. The Hundred had betrayed her, as well as Elinor.

"You were very well informed," Guise commented. "For a dead man."

"I'm not dead. Idiot."

"Not yet. But you are dying, aren't you? The human body is not meant to look like that, or move like that. How long do you have left? A few days? Hours?" Yvonne asked, another fire spell ready in her hand.

"Not dying. They promised. Going to live. Longer than you will."

"Who promised?" Guise asked the question before Yvonne could.

The lord hesitated, for the first time, and stared up at Guise, not seeming to care that Yvonne had another spell ready, or that Guise had his sword in his hand. The silence stretched as he tilted his head to a strange angle, almost as if he was listening to something that they could not hear. The pause lasted for several heartbeats, time enough for Guise and Yvonne to exchange glances, neither of them knowing what to make of it. And then, just as Yvonne was about to press her horse forward, the lord came back to life, blackened teeth revealed again in a parody of a smile.

"Can't catch me," he said, and took off at a run, far faster than any two-legged creature should be able to manage, heading away from the town, out across the common grazing land. The cattle, which had carried on grazing peacefully, with barely a glance, as Guise and Yvonne's horses galloped through them, reacted in terror, a ripple of panic moving through the gathered herd. The cattle started moving away from the running lord as quickly as they possibly could, heading in the opposite direction, which happened to be towards the town. Among the grasses, cries of alarm went up. The herdsmen, who had perhaps been dozing through the afternoon, panicking as they saw their livestock run away from the grasses towards the town.

"I don't think it's a good idea for you to go after him on your own," Yvonne said. "He shouldn't be hard to track, looking like that. I want to speak to Pieris first."

Guise made a low, growling sound in his throat, but stayed where he was, not going after the lord, who had disappeared from view, only the cattle's disturbance leaving a visible trail.

Satisfied that the herdsmen would, eventually, get their cattle under control, Yvonne turned Baldur back towards the town. The supposedly dead, corrupted lord of Coll Castle had come looking for her, or more likely for Guise, in Elinor's hometown. A place that very few people knew where she was, let alone Guise. And that same lord, who was supposed to have been dead, was suddenly using magic in the same way as the Hundred. She hoped that Pieris was done with questioning the suppliers of poison, because she had questions of her own.

Chapter Twenty-Two

They arrived back at Elinor's house to discover that, not only had Pieris returned from his errands, but there were more visitors waiting. Yvonne recognised the horses as soon as they came through the gate.

She left Baldur for a moment, going into the kitchen to find Mariah and Joel unpacking what looked like a month's worth of food, and Pieris and Renard in close conversation, settled at the kitchen table, the sugar bowl, now empty, sitting between them.

"Is everything all right? Are you all right?" Yvonne asked, going from one of her children to the other.

"We're both fine," Joel told her. "And Lothar is healing well. He wanted to come with us, of course, but we left him at the Tavern. The stable hands were arguing over who would look after him first when we last saw him."

Yvonne couldn't hold in a smile. Her old warhorse would love the attention, and being in a bustling stable yard would keep his mind occupied. He might not want to leave when she went back for him.

"We were worried about you," Mariah said.

Yvonne exchanged brief, hard hugs with her children, assessing the truth of that statement. They had been worried. Not just about her. They were giving Renard uneasy glances as they moved about the kitchen, unpacking the foodstuffs.

"Did you buy the entire market?" she asked, trying for a lighter note.

"Not quite," Joel said, a hint of colour in his face. "We were quite hungry when we went shopping."

Always a bad idea, Yvonne knew from experience. She accepted the explanation for now and watched, with some amusement, as Joel got out the chopping board and a knife, and began to sort through the vegetables that they had bought. Both of her children could cook, she had seen to it, so they would not starve, but Joel was not fond of being in the kitchen. He would rather be outdoors. And he did not really seem to mind what he ate, either, whereas both she and Mariah preferred well-cooked food.

"If you will make me some tea, I'll do that," she told him, and had to bite her lip at the relieved sighs from Mariah and Pieris, who had both experienced Joel's cooking before. "But we need to settle the horses first."

Yvonne and her children left Pieris and Renard settled at the kitchen table, Guise keeping an eye on them, with his shoulders propped against the wall, not speaking in response to Pieris' questioning look.

By the time horses were settled and they were back in the kitchen, both Pieris and Renard were silent, having worked out that something was wrong.

"We met an old acquaintance out riding today," Yvonne began, picking up one of Elinor's knives to begin chopping vegetables. She glanced up to make sure she had Pieris' and Renard's attention and, satisfied that she did, continued. "The lord of Coll Castle."

"He's dead," Pieris objected. "Sillman killed him in the castle. You saw his body. We all saw his body."

"He was walking, and talking, and throwing fire spells not that long ago," Yvonne contradicted, her voice flat. "Definitely not dead. And not burned, either."

"That's impossible. He bled to death on the castle floor. We put him with the others and burned them. He was on the funeral pyre," Pieris said. He half rose from his chair, held back by a low, menacing sound from Joel, and a subtle shift in position from Guise.

Pieris settled back in his chair, moving slowly, face paling. "I was sure he was dead."

"Did you actually see the body on the funeral pyre, or was it just the robes?" Yvonne asked. She believed him. But then, she had believed, and trusted, the Hundred without question for a long time. She was no longer sure of her own judgement where they were concerned.

She saw, by the arrested expression on Pieris' face, that she had given him something to consider.

"Just the robes," he said slowly. "But what you're suggesting can't be true. It would mean that one of us hid his death. And lied to the others." He was white when he finished speaking, fingers trembling as he shoved them through his hair.

Yvonne stared at him, assessing. He seemed utterly honest. He had not been part of it. Whatever it was. She felt a moment's sympathy for him, for the unhappy realisation that at least one of the people they had trusted most in the world had betrayed them. And had betrayed Elinor in the worst possible way.

Her shoulder ached, the phantom trace of the Hunar's symbol pressing into her flesh. Elinor was dead. The Coll lord was alive. She had been sundered. And there was something rotten in the heart of the Hundred. She was furious and heartsick at the same time.

"It goes back further than that. Elinor died a year ago," Yvonne reminded Pieris.

She saw the puzzled expression being exchanged between her children, but kept most of her attention on Pieris. She wanted to believe that he had nothing to do with the Coll lord, or with Elinor's death.

"I was right, wasn't I?" Renard asked. He seemed to have aged even in the short time since Yvonne had last seen him, and she thought he would be hard-pressed to defend himself, if needed. No wonder her children had been worried.

"Yes. Elinor was poisoned." She had a feeling that he and Pieris had been discussing this, the sugar bowl between them, but he wanted her to say it, for some reason.

"I found the seller," Pieris said, reaching into one of his pockets and pulling out a glass bottle, sealed with wax. It was one of the small, square, dark glass bottles used by apothecaries. The shape and colour usually meant that the contents were dangerous. "In very small doses, combined with other medicines, it can be used to treat some conditions. There is also a counter-agent." He pulled another bottle out of his pocket, this one slightly larger, rounded, made of clear glass with a clear liquid inside. He put both bottles on the table and pushed them forward, away from him, and then sat back. "This should be enough here to treat anyone who is still affected. It doesn't taste nice, but two spoonfuls should do it. Assuming, of course, that it's been a low dose. A higher dose, over a longer period of time –" His voice cracked at the end. He did not need to finish. A higher dose over a longer period of time, like the one Elinor had had, would be fatal no matter how much antidote was provided.

"Too late for her," Renard said, speaking mostly to himself, staring at the glass bottle on the table. He was so frail, she thought, chest aching. His skin was pale, the fine lines around his eyes and mouth more pronounced. Easy to see why her children had been worried. Far from getting better, he had grown worse.

"But not for you," Yvonne said. "We need you around." She handed him a spoon. For a moment it looked like he was not going to take it. He stared at the bottle, face hollow with age and grief. He and Elinor had been together for a long time. Far longer than Yvonne had been alive.

"We still need to catch a killer," Guise said.

Renard looked up, his attention caught, and Yvonne saw his jaw set in determination. He took the spoon from her, opened the clear glass bottle and took the required two spoonfuls, grimacing at the taste. Mariah went, unasked, and fetched him a glass of water which he took with a word of thanks.

It might just have been her hope, and imagination, but she thought Renard looked brighter as he sat back in his chair. An antidote. He would not have had as large a dose as Elinor, and his wulfkin nature would also help the healing.

Too late for Elinor, though.

"I don't think anyone else is still ill, but we can certainly ask." Yvonne turned back to preparing the meal for a moment. She was crying again.

There was an awkward silence behind her in the kitchen that stretched until she turned, preparation done, the stew simmering over the fire, and accepted a mug of tea from Joel before settling at the table with the others.

"Elinor was really killed?" Mariah asked, sounding quite unlike herself, shaken and subdued.

"And you spoke with a dead man today?" Joel added a question of his own.

Yvonne looked up and met Pieris' eyes across the table. He had such sad eyes. She thought about his fascination with magic, with how it worked, wanting to break down and analyse every spell, and rebuild it to be better. Try as she might, she could not imagine him plotting to kill someone in cold blood, and not by poison, in so cruel a way, using Elinor's sweet tooth against her.

"One of the Hundred did this. Not Pieris. One of the others."

She saw the emotion on Pieris' face. As sickened by the thought as she was, and also relieved. She was right. He had not had anything to do with Elinor's death, but he had been frightened he would not be believed. Would not be trusted.

"Whoever did it, they have betrayed all of their oaths and forgotten what it means to be Hunar," he said, his voice hoarse. He looked up and met her eyes across the table, and spoke in the language of the Hundred. "To serve, without asking anything in return."

It was a core part of the Hunar's oaths, that they all had to swear when they had passed the final test and been accepted. Yvonne opened her mouth to repeat the phrase back to him, in recognition, and her throat closed up. She was no longer Hunar. Speaking the oaths did not seem right.

"We need to find Sillman first," Guise said.

The most likely candidate, Yvonne knew, even as her entire being revolted at the idea. Sillman had been leading the Hundred for a long time. They had all placed their trust and faith in him time and time again. The idea that he could have betrayed their oaths and poisoned Elinor was unthinkable. But it was unthinkable that any of the Hundred had done it, and yet that was what the evidence suggested.

"Well, that shouldn't be hard," Mariah said. "I'm sure we passed him on the road."

"Sillman is here?" Yvonne asked her children, receiving silent, wide-eyed nods in return.

She looked at the empty sugar bowl on the table, wondering what business Sillman could have here, and thinking that it was no coincidence that he was here at the same time as the Coll lord had shown his face.

The grief and ache in her chest warmed, transferring into anger. A slow-burning anger she had rarely felt. Elinor dead not long after Sillman's visit. And now he was here again. She very much wanted to see Sillman, to see what was in his face when she asked the questions spinning around her mind, and to hear his explanation. If he could, in fact, explain himself.

"We'll start looking for him tomorrow," Guise said, face and voice grim. "There are questions he needs to answer."

Chapter Twenty-Three

Over breakfast the next morning they divided up the town into areas to search for traces of Sillman. They ruled out the poorer areas to start with. Sillman's expensive tastes were well known. Willowton was a large town, though, so that still left huge areas to cover. It would take time, unless they were lucky.

Pieris and Mariah left in one direction, Renard, who was looking healthier, and Joel in another. Her children had wanted to help. This way, they could help, but not on their own.

Yvonne was heading out with Guise when she saw a familiar figure striding along the street towards them. The cloth merchant. Dressed in navy this time, another outfit that accentuated her curves and moved with her as she walked. She was accompanied by a burly man who bore all the appearance of a hired thug.

Lita nodded to Yvonne by way of greeting. "Guise. Glad to see you're still in one piece. None of your relatives have skewered you yet?"

"Not for want of trying. Do you have something for us?" Guise asked.

"Yes. But we should talk as we walk. There may not be much time."

Intrigued, Yvonne fell into step with Lita and Guise.

"Is he coming with us?" Yvonne asked as the hired thug kept pace with them.

"Unfortunately, yes. Apparently, some of the other guild merchants don't like the way I do business."

From the very little that Yvonne had seen of Lita, she thought that was likely an understatement.

"Any more attacks on the property?" Guise asked.

"No. Not since you had words with the law keepers," Lita answered. "But I've had visits to my home. So," she tilted her head to the man walking a few paces behind them, "I don't walk around the town without an escort. There are four of them, working in shifts," she added, perhaps anticipating a question from Guise.

"I had no idea that guild members would be so ruthless," Yvonne said. Not all merchants belonged to the guilds. The guilds demanded a certain standard of behaviour from their members, and she was confident that threatening another merchant would break those standards.

"Well, I've managed to upset the weavers and cloth merchants," Lita said cheerfully. "Apparently paying decent wages to people to work in my premises threatens the weavers, who like their craftspeople to be isolated and grateful. And making my own cloth means I can guarantee the quality. Which the cloth merchants don't like."

Yvonne remembered the clack of looms from the upper floor of the blue house.

"But surely it's only the high-end merchants that are affected?" she said. "You're not making every-day cloth."

"No. But they seem to think I will." Lita's tone conveyed her disgust. "I've sent my appeal to masters in Hogsmarthen. And then we'll see. Until then, I have an escort. They also live in my house."

"I know a good lawyer," Yvonne offered. "He might be able to help you with the guild, or the masters if they come."

"Thank you."

"Where are we going just now?" Guise asked.

Lita had directed them away from the main road through the town and onto a secondary street. The houses were still prosperous, the street itself clean. If they kept walking in this direction, they would reach the financial buildings, not far from the law offices.

"I believe I have found your authenticator," Lita told him. "He's not local, and may not be here for much longer. He does not know about my enquiries yet."

"Good," Guise said, satisfaction in his voice.

Nothing more was said until they arrived at the doors of the financial offices.

The financial building had been built some time after the law offices. And, naturally, was larger and more ornate than the law offices. The building was set back from the road with a wide strip of flowers and scented plants around it, reminding Yvonne of Lita's building. This was much larger, though, with doors that stretched at least two storeys above their heads standing open in front of them.

The doors were made of wooden panels, each one with a different carving, and the wood from different lands, so the doors had a patchwork look about them. It was a quiet display of wealth that Yvonne suspected was missed by many of the people who walked through these doors.

Inside, the builders had continued to use materials from all over the lands, from the dark stone from the northlands, carved out of the mountains at great effort, to white stone from the southern lands, which crumbled under too much pressure, used here and there in the walls and pillars, the faintest trace of preservation spells teasing Yvonne's senses.

The building was designed around a great hall in its centre, divided from the rest of the building by a series of pillars, rather than solid walls. Around the central hall and behind the pillars were the offices, three floors of them. Some were tiny, barely big enough for one person to work, while others took up almost one entire side of the building, with armed guards at the doors trying to intimidate passers-by with lowered brows.

Unlike the law offices, Yvonne had been here several times during her stay with Elinor, and afterwards. There were banks settled around the financial offices, the buildings smaller although just as grand in their own ways. The banks' services required far more money than she had ever had. Here, anyone would be served. She could exchange gems for coins, or larger coins for smaller ones.

"He's on the top floor," Lita said, leading them between the great pillars and along the side of the building towards one of the staircases that were tucked away in the building's corners.

They made it up the stairs without meeting anyone else, and Yvonne was interested to note that Lita was as quick on her feet at the top as at the bottom. Clearly, she did not spend her entire life behind a desk.

"Along this way. Second from the end," Lita told them, and stepped aside to let Guise go first.

They had worked together before, Yvonne realised. Enough so that Lita was familiar enough with Guise to know he would want to lead. Yvonne was distracted by a strange sensation in her chest. It was an uncomfortable feeling. A bit like unease but with a sharper edge to it. She could not remember feeling anything like that before.

Guise was still stalking ahead of them, so she forced the unusual feeling away and kept going, hand going to her sword hilt. There wasn't much room for fighting here, but she had learned long ago not to take any chances.

There was no one else along this corridor. One side was open, a low, wooden balustrade between the occupants and a three storey fall to the stone floor below. On the other side, wooden walls enclosed the offices, leaving the walkway in shadow apart from the light from open doors. At this level, and in this particular corridor, they were all small offices accessed by single doors, many of them ajar, showing clerks settled with their ledgers.

The door Lita had directed them to was wide open, light spilling into the corridor. There were shadows moving in the light. Their quarry had company.

They were still several paces away from the door when two men appeared. One was clearly the authenticator, dressed in the close-fitting, drab garments that many of the workers here adopted, his head shaved. The other was an Ashnassan tribesman. Not the Slayer. Yvonne thought she recognised the warrior as one of the deputies.

The tribesman caught sight of Guise bearing along the walkway towards him and spat a curse in his own language that Yvonne was sure was very impressive, before taking off at a run along the rest of the walkway towards the corner of the building and the stairs there. He disappeared out of sight in moments.

The authenticator's dark-skinned face had paled, mouth open in shock and fright, before he, too, turned and ran for the stairs. He was surprisingly nimble for a finance worker. But then, Yvonne thought, working for the Ashnassan carried risk. And she doubted the Ashnassan were his only dangerous clients. He might be ready to run at all times.

By the time Guise reached the door of the office, the authenticator was also out of sight down the stairs.

Guise muttered a curse.

"Stay here and make sure no one goes in or out of the office," he told Lita. She didn't blink at the order, simply nodding once to show she had understood. Her bodyguard was some distance behind them on the walkway, clearly not as used to stairs as Lita.

Guise turned to Yvonne. "Mristrian, I think we should follow these two."

"Yes," Yvonne agreed. That sharp and unsettled feeling was back.

"If you will forgive me, there is a quicker way down than the stairs."

Before Yvonne quite knew what he was doing, he had picked her up as easily as she might lift her horse's saddle. One arm behind her back, one under her knees.

She had no time to react, or do anything apart from draw in a sharp, shocked breath.

He jumped.

Over the wooden balustrade and into the open air of the three storey drop to the floor below, his greatcoat billowing around them as they fell so that her impressions of falling were the weight of his arms underneath her and the dark silk lining of his coat catching the light as they fell.

Even as they fell, he said a command word, goblin magic rising around them.

They kept falling. Three storeys. Yvonne's heart was trying to fight its way out of her throat. There was no breath in her.

Then they landed, goblin magic surrounding them.

As softly and gently as if she had slid off her horse.

Guise put her down with the same care he had picked her up with, made a small, formal bow to her, and took off at a run.

Leaving Yvonne standing, staring at his back for a moment. Not quite sure what had happened, her mind still trying to tell her that she was falling.

Then the tribesman, closely followed by the authenticator, arrived into the great hall of the building between a pair of ornately carved pillars, both running flat out for the open doorway.

Guise was there before them, sword ready, fangs descended, a hint of red in his eyes.

Yvonne forced herself to move. She had been still too long.

There were cries of alarm around them as she ran forward, blocking the retreat of the authenticator as he turned, trying to find an escape route that was not blocked by an angry goblin.

His eyes widened as he saw her, sword ready.

"Stand. We just want to ask you some questions," she told him. "Then you can go."

"I don't believe you," he answered. His voice was accented, although she could not place it just now. Somewhere in the southern realms, possibly at the coast. Not Abar al Endell. There was a long coastline, though, and a number of large islands. Somewhere along there.

He tried to run around her. She moved, blocking his escape.

"It will be much easier if you stand still," she told him.

"You're threatening me. With a sword."

"You deserve worse," she told him, voice hard. She dug into her spell pouch, looking for something to tangle him with, the spells familiar under her fingertips. Nothing. It was not something she normally carried. She had the words for an entanglement spell in her mind, but needed a few moments to speak them.

Before she could begin the spell, he tried to rush past her again, and as he did so, a shadow flew past her, heading straight for the authenticator. The Ashnassan tribesman, his sword ready.

He ran past the authenticator, making a casual sweep of his sword as he did so, slicing open the man's throat, and kept going, pursued by Guise, who simply leapt over the authenticator's fallen body, careless of the spray of blood.

Yvonne followed. The authenticator was dead. But they had a living witness to follow.

She ran between the pillars at the other end of the great hall, seeing a sliver of light ahead. There must be a back door to the building. There always was.

Apart from that sliver of light, she was running into shadow and dark.

There was a snarl of rage ahead of her. Goblin temper. Harsh breathing.

Then air moved ahead of her. She stepped back on instinct, sword up, and caught the blow meant to kill her with the edge of her sword, the impact travelling up her arm. The tribesman had put every bit of his strength behind it.

Then there was another low snarl. This one with some satisfaction.

"Are you alright, mristrian?" Guise asked. Despite the snarls, he sounded himself. A little less composed than he usually was, perhaps.

"Yes," she answered, then wrinkled her nose. She was in one piece, but she had been sprayed with blood when the tribesman murdered the authenticator. She wanted a cleansing spell. And a bath. Both would have to wait. "Is he alive?"

"Yes," Guise answered, satisfaction clear. "Come. Let's see what he has to say."

He was moving away from her as he spoke, followed by the sound of something dragging against the floor. Then he opened the door, letting in daylight, and Yvonne saw that he was dragging the unconscious tribesman by one arm. Guise pulled the man outside the building and down the shallow steps at the back.

"If you damage him too badly, he won't be able to answer our questions," she pointed out, following Guise down the steps.

"He is just bruised," Guise answered, but he dropped the arm he had been holding and reached into his coat, producing a length of cord which he used to tie up the unconscious man.

"What else do you have tucked away?" Yvonne asked.

Guise glanced across, a gleam of unexpected mischief in his face. "I should be delighted to let you search me to find out, mristrian," he told her.

She opened her mouth, heat scorching across her face, unsettled, stomach twisting in unease. He was generally unfailing in his courtesy to her. Never seeking to overwhelm her. He had lifted her as if she weighed nothing, bearing them both across the balustrade and onto the floor below, cushioned by magic. If she had needed any reminder about just how powerful he was, in physical strength and in magic, that had been an effective demonstration.

The unease passed almost as soon as it had arisen, although she was still unsettled. This was Guise. However powerful he was, he would not hurt her.

He had also never picked her up before.

"Did you hit your head?" she asked, narrowing her eyes.

He grinned back, eyes still bright, and opened his mouth to answer.

"We should question him before the law keepers get here," she told him, cutting off whatever he might have said.

There was still a gleam in his eye as he inclined his head in agreement.

In the end, the tribesman had nothing to tell them. He refused to answer any questions, even when Guise picked him up with one hand, holding him upside down.

And of course the law keepers arrived in time to see that. They were outraged to find a goblin holding an Ashnassan warrior by his ankle, although they did take the warrior into custody when Guise mentioned a murder.

The law keepers were even less pleased to discover the mess inside the financial offices.

Coming back into the building, Yvonne was not surprised to see crowds gathered. Everyone in the building had come out of their offices and was standing around, leaning over the balustrades on the upper levels, peering between the pillars on the ground floor, staring at the corpse in the middle, blood soaking into the priceless stone floor. Even Lita had put her head forward to have a look, disappearing as soon as she saw Guise and Yvonne coming back into the building. Yvonne could only hope that no one had crept behind Lita as she was distracted, the uncomfortable feeling creeping back as she saw Lita looking at Guise.

She found herself looking at Guise to see if he was looking back at Lita. Guise was in conversation with the law keepers, or at least, the law keepers were trying to question Guise.

Guise was acting every inch the high-ranking Karoan'shae lord he was, not so much refusing to answer the questions that were being thrown at him as seeming to not recognise that they were directed at him. It was an attitude Yvonne had seen before from high-ranking humans. As if they could simply not comprehend that they might need to answer questions.

The law keepers then turned their attention to Yvonne, and she saw, with a sinking sensation in her stomach, that at least a few of them had been on duty the day that the tribesmen had attacked her. They had seen her with corpses twice on the same day. She wanted to tell them that she hadn't killed anyone. None of the tribesmen, or the authenticator lying on the stone floor nearby, had died at her hands.

She kept quiet, judging that the less she said, the better.

The law keepers gathered in the finance offices might have been willing to let a Hunar away with involvement in public murder. An unnamed woman, with well-worn weapons and involvement in at least two previous incidents that the law keepers had been called to, would not be given the same courtesy.

With an inward sigh, Yvonne realised that they were going to arrest her. She could understand why. It would, at least, be a new experience. She had assisted law keepers in the past, but never actually been arrested herself.

Guise intervened. He barely moved. A simple shift in his body weight and the attention of the law keepers transferred from Yvonne back to him.

"You are questioning my wife," he told them, voice cool. "You will stop now."

To Yvonne, it seemed that the entire world stilled and fell quiet, those words echoing out in ripples from their little hub in the middle of the financial offices' great hall, the ripples going across the floor, through the gathered crowds, and up the three storeys of the building to the ornately carved ceiling high above. Even though Guise had spoken in a normal tone, she imagined that everyone had heard.

The law keepers nearest to her, who had been moving closer in preparation for arresting her, took a clear step back, the senior one swallowing, hard.

"Your wife, my lord?" the senior-most law keeper asked into the awkward silence. If the crowds had not heard Guise, they would certainly have heard that.

Yvonne felt the attention of everyone in the building turn to her, then to Guise, then back to her. Doubtless, every one of them wondering what possessed the fine lord to claim any kind of relationship with her. She might be wearing good quality fabrics, but she was dressed for work in a shirt and trousers. Simple and practical clothing. Hair pulled back into a single plait. Carrying weapons.

Hardly the attire of the wife of a Karoan'shae lord.

A sharp contrast to Guise, who was dressed in his usual impeccable tailoring, weapons hidden for the moment. He could present himself at the nearest Royal Court and would be welcomed without a blink. Yvonne would be stopped at the gates and turned away.

And this fine lord had claimed her, in public, as his wife.

She wanted to stab him. She wanted to run away to somewhere that no one would ever know who she was. She wanted to scream. She wanted to cry. Again.

They might have created a goblin bond, but she still was not sure what, if anything, she wanted to do about that. And Guise had said nothing needed to change. And now he claimed her publicly as his wife.

She was furious with him for speaking. It did not matter how much truth was in it.

Her stomach was twisting as though she were facing overwhelming odds in battle. Her legs were weak, as though the ground were shaking under her feet.

Time seemed to have stretched, extending the pause between the law keeper's question and Guise's answer.

She wondered if he would deny the claim. Or accept it. And wondered, too, what she wanted him to do. Say no, he had made a mistake, and let them take her away to the prison, publicly dismissed. Or say yes. Keep her away from prison, and bring their connection into the public light.

"Yes," Guise said, one brow lifting. "You are questioning my word?"

No, Yvonne thought. They were questioning his state of mind.

"Not at all, my lord. My lady," the senior law keeper bowed to her. "Our apologies for the misunderstanding. Of course, you are free to go."

"Good," Yvonne said. He had bowed to her. Called her a lady. Before Guise had spoken, the law keeper had spoken to her with a sneer in his voice, not believing a word she had said. Ready to arrest her and take her to the town's only prison.

Now, Guise had spoken. And suddenly she was free to go.

She definitely wanted to hurt someone. Perhaps a particular goblin lord, apparently unruffled by events.

Before she could give in to the impulse, she turned on her heel and stalked towards the pillars and the staircase they had used to get to the upper floor.

Interested onlookers, financiers and customers alike, scattered, moving swiftly out of her way.

It was only when she was most of the way up the staircase that she discovered she had her hand on her sword hilt, and a scowl on her face.

"Mristrian," Guise said behind her. Too close. A few steps at most.

She stopped and turned on the stair. They were eye to eye, and she could see the tightness around his mouth.

"I apologise," he said.

"I am not a possession," she said to him, hearing the venom in her voice and unable to stop it. It did not stop the hurt that had taken hold. He had always treated her as equal. Until now. Until he had simply picked her up, and then announced to a room full of strangers that they were married. As if he had a right to do so, to make decisions for her.

"They were going to arrest you," he said, in a mild tone she had heard before, once or twice. He was sure he had done the right thing.

"You thought I needed your protection?" she asked, the edge to her voice turning sharp and hard.

His eyes widened. "Of course not."

"Then what were you doing?" she hissed at him.

She had caught his attention, at least, she saw. He was staring back at her, startled out of his self-assurance into frank surprise.

"Perhaps you could fight another time?" Lita said from above them. "Only, I'm not sure how long it will be before the law keepers want to search the office."

"Yes," Yvonne said, and made her way up the final flight of stairs, brushing past Lita and making her way along the walkway to the office. Lita had left her bodyguard outside it.

The bodyguard took one look at Yvonne's face and moved away, letting her inside.

As she stepped through the office doorway, she caught the tone of a low-voiced conversation between Lita and Guise behind her. She could not hear the words, just the tone. Warm and close.

The unpleasant feeling from earlier surged back, and she finally recognised it for what it was. Jealousy.

She was jealous of the relationship between Lita and Guise. A stab of pain followed. She recognised in their dealings the sort of short-hand language and closeness that she and Guise shared, after working together for so long. With that recognition came the understanding that she had assumed that her relationship with Guise was unique. Discovering that he had another female he also worked closely with made her stomach twist and heart constrict.

Ridiculous. She was being ridiculous. Guise could have as many female friends as he wished, she told herself.

It did not matter he had made her feel as if she were unique, somehow. Not only that, but someone whose opinion he valued. Perhaps he made all of his female friends feel that way.

Another impulse to violence rose again. Guise was quite a large target.

She turned her back on the doorway and forced herself to concentrate on the office in front of her. It was much easier than dealing with her feelings.

The office was almost bare of personal effects, or furniture. There was a waist-high working table, the top a square about half the size of a kitchen table. The surface was covered with plain black fabric, and held tools that Yvonne recognised from previous visits to these offices. A magnifier to examine gems. A tiny scraping tool to check that coins were, indeed, gold. A collection of other instruments she could not immediately identify.

There was a small desk against the wall, an open ledger on its surface, and a well-worn leather backpack underneath, resting against the wall.

Lita had said that the authenticator was not from here, Yvonne remembered. That explained the lack of personal items. He was just visiting.

She wondered where he had been from, and where he usually worked.

The ledger was written in competent, messy handwriting that required a great deal of attention to understand. It was a welcome distraction as Guise came into the office, Lita waiting at the door.

The office was a small room, and seemed abruptly far too small when he arrived and stopped near the desk.

"It's in some kind of code," she told him, flicking back a page or two in the ledger. The last entry named his client as Ash. Turning back the pages, she found previous entries for Ash. Her eyes widened slightly at the numbers. The authenticator, whoever he had been, had inspected a vast number of coins for the Ashnassan over the past few weeks.

"Mristrian," Guise said, moving his weight forward, wanting her attention.

All at once, the office was too small. Far too small. He was too close, and Lita was in the doorway, a watchful shadow.

She stepped away, her back hitting the wall. There was not enough room. Not enough air.

She had to get out.

"Let me past," she said to him. That voice did not sound like hers. Breathless. Too high. Panicked.

He stepped aside at once, without question.

She moved.

Past him, through the door, past Lita's curious stare, past her bodyguard.

By the time she reached the stairs at the end of the walkway, she was nearly running.

Down the stairs, every one of them a reminder of how easily Guise had lifted her and leapt over the balustrade.

The law keepers were still in the building, questioning people. No one tried to stop her, or speak to her, as she went out the front doors. She was walking, but only just.

The streets were full of people, and she imagined every one of them staring at her, wondered if they could see the cracks she could feel across her person, the constriction around her throat, her heart racing. There was not enough air. And she kept going.

She finally stopped when she reached one of the town's green spaces. This one was almost deserted, no one there to witness her rush into the copse of trees, finding the tallest and oldest tree, and leaning back against it. She could feel the age of the tree at her back. It had endured more years than she could imagine, settling into its surroundings. She let its quiet strength hold her.

Her lungs were burning with effort, whole body coated in sweat, legs trembling, heart racing too hard and too fast.

And now she had stopped, she was glad of the quiet and the lack of audience.

She had not lost control like that, in public, for years. The panic might rise close to the surface from time to time, but she usually managed to contain it.

But then, very few people touched her.

And no one had picked her up as if she weighed nothing. Not since the quarrel.

It was not the same. It was Guise. It was an expedient way of chasing their quarry. And in the moment she had been fine. It was everything after that had burned away her self-control.

The public declaration. The change in attitude of the law keepers.

And she had never been jealous before. Not in that way. The echo of it still clawed at her.

She did not want to go back. Not into that building, through the stares and the mutterings. Not into that office, the mere memory of it closing up her throat. Too small. Lita and Guise would need to learn what they could, from the office, and from the tribesman, if the law keepers would allow them to ask questions.

It was all she could do for now to stand and breathe.

Chapter Twenty-Four

She came back to Elinor's house when the afternoon was fading. A cleansing spell had got rid of the sweat, and the traces of blood she had forgotten. One of the town's bakeries had dealt with the gnawing, empty feeling in her stomach. A little bit of time had calmed the panic. It was still close to the surface.

Staying away had been tempting. For a breath or two. But her children were here. And Renard. And Pieris. And she could not hide forever, as much as she wanted to.

She could manage a short apology for her behaviour. At least, she thought so. Running away like a madwoman in the middle of an investigation. She had never done that before, and her skin prickled in shame.

Apart from that, she thought that the sooner she managed to conclude her business here and get back to the house at Fir Tree Crossing, the better. She had a lifetime ahead of her where she was no longer Hunar, and now had enough funds to consider what she really wanted to do.

Except that she could not imagine being anything else, or doing anything else. Not yet. Being Hunar. Wearing that symbol. Working to aid supplicants. It had all felt as natural as breathing.

The others weren't back to the house yet. She could tell that from the house's wards.

She had no time to feel relief because someone was there. There was a ripple in the building's wards, and a glossy-coated horse in the courtyard at the rear of the house. It was the sort of horse a king might ride, and she could not imagine anyone she knew riding such a creature. Very pretty, but impractical. Renard would not approve.

Whoever it was had let themselves in through the kitchen door. It was slightly ajar.

Elinor's wards were there simply to provide an alert to visitors. She had never stopped anyone coming into her house, in all the years Yvonne had known her.

Curiosity roused, Yvonne put one hand on her sword hilt and went inside, stepping out of the threshold in reflex as she did so, only for it to fall away as she saw who was in the room.

The light through the open door revealed Sillman. Dressed as finely as he usually was, in the dark clothes he preferred, white hair swept back from his forehead and falling just below his collar.

He ignored her for a moment, staring at the empty sugar bowl that had been left on the table.

Then he looked up and met her eyes and she could not breathe. He did not show much on his face. It was his eyes. For a moment, they were as hollow and hurt as they had been at Elinor's funeral. Then the hurt faded, a certain hardness taking over. Knowledge. Perhaps a bit of guilt, or perhaps that was what she wanted to see.

"Why?" It was the only thing she could think to say and, perhaps, the most important question she had ever asked him.

"You would not understand. You could not possibly understand."

The twist of hurt made it hard to breathe. Still, she managed to speak. "Try to explain. You betrayed her. You betrayed all of us. There must have been a good reason why."

"You are interfering in matters that do not concern you," he told her, his voice harsh. It was so like him to say that. To think that he was in charge. That he could direct what she did, what the rest of the Hundred did.

She heard a bitter laugh come out of her throat. "Elinor was my friend. More than that, she was my teacher. She taught me what it means to be Hunar. Something which you have clearly forgotten. We are servants. We protect those who cannot protect themselves. We do not make decisions about who should live and who should die among our own people. We are meant to serve, not to rule." Her voice cracked at the end, a wash of fury and grief holding her silent.

"And you can do neither," Sillman told her, satisfaction in his voice.

Her breath caught in her throat, focus sharpening on those words, and the tone he had spoken in. Pleased that she would no longer be Hunar. "Dismissing me was never about Guise, was it? You wanted me out of the Hundred. Why?" she asked, anger chasing away the grief. "I have never betrayed my oaths. Never sought to rule. Not as you did."

"How dare you lecture me? You have no idea, no comprehension. None whatsoever. The life that I have lived, the sacrifices I have made, the choices. And all for what? A pat on the back. The occasional crust of bread. Gratitude." There were spots of colour high on his cheeks, lips a thin line as he spoke, voice shaking with fury.

"Gratitude did not buy that horse outside. Or the clothes you're wearing. Or that expensive wine you like so much. All of those things cost money. You are not suffering." She had not known her voice could be so bitter. So scornful.

He glared back at her. Anger. But also shame. She did not imagine that. He could not quite hold her eyes, dropping his gaze back to the sugar bowl.

"We should not have ties that pull us off course," he said. It did not sound as if he was speaking to her, almost as if he had forgotten she was there. "We should be bound to our oaths and our service. And that should be enough." His face twisted. It looked like grief, although she could not see his eyes.

"But we are human, too," she answered, keeping her voice low. "And having connections reminds us of why we serve." She thought of Mariah's bright laughter, Joel's quiet smile. The contentment of sitting around a table with her family. The knowledge that, no matter what, they would always be her children. They would always find each other.

"Some connections should not be made," he said.

"What do you mean?" she asked, skin prickling. He was not speaking about her. Or Elinor. He was speaking from personal experience. And as far as she knew, Sillman had no personal relationships that could steer him off course. "What have you done?"

He opened his mouth to speak, then froze, tilting his head. As if he was listening. It reminded her of the Coll lord, before he had run away.

She put a hand back on her sword hilt, watching as his expression changed from the distant look to focusing on her again. When he spoke, it was all fury. And yet, it carried none of the heat of before. It was as though he was reading from a script. Words someone else had given him.

"Foolish little girl. I simply came to tell you to keep out of the way. You're not one of us. You don't have the power to stop us." The scripted words. The fury. He might sound sure of himself, and yet she was not convinced.

Yvonne's eyes narrowed. The Coll lord had thought she had lost her powers. And Sillman seemed sure she had. And she realised, too late, that he had not answered her question. Why was she no longer Hunar?

There was no time to think further. He was not finished. "Interfere again, and matters will not go well for you."

He pulled something out of the pouch at his belt and flung it at her, speaking a word she knew. She only had time to duck out of the way before the concussive force of a spell exploded over her head, throwing her off her feet and across the kitchen, thudding into the wall. By the time she got back to her feet again, Sillman was gone, the door left open behind him. She ran out of the kitchen, unsteady, her ears ringing with the aftermath of the spell, and straight into Guise. He put his hands on her shoulders in reflex, steadying her for a moment before letting go, taking a step back to give her room.

"Mristrian? What's wrong?"

"Sillman was here. Did you see him? And his stupid horse? Which way did he go?"

"I saw no one. The gate was open as I came in."

Yvonne tried to run towards the gates to see if she could follow Sillman's trail but was off balance at once, putting a hand on the wall of the house to steady herself.

"What did he do to you?" There was anger in Guise's voice now, which she could hear despite the ringing in her ears.

"Concussive spell," she told him, the words sounding distant in her ears. "I think I need to sit down."

There was a moment of blackness, then she blinked, opening her eyes to a starlit sky above, and a darker shadow by the wall.

"I have waited a long time for you, daughter," the shadow said, voice so deep it vibrated through her.

She knew that voice. She knew this place. She knew those stars above, and the faint scent of liquorice in the air. There was something important here. Something she needed to remember.

She closed her eyes against a wave of dizziness, then opened her mouth to answer the shadow, heart thudding in her ears, and blinked again.

The stars were gone over her head and she was, instead, staring up at the ceiling of Elinor's kitchen, a sight she knew well. She had spent a lot of time lying on this makeshift bed during her training, muscles aching from the drills that Elinor had insisted upon.

The kitchen was full of the sound of voices arguing. Her children, Renard, Pieris and Guise. The voices were all running on top of each other so that she could not work out what, precisely, they were arguing about.

She sat up and put a hand to her head, and had a moment's displacement, remembering sitting up on another occasion, with cold stone underneath her, with a pounding head. The castle's dungeon. Where she been trapped with Guise.

The rest of the memories were there, she could feel them. But they remained stubbornly out of reach. For now. Along with the rest of that night under the stars.

"Kalla. Are you all right? Did Sillman hurt you?" Mariah wanted to know, paler than normal, voice trembling.

"I'm fine. Just the edge of a spell, that's all. Did you have any luck finding him?"

The rest of the room shared dark glances. Nobody else had seen Sillman, or found any trace of him in their ventures around the town. He was managing to disguise his presence very effectively, even from three wulfkin who knew him and one of the Hundred. Guise said that none of his contacts had found a trace of Sillman, either.

That took considerable skill.

"He must have help," Yvonne speculated, coming to stand with the group who were gathered around the table. She noticed then that the sugar bowl had shattered with the force of Sillman's spell, bits of pottery scattered across the table's surface. It seemed fitting, somehow.

"He is one of the Hundred," Pieris commented, his voice dry. He lifted a brow when Guise glared at him. "What? It's the truth. We are legends, don't you know? People tend to help us, if we ask them to. Although, we don't normally ask."

"He's up to something," Yvonne said, settling into her usual chair. She had to crane her neck to look up at everybody standing around her, but her legs were still wobbly from the after-effects of the spell. "He didn't want me to interfere."

Her eyes fell on the shards of pottery. Her chest constricted, an echo of the grief of Elinor's death running through her again. Sillman had killed her. He had all but admitted that. He had poisoned Elinor's sugar supply. And would not say why.

"He must be insane," Pieris said. "What can he possibly be thinking?"

"It's Sillman," Yvonne said, shaking her head again, and wishing she hadn't moved as the room spun slightly around her. "He always thinks he is right, even when he isn't. Elinor was the only one who could get him to listen."

Pieris could not argue with that, although it was clear from his expression he did not like it. None of them did.

Yvonne rested her head in her hands for a moment as the room spun again. She might have avoided the worst of the concussive spell, but it had been one of Sillman's most powerful ones and she was still feeling the after-effects. And, for some reason, her mind kept trying to take her back to her dream. The stars overhead. The testing place. The shadow. No more details came to her waking mind, and her memories skipped ahead. She remembered being in the marketplace, when she had first seen the Coll lord. The watching figure outside the law offices. The fragments of the dungeon cell. Everything mixed together and nothing made sense. Perhaps it was an after-effect of her earlier panic, that her mind would not make sense of anything. Perhaps she was going insane. She had a head full of things she did not remember, and did not understand, just now. Insanity was a real possibility.

She did not want to be alone in her head and looked up, trying to focus on the conversation that had been going on around her, everyone speaking on top of each other.

As she looked up she looked straight ahead and saw, in the courtyard out of the window, the shape of a man wearing elaborate red robes. Red robes she had seen once before, in Coll Castle. She stumbled to her feet, a cut-off sound emerging from her throat, and moved towards the door, the others following, weapons drawn as they caught her alarm.

Of course, when she got outside into the courtyard, there was nothing there. Nothing that they could see, or sense. Renard, Joel and Mariah all reported a foul stench in the air, but could not follow it beyond the gate.

All the horses were anxious in their stalls, more than a few of them with white around their eyes.

The Coll lord had said that he was getting his robes back, she remembered. She had not believed him. The robes had been burned, supposedly along with the rest of him.

It was late at night by then, and the others set a watch rota, excluding her. She had an impulse to protest and held the words back. Her head was still spinning with the after-effects of Sillman's spell, and whatever dreams and memories were trying to push themselves into her mind. She was not sure she could be trusted on watch.

She woke deep into the night from a confusing dream involving her children and a livestock dealer she remembered from several years before, when they were buying new horses for Mariah and Joel. The same horses they had now, in fact. There had been impossibly fast exchanges of coins and mad laughter in her dream. The laughter had been real. The livestock dealer might have known his trade, but he had a weakness for some of the more potent plants available from the southern realms, and a lot of what he said had not made sense, interspersed with the manic laughter.

There was nothing sinister about that dream. It was just one of those random dreams that happened from time to time.

It was a sad reflection of her life that she was relieved to have had an ordinary nightmare.

The house around her was quiet and still. Every bed and every room was occupied, including Elinor's room, which Renard had, reluctantly, agreed to take. It had been his sleeping place when he had been here, after all. He had taken the letter Yvonne had found and retired to his room with slow, reluctant steps. Yvonne understood the reluctance. To read those final words and know that there would be nothing more.

Even so, the house was full of life. Elinor would have loved that. She had always welcomed company.

Despite the peace, her skin was crawling with the certainty that something was badly wrong, somewhere nearby, and she needed to be up and about. She got dressed as quickly and as quietly as she could, and made her way downstairs.

Renard was on watch in the kitchen, looking up as she came in, taking in the fact that she was fully dressed, and armed.

"You are remembering, aren't you? Your final test?" he asked. "I saw your face earlier."

"Bits and pieces," she said, touching her forehead. "None of it really makes sense at the moment."

"Don't try and force it," he advised. "It will come when it's due time, and when you're ready."

"You know the story? Wouldn't it be easier to simply tell me?" Even as she asked the question, she knew the answer. Memory was far more powerful than someone else's story. So it was not really surprising when he shook his head.

"Guise is awake too. You should take him with you. For back-up."

It was a sensible suggestion. But then, Renard had not got to his age as a lone wulf with no range to protect him by taking unnecessary risks.

It might be sensible, but her body seized with reluctance, shame crawling through her. She had run away from Guise in a panic earlier.

Company would be sensible, though. And whatever else he might be, Guise was excellent back-up.

She was about to ask him where she could find Guise when the kitchen door to the courtyard opened, and he stepped in. "Are you feeling better, mristrian?"

"Much better, thank you. But we need to be moving."

"Ready when you are."

"Shall I wake the others?" Renard asked.

Yvonne thought about that for a moment. It did not feel right. She shook her head. "Not yet. I think you'll know if you're needed. You might want to wake Pieris to keep you company, though." That felt right. Between them, Renard and Pieris could manage most threats. And although she was feeling better from the short rest she had managed, she had a feeling that Renard was right, and she would need back-up.

Chapter Twenty-Five

It was dark and cool when they stepped outside, one of the horses making a low sound. It was more like a query for food rather than an alarm. Probably Joel's horse.

Yvonne remembered vividly coming home late one night to find that Joel's horse, far from being dozing in the field with the others, had somehow managed to get into their harness room and the barrel of feed. He had managed to work his way through about a month's supply of feed by the time Yvonne found him. Despite being horribly ill, it had not put him off, and they now secured the barrel with the sort of locks more commonly found in treasuries.

Not surprisingly, there was no one else around on the streets as they went through the gate. Sensible people were tucked up in bed, sleeping. They were not creeping out into the night with only a single person to back them up, looking for a corrupted and possessed human and the leader of the Hundred, who had killed one of his oldest friends.

"Do you have a way to track him?" Guise asked. He always had good questions, Yvonne thought.

"I realised something. When the lord ran away from us earlier, it looked like he was listening to something before he went. And Sillman did the same thing, in the kitchen. I think there must be a way of communicating. There is a street corner not far from here which joins onto the main roads through the town."

Nothing more needed to be said. And yet there were words behind her teeth. An apology. She should speak it. She had never run away from an investigation before, and still could not quite believe she had done so.

Guise kept pace with her, silent and deadly.

She opened and closed her mouth, but the words would not come out.

They made their way the short distance to the corner, strides evenly matched, and Yvonne could not help but realise that, if she was only permitted a single person as back-up, she would have chosen Guise. He was the most formidable fighter she knew. He was also ruthless and cunning and one of the few people in the world she trusted, after her faith in the Hundred had been shattered.

The corner was famous not only for being at the heart of the town, but also for having four taverns clustered together. Even the taverns were closed at this hour, not even a maudlin drunk left on the street. She made her way to the biggest of the tavern buildings, and set her back to the wall. From here, she could see down the three main roads through the town.

"I'm sorry I ran," she said, staring into the night. Not looking at Guise.

"There is nothing to apologise for, mies maisredayenni," he answered, voice shading to warmth.

She bit her lip against that warmth. It called to her, a promise, if she would only turn towards it. She kept staring straight ahead.

Guise was silent for a while, still and quiet in the night, blending into shadows. He did that very well. Kept to the dark.

"Did you find anything useful? You and Lita?" she asked.

"Entries going back months," Guise answered. There was something under his calm voice that she could not read. Irritation, perhaps. He might have side-stepped her apology. It did not mean he was calm about her running away.

Shame prickled across her skin, the memory of the panic in the too-small office rising up again, quickening her heartbeat, constricting her throat.

"Months? A lot of girls, then," she heard herself say.

"A fortune in golden crowns. Each one real. And each one inspected by the authenticator."

"A tidy sum for him," Yvonne commented, shaking her head, self-disgust finding a new target. "He had to have known something was wrong. Do we know where he was working before here?"

"Closer to the Ashnassan borders. It makes sense they found him. Lita is making more enquiries. Making sure he was the only one involved."

"Good. She is very competent," Yvonne said, proud of her calm, even voice. Rational. Reasonable. Nothing like the clawing hurt inside her.

"That she is," Guise agreed, that undertone back in his voice. He shifted his weight slightly, and Yvonne found herself tensing, forcing herself to relax. Guise would not hurt her. No matter what else was true. He would not hurt her. "Lita asked me to tell you that she has several bottles of wine ready. I assume that means something to you?"

For a moment, Yvonne could not think what it might mean. And then she remembered Lita's easy invitation. To drink wine, and to discuss Guise's failings.

Something eased inside. Some hurt lessened.

"Another time, perhaps," Yvonne said.

"She is a valuable resource," Guise said. There was something else in his voice then. He did not normally volunteer information like that.

Yvonne tilted her head, not looking at him.

"You seem to be friends," she said. Calm. Almost detached. Hiding the messy knot of feelings inside.

"Yes," he said, the word lengthened as if he was thinking. A pause dragged on. Then he moved, intake of breath audible in the night. "You thought there was more. No. I would not. I mean, there is nothing."

It was a rare day that Guise sounded unsettled. Goblins took pride in their self-control. She should leave it alone. She really should. And yet, she did not want to.

"I've met your assassin, remember?" Yvonne said.

"Yes. No. Not mine. A long time ago. Long before I met you," he added, still sounding off balance.

For a moment, Yvonne was not sure whether to laugh or cry. He had publicly claimed her as his wife. It was a label that carried so many meanings among humans. Not something she had ever thought would apply to her. It did not describe their connection, whatever it was. And she still felt raw from his public announcement, even past his apology.

"It's not really my business," she said, folding her arms across her middle.

"I disagree," he said, sounding more like himself. "What do you wish to know?"

She stayed silent for a moment, not sure what to say, or how to say anything without sounding petulant and childish. She wanted to tell him that she did not want to know anything. But she would not lie. Hunar did not lie. And the habit was ingrained into her. And this was Guise. Who did not lie to her, even if he did not tell her the truth.

"I don't know," she said. The truth.

"I helped Lita get a blood price for her sister. Did she tell you that her sister was taken by the Ashnassan?" Guise asked.

"Yes. And her body returned."

"I have a reputation in some circles for granting favours," he went on.

Yvonne tilted her head to him, interested despite herself. He was telling her more than she had known before. And it explained a number of things. How he found his informants, for one. A favour granted, a request in return.

"A blood price would have helped Lita set up the blue house," she speculated.

Guise laughed, softly. "It did."

"And you gave her the rest? And now she works for you when you need her to?"

"Something like that. It has served us both well for several years. She has no debt now."

Not money, perhaps, Yvonne thought, but the weight of a favour granted and repaid, many times over, was still there. Along with a friendship that was just that.

"Do you have any male friends?" she asked. It was not the question she had meant to speak, and her face warmed.

Guise stilled beside her. "Yes. Several."

He had more to say, she thought, and kept quiet, biting her lip to hold in a torrent of words.

"They are mostly considered to be both charming and handsome," he added at length, sounding reluctant. "I do not want to introduce them to you."

Yvonne could not help it. She laughed. The knot inside loosened, her shoulders relaxed, and suddenly all was right with the world.

"Do you think they will tell me tales?" she asked, still laughing.

"No. I think they will try and charm you away," he said, sounding grumpy. It was a very human tone. One she had heard from her children more than once. Usually when there were chores to be done and they would rather play, or lie in the sun, or do any of another dozen things that did not involve work.

She laughed again.

"I don't think anyone has ever tried to charm me," she said, her voice light. "It might be a novel experience."

"I have been charming. On many occasions," he said, still sounding grumpy.

She choked on another laugh. "Is that what you call it?" she asked.

"I did not think you noticed, mristrian," he said. If she had not known him so well, she would have missed the trace of laughter in his voice.

"I wonder how Brea and Thort are getting on with digging the ditches," she said, changing the subject as she settled her shoulders against the wall. Ditches being made in preparation for the Karoan'shae's arrival. A site chosen by Guise's mother. The closest goblin palace to Guise's human bond partner. She had a dozen questions to ask Guise.

"We had called in some help," Guise said, still standing a few paces from her. Of course he would not give her more information. And of course he would not do anything as pedestrian as lean against a wall. He was standing straight and tall, and watchful. "I think Brea was looking forward to having her own group to command again."

"She would make a formidable leader," Yvonne said, thinking back to her first meeting with Brea, when the lady had accepted the arrival at her house of a strange group of travellers, one of them injured, without a blink, organising them with grace and calm.

"She is," Guise confirmed.

Which just led to a dozen more questions in Yvonne's mind. Leaders among the goblins rarely quit. And Brea had chosen, along with Thort, to leave their homeland. To settle in a town known for its artistry and beauty. And to take their surviving daughter with them into their self-imposed exile. Away from others of their kind.

Those secrets, and answers, belonged to Brea and Thort, though, not to her. She might be curious. She did not have a right to any answers.

And there was work to do. They had been talking too long.

She and Guise fell silent for a while, Yvonne extending her senses with a low-level spell that would not use too much of her energy. She remembered the lord's surprise that she still had her magic and wondered, again, who had told him that she would be helpless without the Hunar's symbol. People were called to the Hundred because of their abilities and magic, Elinor had told her more than once. Anyone called did not decide to become a member of the Hundred and then, miraculously, develop abilities and magic. And some of the Hundred in the past had possessed very little, or very limited, ability with magic, but had managed their service perfectly well.

For the first time, Yvonne wondered if Elinor's teaching had been different to Sillman's. She was confident that Elinor had held different beliefs, and had had a different way of looking at the world than Sillman. Elinor had been kind, and determined to see the best in people. Sillman had always seemed more cynical. Still a Hunar. Still sworn to help those in need.

As far as she knew, Sillman had never had an apprentice. Elinor had trained two. Pieris, and then Yvonne. Decades apart. But Sillman, despite his long service, had never taken on an apprentice.

Yvonne could not help wondering what Sillman's apprentice might have been like, and what the apprentice might have learned.

The Hundred were scattered far and wide across the lands. Even on the rare occasions where there was more than one apprentice, it was unlikely they would get to spend much time together. There had been no other apprentices when Yvonne was training, and Idal did not have anyone to speak to, either. Yvonne thought about Suanna's failed attempt to train Dundac. Suanna might not be the warmest of people, and she might not be capable of bearing the full burden of training a new Hunar. But she had valuable lessons to teach, nonetheless.

While Yvonne's mind had been wandering, her senses had been gradually curling out, and now found something to call her attention.

There was a low resonance in the air. Like the deepest note of a horn. Too quiet to be heard over the everyday bustle of the town, or if she had not been listening for it. Now that she had heard it, the sound teased at her extended senses, growing louder.

"Can you hear that?" she asked. "I think it might be what Sillman and the Coll lord heard."

"I don't hear anything out of the ordinary."

"It's like a deep note." She touched her breast bone, feeling the vibration of it through her. "Like the deepest horn has sounded, and it's echoing across a plain."

"I still don't hear it," Guise told her. "Can you track it?"

She focused on the noise for a while, initially completely overwhelmed by it. It was so vast. It seemed to be coming from all around.

And then, as she listened, she realised it was not all the same. It was not language. Not precisely. But there was an odd cadence to it. Not a regular rhythm, or regular beat. Some pattern that she did not know. When she had recognised that there was a system to it, she realised it was coming from a particular direction.

She set off on the way, trusting Guise to follow.

The trail took them through the town, streets deserted apart from the occasional startled cat or dog scavenging for food. The animals fled into the shadows as they approached.

They passed by houses and workshops and barns, and another pair of taverns before the trail took them off the main road, along a side street that led, Yvonne knew, to the largest houses in the town. An area that none of them had searched yet.

It made sense. The Coll lord was used to the finer things from his human life, whatever he might be now. And Sillman had always had a weakness for luxury.

The trail led them to a property surrounded by high walls, a gate as tall as Guise blocking their way.

The house was larger than the one Yvonne was renting, or the annex that Guise was living in. It stretched into the night ahead of them, apparently unoccupied.

Except that the resonance was coming from that house, and the house itself seemed disturbed. With her enhanced senses, the spell still working, Yvonne could see the fragments of the ward spells, crudely broken, and the shadows inside the house.

"This is the place," Guise said. It was a statement, not a question. He lifted a brow at her. "I cannot hear what you can, but there is at least one living thing in that house trying to hide from us. It feels like Sillman." There was a dark undertone to his voice.

"I'd like some answers," she said, voice mild.

"As would I. Shall we go?"

For a moment, Yvonne considered summoning the others. A Hunar and three wulfkin, even with Renard recovering from the poison, would be useful back-up. But two of the wulfkin were her children, and she did not want to put them in any more danger.

Decision made, she nodded to Guise and watched as he took hold of the iron gate and ripped it open. The grating of metal against metal and stone sparked a fresh memory of the dungeon cell. Guise chained to the wall, struggling with the manacles. And her, asking what needed to be done.

The memory was gone with the next breath and she shook herself, following Guise up the path to the house's front door. There was no sneaking in this time.

The front door received similar treatment to the gate, the wood giving way under Guise's boot, letting them into a darkened hallway.

A murmured spell, and Guise sent lights out ahead of them, rising towards the ceiling.

Apart from the dark, the first thing she noticed was the scent of decay. Something had died in this house. The stench of decay almost swamped the other smell. The flat metal taste of blood in the air.

She and Guise had their swords out without speaking, creeping forward. They were moving towards the scent of decay, her nose and mouth coated with it.

Guise opened the first door they came to and a flood of foul odour poured out, making Yvonne's eyes water and her lungs seize. She managed a quick glance around before her streaming eyes forced her back. It was a site of slaughter. Too many bodies in a room that looked like it had been designed for pleasure, with heavy drapes over the windows and soft furniture now hosting the dead.

"Eight bodies," Guise told her a moment later, voice harsh. "They did not die easily. And their blood has been taken."

She trusted his word. His night sight was far better than hers, even when she wasn't blinded by tears.

Guise closed the door again, and tilted his chin further down the corridor.

She tilted her head, listening. Nothing. But she was back to her normal human senses and his hearing was sharper than hers.

She wiped her eyes with her shirt sleeve, ignoring her racing pulse.

As they moved further along the corridor, she heard it too. An irregular sound. Like branches on a windowpane.

The rest of the rooms along the corridor were empty, doors open. They paused at each one, checking inside, before moving on.

The end of the corridor was a closed door. The tapping sound was louder.

Guise opened the door and stepped in, alert but not alarmed, sword ready. Yvonne followed.

They had found the house's kitchen. It was as large, and beautifully crafted, as she would have expected from a house of this stature. There was a giant oven that took up most of one side of the room, and a vast kitchen table around which several cooks would have been able to work without getting in each other's way.

The room was almost empty.

The only occupant was Sillman, sitting at the other side of the kitchen table, a glass in front of him. For the first time that Yvonne could remember, he looked dishevelled. In the single day since he had thrown a concussive spell at her, he looked like he had suffered. His hair was a tangled mess. It looked dirty, and as though he had not combed it for several days. There were dark circles under his eyes, betraying a lack of sleep, and he was paler than she had ever seen him before.

He was staring into the glass on the table as though it held an answer he was seeking, tapping the side of it from time to time, making the small, irregular sounds that they had heard from the corridor. It was an odd sound to carry, and made Yvonne aware of just how quiet the house was.

"There's no one else in the house, is there?" she asked.

She wasn't sure if she was asking Sillman or Guise.

Sillman looked up and, with a small shock, she realised that he had been crying. She did not think she had ever seen him cry. Not even at Elinor's funeral. He had been grieving, like the rest of them, but had held in his tears. Now, though, he looked heartsick and heartbroken.

An odd sympathy rose in her. He looked like the foundation of his world had been stripped away from him, and he was trying to make sense of what he had been left with. She remembered that feeling well. Huddled on the ground outside her house, her shoulder raw and bleeding from where the symbol of the Hundred had been taken from her. And Sillman standing over her, face implacable, backed by Suanna and Mica.

"Who are the dead?" she asked.

"Which ones?" he asked in return, his mouth twisting in the parody of a smile.

"The ones lying in the room along the corridor, with their blood drained," she answered, her voice hardening. He might be broken, but he was still hiding something.

"They were not wanted. Not anymore. Still, they will serve a purpose."

"What purpose could it possibly serve to kill eight people, and drain them of their blood?"

Sillman flinched back from her question, his head turning to one side, and she saw that, as well as the tears, he had also been in a fight. There was a deep cut along one side of his face, a bruise forming around it. It had not been there the day before, she was certain.

It was hard to imagine the usually dignified leader of the Hundred getting into a common brawl, but that was what it looked like.

"And what purpose do you serve?" Guise asked. Yvonne caught an odd note in his voice, as though he had picked up on something she had missed, and the answer Sillman gave was very important. Not just an idle question.

Sillman's mouth pulled down at the corners, his fingers continuing to tap the glass in front of him. "I don't like you," he said, in a conversational tone. It was not his usual manner, and Yvonne's eyes narrowed. He was hiding something.

"I don't like you either," Guise answered easily. "What purpose do you serve?"

Sillman flinched, as though the repetition of the question caused him pain, his head turning again so that she could better see the cut on his face. Next to her, Guise hissed in a breath and, to her surprise, took a step towards her, so that he was between her and Sillman.

"You have been meddling in dangerous matters, human," Guise said, a growl in his voice. "Where is he?"

"I cannot tell you." He sounded defeated, Yvonne realised. As though the single strike to his head, evidenced by the cut on his face, had left a profound impact.

They had all been in fights before. Impossible to be a member of the Hundred and avoid conflict. This was different. Sillman sounded as though he had been utterly destroyed.

"Where is everyone else?" she asked. Eight people killed and drained of blood. She did not believe Sillman had done it, even now. There had been at least one other person here. Possibly more than one.

Sillman's mouth moved and he shook his head. "I cannot tell you."

"Your master has commanded you," Guise said, voice bitter.

"What is it?" she asked Guise. His lips were drawn back in a silent snarl, his fangs descended. A sane or sensible person would have backed away from him. She held her ground.

"He has been poisoned," he said. "There is magic in that cut on his face. Magic he cannot possibly have known about."

Yvonne felt a chill run through her. Guise was worried. It was a rare day, indeed, that he was worried by anything. She tightened her grip on her sword, even though she suspected it would do her no good.

Sillman made a dry sound that she recognised after a moment as a laugh, with no humour in it.

"You sound worried. You should be. You are going to lose." Sillman's face twisted, and his voice cracked. "We are all going to lose. It's too late."

"What are you talking about? Does this have anything to do with the Coll lord? He's just one being."

Sillman made another bitter, harsh sound that was probably supposed to be a laugh. "You don't know. You don't understand. It's too late for all of us."

"I don't accept that," Yvonne told him, voice flat. "Sillman, what have you done? What connection did you make that went so wrong? Why did Elinor need to die?"

His mouth worked, lips trying to form words, although no sound came out. For a moment he reminded her of someone in the grips of the sight, trying to pass on whatever message the sight had for her. But he was awake and aware. Something else was stopping him from speaking.

"Too powerful," he said in the end, words distorted, slurred.

"Who is?" Yvonne asked.

He shook his head, tears rolling down his face. Yvonne had a moment of unexpected sympathy for him, and dismay at the transformation of the once-proud and confident leader of the Hundred to this old, disorientated man in front of her. He was still tapping the glass he held, staring at it. He made a low sound in his throat, like something in pain, and closed his fingers around the glass.

"I killed one of my dearest and oldest friends," he said, voice hoarse. "Too many questions. She would not stop."

"Questions?" Yvonne echoed. "She asked questions all the time." Then she remembered the notebook, with the random scraps of information. Bits and pieces gathered. "What questions in particular?" she asked Sillman.

"Too many," he answered, words forced out. He blinked and more tears fell down his face. "I have served my purpose."

He lifted the glass and swallowed its contents in one go, even as Guise surged forward, trying to knock the glass out of his hand. Before Guise could reach him, Sillman was dead. Present and alive in one moment and utterly gone in the next, his body limp, his eyes sightless, the glass falling to the ground from his limp hand. Yvonne surged forward. It was too late. She could see that it was too late, but she still tried to get to him, blocked by Guise's shoulder and his hand held up in front of her. He did not touch her, but the raised hand was enough to make her stop.

"He is still dangerous," Guise said, his voice grim. "Look at the cut on his face, but do not touch it."

Yvonne took a step forward, careful to stay away from Sillman's body, and looked at the cut. At first, she could not see anything out of the ordinary. It looked like any injury that might happen in a fight. But, from Guise's reaction, she knew that was not the case. She took a moment to speak a spell to enhance her senses, and recoiled at once.

Far from being an ordinary wound, it was crawling with darkness, little black tendrils that were still moving even after Sillman's death.

"What is that?"

For a moment, she thought Guise was not going to answer her, and turned to look at him. He looked much as Sillman had done, before he had swallowed poison. Defeated. As though a core certainty of his life had been taken away.

"It is forbidden magic. Bone magic."

She had a moment of displacement, remembering being in the great hall at the castle and Guise wanting to know something about bone dust.

"Goblin magic," she said, voice tight.

"It is now. And forbidden," he repeated.

Yvonne looked at the wound on Sillman's face again and saw, this time, not only the tendrils of black, but the remnants of other spells as well, worked into his flesh. More forbidden magic, spells that she recognised but had never thought to see in use.

"Someone used the bone magic to control him," she said.

"To make him kill himself. Yes. I believe so. I do not think that Sillman would have taken his own life otherwise. He would have tried to find a way around it."

Yvonne's stomach turned. Bone magic. There were superstitious beliefs about using bones for protection, but this was not superstition. The tendrils of black crawling through Sillman's flesh even after his death were vivid, powerful evidence of magic use.

"Is this the Coll lord's master?" she asked aloud.

"I fear it is," Guise answered.

"He is risen," Yvonne quoted, a shiver running up her spine. The first enemy. The first Hunar's brother. She remembered the vast depth of the mine, and the dark pit at the bottom. All covered by the Firebird. It seemed impossible that anything could have survived that, or could have reached the surface. And yet, the sight had never lied. "How do you combat bone magic?"

Guise was silent too long, and she looked across to find him staring at Sillman's body, his expression bleak.

"It is almost impossible to do," he told her. "Bone magic is the most powerful magic we know of. There has never been a single magician powerful enough to combat it."

"He never answered you. Or me," Yvonne said, her mind turning over too many things at once. How it was that Sillman came to have been infected with bone magic, with only the mark on his cheek to show for it. Who else might have been in the house. Where the blood was. And that Sillman had never given Guise a clear answer.

"That is true." Guise sounded troubled. "He was probably told not to answer questions."

Yvonne shivered again at the thought of a magic so powerful it could compel obedience from one of the Hundred, among the more powerful sorcerers alive.

He had tried, though. She remembered his mouth working, trying to speak. Elinor had asked questions, he had said. Yvonne wondered what questions Elinor could have asked that would have led to Sillman poisoning her. And remembered that Suanna had come to visit Elinor after Sillman. And argued about betrayal.

She looked at the body slumped across the table, the fine robes that Sillman had taken such pride in, the white hair swept back from his face, all the life gone from his body. Her heart ached, remembering the first time she had met him. He had seemed a lot younger then, more carefree, delighted to meet a new apprentice. There were too few of them, he had told her then, something the others had often repeated. Too few Hunar for all the need in the world. Still, he had shared a meal with them, laughing as often as Elinor.

She could not remember when that had changed. When the laughter had faded, and his pride had grown. Somewhere along the way his conversations with Elinor had become more combative. And there were still too few Hunar.

He had been so definite in his opinions, though, certain he was right. She could not imagine how that conviction had led him here, to this empty house and the glass full of poison.

Yvonne's eyes stung. Sillman was dead in front of her, and she had no good answers. Just an idea of where to go to find them.

"We need to search the rest of the house, and then burn it," she said. Guise raised a brow. "I'm assuming burning will deal with any residue from the bone magic?"

"Yes. It should."

It did not take long to establish that the rest of the house was empty. One of the bedrooms showed signs of occupation, with rumpled sheets. But there was no trace of whoever had been there. Yvonne tried to open her senses, to see if she could find a trace that she might be able to follow, and got nothing but a headache for her troubles. Whoever had cleaned the place had done so using magic that interfered with any trail that had been left.

They were coming back down the corridor towards the kitchen again, to destroy the house and Sillman's body, when a cry of alarm sounded in her ears, causing her to stumble and catch her balance with a hand on the wall.

She had her sword out, looking around for the threat a moment later, only to realise that the alarm had not been in the house, but in her mind.

The alarm sounded again. The shriek of the Firebird. In her mind, Yvonne could see her, rising into the air, wings extended, golden eyes blazing with fury.

Next to her, Guise was also armed, eyes searching the shadows.

"We need to go. Something is badly wrong."

Guise did not question her, simply drew a few spells of his own from inside his coat, and set them alight in the kitchen so that by the time they reached the front door, the house was fast catching fire. Left unchecked, it would burn to ashes in a very short space of time.

By the time they reached the street again, Yvonne was running, urgency taking hold of her. There was something badly wrong. Someone that she loved was in danger.

Chapter Twenty-Six

They reached Elinor's house in a fraction of the time it had taken to leave, and found chaos waiting for them.

The house was on fire, reminding Yvonne of the blaze they had just left. The flames had the brilliant blue edge that told her someone had used crude magic to start the fire. Impossible to put out without a great deal of magic, and spells she did not have time to work just now.

Someone had managed to free the horses from the stables and gather some of their belongings, and there were piles of clothing and saddlebags on the other side of the street from the house, out of reach of the flames.

None of the neighbours were out on the street, although Yvonne could see the outlines of faces at various windows around the street, picked out in the light from the flames.

No one wanted to come out into the night.

The Ashnassan were back. In greater numbers than before, intent on killing.

In their midst was the Slayer, apparently healed from his injuries and leading his men. And a few paces back from the Slayer was a now familiar figure, with blackened skin, and blackened teeth, shown as he snarled at his intended targets.

Yvonne's heart was racing so fast she could barely breathe, seeing Mariah and Joel were in their animal forms, wolves with eerie, glowing eyes, long fangs bared in defiance as they faced their attackers, easily darting out of the way of swords thrust in their direction.

She wanted to scream at the Ashnassan, at the Coll lord. Her children were not meant for war. They were not meant for this.

Nearby, Renard had stayed in human form, fighting shoulder to shoulder with Pieris. Both of them expert swordsmen.

Renard was tiring, though, the effects of the poison still strong in him and, even with the spells he had, Pieris was only one man against the onslaught of highly skilled warriors.

The wulfkin and Hunar were already backing up towards the burning building. Not close enough to burn. Not yet. The Ashnassan were showing no mercy, pressing ahead with their attack.

Yvonne did not hesitate, freeing her sword and her long dagger, and attacking the tribesmen from behind where they were trying to kill her children and her friends. The tribesmen, as they had before, looked startled to see her, turning their backs on her children and her friends for a moment. Long enough for them to move away from the house, away from the threat of the fire, and out into the street, Yvonne slicing her way through the Ashnassan to join her children, Guise keeping pace with her.

The tribesmen stepped back, regrouping, moving away from the fire. More than twenty of them, at a quick count. They had brought reinforcements after their recent losses.

Regrouped, they would have moved forward but were interrupted by a low, furious sound from the Coll lord.

"You were supposed to be elsewhere," he said. "We are not prepared. We planned a better welcome for you."

Yvonne glanced at her children, crouched low, hair standing up along their backs, teeth bared, and then across at Renard, breathing hard, and Pieris, face drawn, sword ready.

The Coll lord was not ready for her. Her stomach twisted, guessing his meaning.

Her children, and her friends, were still alive despite the overwhelming force of Ashnassan against them.

Not prepared.

There was no line of corpses to greet her. To make her more vulnerable to attack.

Yvonne thought about Sillman's odd manner, the tapping on the glass, staying seated at the table when they had arrived, evading Guise's questions about his purpose.

Now she knew what his purpose had been. A distraction. Nothing more, nothing less. The leader of the Hundred, who had betrayed his oaths and killed one of his brethren, reduced to nothing more than a distraction before he took his own life.

There was no time to feel anything else, or think anymore.

"Maybe you did not have such control over Sillman as you thought," she said, facing the Coll lord. He was easily provoked, she remembered, and prone to making mistakes when angry. "He did not delay us that much." The lord's lips peeled back in fury, and Yvonne almost recoiled at the stench. Whatever was working through him had tightened its grip on him. She thought there was barely anything left of the original lord. Just enough arrogance to make him careless. Whatever had a hold of him had not changed his basic personality.

"He was disposable. As you are. Nothing more than an irritation. Something to be disposed of."

"I don't believe you," she answered. "All that effort. Gathering the bones. Preparing them. That spell working. A lot of effort for something that is supposed to be disposable."

And all this effort to dispose of her, too, she thought. The burning house behind them. The plan to draw her away, then kill those left in the house. And all for what.

So that they could have their time with Guise, that they had wanted in the castle? It did not fit.

He snarled again, lips peeling back, and in the light of the flames burning Elinor's house, she saw that most of the inside of his mouth was black, too. There was very little of the original lord left.

"Foolish, to play with something you don't understand," Guise said, his voice calm. Yvonne was quite sure he felt anything but calm, but he was wearing one of those masks he was so good at. "He still resisted you. Despite the effort you put in."

The lord's response was a silent snarl. Guise had touched a nerve.

"And this plan has gone wrong, too. My children and my friends have been a better opposition than you were expecting," Yvonne said. "More than twenty warriors and a walking corpse? You thought you could defeat them. And yet, they are all still alive."

The lord roared at them, teeth bared, black veins standing out against his corpse-pale skin, lit by the burning house.

Yvonne recoiled instinctively from the waft of his breath.

"Walking corpse was right," she said, turning her head to one side and coughing. It was not as bad as the skunk oil that the Slayer had used on her before. It was still awful.

"You presume much. Kill them." The last words were spoken in a casual aside to the tribesmen.

The Ashnassan. Who had been motionless. Standing, weapons out, facing their enemy. Waiting. It was out of character. The Slayer was not one to take orders.

She cast her eyes over the tribesmen as they moved forward, readying an attack. She didn't see the pair who had been caught and sent to the law keepers with the Slayer. But then, the Slayer had no problems with killing his own people. She wondered who he had got to do the deed this time, with the deputy already dead. She doubted he had done it himself.

The Slayer was in the middle of the group, apparently fully healed from their last encounter and Guise's sword. Something was different, though. There was a dark mark on one side of his face. The side with no tattoos. It reminded Yvonne of the bone magic set into Sillman's face. Bone magic that had controlled a powerful sorcerer. Even as her skin crawled, she wondered how much more effective the magic might be on a warrior with little, if any, magic of his own.

The rest of the tribesmen just bore their usual tattoos, but they were keeping a distance from their leader, and the ones closest to the Slayer were the more junior warriors, a few with barely any markings on their faces. The senior warriors were as far away from their leader as they could be, some of them perilously close to the burning building. Interesting.

None of them looked eager for the fight ahead, facing her and the others with flat determination on their faces. For a people who lived for fighting, it was strange.

They were also trying to keep their distance from the corrupted lord. Yvonne did not blame them.

"It's quite sad, really," she said to Guise. "I was quite looking forward to a decent fight, with worthwhile opposition. This doesn't seem fair." She saw sideways glances from Joel and Mariah, doubtless wondering if she had hit her head.

"I agree, mristrian," he answered. "They are rather weak. I suppose I could consider this to be practice."

Yvonne bit her lip against an unexpected and inappropriate smile as one of the tribesmen towards the edge of the group, one of the more senior, made a low, enraged sound in his throat.

The Slayer was looking at them with narrowed eyes, expression tight. The predator she had seen before, that had chilled her all the way through, was absent. Instead, he looked ordinary. Just another hired sword. With a bit of forbidden magic on his face.

Her breath caught. A mercenary. That was what he had been reduced to.

"Where is your god now?" she asked him. "Does Nassash protect sell swords?"

There was a ripple of unease through the tribesmen. A superstitious people. They worshipped their gods with the same single-minded determination they used in weapons practice.

"Nassash is always present," the Slayer answered. Except that his voice was flat, words hollow.

"You don't believe that. Nassash has deserted you. Probably because you left the path he had set out for you," she added, prompted by instinct, and the uneasy glances that the senior tribesmen were sending between their leader and the Coll lord, hissing in fury nearby.

"We fight for his honour," the Slayer answered, baring his teeth. It was a good show. Yet there was no heart in it. None of the fanatical belief from their first meeting.

"And for wealth to celebrate him," she prompted. "Don't forget that. All those golden crowns." She tilted her head, eyes travelling between the Slayer and the Coll lord. "Or did he forget to pay you?"

"Difficult to pay his sell swords when his money is under guard," Guise added, in the manner of someone trying to be helpful. The lock box hidden in Coll

Castle, under watch from people loyal to Guise. The lord had not been back to collect its contents since Yvonne, Guise and the Hundred had been there.

"That's true," Yvonne said, as if she had only just realised that. "And experienced warriors like the Ashnassan will expect a premium payment."

"What is being paid is irrelevant," the Coll lord said, voice rasping. "You have a job. Kill them."

Yvonne exchanged glances with Guise. Confirmation. As if they had needed it. The Coll lord had hired the Ashnassan.

"So, you like little girls?" she asked the Coll lord.

To her surprise, he laughed, a dry sound that grated in her ears.

"You think you're clever. Silly witch." He laughed again.

Yvonne lifted a brow. Petty insults seemed out of character. He was deflecting.

And the flames were getting higher, Elinor's house burning while she traded insults with creatures who would have killed her children and friends.

"What does your master want with young girls?" Guise asked, taking a step forward. Perhaps he was getting warm, too. Or perhaps he was single-handedly trying to intimidate the Ashnassan. He had killed a number of them already.

She took a step forward to stay shoulder to shoulder with him, conscious of her children, Pieris and Renard moving with them. A show of strength. Six of them against over twenty tribesmen and a mad, corrupted human lord. If they had all been trained fighters and in good health, it would have been enough. But Mariah and Joel were not warriors. And Renard was struggling. Still not free of the poison. She could hear his harsh breathing even over the crackle of the fire behind them.

"I have no master," the Coll lord answered, mouth twisting in a grimace that might have been intended to be a sneer.

"You're lying. You said they promised you a long life. They lied. You're dying," Yvonne told him. "So, what does your master want with young girls?"

"Get on with it!" The Coll lord lost his temper, shrieking at the tribesmen. "You're being paid to fight."

"There's been no payment for a while," the Slayer contradicted, turning his attention from Yvonne and Guise to the Coll lord. His face twisted, as if the mark was hurting him. "We don't work for free."

"Mercenary cowards," the Coll lord growled, voice lower than it should have been. He bared his blackened teeth. "Fight and be paid. Do not fight and die."

"We've lost some of our finest warriors working for this creature?" one of the senior tribesmen said, from the opposite end of the line to the Coll lord. "It's not even human."

"You will do as I say."

Strong words. Except that they came from the Coll lord. And not from the Slayer, who was watching the Coll lord with narrowed eyes. Yvonne could see the predator shifting under his skin, coming to the surface again. Whatever had been done to him, with that bit of unclean magic in his skin, it was not strong enough. The Slayer was used to being the absolute ruler of his people.

"No one orders the Ashnassan but me," the Slayer said, voice soft and lethal. "And you've been lying. Nassash has not spoken to you. We will not follow you anymore."

He straightened from a fighting stance, face flat, and put his sword away, tilting his chin to Yvonne for a moment.

"I can kill you another time."

"You can try," she answered.

"You are not being paid to run," the lord said, his voice dark and laced with some other power that made Yvonne's skin crawl again.

"There's no honour in this," the Slayer answered, lip curling. "And we fight for the glory of Nassash. Always."

"You'll find it hard to move away," the lord said, voice hissing in threat.

"This?" the Slayer waved a hand at his cheek. "I will cut it out myself. Pathetic foreign magic. Nassash is with me." And there was the belief she had heard before. The absolute faith in his god. Shoulders square, back straight, he was back to the leader she had first met.

And his men saw the difference.

Following their leader's cue, the rest of the tribe began putting their weapons away, taking steps back from the conflict.

As the tribesmen turned to go, the Slayer the last to turn, the lord made another sound of rage and spoke a few phrases in a language that he should not know.

Before Yvonne could do more than utter an inarticulate sound of protest, the spell he had spoken had been released. A death curse. The most powerful one she had ever seen. It rolled out from the lord's blackened tongue, across the short distance to the tribesmen, a snake of dark in the night, picking the tribesmen out one by one.

One by one, the Ashnassan warriors screamed as the curse bit into them, bodies twisting in agony as the magic ran over them, working its way up their bodies until it slipped into their open mouths. One by one, they dropped to the ground, sightless eyes staring up at the sky.

Even the Slayer, who stood straight and tall among his men, sword lifted as though he would cut the death curse down as it trailed towards him. Even him. The fiercest warrior among the Ashnassan. The strongest in his belief in their gods. The dark snake of the death curse slid around his sword, up his arm, despite him trying to move away, and formed a noose around his neck before sliding into his open mouth, cutting off his cry of defiance before it had been uttered.

Yvonne watched, unable to do anything, feet rooted to the spot, as the death curse bit into the Slayer, as his body arched in agony as the unclean magic took hold, a raw cry of grief and hurt and anger coming from his throat before he, too, fell.

She heard the dull thud as the Slayer's body hit the ground, the clatter of his sword falling, too, one of the last of the Ashnassan to fall.

All that anger. All that greed. All that ambition. All that belief. All that cruelty. Gone. In moments. Cut off by unclean magic from an undead lord.

She could feel no grief at the Slayer's death. All the harm he had done in his life. All those girls, taken for money. The women stolen to be brides. His own men, dead by his orders.

And all so that he could die, here, on the street outside Elinor's house.

As the last of the Ashnassan fell, the death curse faded away, its purpose complete.

It seemed to take forever, and yet it happened so quickly Yvonne had no time to get a counter-spell from her pouch.

"No one betrays me," the lord said, surveying the bodies. He reached into a pocket and produced a pouch, spilling some fine powder out into his hand, speaking words that Yvonne did not know and did not understand.

Guise did, though. He hissed in a breath.

"Bone magic," he said. "We need to stop him."

"I'd be delighted," Yvonne said, voice tart. "Suggestions?"

The lord had finished his spell by then, and walked among the dead, scattering the bone dust over the corpses. One by one, the Ashnassan dead twitched, limbs quivering as the spell worked on them. Even the Slayer, his face slack in death, fingers closing around his sword.

Yvonne did not wait for Guise's suggestion, pulling a fire spell out of her pouch and throwing it across the distance to the Coll lord. He batted the fire aside with a sweep of his hand. The fire landed on one of the corpses, catching it alight. Even as the corpse burned, it was sitting up, obeying whatever spell the lord had used.

"He should not be able to do that," Guise said, voice grim. He was rummaging in a pocket for a spell of his own. "I don't have anything to counter this."

Bone magic. Forbidden and powerful.

The Coll lord turned back to them, baring his rotting teeth in a grin. Around him, the Ashnassan dead were getting to their feet and drawing their swords, their movements jerky and uncoordinated. Whatever dark magic the lord had used to animate the dead, it did not give them weapons skills.

"I will enjoy watching you die," he said in a conversational tone.

"Do you think he's talking to you or me?" Yvonne asked, scrabbling in her pouch for one of the counter-spells she had. It might not work. But she had nothing else to try.

"Could be either," Guise said. He was standing straight beside her, vial held in one hand. "Ready?"

"Ready." She had her counter-spell to hand.

They threw their spells together, catching the nearest of the corpses. The corpses twitched, limbs disoriented, collapsing to the ground. Not fully dead. Just incapacitated for a moment.

Until the Coll lord growled another spell, the tone of which made Yvonne's skin crawl. The bodies gathered their limbs and stood up, swords out, sightless eyes turning towards her.

She had her own sword out. She did not remember drawing it. She held her ground, watching the corpses walk towards her, lit on one side by the fire, cast into pitch shadow on the other. The fire was billowing smoke, too, and it stung her eyes.

"Counter-spells slow them down," she said, her voice calm. "Do you have any more?" she asked Guise, standing beside her.

"Two."

"Pieris," Yvonne said over her shoulder, "do you have any counter-spells ready?"

He didn't answer, and she turned, concerned, to see him staring at her, arrested expression on his face. He was holding his sword in one hand, other hand resting just above his belt.

"Are you all right?" she asked.

"No." He moved his hand, and only then did she realise that he had been covering a wound in his abdomen. "I'm not going to be much use in this fight."

"Counter-spells?" she asked again. He might not be able to fight, but they could still use any counter-spells he had.

"Something better," he said. "You don't feel it?"

"Feel what?" she asked, distracted. The lord was standing behind his undead army now, a smile on his face that set her teeth on edge. He thought he had won. More than twenty Ashnassan corpses. Against her small band.

Joel and Mariah were growling to one side of her. She glanced down and saw them both huddled close to the ground, eyes fixed on their enemies ahead. Her heart swelled. Her children. Terrified, but facing their enemy.

"Don't bite them," she said, panic rising in her. "They might be poisonous."

Joel looked up at her, teeth bared, fire catching the power in his eyes. For an awful moment, that seemed to stretch, she thought he had not understood her, that the predator had taken hold. Then he snapped at the air and moved backwards, still facing his enemy, nipping Mariah on her flank when she did not move with him.

"Pieris?" she prompted, trying to remember if he had any other wounds. They were facing overwhelming numbers, and he was focused on her, not their enemy.

"You're surrounded by power," he told her.

She turned to him, frowning.

"I have magic of my own," she told him. "Sillman seemed surprised, too."

"Not like this," he said. He was pale even in the firelight, and she could see blood seeping through his fingers where they were pressed against his side.

Her stomach churned. He would not be able to fight.

Mariah and Joel, back in human form, came to stand either side of Pieris. They had bows and arrows ready, swords by their sides.

"Use fire," she told them. Even the undead would burn. She hoped.

"We are overwhelmed," Pieris said, voice fading. He was leaning to one side, the symbol at his shoulder barely visible.

"I know," she answered. "You should stay back." He might not be able to fight, but he could still throw a spell or two.

"We are overwhelmed," he said again, still in that faint voice, sounding at the end of his strength. "Hunar, help me."

Yvonne opened her mouth to ask how hard he had hit his head, thinking that he was going to get the aid of the Hundred, when he was the only Hunar in reach.

Before she could speak, an invisible force slammed into her, knocking her to her knees, a wind rising around her, catching the wisps of hair that had come loose around her face, tugging the scarf at her neck. As she fought the wind, trying to stand, a familiar magic poured over her. The magic of the Hundred. It coursed through her, focused on the spot at her shoulder where the symbol had sat, the strength of it sending her back to her knees, gasping for breath.

Blinding and perfect and familiar and impossible.

She glanced down at her shoulder and saw the Firebird's symbol across her shoulder, blazing with the vivid green of an emerald's heart. "I don't understand."

"The Firebird. She had never appeared before. Not in my life. And I saw her all around you at the mine. And now. We don't get to decide who is Hunar, and who is not," Pieris said softly, eyes bright. He was gasping for breath, the symbol at his shoulder faint. "The magic decides who is worthy. And the magic decided a very long time ago that you were Hunar, and you are worthy of it. Now, you need to defend us and send these unnatural things to their graves once and for all."

Yvonne couldn't think of a good reply to Pieris, turning instead towards the walking corpses and the corrupted lord, who was glaring at her. Yet again, she was not behaving according to his plans. Every time something happened to spoil his plans, he grew more furious.

She found she was smiling. There might be corpses animated by bone magic shuffling towards her, and a creature with corruption riddled through him behind them.

Minor concerns.

She was whole again. The symbol at her shoulder. The familiar power of the Hundred running through her. The Firebird's shriek in her ears familiar and welcome.

Light and life and love and laughter poured through her. Whole. Every part of her complete. The magic and the power of the Hundred. The fury and heat of the Firebird. All within her. All there for her use. The Firebird, the bringer of justice. And the Hunar. Servant. There to give aid where it was needed. All in one.

The lord threw a death curse at them. She deflected it with a spark of lightning from her fingers. She was bubbling over with power. The extraordinary power of the Hundred. Sparked by Pieris' plea.

The power was in her veins. It was in her breath. It was coursing over her skin in a static charge, raising hairs all over her body and filling her up. It was the most glorious thing. It was there, ready and waiting to be used. Enough power to level the entire army before her.

She did not move. She had not forgotten her oaths. The Hundred did not simply kill or destroy. Their business was justice, not slaughter.

She spoke instead.

"I will give you a chance. If you leave. If you let these warriors die. If you go from here immediately. If you promise never to return, never to harm another living being, you may live. You may go, and I will not stop you and nobody else will either."

The lord flung back his head and laughed, the blackened veins on his skin rippling.

"Is that your best offer? Little witch. You cannot stop me. You will die. And everyone else will die. And there will be nothing to stop me."

The army shuffled forward more quickly at his command.

Yvonne raised a hand and the power of the Hundred surged through her, lightning dancing out of her fingers, finding the bits of bone dust and the forbidden magic the lord had used, setting the corpses alight and cleansing the dark magic with fire.

The lord screamed as the corpses fell, one by one, bodies becoming lifeless again. The lightning could not remove the death curse. The Ashnassan were still dead.

The Firebird's wings beat once in Yvonne's ears, the soft displacement of air all she could hear as the Coll lord surged forward, hands raised, lips moving in another spell. Another death curse, perhaps. She did not wait to find out.

The Firebird shrieked in her mind. Deafening. She had so much power in her. More than she had ever had before. Just waiting to be used. She lifted a hand again. More lightning spat out, spinning across the distance between her and the lord, cascading over him. He screamed in disbelief, and in agony, as the power of the Hundred bit into him, body twisting and writhing, expression changing from one of arrogance to one of disbelief and horror.

The Coll lord burned. All the blackened blood in his veins. All the corruption that had riddled through him. The clawed hands. All caught fire.

The bone magic he had worked could not save him.

Whatever promises had been given to him, could not save him.

Everything surrendered to the Firebird's power, Yvonne trembling with the after-effect of holding so much inside her.

The lord seemed to burn forever, and yet the fire died quickly, reducing the lord's body to ash. Not even bones left. Just a pile of black ash, which stirred in the heat of Elinor's house burning behind them.

The remnants of the lord scattered even as she watched, flaking to tiny pieces, floating into the air. There was no corruption anymore.

Nothing left. Every rotten part of him reduced to ash. All that venom and bitterness, gone. All the ambition, gone. The gleeful use of unclean magic, gone.

The air felt fresher around her, the world whole again.

And in her mind, she could hear and feel the Firebird. The wordless shriek of triumph. The beat of her wings as she rose, faded away. Task completed.

Yvonne turned away from the reducing pile of the Coll lord's ashes just in time to see the roof of Elinor's house collapse, unable to stand any more with the intense pressure of the fire. The spell that had started the fire was still at work, confined to the building. She had no energy left to combat it. Nothing to stop Elinor's house burning.

The road all around was littered with the dead. The Ashnassan, whose leader had made a poor bargain for them. Dead by forbidden magic, betrayed by their paymaster. She could not help wondering how Nassash might view that. The Slayer, who had taken payment to kidnap children. The warriors who had followed him willingly. The warriors who had followed him through fear. None of them had been innocent.

And still, her heart ached. So much death.

Her eyes were gritty with smoke and with unshed tears.

The lord of Coll Castle was dead. Finally.

And in a house not that far away, also burning, Sillman was dead. Elinor's killer.

It was justice.

But the price had been high.

The Hundred could not be the same. Not ever. Not when one of their number had killed another, betraying their oaths.

It hurt too much to think of that, of what might be.

She glanced behind her at the ashes still scattering in the breeze. Her mind was trying to tell her that she had missed something.

But the lord was still dead. As were the Ashnassan. There was no threat there.

Relief made her legs shake, her eyes fill up. The danger was past.

A rush of movement behind her drew her attention away. She turned, alarmed, to find Mariah and Joel coming towards her at a run. For the first time in over a decade, they did not wait for permission, but simply threw their arms around her and drew her into a hug. She braced herself, breath catching in her throat.

And the panic did not come.

There was just the familiar weight and warmth of her children. The scent of wulfkin. The straight blond hair that was Joel's. The curly dark hair that was Mariah's.

She hugged them back, as tightly as she could, patted Joel's shoulder, stroked Mariah's hair, and ignored their damp cheeks as they were ignoring hers.

Over their heads, she could see Renard and Guise crouched over Pieris, Renard holding a cloth to Pieris' side. Renard looked haggard, lifting his face for a moment to look at the burning building, tears coursing down his cheeks. The last little bits Elinor had left in the world were burning before their eyes.

Yvonne hugged her children closer again, closing her own eyes for a moment before they turned, in mutual and silent agreement, and looked at the burning building. It had been a resting place for all of them, for a long time, and it was soon to be completely gone. Like Elinor.

The Coll lord might be dead, but the price was high.

Chapter Twenty-Seven

She asked her children to stay with Pieris and set herself the grim task of inspecting the dead, just to be sure they were all gone and none could be saved.

When she had finished that, she found that Renard had been collecting the horses and Guise had been organising accommodation for them and a litter for Pieris, so that the entire group moved to the most luxurious and expensive tavern in Willowton. Yvonne did not know why she was surprised. Guise had organised it, after all.

The stable hands seemed overwhelmed to be receiving horses into their care from Renard and, from the critical eye Renard cast over their work, Yvonne was quite sure that the horses would have the best possible care.

Yvonne used the last of her healing spells on Pieris, and saw his face ease into normal sleep, leaving him to rest.

By then it was early morning. Her eyes were gritty from lack of sleep, a leaden weight in her chest again as she thought about the smouldering ruin that had been Elinor's house. She did not want to go back, but knew she would have to. She owed that much, and more, to Elinor, to inspect the remnants of her home. See if it could be rebuilt. See what could be rescued.

After a long and thorough bath in one of the tavern's splendid private bathing rooms, and a dose of cleansing spell across her clothes, she was feeling a little better. The day was approaching noon. Too early for bed. But none of them had eaten yet.

Guise and Renard were nowhere to be found. Pieris was resting in his room.

She found one of the tavern's staff and sent an order to the kitchens that should keep them busy for a while, including a tray for Pieris, then went to find her children.

Guise had secured a private sitting room for them upstairs, with a view over the street, and she found Mariah and Joel in a window seat that looked out onto the street below. Mariah was engaged in one of her favourite pastimes, critiquing the outfits she could see, Joel making the occasional noise that might have been agreement, or amusement.

"Kalla," Joel said, spotting her. He rose to his feet and came across the room. "You are Hunar again."

"I am."

She came into the room, closing the door behind her, not wanting a casual audience, then settled in a chair near the window, not sure where to begin.

"Sillman is definitely dead?" Mariah asked.

"Yes. Quite definitely dead."

"What was that thing last night?" Joel wanted to know, teeth bared for a moment. He was a powerful wulf. One day he would rival Renard, and possibly also Sephenamin. And powerful wulfkin liked to know their enemies.

"That was the lord of Coll Castle. Something had a hold of him, though."

"He smelled dead," Mariah commented, not looking away from the window. She swallowed, imperfectly hiding her fear. Mariah was not a fighter. She preferred a needle and thread, and conversation, to sword play.

"I think he was dying already," Yvonne confirmed. "I'm not sure what happened to him," she added, before Joel could ask. She had a single guess, which she thought was right, but she also had a lifetime of protecting her children behind her, and a habit of not telling them everything which was hard to break.

"Do people try to kill you a lot, Kalla?" Mariah asked, her voice brittle.

"Quite often," Yvonne answered easily, keeping her voice calm. She moved to sit next to Mariah on the window seat, and touched her arm. "But I am still here."

"I didn't realise," Mariah said, turning to face her, a tear rolling down her face. "I know you never tell us everything. But I didn't realise. Not really."

"I don't want to worry you," Yvonne said gently. "And I've never faced anything like the Coll lord before."

"I'm glad he's dead," Joel put in, coming to sit at her other side. "But I am sorry that Elinor's house is gone."

Yvonne agreed, and touched both their hands.

"It's hard. I miss her every day. But, I have something to tell you."

Distracted from her fears, Mariah looked at her with bright, enquiring eyes. Joel lifted his brows, waiting, not so easily distracted.

"Elinor left her wealth to me," Yvonne said, the words sounding strange to her ears. "Something for Adira, and Renard, but the rest to me."

"So, the house was yours?" Joel asked. Trust him to reach that fact sooner than she had.

"Yes."

"I'm sorry, Kalla," Mariah said, her face and voice sad. "It was a lovely house."

"Will you rebuild?" Joel asked.

"No," Yvonne said, shaking her head, the definite answer out of her mouth before she realised that she had already made the decision. "That was Elinor's home. And rebuilding it would not be the same. I might sell it," she added, speculation in her tone. "We could buy the house at Fir Tree Crossing. Or another one, if you like."

"Can we afford it?" Joel asked bluntly.

They had grown up with very little, as there was often very little to be had. Barely enough to keep them clothed and fed, a lot of the time, and they all had memories of one particularly hard winter when they had needed to hunt and forage for food to keep them going.

"Yes," Yvonne told them. "I saw Elinor's lawyer the other day. She had a lot of money. She was a clever woman."

"She was," Mariah agreed, straightening, focus sharpening. "Elinor was wealthy? I mean, we knew she was not poor. But, wealthy?"

"Probably not by Guise's standards," Yvonne said, a laugh catching in her throat, "but by our standards, yes. Enough for a house. Enough that none of us need to work. And I can have some very fine wine." Another laugh escaped as she imagined travelling the lands with a selection of wine bottles in a specially made case, with wine glasses too, as Guise apparently did.

Both her children were staring at her, wide-eyed and startled, when the door opened and Renard came into the room. He was looking better, Yvonne saw, even after the long and awful night. The antidote was working.

"Renard, we're rich," Mariah proclaimed, dancing across the room to him, taking his hands and spinning him around. "Properly rich."

Renard spun Mariah a few more times, an indulgent smile on his face that faded to sadness as he let her go and turned to Yvonne.

"You found Elinor's will," he said.

"I spoke to her lawyer, yes," Yvonne answered, her chest constricting again. "I would give it all to have her back," she added.

"I know. She loved you. All of you," he said, eyes travelling around the room. "She would be delighted to know that her legacy will make a difference to you all. Although," he added, mischief crossing his face, "I do believe the legacy was for Yvonne."

Yvonne smiled back, constriction loosening, and shook her head slightly. Few people got to see this side of Renard, this quiet mischief.

"If that's true, you'd best mind your manners, little sister, in case Kalla decides not to give us any," Joel teased.

Mariah was staring at Yvonne with an arrested expression, face pinched for a moment, brows together as she thought, hard. Her face melted into a smile.

"Of course Kalla will share. Won't you?" Mariah said, sidling up to Yvonne and resting her head on her shoulder.

"Mariah, you know that doesn't work with me. Does it work with anyone?"

"Not so far." Mariah sighed, shaking her head, then brightening. "But perhaps I just need some more practice."

Before Yvonne could react, stomach twisting at the thought of just how much trouble a flirtatious, wheedling young wulfkin could get into, she met Joel's eyes across Mariah's head. He rolled his eyes. Aware of the dangers his sister was courting. And not worried by them.

"The range are careful," he told her over Mariah's head.

The range. That meant Sephenamin and the other wulfkin at Fir Tree Crossing. Yvonne felt her shoulders relax, stomach easing. The range were used to dealing with precocious youngsters.

"I was going to go look at the house," Renard said, changing the subject, the humour in his eyes fading. "See if there's anything else we can salvage. Do you want to come?"

No, was the honest answer. But she knew it was the right thing to do.

"After lunch," she said instead. And, as if on cue, there was a knock at the door and a half dozen of the tavern's servants entered the room bearing enough food for a small army. Or, she hoped, three hungry wulfkin and one Hunar. Pieris was still sleeping. There might also be enough to feed a goblin lord, if Guise turned up for lunch.

The house was still smouldering when they returned. Most of the roof was gone, slates scattered into the street, a few still supported by the charred remains of roof beams. There were bits and pieces of the walls left, darkened with soot, tangled with the remains of the upper floor. And here and there a spot of brightness. Part of a wall covering, or rug, that had somehow managed to survive. Testament to Elinor's preservation spells.

The fire was out, though, the ruins cool enough to walk through.

Yvonne let Mariah, Joel and Renard go ahead of her into the remains of the house, standing back a moment to consider the structure, and the extent of the grounds around it. The front door might open straight onto the street, but there was land to either side, and a large swathe behind.

"What will you do with it?" Guise asked.

He had arrived as the table was being set for lunch, with no explanation as to where he had been. Yvonne shook her head slightly at the thought. He did not owe her any explanation. And when he had learned that they would be visiting the house, to see what might be rescued, he had simply come with them.

After they had eaten every scrap of food the tavern kitchens had provided, she had gone to check on Pieris, taking a tray with her. He was alert enough to wake up briefly when Yvonne had checked on him, eyed the food she had brought without much interest. Despite the healing he'd received, he still looked worn. And heartsick. Yvonne understood. It was one thing to speculate that one of the Hundred had been involved in Elinor's death. Quite another to have it confirmed, and lose another one of their number. She had left him to rest.

"Sell it, probably," she answered Guise, dragging her attention back to the here and now. "I don't think the house can be saved. And rebuilding would feel wrong. It's not Elinor's house now."

She made herself look again. At the charred remains of the house. The stables, which might be repaired. And the swathe of green. Elinor's garden. Much of it practical, for herbs and vegetables and fruit. And some of it just because. Because flowers were beautiful. Because she had wanted somewhere lovely and peaceful to sit after a particularly difficult task. Because she had loved that plant's particular scent, or another plant's shape of leaf. Yvonne's chest ached again. Elinor would never walk the paths again, and the garden had grown neglected and wild in her absence.

Elinor had often grown too much for her own use, freely sharing with her neighbours.

Yvonne looked around the site, and the houses nearby. Mostly smaller, with smaller bits of land, if any. And Elinor had always opened her house to her neighbours.

"It could be a garden," she speculated aloud, looking around the plot with new eyes. It already produced a variety of herbs, vegetables, and fruit. If the house was taken away, there would be room for some fruit trees, and more vegetables. "For the neighbours."

"Elinor would have loved that," Renard said, appearing next to her. He had a pile of books in his hands that looked familiar. "Her recipe books. They were in the cold safe in the pantry. Only slightly singed. She would want you to have them."

Chapter Twenty-Eight

Working through the remains of Elinor's house had been just as sad as Yvonne had thought it would be. There was precious little left of her mentor, and no trace of her vibrant personality in the blackened and charred timbers or soot-covered stones. Very little could be recovered, although Yvonne was pleased to find the box of correspondence she had put into the kitchen had remained mostly intact, the preservation spells in the box keeping the letters safe even if the box itself was ruined. Adira and Renard could have their letters to Elinor back, at least.

They carried away what they could in one trip, not even needing a cart. There was still some light left in the day, and Yvonne decided she could not be still, setting out again for the law offices. Some work would be needed to take down the remains of the house, and to transfer the title of the land to the neighbours.

Elinor's lawyer, or her lawyer now, she supposed, was apparently delighted to see her. He seemed highly resourceful, listening intently when she set out her plans, promising to deal with the necessary arrangements as swiftly as possible.

It was a bittersweet meeting. Renard was right. Elinor would have loved the idea of her neighbours having the land. And Yvonne did not want it. She had a head full of memories of her mentor.

Still, it was a difficult discussion, settling matters that she would rather not have to deal with, conscious that there were other difficult things she needed to do. She was feeling restless as she left the lawyer. Although they had not made any arrangement, she was somehow not surprised to find Guise waiting for her in the great hall. He was standing in his own pool of quiet, receiving sideways glances from a number of the other people present. It was rare to see a goblin lord in a building dedicated to human laws. The Karoan'shae had their own way of doing things.

Her heart lightened as she walked towards him. He was perfectly aware of the glances he was getting, and was putting on a performance for the watchers, although they might not guess it. Standing straight, hands tucked behind his back, apparently fascinated by his surroundings.

When she reached him, he suggested a walk. A perfectly plain and ordinary suggestion. And nothing like the sorts of things they normally did. Investigating crimes. Chasing tribesmen. Rescuing slaves. She almost asked him if he was feeling well, but plain, ordinary movement suited her, so she fell in beside him as he chose their path.

They ended up walking through a large expanse of trees and carefully planted shrubs that crossed the heart of the town. A place for townsfolk to rest, it was often filled with children playing, couples walking, people crossing from one side to the other to get to their business or appointments.

Today it was mostly deserted, giving them some privacy to talk, away from the tavern and the curious eyes and ears not only of her children but also Renard and Pieris.

She felt strangely out of balance. Wealthier than she had ever been. Her children's futures secured. It was a significant worry lifted. She should have been content. And yet, her feet did not want to stay still, her mind turning in different directions. This bond, whatever it might be, was troubling her. She had the sensation of being at the edge of something, not knowing if she wanted to step forward onto unfamiliar territory, or stay where she was, where things were different but still familiar.

Guise was keeping pace with her with easy strides. Despite the peace in the air around them, she knew that he, like her, would have part of his attention on their surroundings, watching for threats.

"You said nothing needs to change," she said abruptly, unable to look at him. She sensed his full attention coming back to her.

"That is so," he agreed.

"But that is not what you want." Her face was burning, stomach twisting with nerves as if she was facing her first real fight, not knowing if she might survive.

Unlike that fight, she did not have any training to support her through this. Just instinct and a reluctance to leave the matter alone. She and her children would be heading home soon, probably the next day, and she wanted some kind of understanding, if not a resolution.

He sent out a breath in a near-silent sigh that she might have missed if she hadn't been paying such close attention.

"What I want is not the issue," he said at length. He did not sound entirely like himself. The smooth voice was restricted, as if he were holding something in.

"I ..." And now it was her turn to blow out a breath, frustration and unease mixing together. She wasn't sure what she wanted. But she did not think things could stay the same.

"I know," he answered.

She looked round, startled, and only then realised that she had spoken aloud. There was a small smile on his mouth, a joke of some kind at his own expense, and the gold was back in his eyes. He had his hands behind his back, keeping a respectable distance between them as they walked.

"I don't ... I never thought ... I mean ..." She ducked her head away, heat in her face again. She could not remember the last time she had been so awkward. She waved a hand in a useless gesture. "I was not looking for anything."

"I know," he said again, still with that wry tone. "And I would have waited. Have waited."

"For what?" she asked, curiosity overcoming her embarrassment. She stopped walking, turned to face him and looked up to see what was in his face. He had a thoughtful expression, considering her question.

"I'm not sure," he said, perhaps the most honest he had ever been. "You have never sought attention from anyone," he went on. "And perhaps I was waiting for that to change."

"And instead, here we are. With this bond." And with her entire being revolting at the idea of seeking attention from anyone else.

Her chin lifted, eyes staring into middle distance.

Anyone else.

The day fell away and she was back in the dungeon cell, with Guise chained to the wall, her heart thudding, face bruised and bloody, her head a mass of agony and the words that he had given her to say ringing through her mind. She had barely been conscious, then. Now, she remembered the words, and they rang through her entire being.

"I didn't know what it meant," she heard her voice saying. "I just wanted out of the cell."

"You've remembered," he said, voice flat. "I apologise for my lack of self-control."

"Hadn't you been poisoned?" she asked, using a dry tone that she had heard from him more than once. She focused on his face, and saw that wry smile was back, along with a touch of colour. It was a rare day indeed that a member of the Karoan'shae blushed.

"That is so," he agreed. "It is long past," he assured her, "and I would not harm you."

"I know. And we're not in a dungeon cell now," she added.

He went still. Utterly motionless, only his eyes alive, the vivid green twined through with gold.

"That is so," he agreed, voice low, as if he did not want to startle her.

"And we have agreed that things cannot remain as they are."

"Indeed."

The heat was back in her face again, and she could not quite meet his eyes. "I don't know what I want. I ..." She waved her hand in another useless gesture. "I don't know anything about ..." She broke off, face burning.

"There is time. As much time as you might require. Among the Karoan'shae, some courtships move slowly. It can take several years."

"Years?" She blinked, startled. And realised that he had anticipated one of her fears. It had not been that long since they were in the dungeon, exchanging the words of a goblin bond while a madman plotted her death and Guise's torture.

Maisre. That was the name. A maisre bond.

A lifetime bond. A commitment made without reserve or hesitation by Guise. And in desperation by her. Not the best of starts.

And he had been trying to tell her, in his words, in his actions, that there was no rush. And she had not understood that. Until now.

"Thort and Brea's courtship lasted nearly a decade," he told her, mouth curving in remembrance. "She was not impressed with him when they first met."

Yvonne felt a tentative smile on her face. She could well imagine Brea looking down her nose at Thort. Somewhere in that decade, though, things had changed.

"Courtship," she said, testing the word. It sounded archaic. "I am no fine lady to be courted," she said. It was true. She might be well dressed just now, but that was thanks to his gifts, and she was still armed, hair back in its usual plain style.

"You are much more than that, mristrian," he told her, voice shading to a warmth that made her heart skip again. "A remarkable and beautiful woman."

Heat scorched her face, rising up to her hairline, and she could not look at him. He had called her beautiful before, in much the same manner. Stating a basic fact. No one else had ever thought so, or said so.

She trusted his judgement on many things. Not on this. She opened her mouth to argue, then shook her head. They were tied together.

Perhaps she should see this as another gift. Like the time to consider what she wanted.

A tightness in her chest released and she could breathe more easily, until a disturbing thought occurred to her.

"Please tell me there's no poetry involved?" she asked, nose wrinkling in distaste.

Guise laughed. It was a splendid laugh. Rich and warm, full of something that she still did not want to name. It drew a better smile to her mouth, and lightened something inside her.

He held out his hand and she put hers into it without hesitation, not knowing what he might do. Or not do.

"No poetry," he promised her, eyes dancing with amusement. He lifted her hand to his mouth and kissed the back of it.

Her whole body stilled, a shock coursing through her. Like static, only with more warmth.

Before she could pull away, not sure what to do with the sensations and feelings working through her, he let go of her hand and made a small bow.

"I cannot promise no wine, though," he said, apparently quite serious apart from the laughter still in his eyes. Green and gold danced together. It was a fascinating mix, and distracted her from the tingling sensation at the back of her hand.

"I like wine," she answered.

"But not poetry," he returned, smile curving his mouth. "Or beer."

"Ugh. No."

"Perhaps you should tell me some other things you dislike?" he suggested, his tone light. He waved a hand, a silent invitation to continue walking, and she fell into step beside him, shaking her head.

"I am not going to bargain with you," she told him, the words familiar and easy off her tongue.

"A challenge," he answered, sounding like he relished the prospect. "Very well."

She almost stumbled in her stride, wondering for a moment just what she had done and what she had set in motion. Another step, another breath, and she remembered that this was Guise. Who would never hurt her. And who she trusted with her life.

"Does goblin courtship consist mostly of bribery, then?" she asked, voice light.

He laughed, another rich sound full of warmth that curled through her.

"We are a people who love a bargain," he admitted, voice still carrying amusement. "But you will not bargain with me. So, I shall have to find another way."

For perhaps the first time in their dealings, Yvonne could not think of a single thing to say to answer him.

Chapter Twenty-Nine

After the day of dealing with Elinor's house, the lawyer and her awkward conversation with Guise, Yvonne was surprised to sleep at all. But sleep she did, later than she had planned, arriving at the breakfast table the next day to find everyone there, including Pieris, who was slightly pale. Healing took a great deal of energy. Despite everyone's presence, no one seemed relaxed.

"What's wrong?"

"There's a message for you," Joel said, tension in his voice. He tilted his head to a small table next to the door.

The table was a beautifully made bit of furniture, but that was not what had disturbed Joel. On the table surface was a roll of parchment, sealed with wax and tied with an ornate ribbon that she was sure Mariah would want to have for her collection.

Yvonne moved across to the table and caught the faintest scent as she did so. Not human. Only goblins used that scent. She looked across the room and saw that Guise was holding himself quite still, and would not meet her eyes. That was never a good sign.

She picked up the parchment, feeling the weight of the paper in her hand. She had seen a few official messages from kings before, and this had all the weight of one of those.

She turned it over, putting off the moment she would have to break the seal, and saw that it was addressed to Yvonne of Fir Tree Crossing. Not to Yvonne, one of the Hundred, or to her as a Hunar.

"That is from my mother," Guise said into the awkward silence. She turned to find that he, and the others, were openly staring at her, attention focused on the parchment in her hands. "You do not have to open it."

He was worried, she realised. It was unlike Guise to be worried by anything. They had faced down creatures in the mine, the corrupted Coll lord and almost impossible odds, and he had barely blinked. One letter from his mother, and he was openly worried.

Family was different, though. She knew that herself. Family pulled on all the weak and vulnerable spots. So much history in every simple exchange. And Guise's family was at the heart of the Karoan'shae, inside the tangled net of goblin politics.

She turned the parchment over again, and broke the seal with her thumb, releasing a tiny spark of magic. It had been sealed for her, she realised, watching the magic disappear into the air. Powerful magic. The wrong person opening this message would have been lucky to receive only burns.

She spread open the parchment and saw that it was written in the human language. A polite consideration. Perhaps Helgiarast had made enquiries of her own, and learned that, despite her extensive travelling, Yvonne had never spent any time in the goblin lands. Humans were permitted within the borders, of course, as goblins loved information and loved to trade. But, within goblin lands, only their own tongue was spoken. The human language was an extraordinary courtesy.

Then she started reading, and forgot about good-manners and language, her eyes widening as she read.

The letter was written in what she suspected was Helgiarast's own hand and extended, in flowery language, an invitation to Yvonne to attend the confirmation of the new Head of House at the Karoan'shae palace, not only as her younger son's bond partner, but also as Helgiarast's personal guest.

At first, Yvonne could not remember what the confirmation was, then the conversation with Guise in the garden at the annex came back to her. A new Head of House. The old lord someone he had admired. And the feel of his hand under hers, texture faintly rough, skin warm against hers, the memory lingering.

The confirmation. The circus that Brea had referred to, which could get bloody if things did not go well. And Helgiarast was inviting Yvonne to attend.

Yvonne read the letter twice more. It was not extremely long, but she had met the current star of the Karoan'shae, and knew that every single word would have been considered and carefully thought out. Not only that, but Helgiarast had written it in a language that Yvonne could understand, and chosen words that carried different weights in the human language than in the goblin's own language.

It was not so much an invitation as a summons.

Her heart was racing too fast. She had only just remembered the dungeon, and the forming of the bond. They had only just begun to work out what that might mean. She had the sensation again of standing on the edge of something, the push of wanting to stay where she was, where everything was familiar, and the pull of the unknown ahead, not knowing where that might lead. Guise had promised her there was no need to rush. She had time to consider the implications. Time to consider the tangle of feelings that knotted her insides when she even considered that there was a bond there.

Reading his mother's words, Yvonne remembered that, as much as she did not want to be tied to Guise, she had been unable to speak the words that would sever that tie. And now, remembering what they had said to each other in the castle, she knew she would never speak those words. There had been no deception. No lies. With his control stripped down by the poison, Guise had said what he wanted. Nothing less. Nothing more. And she had agreed. Even if she hadn't understood what she was agreeing to. For better, or for worse, she was tied to him. And that meant that she was well within the influence of the star of the Karoan'shae.

She read the letter again to make sure she had not missed anything. No. It was definitely a summons. Beautifully written, carefully worded. But, a summons nonetheless.

"What does she want?" Guise asked. He was worried. As well he might be.

She glanced up to see his question reflected on the other faces, and a crease of worry between Mariah's brows. Joel's jaw was set, trying to hide his own worry.

"An invitation," she told him, rolling up the parchment. She was not sure she wanted to show it to him, despite it being from his mother. There was nothing untoward in language, and yet she had a sense that he would want to intervene. And she wanted to make up her own mind.

"Breakfast," Pieris suggested, voice calm, breaking the tense silence. "I don't know about you, but I am starving."

"An invitation to what?" Mariah wanted to know as they took their places around the dining table, everyone with a full plate.

"A matter of goblin business," Yvonne told her, glancing briefly at Guise and seeing that he understood what she was referring to at once.

"Will you go?" Joel asked.

"Where?" Renard asked at the same time as Joel spoke, the words carrying quiet emphasis.

"The Karoan'shae palace near Fir Tree Crossing," she answered Renard, and shook her head slightly. "I will need to think about it," she told Joel. She couldn't read the expression on Guise's face. He was wearing one of his masks, only the brightness of his eyes betraying that he was not as calm as he appeared.

She could see a dozen objections on Joel's lips, and his sister's. She understood. The symbol of the Hunar meant almost nothing in goblin lands. She would simply be another human, among deadly and skilled adversaries.

"Do we need to call her Grandmama?" Mariah asked, nose wrinkling in distaste. Yvonne stared at her daughter, taken aback. There had been no chance to speak to either of her children since her conversation with Guise the day before. Not that she knew what she might have said. That Guise was courting her? That they had reached an agreement? Except that neither of those things felt right, and she could not imagine speaking those words to anyone, even her children.

"Pardon?" Guise asked Mariah, blinking in what appeared to be genuine surprise.

"Don't worry. I am not calling you Papa," she told him, nose still wrinkled.

Renard and Pieris choked at the same time, turning their laughter into unconvincing coughs, Pieris ducking his head to his plate, Renard taking a sip from his glass.

"You don't think that Guise would like being called Papa?" Pieris asked, looking up with an expression of false innocence on his face.

Yvonne found her jaw open, staring at one of her oldest friends. His eyes were dancing with humour.

"Papa Guise," Renard said, then choked on another laugh.

Yvonne glanced across to find Guise looking at the pair with an expression of horror. The others caught the look and dissolved into laughter.

"I'm not calling you Papa, either," Joel added, over Renard and Pieris' laughter, in the tone of one trying to be helpful. "What?" he said, in response to Yvonne's glare. "It's important to understand these things."

"If you ever meet her, you should call her my lady, or Lady Helgiarast," Yvonne told her children, shaking her head slightly, trying and failing to imagine the lady's reaction to two wulfkin she did not know calling her Grandmama. "Particularly if you want to inspect her clothes," she added to Mariah.

"No," Guise said to Mariah, voice faint as if the breath had been knocked out of him. "My mother would not want to be called Grandmama. And …" his voice trailed away, lips moving but no words emerging. His nose wrinkled slightly. "Just no," he finished.

"Good," Mariah said, eyes dancing with mischief. "I'm so glad that's settled."

Yvonne narrowed her eyes at her daughter across the table. Mariah smiled back, unrepentant.

"So, that's no to Grandmama. And Papa. I'm sure we can come up with something else," Pieris said, eyes still full of mischief.

Yvonne shook her head, face warm. She might be embarrassed, but she was also hopeful. It was a long time since she had seen mischief in Pieris' face. He had been sad a long time before his winter in the mountains.

"My lord will suffice," Guise said, adopting his haughtiest manner. Yvonne was not fooled. There was laughter in his eyes.

Mariah and Joel laughed back, shaking their heads.

Yvonne opened her mouth to reprimand her children, thought better of it, and instead set the rolled parchment on the table cloth beside her plate, asking about everyone's plans for the day.

No one particularly wanted to talk about their plans, but, to her surprise, they respected her wish to change the subject. Mariah and Joel wanted to revisit some of their favourite places before leaving the next day. Yvonne suggested that Mariah might want to visit the cloth merchant in the blue house. Mariah's eyes widened, and Yvonne wondered if she would need to drag her daughter out of the building later. Renard simply said he had some business, and Pieris was proposing to spend much of the day sleeping, still feeling the effects of his injury and the healing spell.

Yvonne discovered that Mariah and Joel had invited both Renard and Pieris to come and stay with them for as long as they wanted, and had no hesitation in endorsing the invitation when Renard lifted his brows at her. She saw something shift in Pieris' face and realised that he had not expected to be welcome in her home. Sillman's shadow lay between then, invisible and unacknowledged.

At the end of the meal, the others left about their business. Apart from Guise, who simply stayed in the room while the others left. He had been unusually silent through the meal, eyes straying from time to time to the parchment at Yvonne's elbow.

"It isn't really a request," he said, when the door had closed behind Pieris, the last to leave.

Yvonne laughed, a release of tension at hearing her own thoughts reflected. "No, I did not think it was. Here." She held the parchment out to him. He took it and unfurled it, reading slowly. And then, as she had done, re-read the words.

"Most interesting," he said at length, handing the parchment back to her. His mood seemed to have lightened, although there was no outward change in expression.

"Please explain," she requested. Despite the words being in the human language, it was possible she had entirely missed some meaning.

"Extending an invitation to you as her personal guest puts you within her care," Guise explained. All the tension had gone from him. Whatever had worried him, was no longer of concern. "It means that she, and her household, will look after you. It's as close as you can get to a guarantee of safety within the Karoan'shae," he added. "She really wants you to be there."

Yvonne sat back in her chair, considering that. There had only been one, brief and awkward, meeting with Helgiarast. Helgiarast had left abruptly. Yvonne had been left with the impression of a strong and capable woman, used to getting her own way. And, she had thought, less than pleased with the bond her son had made.

"What advantage is there, to her, if I am there?" Yvonne asked slowly.

She saw, by the gleam in Guise's eyes, that she had asked a good question. One that he considered good, in any event, and he had a lifetime of experience in the Karoan'shae behind him.

"That is the question, isn't it?" he said.

Yvonne looked down at the parchment beside her. Based on what had been said, and not said, she thought that Guise had already been under pressure from his mother to request Yvonne's presence.

She remembered the assassin's warning. There was unease among the Karoan'shae at the bond she and Guise had formed. They may both be in danger.

And yet, Yvonne had the direct, and personal, request of the current star of the Karoan'shae to attend.

Her stomach twisted at the thought. There were so many practical obstacles. She had nothing to wear. She did not speak the language. She did not understand the manners of the Karoan'shae.

Those were concerns. By far the biggest issue was whether she wanted to go.

She stared at the parchment, with its ribbon and the broken wax seal. Helgiarast se'laj Krejefell was one of the most powerful women in all the lands. It would be unwise to offend her. Particularly after the star of the Karoan'shae had extended a personal invitation. In her own hand.

That was, of course, one of the reasons why Helgiarast had penned the letter herself. And chosen her words so carefully, trying to convey meaning that a human would understand.

Yvonne's breath caught in her throat. She was considering it. Actually considering putting herself in the middle of the Karoan'shae. She could admit to herself that she was curious. It was a place very few humans would ever go. And fewer still come out alive. And she had an advantage. A bond with a goblin lord. Helgiarast's son, no less.

"I'll need to think about it," she told him and received a calm acknowledgement. It wasn't quite true. She had almost made up her mind to go. She just wanted more time. To convince herself to cross over that edge, to step ahead into the unknown.

Chapter Thirty

Before they could leave the next day, there was still one, vital, task left to her.

Elinor's letter to Adira was still intact after the fire, and Yvonne also still had the letters that Adira had sent to Elinor over the years, so carefully preserved by Elinor. Renard had taken his letters back already. With her head and stomach unsettled with what might be excitement and might be fear at the thought of what she and Guise might, or might not, have promised each other, and the prospect of a visit with the Karoan'shae, Yvonne settled at the writing desk in the tavern's private room and spent some time writing a long letter to Adira, the activity calming her, and bringing her grief back to life.

The Sisters of the Stone Walls were used to dealing with difficult things, and heartache, so she set out everything she could in the letter. How Elinor's death had not been natural, how one of the Hundred had been persuaded, somehow, to add poison to her sugar. She also set out the detail of the poison, and the antidote. She did not think that Adira had been to visit Elinor in the months before her death. But just in case. Pieris had undertaken to visit the neighbours to make sure no one else needed the antidote.

Yvonne told Adira about finding the letters, enclosing hers, unopened, and that the lawyer would be in touch about a legacy from Elinor.

She left the tavern to make arrangements for the letter to be sent, heading for the trade guilds' offices which handled correspondence. The clerk lifted her brows slightly at the address, but accepted the commission without question.

As she was leaving the offices, she caught sight of her reflection in the glass of the doors and saw the faint glimmer of the Hunar's symbol at her shoulder.

She stilled, feeling her mouth lift in a smile. Hunar. The clerk had used her title and, aching with loss and the weight of her words to Adira, she had not paid much attention.

She put her hand to her shoulder. The mark was spun of magic and she could not really feel it. If she looked with enhanced sight, she would see the bright spark of magic that held the symbol there. It was real. And her shoulder no longer ached in memory of Sillman's spell tearing the magic out of her flesh.

Hunar again. It had been her identity for a long time. Since she had first met Elinor, seen the magic around her, and learned that it might be possible for her to be one of the Hundred, too. She had been an apprentice and then Hunar for more than half her life. The rightness of it settled around her. More than a label she wore. It was part of her, a calling she could not ignore.

She had managed without it for a while. She had tracked the Ashnassan, sought answers to Elinor's death, and fought warriors without the symbol. The symbol itself helped, but was not what really mattered.

In searching for answers, she had discovered that at least one of the Hundred was not at all who she had thought they were. That they had forgotten what being Hunar meant, the very word defining their role. Servant. Sworn to help those in need.

The symbol settled at her shoulder. It felt permanent, as though it had bound itself more securely into her being so that no one could take it away from her, no matter what spell they used. It was a symbol for others, reflecting who she was.

She remembered the night before. The course of light and life and love and laughter through her when her symbol had returned. Part of her. As if it had never been taken.

As she stared at the reflected symbol, something behind her, seen across her shoulder, caught her attention.

She turned, moving out of the doorway to the steps of the building, and saw a figure standing in between two buildings on the other side of the street. A tall, male figure, with red robes gathered around him, and a wide-brimmed hat pulled low so she could not see his face.

Her heart stopped. Not the Coll lord. He was dead. In ashes.

And the Coll lord had not been wearing the robes when he died. He had been promised replacements. None had been provided to him.

Red robes.

That was what had been missing from the Coll lord, what her mind had been trying to tell her when she was watching his ashes scatter to the wind. The Ashnassan had been looking for red velvet. And the Coll lord had been confident that replacement robes would be found for him. But he had been in ordinary clothes.

The red robes had never been meant for the Coll lord. Twisted by the corruption in him, he had never suspected that he was being used. As the Ashnassan were. As Sillman had been.

The robes had been meant for someone else.

The figure standing across the street from her.

As she stood still, pulse racing, the mark at her shoulder flaring in the sunlight, there was an echo in her chest. The resonance that she had followed to find Sillman in the house with the bodies. The rhythmic note, deeper than the lowest horn. It rang through her, calling her forward.

He is risen.

The resonance vibrated through her, low and familiar. As if it had always been there, just waiting for her to listen.

Red robes.

He is risen.

And the power she could sense through that resonance.

Her mind shied away from the idea, yet she could not deny it.

The first enemy of the Hundred. The first Hunar's brother. The ancient enemy.

As if naming him, even in her mind, had cut their connection, the resonance vanished as swiftly as it had arrived. She moved forward of her own free will, going down the steps at a run, heading for the gap between the buildings.

She must have taken her eyes off him for a moment, no more, to check her footing, and when she looked up, he was gone.

There was nothing between the buildings. Empty space.

When she reached there, she found nothing. No scent, no trace, no footprints. Nothing to suggest that the first enemy of the Hundred was alive and well and prowling the streets of Elinor's town.

There had been nothing.

But, when she looked again, eyes travelling all over the space, from the sky to the ground, she caught sight of something. A trail of ribbon. Bright blue. The sort that a young girl might wear in her hair. It was tied around a lock of shining golden hair, each end of the lock cut precisely, the bundle as long as her hand.

A message. A warning.

She picked it up. Fear washed over her. Not her fear. Someone else. The one who used to have this hair. A girl. If Yvonne had to guess, she would say nine years old.

She had a confused series of impressions from the girl, all tainted with fear. Taken from her parents' house. Men with horses, and tattoos on their faces. Riding into the night.

A building with high stone walls. There were narrow windows in the walls, open to the air, with no glass, and metal bars across them.

The poor light from the windows showed little of the room itself.

The frightened girl was not alone. There were other girls there. All the same age. From all across the lands. Faces marred with dirt and tears. Clothes dusty and some of them torn. A dozen at least.

The impressions faded as quickly as they had taken her over.

The girls were together.

The first Hunar's brother was walking the world.

Yvonne stared down at the ribbon and hair. There was nothing left in it. No impressions. No life. No fear. It was simply a twist of hair and ribbon such as a parent might have for a keepsake.

She found a clean cloth in one of her belt pouches and wrapped the hair and ribbon inside, tucking it away.

When she looked back up, her jaw was set, eyes hard, making a promise in her own mind.

The girls were terrified and in need of rescue. No one else was looking for them. Not really. But, with the symbol at her shoulder she could cross borders. She could ask questions.

She would find the girls. She would see them home, if that's what they wanted, or to the Sisters, if they preferred.

And she would send the first Hunar's brother to his death, finally. Perhaps back to the corrupted pit he had been lying in for hundreds of years. Perhaps she would find a more suitable resting place for him. He would find out how much had changed since he was thrown into his grave.

The symbol at her shoulder flared, the promise sending a fresh wave of magic through her. No one had asked her for help, but the magic responded anyway, recognising the binding promise.

Whatever else was true, she was Hunar.

THANK YOU

THANK YOU VERY MUCH for reading *The Sundering*, The Hundred - Book 2. I hope you have enjoyed spending more time with Yvonne and Guise.

It would be great, if you have five minutes, if you could leave an honest review at the store you got it from. Reviews are really helpful for other readers decide whether the book is for them, and that also helps me get visibility for my books - thank you.

Yvonne's story continues in *The Reckoning*, The Hundred - Book 3, also available at Amazon.

If you want to know what I'm working on and when the next book will be available, you can contact me and sign up for my newsletter at the website: www.taellaneth.com.

CHARACTER LIST

Note: to avoid spoilers, some names may have been omitted, and some details left out.

Adira - human, senior head Sister in the Stone Walls
Annabelle - human, one of the Hundred
Baldur - warhorse
Brea - goblin, wife to Thort and mother to Jesset
Cressin - human, tanners, from Silverton
Dundac - human, one of the Hundred
Elinor – human, deceased at start, formerly of the Hundred
Ella - wulfkin, in Sephenamin's range
Firon - human, one of the Hundred
Frida - human, dressmaker, from Fir Tree Crossing
Grayling- human, head of law keepers at Fir Tree Crossing
Guise - goblin
Handerson - human, potter, from Fir Tree Crossing
Idal - human, apprentice Hunar
Jesset - goblin, Brea and Thort's daughter
Joel - wulfkin, one of Yvonne's wards and Mariah's brother
Keffle - human, potter, from Fir Tree Crossing

Lothar - Yvonne's horse

Mariah - wulfkin, one of Yvonne's wards and Joel's sister

Mica - human, one of the Hundred

Modig - mixed heritage, hotel manager in Three Falls

Renard - wulfkin, of no range, horse trainer

Pieris - human, one of the Hundred

Sephenamin – wulfkin, cerro in Fir Tree Crossing, owns The Tavern

Sillman - human, one of the Hundred

Slayer - leader of the Ashnassan

Suanna - human, one of the Hundred

Thort - goblin, Brea's husband, Jesset's father

Ubel - human, deceased at start, merchant

Viola - human, herbalist in Fir Tree Crossing

Yvonne - human, one of the Hundred, legal guardian of Mariah and Joel

PLACES

Abar al Endell – southernmost city, at the edge of the desert, near the Forbidden Lands

Coll Castle - part of Kingdom of Valland

Fir Tree Crossing - busy trading town on the Great River

Forbidden Lands - desert territory beyond Abar al Endell

Hogsmarthen - closest city to the Sisters in the Stone Walls, on the Great River (upriver from Fir Tree Crossing)

Karoan'shae Palace - goblin palace and territory a short distance from Fir Tree Crossing

Kelton - artists' town on the Great River between Hogsmarthen and Fir Tree Crossing

Royal City - home of the Valland Kings, furthest upriver on the Great River

Silverton - small trading town upriver from Fir Tree Crossing

Stone Walls - home of the Sisters in the Stone Walls, a high-sided mountain valley not far from Hogsmarthen

Three Falls - city state near Valland

Valland - largest Kingdom in the lands, holds the Royal City, a lot of the Great River and Coll Castle

Willowton - Elinor's home town

ALSO BY THE AUTHOR

(As at May 2023)

The Hundred series (complete)
The Gathering, Book 1
The Sundering, Book 2
The Reckoning, Book 3
The Rending, Book 4
The Searching, Book 5
The Rising, Book 6

The Taellaneth series (complete)
Concealed, Book 1
Revealed, Book 2
Betrayed, Book 3
Tainted, Book 4
Cloaked, Book 5

Taellaneth Box Set (all five books in one e-book)
Taellaneth Complete Series (Books 1–5)

Ageless Mysteries
Deadly Night, Book 1
False Dawn, Book 2
Morning Trap, Book 3
Assassin's Noon, Book 4
Flightless Afternoon, Book 5
Ascension Day, Book 6

The Grey Gates
Outcast, Book 1
Called, Book 2
Hunted, Book 3 (expected to be available mid-July 2023)

ABOUT THE AUTHOR

Vanessa Nelson is a fantasy author who lives in Scotland, United Kingdom and spends her days juggling the demands of two spoiled cats, two giant dogs and her fictional characters.

As far as the cats are concerned, they should always come first. The older dog lets her know when he isn't getting enough attention by chewing up the house. The younger dog's favourite method of getting her attention is a gentle nudge with his head. At least, he would say it's gentle.

You can find out more information online at the following places:

Website: www.taellaneth.com

Facebook: www.facebook.com/taellaneth

Printed in Great Britain
by Amazon